WHEN THE PHOENIX RISES

BY

NESLY CLERGE

"When the Phoenix Rises"

(Print) ISBN: 978-0-9993235-0-2
(Electronic) ISBN: 978-0-9965017-9-8

Publisher: Clerge Books, LLC

Editor: Joyce L. Shafer (http://editmybookandmore.weebly.com)

Cover and Interior Book Design: Damonza.com

E-Book Formatting: Ebooklaunch.com

ALSO BY NESLY CLERGE

When the Serpent Bites
(Book 1 of The Starks Trilogy)

When the Dragon Roars
(Book 2 of The Starks Trilogy)

End of the World: The Beginning
(Book 1 of a Serial - Amazon #1 Bestseller)

The Anatomy of Cheating

ACKNOWLEDGMENTS

Just as no man is an island, no author succeeds without a team that supports him or her, from typing the first word, to sharing the result of all their cumulative efforts with readers.

I wish to thank my editor, Joyce L. Shafer, for assisting me with the first two books, as well as the completion of this last book in The Starks Trilogy. We share quite an adventure, getting all of my novels into the world.

My sincerest gratitude to Tierra Guy, my significant other. Your support and encouragement make this experience all the more engaging and rewarding.

A big thank-you to Shayla Eaton, for her exceptional marketing skills that make a significant difference in my books reaching many.

And that leaves my readers to thank, from my Goodreads friends, reviewers, and newsletter receivers, to every reader who has given my novels a chance, as well as exceptional reviews.

Special thanks goes to Lynn Mccarthy, Sue Leonhardt, Hillary Validia Earl, Kay Smillie, Rebecca McNutt, Dee Cherry, Veronica Joy, Patricia Brooks, Kimberlie Lashley, Brenda Telford, Nicki M, C.P. Bialois, K. Morton, Anthony Richard Parsons, Dianne Bylo, Linda Strong, Brenda Bradshaw, Sue Ward, Dawn P. Harrell, and Diane Lybbert.

My heartfelt thanks to you all.

"There are two ways to be fooled.
One is to believe what isn't true;
The other is to refuse to believe what is true."

~ Soren Kierkegaard

CHAPTER 1

Frederick Starks's heart pounded against his chest. The hope he'd clung to shattered. "What the hell do you mean, my appeal was denied?"

He flew from the lower bunk. Pacing the six by eight enclosure, cell phone pressed to his ear in a white-knuckled grip, he struggled to suppress his rising panic. Starks continued to pace, oblivious to the risk. Until he caught his reflection in the small mirror bolted to the wall above the insufficient sink. The last thing he needed was for the wrong guard or inmate to catch him with the illegal device.

Starks's eyes darted up and down the corridor. Of the few inmates present in their cells, none paid attention to him. He returned to his bunk, sat with his knees bent, and placed the heavy book back on his thighs.

His attorney had remained in silent understanding of his frustration. Starks rubbed the back of his neck and said through tight lips, "The clock's ticking down. My wife's dying. Kayla needs me. Our kids need me. Fix this, Parker. I've got to get out of here. Bribe someone, if you have to."

"I'm obligated to adhere to the law. You know this well enough."

"And you know where you can stick the law."

"I made every effort to get Solomon to recuse himself."

"Obviously, it wasn't enough."

Parker cleared his throat. "You don't understand how these things work. Standard Massachusetts practice is that the appeal goes before the judge who presided over the criminal trial. Solomon should have recused himself, upon my request. However, the law states it's his choice."

"It was clear at my trial that he wanted to stick it to me."

"It seems he still does."

"How can he get away with this?"

"Granting a new trial is at his discretion."

"What about the new evidence?"

"He doesn't feel it casts doubt on the decision. Said the appeal has no merit."

"That should be left up to a new jury. Shouldn't it? Isn't that my right?"

"Another way to say it is, he doesn't want to overturn his decision."

"I'm screwed."

"Don't give up. I'm not. There are still recourses. I'll get started on another appeal. I'll do whatever I have to, to get him to recuse himself, or take your appeal to a higher court."

"How long will this take?"

Parker hesitated then said, "A couple to several months. Possibly longer."

"What the hell am I paying your exorbitant fees and my left nut for, if you can't move any faster and more effectively than that?"

Starks knew Michael Parker well. Knew Parker had his head back, eyes aimed at a point on the ceiling, while he worked his jaw in an attempt to contain his temper. If he were any other client, Parker would tell him to kiss his ass and find another attorney to torment. But he wasn't just any client. He was Parker's best-paying client, and they'd been friends a long time.

"I'm sorry, Mike. You don't know what I'm going through. Maybe you're in a tight spot, but I also know you've got pull. Damn it, it's not just me I'm fighting for."

Parker exhaled in frustration. "I'm aware of that. Perhaps I can call in a few favors. Or obligate myself in some way I may regret."

"Whatever it takes."

"Don't lose hope, Starks."

"Easier said than done."

A weight of worry settled into Starks's bones. The several-inches-thick book he'd stolen from the library remained against his thighs. He placed the phone into the recess he'd cut into the pages and slammed the book closed. Dragged himself from his lower bunk to his small vinyl desk placed against the opposite wall, where he kept the book among others, and began to pace the matchbox cell in C Block of the maximum security prison. Sands Correctional Facility. Nothing resort-like about it. The *correction* that went on inside more often deadly than not, and more often than not dealt by inmates, themselves.

Don't lose hope.

Right.

He was screwed, and they both knew it. Parker could make all the appeal attempts the law would allow, fail, and still collect fees, while his client suffered.

Starks drifted to the entrance of the cell and into the corridor. There was no place he wanted to go, no one he wanted to see.

That wasn't true. The one person he desperately wanted to see, to talk with, to play catch or basketball with—to protect with his life—had been taken from him.

He yearned to turn back the hands of time, to prevent what had happened. Almost three months now. Exactly how far back he'd have to twist those clock hands to the left, and how many times, hit like a hard punch.

Starks faced the interior of his cell and the empty top bunk. He shut his eyes and replayed snippets of conversations he'd had with Kane, the times they'd laughed, or argued, including after Kane's big reveal—*I'm your son.*

It was as though some entity sucked all the oxygen from the air. Ache mixed with raw panic inside his chest expanded.

Parker wanted him to believe a chance remained that he'd get out, but he knew the truth. He wasn't leaving this godforsaken place until his fifteen years were up. Unless some other crime he got caught up in, landed him with a longer sentence to serve. Or he left in a body bag. Both were options that increased in possibility every day he opened his eyes.

A moan started in his throat and escalated. Bellowing curses, Starks grabbed the plastic chair tucked under his desk and slammed it repeatedly against the wall. A jagged piece from one of the legs flew off, making a thin slice in the dragon tattoo that started on his right hand and climbed to his shoulder. Bits of concrete splintered from several gray cinderblocks that walled him in on three sides.

Rubber-soled shoes rapidly slapped against the concrete corridor floor. Unable to cease flailing and shouting, he ignored everything but his pain. Didn't look at or acknowledge whoever stood at the threshold of his cell.

"What the hell are you doing, asshole?" When no answer came, the corrections officer placed a hand on the Taser clipped to his belt and said, "If you won't stop on your own, maybe a few jolts will do the trick."

CHAPTER 2

Starks flung the chair toward the bunk beds. He'd had electricity zapped through him, reducing him to a twitching mass for a period of time. Having barbed prongs dug from skin and muscle was an experience he didn't care to repeat. Once was enough. Not that he didn't deserve whatever pain anyone dealt him.

The guard made *tsking* sounds. "Destroying prison property. That's worth a few privileges being revoked. Maybe even a couple nights in the Hole."

Starks glared at him. "Who the hell are you?"

"Officer Stone. You, ass-wipe, are out of line talking to me like that. Maybe you need a lesson that sticks." He sneered as he extracted his Taser and took aim.

CO Roberts sprinted into the cell. "Put it away, Stone."

Stone flicked a surprised glance at Roberts before returning his focus to Starks. "Bastard deserves it."

"Put it away and get out."

His expression incredulous, Stone shifted his gaze from Starks to Roberts. "What the hell's going on here?"

"I'll explain later."

"Better be good, or I'll report this." Stone shoved the Taser back onto his belt, glared at Starks and retreated into the corridor.

Roberts stood at the entrance and waited until Stone was far enough away before facing Starks. "Rookies. Easier to train a new puppy not to pee inside or eat your shoes." He studied Starks for a moment. "Your arm's bleeding."

Starks, jaw tight, glanced at his right arm and shrugged.

"Wanna talk about it?"

Starks righted his chair and dropped into it. "The author of my life has it in for me."

"That would be you. You may not like hearing that, but …"

Starks studied Roberts through narrowed eyes. The words could have flowed from Sands' mafia don-slash-philosopher, Gabe Bianchi. "You sound like someone I know."

Roberts cast his gaze to the top bunk. "Kane Sandler. Why the different last name? How come you didn't tell us he was your boy?"

"I didn't know. He told me a couple days before … before what happened. I called him a liar. Then I got proof he was mine. DNA doesn't lie."

"How'd you manage that? Nevermind. I'll set the rookie straight."

"I don't need punks like him coming after me. I've already got enough grief in this place." Starks scrubbed his forehead with his hands. "Over and over in my mind, I see Kane in the condition he was in when I found him. I imagine how terrified he had to be. How alone he must have felt."

"No parent should lose a child, especially not like that. But thinking that way isn't going to help him or you."

"His death is my fault."

"It's the fault of whichever bastard beat him with a steel pipe."

Starks grew still. "You found the weapon?"

"Eventually. Bastard who did it was careful. No fingerprints."

"Why didn't you tell me?"

"You had enough to deal with."

Starks shook his head. "The only reason he was in here was because of me."

"I don't follow."

"Committed a crime to be near me, the father who never knew he existed. And what did I do? Rejected him when he told me. Had to have proof. I got it. Too damn late to do anything but hold him until he died." Starks locked eyes with Roberts. "Seconds. That's all I had. At least I was able to tell him I claimed him as mine before he …" Tears filled his eyes. He turned and faced the back wall. "I need you to go."

"Let me know if there's anything I can do." Roberts started to leave. "One thing I need to mention. It's not the best time, but while

I'm here, every now and then, use the regular phones so the wrong people don't get curious."

Starks responded with a nod.

There was nothing that could be done about Kane. Kayla was dying, and there was nothing he could do about that, either. Or about helping her and their three children, other than what his wealth could buy.

He'd failed them all.

Starks stumbled the short distance it took to reach the bunk beds. Stretched his arms across the cold, thin plastic-sheathed mattress on the top bunk and wept, unable to care if he was heard or not.

CHAPTER 3

B reakfast shift over, Ronald Jackson tossed the grimy, sodden dishcloth into the laundry hamper. The odor of inedible excuses for food permeated the kitchen and his yellow scrub set, identical to the ones each inmate was forced to wear. He had the rest of the day to himself.

Jackson nodded at a few of his co-workers, who dripped sweat as he did. A result of rushing around for two hours near ovens that would stay hot until after the dinner shift. His destination was C Block, middle cell on the left. He and Starks had discussed his moving back in, now that Kane's bed lay empty. Then Starks had asked him to hold off. But for how long? They had things to do and discuss, actions better facilitated if they shared the same space.

He'd intended to announce his arrival in some clever manner that might elicit a smile from Starks, even if thin, but stopped himself from calling out once he reached the cell entrance. Starks's arms were draped across Kane's vacant mattress, his sobs subtle but evident by the movement of his shoulders. This wasn't the time.

Jackson hoofed it to the yard. A cool mid-autumn breeze teased the sweat from his skin as he stepped onto the flat, dirt-packed stretch of ground where inmates often vented frustration through rowdy football or basketball games. Or worked on their anger or muscles with weights set up in the southernmost part of the secured enclosure. He excluded himself from this latter activity, relying more on his brains than his brawn, if he needed to fend off an attack. He glanced at the wooden bleachers located yards from the northwest corner. Pete, Tommy, Stinky, and Tank occupied the bottom riser, displaying minimal interest in the games.

Four pairs of eyes, set in faces pigmented shades lighter and darker than his own deep bronze, focused on Jackson as he approached. He sat on the empty riser above the men, all members of the gang Starks had started; though, Starks preferred they be called a crew, like on a ship, with him as their captain. Their leader was temporarily down, or perhaps permanently. No one would know for certain, not until Starks emerged again.

Pete swiveled around. "What's the word on the Dragon?"

Jackson squinted against the sunlight. "Started to talk to him. Wasn't a good time."

Tommy propped his elbows on his thighs. "Warden ain't gonna let that bed stay empty. Good time or not, move your shit in. Before someone who's not one of us bunks in there."

Jackson nodded. "It's not like the line feeding people into here ever stops. They've started putting three and four to a cell in A Block."

Stinky scratched his crotch. "Starks need to be snappin' out of it."

Tank swatted the back of Stinky's head. "The man is in a world of hurt." He adjusted his bulk on the riser. "Show some respect."

"Respect only go so far. How long you think Seth gonna hang back?" Stinky gestured with his chin at inmates mulling about the yard. "Same for any of these assholes. They decide Starks's lost his position, the shit'll hit the fan. We be in the way of that mess."

Tank glared at him. "Takes time to come back from loss. You never the same. The damage been done. Just can't let it drag you down so far you can't come back up."

Pete shot Tank a look. "Where's this shit coming from?"

Tank pursed his lips and cast his eyes downward. "Lost my little girl. That kinda loss is different. Walks with you like a splinter you can't get out."

Pete toed a pebble then kicked it into the field. "How come you never said nothin'?"

"Not the kind of thing you drop to just anyone."

"We not just anyone."

Tank glanced at Pete. "Don't want no one feeling sorry for me. People think that make a man weak. Me and Starks ain't weak. Hurtin' ain't the same as weak."

"Still," Stinky said, "Starks's time runnin' out. Seth ain't gonna wait much longer for him to make a move."

"He try anything," Tank said, "we take care of it. That mother good as dead, anyway. Kill a man's son, you gotta pay."

Pete cleared his throat and spit. "Maybe Starks only think he know what he doing. We come from the streets. He some big-time executive. What he know about the fight?"

Jackson leaned forward. "You assholes suffering from memory loss or something? Starks is set to win. And he's carrying all of us with him. When he's ready to deal with Seth, he'll come up with a plan that settles the score. In the meantime, let that lion-tattooed sonofabitch piss his pants wondering when it'll happen and how bad it's gonna be."

Tommy stretched his arms overhead and yawned. "Starks's body count keeps going up. Five deaths, and he ain't even been here a year. Make that six. If you count Skullars Bailey."

Tank jabbed him. "He only did Big Bo. Kane and Skullars were done because they were with Starks. Get the facts straight or keep your mouth shut." He raised his finger to jab the inmate a second time.

Tommy moved out of Tank's reach. "Maybe he only did Big Bo himself, but the other five still on his head."

Jackson jumped from the second riser and kept his back to the men. "Starks is down, but not out. I know him better than any of you." He pivoted. "Anyone who doubts him is free to leave his protection. Like I said, always more bodies ready to fill a spot." He turned to leave, halted and smiled, as apologies from all but Tank poured forth. Tank excelled at keeping the crew in line. But so did he.

Still, if Starks didn't come out of his funk soon …

Possible scenarios whirled in Jackson's mind.

He shuddered.

CHAPTER 4

Starks swiped his shirtsleeve across his damp eyes and face. He stepped to the lidless, seat-less toilet near the cell entrance. Turned on the tap of the small sink mounted atop the stainless steel unit. Cleaned the blood from his arm then filled the palms of his hands with cold water and buried his face in it, until the water drained from between his fingers.

Red-rimmed eyes, shadowed by swollen circles underneath, stared back at him from the small mirror. He raked a hand through his scraggly dark hair and across his unshaven face. No one who knew him from his former life would recognize him. He barely recognized himself.

Starks tore off a sheet of paper towel and began wiping up the splashed water. Disgusted with the compulsion, he wadded the paper and tossed it into the plastic receptacle. How many times had Kayla complained about his need for life to be neat, reminded him it was not only impossible, but an imposition?

He ran his hand along the dragon tattoo that had taken Joe "Tat Man" Reynolds four hours, intended to represent a threat to anyone who thought to challenge him. He was trapped between two worlds, where some things still mattered and some things didn't. He was certain which was which about only some of them.

His grandfather had told him that memories didn't belong to a building or a house. They belonged to us, and it was up to us to decide what to do with them. But what was he supposed to do with memories—past and recent—that ate away at him like acid?

Gabe Bianchi would remind him to be like the phoenix and rise from the ashes. That doing so was his choice. That is, if he wanted to climb out of any hole he'd fallen or been pushed into. Or dug for himself.

The mythical phoenix birds regenerated from the ashes because that was their nature. They had no other option. That, of course, was Gabe's point: He had the option. But whereas it was rebirth for the phoenix, it could only be a lesser form of renewal for him. Because of all that had happened, as well as what was inevitable, substantial regeneration remained out of reach.

Inmates began filing into the corridor. Starks glanced at his clock. The red digital numbers showed it was 10:59.

He took his position outside his cell, keenly aware of Kane's absence at his side, like phantom-limb syndrome. If Kane's mother knew he felt this emptiness, she'd say he had no right to that emotion. She'd be justified in saying so. But that didn't stop the sensation from piercing his consciousness.

Jackson jogged to his place in front of the cell left of Starks's. "How's it going, man?"

Starks shrugged.

Seconds later, a voice boomed, "On the count," over the intercom.

Starks's mind wandered to a different time and place. The guard ticking off inmates' names, as well as the one handing out mail, had nearly finished in their corridor by the time he noticed they'd passed him.

Jackson sidled up to Starks as soon as the count was over. "Want to grab lunch with me and the guys?"

"There's something else I need to do."

"Anything I can help with?"

"Not this time."

"You gotta show up at some point, man. Gotta let the guys know everything is okay. That you're still in charge."

Starks remained where he was and didn't respond. Jackson shrugged and started up the corridor. Starks returned to his bunk.

Nothing was okay. No longer was he confident that he was in charge, starting with himself. An attitude he needed to get past, and soon. If he was to be stuck here for another fourteen years, or longer, he couldn't afford to falter. Power equaled strength. Strength gave him a chance. Not much of one, but he'd take what he could get or create for himself. Even if it meant using force, which it would.

Seth had made certain of it.

CHAPTER 5

S am Carson cleared his throat and waited just outside the cell entrance. Starks swung his feet heavily to the floor. "Come on in."

Sam pointed to the chair nearest the bunk beds. Starks nodded. "You okay?"

Starks shrugged and exhaled hard. "Better than maybe I deserve."

"Sorry about your boy."

"Appreciate it."

"Should've come sooner. Never did know what to say at times like these."

"You're here. That's enough."

Sam linked his fingers, stared at them and nodded. "Realized how bad it was when you didn't get word to me about working your shift in the library."

"Sorry. I should have thought about how my absence might inconvenience you."

Sam waved a dismissive hand. "I knew what happened was rough on you. Nothing like work to clear the mind. Or numb it for a while." He cleared his throat again. "Only time you miss work is when you're sick or someone's cleaned your clock. And now, of course."

"Or when I'm locked in the Hole."

The corners of Sam's lips turned up slightly. "Or that. The thing is, you got a work ethic like no one else in here."

"My grandfather instilled that in me."

"He still alive?"

Starks shook his head. "Thankfully, he checked out before I checked into this place."

Sam slapped his hands on his thighs and stood. "Besides my condolences, I wanted to see if I could get you to come back sooner than later. Now that I see you, take your time. I'll cover for you until you return. But," he waited for Starks to look at him, "try not to wait too long. Even I'm not as accurate or disciplined as you are. Plus, the animals behave better when you're there."

Starks got to his feet and extended his hand. "You're a good man, Sam. One of the few in here."

Sam's face colored as he shook Starks's hand. "Some might say that's debatable."

"I'll debate them any day of the week."

"Yeah, well …" Sam released Starks's hand and shuffled toward the door. He paused at the entrance. Without looking back he said, "I'm really sorry, Starks."

Starks sat on the edge of his bunk. It seemed unfair, perhaps even unrealistic, that this time couldn't be all about him. At least, not for much longer. There were people here who relied on him. His grandfather had told him he'd know, without a doubt, the day he became a man, because others would depend on him, and he'd do what was expected.

It was time to find within himself, a way to return to that place again, before failing and giving up became too easy.

The guard at the barred gate scowled. "You don't got an appointment, you don't get in to see the counselor."

Starks balled his hands into fists. "I need to see Demory. Either ask him or let me in. You know who I am?"

The guard shifted in his chair. "Yeah."

"Then you can understand why this is important."

The guard stared at Starks for a moment. "Lemme see if he's busy." He punched in a few numbers on the phone, whispered into the receiver, and then placed it back in its cradle. "He'll see you."

A button was pushed. The electronic gate groaned open.

Starks passed through, wondering if this was a good idea or not. He never knew what he'd get from the counselor.

He paused to peer in through the double-paned security glass at the top half of Demory's office door.

What could he lose that hadn't already been taken from him, or was about to be?

He made a fist and knocked.

CHAPTER 6

Matthew Demory waved for Starks to enter. He shot out of his brown leather swivel chair, hand extended. "I'm relieved you decided to see me. If you hadn't by next week, I was going to insist." He gestured toward the chair positioned in front of his desk. "I've been worried about you, Starks. How are you doing?" Seated again, Demory picked up his pen and held it poised over the tablet in front of him.

Starks lowered into the chair. "How do you think?"

"There are any number of questions I'd like to ask—need to ask, but I think it's best if you lead the conversation."

Starks fixed his gaze on the pen. "I'd prefer not to compete with your scratching on paper while I talk. This is hard enough."

Demory put the pen down, leaned back and waited.

Starks nodded once in appreciation. The last time he'd sought assistance from Demory, it hadn't gone well. He'd all but stormed out, proclaiming he was done with the man. Yet, here he was again, seated across from the pudgy prison counselor, who was mostly kind to him, often annoying, and sometimes clueless.

Drops of rain splattered against the small square window positioned high on the wall behind Demory. Several splotches of coffee stained the counselor's shirt. Starks glanced left. As usual, folders protruded from open filing cabinet drawers. It should have been comforting to know that some things never change, but it wasn't. Eventually, everything changed. Any belief otherwise was an illusion.

Demory had told him once that the color scheme of blue walls with the lighter aqua wavy lines was deliberate, meant to represent the seashore. Meant to offer a more calming ambiance for inmates who needed his assistance, as well as a break from the ubiquitous gray permeating the prison interior. This time, the beach-like scheme ignited a different reaction.

"Your expression," Demory said, "just shifted in an odd way. What's that about?"

"Kyle."

Demory nodded once. "Your son who drowned when he was five."

Starks faced him. "Don't you really mean my *other* illegitimate son?"

"I wouldn't put it that way."

"I can't tell you how many times I forget to think about him, to remember he was a part of me. Because I made damn sure he wasn't a part of my life, except occasionally. But every now and then, *wham*. The truth about his brief life, and his death, socks me in the gut. But, Kane? Kane haunts me all the time. Will for the rest of my life. Punishment for every sin I ever committed."

"I don't know that you can assign—"

"The nightmares don't stop. They just change characters. Sometimes it's like a bizarre gathering, or parade. Everyone I've destroyed in some way, makes an appearance. The innocent ones are always in danger, always terrified, and I can't reach or help them. Sometimes it's me holding Kyle under the water, until he dissolves, so the fact of him isn't revealed. Or me wielding the weapon that destroys Kane. Those are only a few of the numerous images that wake me soaked with sweat. I'm afraid to close my eyes." He glanced at the wall. "That doesn't help. The images still swim in front of me when my eyes are open."

"It's understandable that these dreams are happening. Especially because of what you experienced with Kane."

Starks picked at his cuticles. His voice came out thin as he said, "I told him I knew he was my son. I don't know if he was able to hear me or understand." He wiped at tears that refused to be held back. "On my way to find him, I made such plans for him. For us. I was determined to make him a part of my life. To make it up to him. The way I couldn't make it up to Kyle."

"You established a dream about your relationship going forward and built it up in your mind."

"I saw it as a measure of redemption."

Demory leaned forward and nodded. "You want to be released from your sins."

"Another impossibility."

"That's the definition, you know. Usually followed by a fresh start. If you feel Kane's death was punishment for your sins, and if you believed forming a relationship with him, claiming him as yours, would redeem you in some way, it sounds to me like you want to be redeemed. Maybe you want redemption for everything."

"Looks like that's not going to happen. Not in here."

"Isn't that up to you?"

"Not if my enemies have anything to do with it."

Demory inched to the edge of his chair. "Who are your enemies?"

"It's a long list. Too long."

CHAPTER 7

"It used to be that your wife," Demory said, "was the primary target of your enmity." His attention sharpened in response to the pained expression on Starks's face. "Or is Kayla now your ex-wife?"

"There isn't going to be a divorce. No point now."

Demory sat up straight. "What's changed?"

"Cancer. It's what caused her to lose Bret's bastard baby. And Bret. The disease is winning, not that she's fighting. "

"I'm sorry to hear it, Starks."

"They gave her months. I can't believe there's so little time left. I always thought …"

"Doctors are sometimes wrong about their prognoses. Some people's will to live keeps them going longer than anyone anticipated. Some of them outlive their doctors."

Starks leaned forward, shoulders hunched. "Jeffrey had to tell me. After I treated her like crap when she came to see me. Ripped into her so viciously, she left without saying a word about it. I didn't give her the chance. Even told her I'd be better off if she died." He cradled his head in his hands.

"Maybe you're ready to forgive her for her indiscretions."

Starks dropped his hands and shook his head. "Is that what you call twenty years of giving it to other men, making me look like a damn fool because I believed she was faithful?"

"After all this time, you still have a one-sided mindset about this. Not only did you cheat on Kayla, you had two illegitimate children, one while you were married to her."

"And she had one while married to me. Let me believe Blake was mine."

"She's admitted that to you?"

"I haven't told her I know. I'm not even certain she knows he's not mine."

"What a convoluted web people entrap themselves in." Demory picked up his pen and tapped it against the tablet. "How can you expect to cope with what's happening to her, if you can't even be fair with the truth?"

"How many times do I have to tell you that I can't forgive what I can't forget?"

"Then why mention redemption at all? What's the point?"

"Kane was my son. It's different when it comes to your children."

"That's selective reasoning. Convenient, but not accurate. Redemption is all about forgiveness, Starks. You can't expect to receive it if you can't give it. You might receive it from others for a while, but if that incoming column is full and the outgoing one is empty, the ledger tips or crashes."

Starks curled his lips in contempt. "Sometimes talking to you is like talking to a brick."

"Ditto." Demory relaxed his face and sighed. "That was inappropriate for me to say. I apologize."

Starks shrugged and stared out the window.

"I know what your problem is. You still love her."

"I was so sure I didn't. Then I realized I was going to lose her. Really lose her. All the times I said I wished she were dead. Now I'm going to get my wish, no matter how much I want to take it back. Whatever else she may have deserved, she doesn't deserve this. Neither do our kids."

"You said she's not fighting it. Isn't she getting treatment?"

"Jeffrey said no. Because it's too advanced. I need to check in with him about how things are going. I haven't talked to him recently. Wasn't up to talking to anyone." Starks stood and began to pace. "It should have been me."

"What do you mean?"

"Kane was killed to get back at me."

"For what reason?"

"People in here, the worst ones, get pissed at someone, they punish them, directly or indirectly. It was obvious I'd taken Kane in, was looking after him. Nineteen. Hadn't started to shave yet. I don't even know when his birthday is." He slammed his fists against the wall. "The kid was so green. Thought he was so damn smart getting himself tossed in here so he could be with me. Did you ever see him?" "No, but I wish I had."

"Had my dark, wavy hair, and brown eyes so like my son's. Nathan, I mean. Kane was average-sized, like me. No way could he defend himself against …"

"Against who?"

Starks turned away. "Against whoever did it."

"You *do* know, don't you?"

Starks avoided looking at Demory. "A number of people took credit. Until they learned I was Kane's father. Then they shut up and slunk back into their holes." The lie was easy. Necessary.

There was a knock at the door. Demory gestured for the person to wait. "Sorry, Starks. My appointment is here." He pulled his calendar toward him. "Let's meet every Thursday at four thirty. Any conflict with that day or time?"

"None I can think of." Starks stepped toward the door. He pivoted and said, "One of the lessons I've learned in here—and you'll have to excuse the alliteration—is that prison is a petri dish of pain."

"It's not like that for everyone."

"Seems I drew the short straw."

CHAPTER 8

He'd been as honest as he felt it safe to be with Demory, but one thing had been deliberately omitted regarding his nightmares: They no longer included the one inmate he'd personally killed or the three he'd prompted others to kill. What did that say about him?

It was too complex a question to deal with at the moment. Denial was more expedient.

Halfway to his destination, Starks halted his steps. The cell had been his refuge for months. Jackson had said he needed to make an appearance. Ready or not, it was time to ease back into life, as dismal as it was.

His grandfather, as the old and odd saying went, had probably turned over in his grave to know the grandson he'd raised had not only retreated from the world, but had also missed working his shifts in the library. That wasn't Ryan Lee Morgan's way. His grandfather had taken off work the day of his wife's funeral, and had returned to the factory the next day. "What am I going to do," he'd said, "sit around moping at home? Make myself available for a bunch of old biddies to wag their nagging tongues at me?"

Later, once they'd been alone, his grandfather had told him, "Freddie, crap happens in life. Some piles are bigger than others. You've got to shovel your way clear. Otherwise, you'll get buried. And, believe me, boy, you won't like the smell."

There was one major difference: his grandfather had never held his brutalized child in his arms until the last shattered breath left him.

Fetid odors, mounting obligations, and wretchedness pressed in on him. He needed air that wasn't contained or contaminated.

He needed to feel alive again, even if only by a sliver. He owed it to Kane. He owed it to the men who relied on him. And he owed the bastard who'd slaughtered his son.

Starks forced his feet to move, to take him to the double doors that opened to the yard.

A diversion, even a brief one, would take his mind off his troubles. Shock and grief had paralyzed him long enough.

He pushed the door on the right open and stepped outside for the first time since minutes before that day in the laundry room.

Maybe the fresh air would cleanse him of something.

Tell yourself another one.

CHAPTER 9

It took only seconds for heads to swivel and voices to drop to near whispers. Starks made a visual assessment of the yard—the bleachers, the packed-dirt area used as a basketball court, and around the fenced area, where several inmates stood alone or in clusters. A few of the men ate sandwiches purchased in the commissary. That explained the few men outside: It was lunchtime. Hunger no longer gnawed at him as it once had. Nor had he paid much attention to the time recently. Life had become a never-ending miasma of emotions, so why count the minutes.

Not one of his crew members was outside, not that he was in the mood for companionship at the moment.

No one was using the weights. It would be a relief to lose himself in the focus required to lift something other than his grief. Although no one was available he'd trust to spot him, he decided to start with the bench press. Two hundred pounds to start with should do it. Once in position, he began to count, his eyes squinted nearly shut against the sunlight. He paused to add additional weights, noting more inmates had filtered into the yard during his reps.

He wanted to feel his muscles work, his lungs breathe, his heart pump—to remind himself he was still alive, so made his movements deliberately slow. Sweat beaded and ran down his face and neck, pooled behind his knees and in the crooks of his arms.

He put the barbell away, grabbed a twenty-pound dumbbell and positioned his left knee on the bench, leaning over his knee before beginning reps with his right arm. A shadow fell over him from his right. Starks glanced at the inmate he'd seen around, but didn't stop what he was doing.

"You've been at it long enough," the inmate said. "Time to move on."

Starks made eye contact with the man and continued doing his reps. "I'll leave when I'm done."

The inmate grabbed the dumbbell in Starks's hand. When Starks held on, he said, "Maybe I wasn't straight enough. You're done."

Audible gasps and murmured comments came from inmates near the area. They edged closer.

Starks put both feet firmly on the ground. His grip tightened on the dumbbell. "Remove your hand and go away. Or risk losing your arm. Up to you."

The inmate attempted to wrench the weight from Starks. Starks flung the dumbbell to the side, grabbed the man's arm and twisted it, bringing the inmate to his knees. The several jiu jitsu lessons he'd had with Felipe came to him automatically, despite the recent absence of practice.

Inmates shouted and crowded around the two men. Threats laced with obscenities spewed from the downed inmate. Repressed rage welled inside Starks. He kicked the inmate, who landed on his back. A few inmates dragged the man to his feet. One of the men restraining him said something too low for Starks to hear. The man's eyes widened.

The inmate shook off the others and said, "Didn't mean anything, Starks." He gestured toward the bench press. "If you're not done, I can spot you."

Pulse racing, Starks glared at him. "It's all yours."

Disappointed at the absence of a brawl, the crowd began to disperse. Starks wended his way through them. For the first time in too long, his appetite nudged him. He'd make a quick trip to the commissary, and maybe stop at the library to discuss with Sam, when he might be ready to resume his shifts.

Halfway across the yard, silence engulfed him. Like the Red Sea, a cluster of men to his right parted, revealing the only African American at Sands with a white lion tattooed on his arm. Surrounding the inmate were six of his soldiers, who'd once belonged to Big Bo's gang. The man they shielded flashed yellowed teeth at Starks.

Seth.

CHAPTER 10

Starks's hands instinctively curled into fists. Seven-to-one odds sucked, no matter how much rage pounded in his head. But he had one advantage. In mere seconds, and done with slight-of-hand, as Jackson had taught him, the child-size knitting needle, with its poisoned tip, was out of his shirt hem and hidden in the palm of his right hand.

If this was the moment, so be it. He'd face it for Kane. He'd likely get killed, but he'd take Seth with him, or die trying.

First, he'd have to plow through Seth's soldiers, which meant he'd have to use up the poison on a few of them. Once he reached Seth, he'd go for the man's eyes. No matter the blows to his own body, he'd press his thumbs hard, make Seth squeal. Use his hand or head to crush the man's esophagus. That, or puncture his jugular with the needle. It wouldn't be punishment enough, but if this was to be his last act, it would have to do.

He palmed the needle in his other hand. Jabbed it into the thigh of the man on his left. Threw a punch that grazed the throat of the man on his right. The man he'd stuck should have been down, howling in agony, before heading out of this life for an eternity in hell. Instead the man swung and hit him in the jaw. The months-old mixture was inert. But the needle could still be a weapon, if he used it effectively.

Starks returned the needle to his right hand, securing it between the first and middle fingers.

Seth shoved his soldiers out of the way and charged forward.

Starks crouched then sprung upward, aiming for Seth's neck.

Seth ducked, spun, and connected his foot with Starks's groin, sending him curled and gasping to the ground.

Two of Seth's men threw themselves on top of Starks, slamming their fists repeatedly into his body. As the others kicked at him, sometimes missing and hitting their comrades, Starks kept a firm grasp on the knitting needle.

The words, "Break it up," were shouted from Starks's left. Someone got one last kick in, on Starks's thigh, before they all backed away.

Correctional Officers Simmons and Jakes, both on Starks's payroll, sprinted toward him, followed by two other guards.

Jakes shouted, "What the hell's going on here?" A few inmates shrugged, everyone stayed silent. Several of the inmates meandered away. Jakes rested his thumbs on his belt. "Typical."

Simmons holstered his Taser. "Show's over." To Jakes and the other two guards he said, "Get these assholes outta here." Facing the inmates he said, "Move, or lose some privileges."

While this went on, Starks slid the needle back into the slit in his shirt hem.

Simmons stared at Starks, who lay curled in the dirt. "That was some kick to your balls. Can you get up yet?"

"Might need a hand."

Simmons gripped Starks by the arm and pulled him to his feet. "I'm going to walk you back to your cell."

Starks followed Seth's movements with his eyes.

Simmons shook Starks's arm. "Leave it. Unless time in the Hole and nutraloaf appeal to you. I'm not the only one who saw you start it."

"You're right." Starks limped toward the prison door.

Simmons waited until they were inside Starks's cell to speak again. "I know you've had a tough time, but that's no reason to risk getting killed."

"Worried about your payments disappearing?"

"Don't be like that, Starks. You get something out of our arrangement. But if you're going to go looking for trouble, give us a heads-up or something. And don't face off with some asshole when you're outnumbered."

"I don't care about that."

"Got a death wish or something?"

"No death wish. At least, not my own."

"What's your beef with Seth?"

"I didn't like the way he looked at me."

"Yeah. Right. Heard that one before. Look, if there's something we should know about him—"

"Are you done?"

"All right, I'll leave. But you're smarter than this." Simmons shook his head and disappeared into the maze of corridors.

As Sam had said about himself, how smart he was had become debatable.

CHAPTER 11

Minutes later, Jackson stormed into the cell. "First time you leave this cell in weeks, and you have to make it a damn suicide mission? You got a crew chomping at the bit to help you take care of this Seth business, or take care of it for you, and you do this?"

Starks remained reclined on his bed. "It wasn't planned."

"You went into the yard alone. What, were you sleepwalking?"

"I wanted some air."

"Didn't you stop to think Seth might be out there?"

"I knew it was a possibility."

Jackson grabbed the chair under his desk, scraped it across the concrete floor and plopped into it. "Look at you. Cuts, bruises—ones I can see and probably ones I can't. Sore balls. You're gonna have to recover, and hope like hell you do it before the real fight."

"That was real enough."

"Someone catches you alone again, condition you're in, you're ground meat."

"I don't need a lecture."

"Don't expect any sympathy for your stupidity. Several of the guys should be with you at all times, at least until this mess is dealt with."

"That isn't always feasible."

"Feasible or not, Seth's preparing for battle."

"I intend to give him one."

"No yard skirmish is going to satisfy him." Jackson slouched in the chair and folded his arms across his chest. "Shape you're in now, you couldn't give him a pimple. He could come in here right now and take you out."

Starks smiled through the pain in his jaw and face. "You wouldn't let him."

"Don't screw with me, man. This is some serious shit."

"He could do that, but he won't." Starks's gaze met Jackson's. "He wants—make that needs—it to be a show of power. Bet on it."

"I am. He's recruiting and getting takers. His own rainbow coalition, you might say. His numbers are growing, ours are stagnant."

"We doubled when we added Sanchez's men."

"Some of Seth's Hispanic recruits aren't happy with you about that. They wanted to join Los Hermanos. You ruined their ambitions when you ended Sanchez."

"They don't have their story straight, do they?"

"Who it was that sliced his throat open is a minor detail to them."

"That's their mistake."

"Don't make it yours. Or ours. They know you were behind it." Jackson rubbed a hand back and forth over his hairless scalp. "We need more soldiers than Seth has."

"Handle it."

"Now you're talking. But it's going to take more than men." Jackson inched his chair closer. "It's going to take a brilliant plan."

"You have one?"

"Not yet. I've been waiting for the fog you've been in to lift so we could discuss it. Soon as I heard about what happened in the yard, I realized you're not in a fog, you are the fog."

"Whatever that means."

"It means you're flying blind. I wouldn't mind getting into a philosophical discourse with you about that, but one of the guys on dinner shift isn't feeling well. They asked me to fill in. I need to go make sure food that tastes like crap is unrecognizable when it hits the plates." Jackson put his chair back and started for the corridor.

"Jackson."

"Yeah?"

"It'll be all right."

"Only thing that'll make me believe that is when I see you're one hundred percent."

"That could take awhile."

"We don't have that long."

CHAPTER 12

J ackson and Simmons were right, of course. He'd known his and Seth's paths would cross eventually, but it was nothing short of stupidity for him to go into the yard alone, with no one to provide protection. The rage that had climbed up his spine when he saw the man, was hardly an ample weapon. But once they'd faced each other, there was no way he could back down. It would have been a deadly display of weakness. That fact would have hit the grapevine in seconds, and everything he'd worked and fought and bled for would have deflated like a punctured balloon.

Jackson was also right about the need for a strategy, but his mind was blank. Details for Big Bo's execution had been Jackson's idea, planned for months. But it was he who had presented the opportunity, as well as the indefensible weapon.

How do you plan for a battle when too many unknowns exist? They could probably devise a way to take care of Seth without a full-scale war, but the man wasn't going to leave himself open to attack. Unlike what he, himself, had done in the yard. And even if he and his some of his crew succeeded in getting Seth alone or with a few of his men, the rest of Seth's soldiers would take their revenge, and likely in the most brutal way possible.

Starks groaned and held his side as he retrieved the book that contained his cell phone. The full measure of his vanity was made evident throughout his body. Moving like a man whose bones were brittle, he checked the corridor then returned to his bunk. His breath grew ragged at the sight of the extra phone he'd intended for Kane. With his back against the wall and the book resting on his bent knees, he dialed Jeffrey Davis' number.

His long-time friend answered on the third ring.

"Jeffrey, it's me."

"You okay, bro? Gotta say, I expected to hear from you sooner than this."

"I've been dealing with stuff. Speaking of stuff, Mason should've gotten back from his trip overseas a long time ago. I want to make sure I have more powders sooner rather than later."

"He got delayed, but he's back on track now. Should have the powders ready soon."

"How's Kayla doing?"

"I guess if any news is good, it's that she's hanging on longer than anyone expected." Jeffrey paused then added, "Wish I had better news about Blake."

Starks gripped the phone. "What about Blake? God, I can't lose another son."

"What are you talking about?"

"Another time. What's happened?"

"He started hanging around with the wrong kids. Been skipping school with them. Got his ass suspended. Avoids being home as much as possible. Acts like curfew is the sound made when someone sneezes. I'm keeping an eye on him as much as I can. Just wish I'd done more of that before he got into trouble. I'm sure it's nothing more than a phase some fourteen-year-olds go through."

"I don't give a damn how old he is, he can't be doing this to Kayla. Not now. I'd tell you to take a belt to his butt, but that could get you arrested for child abuse."

"Not like the old days, is it?"

"I got licks with a belt one time from my grandfather. It set me straight. I never wanted to make him that angry with or disappointed in me again. That hurt worse than the belt."

"That why you never used a strap on yours?"

"I couldn't bring myself to strike them, even for disciplinary purposes. Still, Blake turns fourteen in a few months. He's too damn old to pull this crap. Not at a time like this."

"That bit about the age was my way of trying to diminish the situation. I didn't want to say this to you—you have enough going on, but I think it's more a coping mechanism for him. Teen or not, he's still a kid, feeling like he's about to lose another parent. I don't think it matters that he has other adults looking after him and carrying the load. I think he feels alone. And as the oldest of the three, he's overwhelmed with feeling he needs to be responsible. Knows he's unprepared."

"Can this situation get any more screwed up?"

"I'll see what I can do." Jeffrey stayed quiet for a moment. "There's something else I want to talk to you about, but I'd rather do it in person."

"That doesn't sound good. What's going on?"

"I'm seeing how I can rearrange my schedule. I'll get over there as soon as I can."

"Jeffrey—"

"I'll look after your family, bro. Gotta cut this short. Running late for an appointment. I'll get there soon."

Starks dropped the phone to his lap. Everything was falling apart. Jeffrey would do his best. A comforting fact, but a small one. Jeffrey, despite his best intentions, was limited. As much as he hated to involve his mother, maybe he needed to. He punched in her number.

"Who is this?" Lynn Starks snapped.

"It's me, Mom."

"I don't like answering without knowing who it is."

"Can't be helped."

Lynn sniffed. "How are you, son?"

"I just talked to Jeffrey. He told me what Blake's been up to."

"What do you mean, 'up to'?"

When he finished explaining, Starks waited for her usual eruption. He wasn't disappointed.

"You can be damn sure it isn't Blake's fault. I blame it on his whore of a mother. Karma's a bitch, and it's after Kayla's ass. About damn time."

"Mom—"

"Don't worry, son. I'll go to the house and see what's what. I'll do what needs to be done."

"I'm afraid to ask what that might be."

"Kayla's mother's too much of a damn libertine to raise my grandson. Proof that the apple doesn't fall far from the tree. Not that she could be bothered with her daughter or grandkids.

"That's it. My mind is made up. Blake is coming to live with me. I'm the only one who can discipline him the right way. He'll cut this crap out, and in a damn hurry."

"Don't do that."

"I'll call the nanny and tell her to pack his things. I can get him by this evening."

"No. You won't."

"Why the hell not?"

"Even if he's acting out, he's still a help with his brother and sister."

"Then all three will come home with me."

"You can't do that. It'll kill Kayla if you take her children from her."

"She's already dying. What's the damn difference? It's not like she took any great interest in them. Had to have a nanny take care of them, so she could act like the whore she is. Those days are over. I doubt she's still putting out. Who the hell would want her now? Still, with her, you never know."

Starks refrained from saying all he wanted to say. "You'll crush them if you take them away from her."

"They won't hurt long. Besides, they need to get used to life without her."

He massaged a throbbing vein in his right temple. "Damn it, Mom. You're making me insane."

"Watch your tone, Starks. Besides, Kayla did that to you, not me." She sniffed. "I'm only trying to help. You're treating me like I'm the one in the wrong."

Forgetting his bruises, Starks rubbed his face and flinched. "Moving them to your house won't help anyone." *But you.* "Just leave it alone. It'll work out. Jeffrey will see to it."

"I'm their grandmother. If you don't want me to act like it, what exactly is it you want me to do?"

"Maybe it's time we all forgive Kayla. Each of us has made mistakes. Everyone deserves a second chance."

"I'll forgive her. Just as soon as they discover the moon really is a big ball of blue cheese. You damn sure never held your tongue about her being a slut. Now, all of a sudden, you expect me to treat her like a martyr. Just because she's dying, which she deserves."

"Mom—"

"Your aunt just pulled up and honked. I can't be late to the hair salon. You'd think I deserved a little gratitude for all I've done and been through because of you two."

Starks moved the phone from his ear when his mother slammed the receiver down.

His family was imploding.

Despite Parker's wishful thinking, it was time to face facts. He'd remain caged here for the duration. Impotent, as far as taking care of his family went. The most he could do about them was make noise from a distance of two hours away.

Seth, however, was a different matter. A matter he could deal with directly. Seth's intention had been to wound him. Damage his reputation. Maybe if he'd known Kane was his son, the bastard might have thought twice. Maybe not. But Seth found himself preparing for a battle that was inevitable. And he'd get one. Shoved down his throat and up his rectum.

Next time he saw Jackson, he'd tell him to call a meeting with the crew. But not in the laundry room. He still couldn't go near that space. Twice, that room had become the drop-off point, the dying place, for two people he'd cared about. One day, he'd have to figure out what to do about the showers, where the attacks had occurred.

Before any meeting with his crew took place, he needed to seek Gabe's counsel.

CHAPTER 13

Muted hammering came from the other side of the heavy metal door that sealed off the workroom occupied by a sole inmate. Starks pounded with his fist and waited. The hammering stopped. Seconds later the bolt was thrown and the door flung open.

Gabe Bianchi's sparse white hair lay plastered to his scalp. Sweat dripped from his chin onto his shirtless torso, disappearing into the few-inch-wide patch of more-salt-than-pepper hair that tapered to a point on his small potbelly. He wiped his moist forehead against his equally moist forearm and raked his eyes over Starks. "You look like I thought you would. Maybe only slightly better. Come on in. I need a break."

"Aren't you overdoing it for a man your age?"

"I'm younger than I look."

"That's discouraging."

"You here to trade insults? I got a few I could hurl at you."

"I'm here for feedback."

"Got some of that, too."

Gabe pivoted and walked to the small table a few feet away.

Starks's eyebrows raised at the sight of a black arrow tattooed on the older man's back. "What's the arrow about? And why does it aim down? Is that a statement like, 'Kiss my ass'?"

"That's my damn business."

"Why so touchy?"

"Also my business." Gabe pointed to the extra wooden chair. He went to a long counter to the right of the door, picked up a bottle of water from a small stash and said, "Want one?"

"I'm good."

"I don't share your opinion." Gabe opened the bottle and spilled half the contents onto his head before guzzling the rest. He tossed the plastic bottle into a cardboard box then plunked into the chair opposite Starks. "You wanted feedback, so that's what I'm gonna give you. I'd ask you what the hell you were thinking, going seven to one, but we both know you weren't."

"It was a reflex."

"Reflex, my ass. You wear your damn emotions on your sleeve and sit on your brains."

"Go ahead. Let's add your lecture to the others I got. Maybe if enough people tell me it was stupid on my part, I'll finally get it."

"Not a bet I'd take. What you did was your first mistake. You survived it then made another one."

"I'm not following."

"You shoulda retaliated, right after you got your ass kicked. You shoulda got your soldiers to hit him hard and fast."

"It only happened a little while ago."

Gabe blew out an exasperated breath. "You screwed up. Now you'll never get him alone. He'll wrap soldiers around him like bacon on filet mignon."

"I already thought of that."

"And yet, here you are, alone. No soldiers standing outside that door that I saw."

"Nothing like an armchair general."

"How about you kiss my ass and get the hell out."

"For your information, I've never seen Seth anywhere, when he didn't have several men with him. Not since Kane. He's not the brightest bulb, but he's not a fool."

"Ten points for him, zero for you."

"I'll do better."

Gabe harrumphed. "Won't see me placing any bets on that, either." He shook his head and sighed. "What else is on your limited mind?"

Ignoring the insult, Starks let the dam inside him burst. He poured out his thoughts and feelings about the two sons he'd lost and Kayla.

Gabe let him talk uninterrupted then leaned his head back, eyes closed.

Starks jumped when Gabe slammed his fist on the table.

Gabe pointed a finger at Starks. "I told you before. I don't like whiners."

"What the hell? I just spilled my guts to you, old man."

"What you did was bitch about your life. Again. What do you want from me? Want me to pat you on the head? Give you a cookie, so you feel better?"

"I thought you, of all people, would understand."

"What I understand is that you need to grow a pair. Replace the little ones Seth kicked into your gullet."

Starks reared back in the chair. "I don't know what this is about, but unless you're schizophrenic, I know for a fact you're not the heartless S.O.B. you act like."

Gabe glared at Starks through narrowed eyes. He sniffed and relaxed his face. "Guess the wounds are still raw." He shifted forward. "There's something you gotta realize. You wanted to be the big boss in here. You're still considered that by some of these guys, but you're hanging on by a skinny-ass thread. Pain and agony, and a lotta crap you could do without, comes with the territory. You gotta deal with it. Or take up knitting."

Starks sat grim-faced, jaw clenched. "I know that."

"You know squat. I had to deal with losing a son. And a wife. Not to mention others I either respected or relied on. But I was a boss." He jabbed at his chest. "Whatever I felt like inside, I was the one people watched. My soldiers watched to see if I still had what it took. My enemies watched to see if I could be beaten or taken out."

"Not everyone can be as cold as you." Starks's chair scraped against the concrete floor when he stood.

"Cold's what you gotta be in that business, and this one. Don't try to act like you didn't feel iced rage when you went after the guys in here who deserved it."

"I knew what they'd done. I had proof. Word is, only thing you had were suspicions about who was involved in your son's death. Still, you executed them or ordered it done."

"Didn't bother me one damn bit. You, however, get your panties in a twist about every damn thing."

"Admit it. It crushed you to lose your son and wife."

"You're right about only one of those."

Starks leaned back against the nearest worktable. "I know your wife cheated on you, *and* what you did to the man, but you still loved her. Am I right?"

"Right up to the seconds before I snuffed the life outta her with these." He held up his hands.

Starks became fixed in place. He studied Gabe's face a moment then said, "You're lying. You don't have to pretend with me. She died of natural causes."

"Of course it looked natural. I'm a professional."

"You're serious."

"Damn straight."

A spasm of contempt crossed Starks's face. "To think I respected you. You're an animal."

Gabe's chair clattered to the floor as he leaped to his feet. He maneuvered around the table, toward Starks, his expression unreadable.

Starks inched left, toward the door. Uneasiness spread from his gut onto his skin.

"You snot-nosed little shit. You don't know shit about that kind of life. You're weak. And you're a problem. A big stinking, steaming pile-of-shit problem."

A sheen of perspiration on his face, Starks held up a hand. "Hang on, Gabe."

"You hang on. You keep company with killers, you gotta know how to kill. And be willing to do it. That includes family ready to stab you in the back when you're not looking. I killed the bitch. She'd plotted to kill me. I just happened to learn about it before she could succeed."

"I didn't know. You never said."

"Learn your damn facts before you judge. You're too damn full of yourself for your own damn good. Always assuming instead of going after facts and assessing them."

"I'm sorry."

"More than you know."

"I've upset you. That's not what I intended. I'll leave you to it. Maybe catch up with you when it's a better time."

"You're not going anywhere."

"What's that supposed to mean?"

"Not until you tell me what you intend to do about Seth." Gabe returned to his chair.

A shaken Starks followed suit. They'd had heated exchanges before, but never like this. Unsure of what to say, if anything, he waited for the old man to speak first.

"We both ran our enterprises out there," Gabe said, "but overseeing a company, like you did, and overseeing a prison gang? They have limited aspects in common."

"I understand."

"No. You don't. Why'd you get Trevor moved outta here instead of taking care of the little twit? He deserved it, not the clemency you gave him."

"He's a kid. A stupid one, but still a kid."

"And Seth? You gonna keep missing opportunities?"

"Word is, he's recruiting. I'm doing the same."

"That's the extent of your grand scheme?"

Starks shifted in the chair. "So far."

Gabe grunted. "You don't deserve power. Know why?"

"I'm sure you'll tell me."

"Because you don't understand what it is."

"You're wrong."

"You're too weak to seek true power, much less deserve it."

"The kind of power you had?"

"Damn straight."

"We have different definitions of power."

"There's only one. And that's why your face is messed up and mine isn't. You're a bigger fool than I thought. Man's the cruelest animal alive. He deliberately goes after who and what he wants. You plan to fight with animals, you better plan to win."

"That's what I intend."

"I got no faith in you about that. The way you handle your enemies, it's lucky you've made it this far."

"It's not as though I go around looking for trouble."

"You don't pick your enemies, they pick you. Then you deal with them. Otherwise, you find yourself six feet under or scattered in pieces the birds eat. It can't matter if it's a kid or a wife." He waited for Starks's gaze to meet his. "Or even a son." Gabe strolled to the door and opened it. "Now you can leave. I don't have anything else to say to you at this time."

Starks strained to keep his countenance and steps measured. Instinct guided him to fake confidence he didn't feel. The door slammed behind him. A soon as the bolt was latched, he moved as fast as his trembling legs allowed.

He'd pushed Gabe.

His grandfather's voice whispered in his mind: stupid is as stupid does.

He needed to wise up.

CHAPTER 14

What was wrong with the old guy? And what did he mean by "even a son"? Starks hadn't dared risk asking, but the words looped through his mind as he returned to his cell.

He stretched out on his bed. Closed his eyes to avoid focusing on the bottom of the top bunk. At night, when he was half-asleep, he often heard his son moving around above him. A habit, nothing more; yet, he wondered when it would begin to diminish. Perhaps it was time to get Jackson back in the cell, for that reason and others.

Even a son. What did it mean?

Gabe enjoyed being a cryptic bastard, but he was in no mood to work one of the old guy's puzzles. Not when more urgent matters clamored for his attention.

Maybe mister mafia man understood running an organization only slightly better, by virtue of being in business—if you could call it that—longer than he had been, but he knew what was what. Granted, Gabe's had been a criminal organization, but they'd both had to hire people; though, their interview processes and operation methods were significantly different. Differences aside, they'd had to build their businesses into a success. They'd had to train and compensate people they'd employed. Had to find ways to instill loyalty. And on occasion, when people had to be fired, they took care of it. Gabe's employee termination policy, however, meant something else entirely.

Because of how well he'd treated his employees at Tendum Enterprises, people leaving his employ had been a rare event. When someone had to be fired, also rare, he'd made it as painless as possible. They understood when he carefully explained why the two of them weren't a fit, were grateful to get a month's pay for each year they'd been employed there, plus an extra month. Those who'd been employed less than a year received two months' pay, rather than the usual two weeks' extra. The few who'd been released left with no hard feelings. They moved on to more fertile pastures.

All except the one guy, but something had to have been wrong with him. Something he'd missed about the man in the interview. This slip on his part had plagued him for a while, after learning what had happened to his former employee. Because he didn't want to believe he'd had any part in the guy not finding or accepting another job—how hard was it, really? Or losing his house. Or the man's wife taking their kids and leaving him to figure it out on his own. He certainly wasn't responsible, in any measure, for the guy taking his life.

Or was this one of those lies Gabe said he tended to tell himself?

No. People were responsible for their choices and the consequences, whether the consequences were rewarding or punitive.

The hypocrisy of that statement stung. But the fact was, he'd busted his hump to become successful. Had done whatever it took in hours and risks. He'd believed in himself, which had kept him going, even when he'd wanted to call it quits. The employee had been missing one or all of those elements in his character. How could he be blamed for what someone else lacked? Why should he be?

Starks massaged his temples.

Sometimes success was as much a curse as a blessing. Like in this hellhole, where inmates had to fight their way to the top of the food chain among the animals enclosed within its walls, or be consumed.

He'd fought something or someone since the day of his arrival at Sands. Fought to regain as much control of his life as he could. Certain inmates, like Seth, repeatedly challenged him, knocked him down. But he always got up. Sometimes it took a little longer to heal and regroup, but he always did.

Seth wanted to take his place, wanted to take over control of everything he'd fought so hard to build.

It was the second grave mistake Seth had made.

CHAPTER 15

CO Roberts, looking left, right, and front, strolled several yards ahead. Starks called his name and rushed to catch up.

Roberts turned around, shook his head at Starks's appearance, and opened his mouth to speak.

"Don't. I've already gotten enough grief about it."

Roberts held up his hands in a gesture of acquiescence. "What can I do for you?"

"I need to talk to Brunson. Is he working today?"

"Yeah. I'll tell him to meet you in your cell. I'll get back to you about the time."

"Take me to him."

"Now?"

"Do I need to say it another way?"

Roberts pressed a few digits on his radio. Amid the static, they heard Brunson respond. Roberts let his eyes scan inmates moving through the corridor. "Starks wants to see you. Wants me to take him to you right now."

There was a moment's pause. "You know where to find me."

They maneuvered their way through a maze of hallways and secured doors, until they reached the office. Roberts knocked on the closed door.

Red Brunson's gruff voice told him to come in.

Roberts turned the doorknob. "Want me in there?"

"No. But wait for me. It shouldn't take long."

Starks nodded at Brunson and closed the door behind him. He picked up the chair positioned against the back wall of the small, square office, wincing as he moved closer to the desk.

"You look like shit."

Starks glanced up, as he eased onto the padded seat. "Wish someone had told me. Always tried to look my best for meetings."

Brunson slouched back in his chair and linked his hands over his protruding middle. "You're also moving like you got it smacked outta you."

"When you're done with your assessments, let me know so I can talk."

Brunson gestured at Starks's face. "If you want me to do something about the guys what did that to you, I'll need names."

"I'm here about Trevor."

"What about him?"

"He's still in the SHU?"

"That's where you wanted him."

"Temporarily, is what I told you. We need to make him disappear permanently."

Brunson scowled and sat up straight. "Just a damn minute."

"Let me explain what I mean. You said you were working on getting him transferred to another prison."

"Like I told you, it'll cost you."

"I made it clear that I'd pay."

"Payment needs to be upfront. If it was just me …" He shrugged.

"Tell whoever that I'm good for it. You know I am."

Brunson pulled on his chin. "They're not as easy-going as I am."

"Persuade them. And do it fast. There's something else I want you to do that's attached to it."

"Such as?"

"First, get the kid out of here as quietly as possible. Then get word out, to inmates only, that you suspect I got to him or had someone else do it. Make it clear you have no proof. You, me, and anyone you involve will be the only ones who know the truth. Tell them they'll be paid to keep their mouths shut."

Brunson leaned back and studied Starks. "Let me get this straight. You want the scum in here to think you're some kind of ruthless sonofabitch who'd off a mouthy kid."

"You got it."

"What are you, nuts?"

"Are you going to handle this or not?"

Brunson half grinned, half sneered. "That'll really cost you."

"It'll cost me more if you don't handle this the way I want you to."

"I'll see what I can do."

"Make it sooner than soon. Then get back to me about what needs to be paid. Don't promise more than a grand to anyone you involve. Your bonus will be triple. That work for you?"

"Make it five."

"Deal."

Starks put the chair back, opened the door then shut it behind him.

Roberts eased away from the opposite wall and unfolded his arms. "Everything good?"

"Time will tell."

He hoped Gabe didn't see through his charade. He wanted the old man to think he could be just as ruthless. Maybe it would fool him. Maybe not. One thing was certain: whatever violence he exacted on any deserving inmate, he was no Gabe, nor would he ever be.

Unless he was wrong about that, as well. Too often, when survival was at stake, the line between good and evil blurred, until it was unrecognizable.

It was a convenient lie, and he knew it. But, what the hell was he supposed to do?

Starks clenched and unclenched his hands. Why should he care what that bitter old man thought about him? Why should his opinion matter?

But it did.

CHAPTER 16

"On the count" blared over the intercom at precisely three o'clock. Starks took his position outside his cell. He nodded at Jackson, who stood two feet to his left. "I think it's time."

Jackson's expression turned guarded. "For what?"

"For you to move back in. And for me to talk to the crew. I'll take care of arranging the former. You handle the latter."

"Ten-four. It'll have to be in the yard. I've added to our numbers. If we try to meet in the laundry room, it'll look like a mob."

Starks stared straight ahead. Jackson's tendency to be realistic and practical saved him from having to admit he couldn't so much as look at or pass the corridor that led to the laundry room.

CO Roberts took the count. CO Simmons handed out mail. As usual, Starks received none. When the guards reached him, he said to Roberts, "Tell Brunson I want Jackson back in my cell."

Roberts glanced at Jackson, who pretended to tip a hat that wasn't there, and then back at Starks. "You're sure?"

"Wouldn't have placed my order if I wasn't."

Roberts looked at Jackson. "You're on board about this?"

"The Dragon's wish is my command."

Roberts rolled his eyes. "I'll handle it. Jackson, move your gear after the count." He moved to the next cell, joining Simmons, who'd gone ahead.

The first time an inmate had referred to him as the Dragon, he'd taken it as a clear sign his efforts to build his reputation at Sands were working. Hearing that sobriquet after these several weeks, felt hollow, yet at the same time, reassuring. As though he might be able to restore some of what had been lost, both with inmates and himself.

Jackson clapped his hands once the count ended, and then bounded into his cell. Starks returned to his. There was nothing left of Kane's to move, so as to make room for Jackson. Someone had taken everything, with the exception of one item, oblivious as to how significant it would be for him. Had done this while he lied to the investigative council about knowing who'd killed his son.

Starks pulled a plain white envelope from under his clock. Lifted the flap and looked inside at the small black comb. Several of Kane's hairs, as dark as his own, remained threaded in the teeth.

Jackson zoomed into the cell. "It's good to be back at the old homestead. You okay, Starks?"

Starks cleared his throat and tucked the envelope back into its place. "Organize your things later. Get word to the guys to meet at the bleachers at four."

Jackson tossed his items onto the upper bunk, and turned, grinning. "Some things never change. I get my small comforts where I can."

"What's that supposed to mean?"

"You're back to giving me orders. How I missed that."

"You're right. Some things *don't* change. You're still full of crap."

"Yessir, happy days are here again. See you at four."

Starks fixed his eyes on the items strewn on the upper bunk. Jackson would occupy that space tonight. No longer would he be alone with his thoughts. Heavy silence would be replaced by Jackson's buzzsaw snores.

Jackson had a point. Inside this gray space, they all had to get their small comforts where they could.

CHAPTER 17

S tarks scanned the faces of the men who aimed their attention at him. Without counting, he guessed about ten were new. His usual crew members sat in close proximity on three risers. All present, with the exception of Ethan. Starks took in a breath and prepared to speak.

Stinky jabbed Pete in his side, nodded toward something to Starks's right and said, "I still think he's the one that offed Crazy D."

Pete frowned. "You mean offed Crazy D's head."

"Whatever. I don't know whether to be scared shit-less of him or buy him an ice cream."

"That's enough," Starks barked. "You know better than to believe or spread rumors about crew members. Or you should."

Heads turned to watch Ethan's approach when the lanky young man emitted a high-pitched squeal. Ethan skipped forward, stopped and waved his arms in circles. He leaped up, as though trying to catch something in the air that only he could see. Grinning, he ran forward, skidding to a stop when he reached Starks. He extended his arm, as though showing Starks what he held in his hand.

Ethan said, "L-l-look, S-s-starks. Isn't it p-p-pretty?"

A number of the new members murmured. One of them said, "What's that freak doing here?"

Tank turned to the man and said, "One thing you gotta learn is, we protect the ones who can't protect themselves. This guy's lacking some things up top, but he's harmless. Like it or not, he's one of us."

The inmate frowned. "Say what?"

Starks gave a subtle shake of his head at Ethan and gestured for him to take a seat. Ethan started toward the top riser. Several new members seated at the top moved to lower levels.

Starks said, "Settle down. You new guys, I'm going to tell you what I tell anyone who joins with me. Loyalty is paramount. Betrayal comes with a severe penalty. However, once you align with me, you'll be looked after. Your families need anything, you tell me or Jackson or Tank. I'll see what I can do to help them."

"How you gonna help them from in here?" one of the new members asked.

"That's between me and whomever. In this crew, we look out for each other. As Tank said, we protect those inside too weak to protect themselves. And, we don't make fun of anyone who has a disability." He glanced at Ethan, who winked at him. "I'm going to let Jackson fill you in on some details."

Jackson left the lowest riser and stood next to Starks. "Everyone knows who Seth is?" The men nodded or said yes. "Seth wants to knock Starks out of top-man position. He knows our cell phone business has taken off big-time. And although I handle the drugs and alcohol side of the business, that's doing well, too. Seth wants it all."

One of the new members said, "We get in on that?"

"Yes," Jackson said. "You can talk to me after the meeting about it. The main thing to know is that Seth wants what Starks has. He also knows he's got a big-ass target on him for," he glanced at Starks, who stared over the heads of the men, "killing Starks's son."

All eyes focused on Starks. He kept his expression blank and met some of their gazes.

Jackson continued. "Seth's adding soldiers. I can't pin down how many he has, but rumor has it, it's more than we have. We're a good number, including the Hermanos gang, and some of you are big enough to almost count as two, but we need more. You're welcome to recruit. But it's me or Tank who approves them. Be careful who you talk to. We don't want any infiltrators."

Tommy looked at Jackson then at Starks. "What are we gonna do about Seth, and when?"

Starks said, "When it's time for you to know, you'll know."

"We could get Wolly to kick in with us. Told me, himself, he's interested."

Tank reared back. "That bunch of skinheads? You outta your Black mind?"

A number of the new members, also African American, protested. One of them said, "No way I'm hooking up with that pack of racist mothers."

Tommy raised his voice over the objections. "There's gonna be a war. A big one. Isn't that right, Starks?"

Starks nodded. "It could be today, tomorrow, next week, or a few months from now. That means we need to be prepared at all times."

One of the new members asked, "How we supposed to prepare for that?"

Starks fixed his gaze on the man then looked at the others. "If you don't have shanks, talk to Jackson. He can set you up. In the meantime, we'll keep adding to our numbers."

Tommy pointed at Starks. "It's gonna be about who stays alive. That's why you gotta take Wolly's offer serious. We wanna win, don't we?"

"I don't know them," Starks said. "Nor am I comfortable about engaging with people who have that kind of prejudice running through their veins."

"Well," Tommy said, "they know who you are. Think you're badass. They're ready to stand with you."

"Who told you this?"

"Wolly. Told him I'd tell you and get back to him. What about it?"

Starks's diverse crew waited, eyes fixed on him. "Tell Wolly I'll think about it." He held up a hand to the grumbling men and gestured toward Jackson. "Meeting's over. Jackson will answer any questions you new members have."

Ethan jumped to the ground, ran in a circle then to the front of the bleachers. "S-s-starks, I h-h-have s-s-something t-t-to show you." He tugged on Starks arm, dragging him far enough away to be out of earshot.

"What's up?"

Ethan waved his arms and dropped the stammer. "I fully intended to settle the score with Seth when he killed Kane. Then I found out Kane was your son. I apologize for not telling you sooner how sorry I am for your loss. Anyway, I came up with something quite special for lion man. But I couldn't get to him. He makes certain he's never alone or outnumbered. One of his numerous annoying habits."

"I appreciate the thought, but—"

"Perhaps it's a good idea to join forces with Wolly."

"Oil and water don't mix. I've got too many Blacks and Hispanics running with me."

"Get him and his miscreants involved just long enough to help you take care of Seth and his men. Then, as you find him and his kind objectionable, tell baldy to go screw himself." He hacked the side of his hand against his neck. "Or let me take care of him for you."

"I'll give your idea thought."

Ethan marched around Starks, who reminded himself that crazy could be useful.

It could also be detrimental.

Shouts came from the northernmost part of the yard. Two Caucasian inmates had a third one cornered. Size-wise, the men were evenly matched. The one being picked on had a mop of ginger hair.

"Ethan, tell Jackson I want to see him."

Ethan zigzagged to the bleachers. Starks kept his attention on the potential altercation. They were too far away for him to hear what was being said, but something was going to blow, unless someone backed down. He scanned the yard to see if any guards were paying attention. CO Simmons watched the inmates from the northeast corner for a few moments then started toward them. Starks caught his attention and gave a subtle shake of his head. Simmons nodded and stayed where he was.

Jackson sauntered up to Starks. "If we had popcorn, we'd be set to watch the show."

"Know any of those guys?"

"I've seen them around, but that's all. The guy with the red hair got here two days ago. You thinking about getting our guys to rescue him?"

"I want you to recruit whoever wins."

One of the inmates shoved the red-haired man. The other one laughed and shoved him from the other side. They bounced the man between them for several seconds. He twisted away, grabbed each man into a headlock and smashed their heads together. The inmates staggered to the ground. He stepped over them and started walking in the direction that would take him by the bleachers.

"Jackson, tell him I'd like to talk to him."

Jackson grinned and hastened toward the man, who went into a defensive stance as Jackson approached.

Jackson spoke to the man and pointed back at Starks. The man nodded and walked with Jackson to where Starks waited. Starks kept his head shake to himself at the sight of toffee-colored freckles competing for space on skin the color of milk. The guy stood out in a way that wasn't healthy for him.

"You have something to say?" the man asked.

"That was a nice maneuver." Starks nodded toward the two inmates, who sat up and looked around until they spotted their opponent talking with him. Their expressions registered surprise then alarm.

The red-haired man said, "They seem afraid of you."

"It happens."

"Am I supposed to be afraid of you?"

"I'd rather you join my crew."

"I'm not a joiner."

"Maybe not, but you are a target. Every new guy is. You, however, with your coloring, are like a lone tree in a desert. There are any number of dogs here eager to run up to you and lift their leg."

"I can manage."

"You'll manage better with a team watching your back." Starks gestured toward the bleachers. "I formed our crew to protect people who need it. That's why you see such a mix of individuals."

The inmate studied the crew members. "I'd like to think about it."

"I'm Starks."

"Blackie."

Starks's eyebrows arched. "How'd that happen?"

"Name's Stan Black."

"Okay, Blackie, here's the deal." He raised his shirt, revealing his scars. When the anticipated reaction came, he said, "Join me, and you'll be on the side of the angels. Don't join me, and you stand a greater chance of being escorted out of here by one, and not in the way you might like."

"What do I need to do?"

"Jackson will explain things to you and introduce you to the crew."

Starks left his second-in-command to handle the details. That was one more man added to his numbers. Now all he needed was about another thousand to feel confident he could win.

CHAPTER 18

The toilet flushed, jolting Starks awake. He'd slept through the night for the first time in weeks. A quick glance at his clock showed the time as 5:47. Thirteen minutes until overhead lights further illuminated their desolation. Locks opened electronically released inmates from the confines of their cells.

He closed his eyes again. "What's on the breakfast menu?"

Jackson turned the tap on and washed his hands. "The usual."

"Then I won't miss anything."

"When are you going back to work?"

"Soon. Just need a little more time."

Jackson shook the can of shaving cream, filled his palm with lather, and smoothed it over his head. Razor in hand, he began to shave his scalp. "I wonder if the skinheads would mistake me for one of them. Ignore the fact that my skin is a lovely shade of coffee with a splash of cream."

"Clever camouflage like that? Sure. It'll fool them."

"The thought of joining that bunch makes me want to grow my hair out. I wonder if I have any gray yet." Jackson studied his reflection. "Wonder if I've lost any. For all I know, maybe I am bald and wasting my time."

"What do you think about mixing it up with them?"

"Not the best idea. Not the worst. It would either piss Seth and his soldiers off or scare the hell out of them."

"I'm not thrilled about the prospect, but maybe a temporary arrangement would work. If Wolly's gang and mine don't try to kill each other first."

"That mean you're giving it serious thought?"

"How many in his gang?"

"Maybe thirty or so. But that's a best guess."

"That's a decent number."

"Wish I had dibs on selling foam and razors to them."

"Your mind runs on one track."

"Maybe so, but I run more than one train on it at a time."

The overhead lights brightened. Locks clicked and barred doors throughout the prison squealed open.

Starks sat up and ran his hands through his hair. "Another day."

Jackson tossed his razor into the trash and splashed his scalp with water. "What are you going to do with yours?"

"Find Felipe."

"And do what?"

"Make sure my investment is still secure."

CHAPTER 19

J ackson left a few minutes after six. Starks decided he'd abandoned his usual morning routine long enough. Working with the weights in the yard had brought that fact home clearly to him. The fight with Seth and his men had proved this even more so.

He stretched then launched into lunges, twenty each leg, followed by forty push-ups and forty ab-crunches. Frowned at the weakness and tightness in his limbs and torso. Ignored the pulls of scar tissue from the dozen knife wounds inflicted several months ago, but felt like a lifetime.

He did the best he could to wash his body and hair in the quart-size lavatory then got dressed. Eventually, he'd have to take a real shower. Several members of his crew would have to be with him. Too many people had a target on his back for him to chance going alone.

That was only one obstacle. The other would be to find a way to block images he couldn't suppress. Both Kane and Skullars had been brutalized on those scarred, over-bleached tiles. Then they'd been dumped in the laundry room to die. He'd have to address this matter soon. He couldn't afford to feel or act like a child afraid of the basement.

A little over an hour remained before the count at eight. Some inmates moved about in their cells, others remained in bed, either genuinely snoring or pretending to sleep. The general feeling shared by most was a lack of an incentive to look forward to their day. That wasn't true for every inmate. Some inmates focused on improving themselves through educational or spiritual courses. This caused them to cling to the hope that their efforts would make a difference in their existence. But he didn't associate with them. He held no judgment in their regard. They coped with their reality in their own way, as he coped with his in the manner he'd been forced into.

He put a small amount of water into a paper cup and carried it to his bunk. His back to the entrance, he pulled the Latex thumbs from his pants pockets and sprinkled a small amount of each powder onto the tiny window sill. Using the child-size knitting needle, he stirred the powders and drops of water into a paste. Twisted the needle in the mixture and blew on it until certain it was dry, before sliding the needle into the hem of his shirt.

Starks cleaned the sill then returned to his bunk and positioned himself so he could peer out the window. Overcast, dismal out. As though the gray interior had leeched through the concrete walls and infected the world.

Little in his life was predictable anymore. So many problems, too few easy solutions.

He stayed where he was until the count was called. Once completed, he joined the stream of inmates moving to the chow hall. Joined the line that inched toward the slot, where trays laden with unappetizing slop got pushed through in anonymity.

Tray in hand, he started for the usual table, where his crew had seated themselves. He paused at the table claimed by Los Hermanos, returned greetings from the men. "Felipe, you have time to meet with me after chow?"

"Where?"

"Gym."

"I'll be there."

He continued forward. Tank's bulk occupied the end of the bench bolted to the floor. Starks gestured with his head for his number-two man to move over.

Tank said to the men on his right, "Shove down."

Starks rapped on the table and took a seat.

Tank stuffed half a hard roll into his mouth and said, "It was time."

"Whether I wanted it to be or not."

"Funny how life is like that."

"It keeps me in stitches."

"You got the scars to prove it."

CHAPTER 20

Felipe sat alone on the bench press. Starks glanced around at the dozen or so men in the gym as he walked toward the Hermanos leader. A few inmates looked his way and nodded. He took a seat next to Felipe. "How's your father doing?"

"He's holding his own at the moment. Papa's strong. More in his will than in his body." Felipe scowled. "Fucking cancer."

"My sentiments exactly."

"What about you?"

"Pretty much the same. Holding my own, I mean."

"About your son … I'm sorry."

Starks nodded and stayed silent.

Felipe nudged Starks. "Say the word, and I'll take care of Seth. And it won't be quick and clean, like I did Sanchez."

"I haven't decided how I want to take care of him."

"He's adding soldiers."

"That includes a good number of Hispanics, from what I hear."

"None of ours. They see you as their savior from Sanchez. Got tired of being cut by *El Razor* for looking at him the wrong way."

"It was my pleasure."

Felipe made eye contact with him. "It was mine even more so."

"Good to know your men are still on my side."

"Your men now."

Starks cast his gaze at the Hermanos working out. "However, I consider you their captain and want it to stay that way."

"The razor is still where I hid it. I can get it, if you want it."

"I'll keep that in mind. You have any sway with the other Hispanics?"

"There are several gangs in here. Some we get along with, some we don't. Want me to recruit?"

"Seems like the smart thing to do." Starks stepped onto the mat a yard away. "How about sparring with me for a few minutes?"

"Amigo, did you look in the mirror? You're still healing from your last fight."

"You think that would stop Seth or any other asshole here?"

Felipe grinned. He lunged forward. In seconds, he had Starks pinned to the mat on his back. "You're out of shape. Physically and mentally."

"Only if it's you or someone you trained."

"Condition you're in, my old *abuelo* could beat you."

"Translation?"

"Grandfather. You need to react quicker. Need to pay better attention to what's going on around you. Should have anticipated my move and dodged or countered it."

"If you've got the time now, how about teaching me some new moves?"

Felipe positioned himself at the center of the mat. "First, let's see how you do with the ones you've learned."

"Go easy on me."

Felipe shook his head. "Like you said, Seth won't."

"Crap."

Felipe held his hands out and flexed his fingers toward his body. "Let's go, amigo. Let's see if you still got chops."

"Just make sure I can walk out of here without help when we're done. If you beat me too bad, you'll screw up my rep."

"Maybe I'll let you win a few times. Let you look good in front of these guys."

"As *you* said, Seth won't go easy on me, so you can't. But don't break anything."

"I'll leave the Dragon intact."

CHAPTER 21

Despite complaints from his bruised body, Starks left the gym pleased with his performance. After being slammed to the mat on his back or face a number of times, he ignored the pain and became more of a challenge to Felipe. He didn't win the matches, but neither did he humiliate himself.

He turned the lavatory tap on in his cell, and then turned it off. With resolute steps, he started for the yard. The previously drab sky had mostly cleared to a pale, partly cloudy blue. An intermittent breeze hinted at the possibility of a cold front. He checked the bleachers first, relieved to see Tank, Pete, Stinky, and Blackie there, cheering crew members engaged in a basketball game.

He joined the men on the bleachers.

Tank wrinkled his nose and said, "What the hell you been doing?"

"Working out with Felipe."

"Damn, Starks. You trying to take over Stinky's title?"

Stinky punched Tank's arm. "Screw you."

Starks pretended to watch the game. "I can't go to the showers without protection. Not with the heat ratcheting up."

Tank puffed his cheeks and blew out a breath. "All it takes is one mother seeing you're alone with your pecker dangling, and blabbing it to Seth." He stood and faced the others. "C'mon. We're on shower duty." He said to Starks, "Let's get your stuff."

"Probably a good idea if you have a weapon or two. We'll go by your cells first."

"We don't go anywhere without carrying. Not no more."

Tank entered the shower room, while the others stood near the entrance. He returned moments later. "No one in there who's got it in for you. That I know of. We'll stay here. Anyone starts anything, yell."

"I won't be long."

Five men stood in front of shower heads on the far left, including Paco, who faced forward, eyes closed, as water cascaded over his thin silver hair. Starks didn't know the other four, so opted for a shower head on the far right. He faced the men as he undressed. Quelled the images insistent on tormenting him.

Paco, eyes still shut, shifted right then left under the stream. Something undefined registered in Starks's brain, but he was in a rush to get clean and out. He put whatever it was out of his mine. Turned the water on and stepped into the stream face-first.

Starks propped his hands against the wall and let the water wash over him. He adjusted the temperature. Tight muscles began to relax.

Maybe Gabe was right. Swim with sharks long enough, you become one of them. Instead of killing deals, he was now killing men. Even worse was that it bothered him less and less. He'd *had* to kill Big Bo. If he hadn't, Bo wouldn't have failed a second time to end him. Still, his conscience had plagued him. Maybe the first kill was like that for others, with the exception of Gabe and several inmates at Sands. Deciding to remove a person from his life, and seeing it through, could too easily become second nature. That would give him another thing in common with Gabe. Despite the hot water, he shivered.

Starks removed his hands from the wall and raised his face to the stream.

He'd entered a vortex where he aimed to take power from someone or they aimed to take power he'd fought to acquire. More and more broken bodies cluttered the interior of that swirling mass. And before long, others would join them.

Doubt filled him as to whether or not his eventual liberation would happen before there was nothing left of his soul to salvage.

Starks shut the water off and grabbed his towel. Paco and two other inmates had already left. The remaining inmates wouldn't be far behind. He hurriedly dressed.

He couldn't get out of there fast enough.

No matter where he went or how fast he moved, he couldn't escape the ghosts that never left him alone.

CHAPTER 22

The crew members stayed with Starks as he dropped off his dirty clothes and damp towel in his cell. "You think the game's still going on?"

Tank leaned his shoulder against the barred door, keeping an eye on the comings and goings in the corridor. "Bet on it."

"Let's head to the commissary. We'll get enough sandwiches and such for our crew."

Pete, who'd been scoping out items on Starks's desk, turned and asked, "You buying?"

"Wouldn't have brought it up, if I wasn't. First, I want to make a quick detour to the library."

After the less than sixty seconds it took to talk with Sam, they made it to the commissary. Starks plucked a variety of bags of chips from the shelves. "Pete, you and Stinky grab some waters. Blackie, you get the soft drinks. Better make it fourteen of each, just in case."

Starks selected twice as many plastic-encased sandwiches from the shelf and added them to the rest of the stash, which filled three small cardboard boxes. He glanced at the clock on the wall. It was close to ten. He'd arranged with Sam to resume his library shift at one, working half-days until he was ready to resume his usual schedule.

They carried the boxes to the bleachers. Starks joined in the cheering. It felt good to behave more normally. Except when he pictured Kane kicking up dust under his feet, as he dribbled the ball and dodged players. Or how Kane had searched his face for approval, whenever he sunk the ball through the net.

He faced a situation similar to when Kyle had died: Being a member of that unique group of parents who've lost a child. Back then, the only person he'd been able to talk about Kyle with was Jeffrey. Even then, he did it only once. And it took getting drunk to make it easier to face his feelings. Then it was back to acting as though nothing had happened. Back to hiding the fact of the boy.

People tended to become uncomfortable, whenever someone spoke about that kind of loss for too long a time after death. How long was appropriate to do so? Weeks? Months? Those not directly impacted by a parent's loss might be sympathetic but tended to get on with lives, and often were as eager for the parent or parents to get on with theirs. Those not intimately affected had no gaping wound refusing to mend, seeping infection into other areas of their lives.

Yes, there was a difference between parents who'd shared their lives with their child since conception, as opposed to his own situation with Kyle. And with Kane. Their wound was larger, but that difference could matter only so much. Some significant part of each parent had been lost, and nothing would ever change that fact.

He snapped out of his reverie when the guys on the bleachers and in the game cheered. His crew members jogged to the bleachers, some of them high-fiving, others scowling as they promised to kick ass next time.

Starks picked up the box filled with sandwiches, took one, and passed it along. "Eats and drinks. There should be enough for everyone. I know it's early for lunch, and that it's hours until dinner, but—"

One of the new members said, "Won't stop me from eating twice. I stay hungry enough to eat a cow."

A different new member said, "That's why the guy they call Chef is doing life in isolation."

Pete turned to him. "Someone got life for eating a cow?"

The inmate shook his head. "His wife. Seems she sucked at cooking. Finally decided he'd show her how it should be done. Not that she was around to appreciate it. She was an extra-large woman. Even after two weeks of meals, police still found more than half of her in the freezer."

Starks left his sandwich wrapped. He'd take it to the library, in case his appetite returned. "I'll catch up with you later," he told them.

Tank, mouth full, said, "Where you going?"

"Library. Think I'll get an early start."

One of the new members said, "We gotta be able to read?"
Tank popped him on the side of the head.
Starks shook his head and walked away.
He wanted out.

CHAPTER 23

Paco occupied the same chair as he always did, in front of the first computer nearest the entrance. Whatever it was that he was reading on the screen, held his rapt attention.

Starks cleared his throat so as not to startle him then asked, "How's it going?"

Paco stood and placed a hand on Starks's shoulder. "About your boy ..."

Starks nodded and lowered his eyes. "How's the memoir coming along?"

Paco grinned and reached for a three-inch stack of pages. "Read it and tell me what you think."

Starks took the stack. He lifted the cover sheet and cringed at the small font size filling the first page. "You finished it already? That was quick."

"Si, amigo. Only took me five years." He laughed. "You read it. You tell me what you think. Okay?"

"I'll get back to you when I'm done."

He left a beaming Paco and started toward the office at the back.

On the other side of the large bullet-proof window, Sam Carson sat behind the desk. He looked up when Starks entered. "You're more than an hour early."

"That okay with you?"

Sam shrugged. "I got no problem with it."

"You don't have to stay, unless you want to."

"Free time. In prison. Yippee." Sam stood. "Not much going on at the moment. Should be an easy first shift back for you."

Starks held up the manuscript. "Paco's memoir."

Sam stared at the stack of pages. "He finished it."

"I'll give it a look and figure out how to say something nice. After all his effort, I don't want to trounce on his feelings."

"You're the soul of compassion."

"And you're an asshole."

"Back at you." Sam walked around the desk. "See you tomorrow."

Starks pulled the chair into position and propped his feet on the desk, ankles crossed. He placed the cover sheet face-down on the desk and started to read.

He finished the first chapter and went to the door. "Paco."

"Si?"

"Get in here."

He returned to his chair and gestured for Paco to sit in the extra chair in front of the desk. "I had no idea you could write like this."

Paco grinned. "You judged the book by its cover, yes?"

"If I'm honest."

"I got a journalism degree in college. But as soon as I got here, I realized I couldn't let others know. You know what it's like with these guys, as well as some of the guards. They resent it if you're more educated than they are, which is most of them."

"You don't win any popularity contests."

"Except for you."

"I'm not popular."

"You're infamous. That automatically makes you popular."

"In a twisted kind of way."

"This is a twisted place."

"Tell me about it."

Paco's smile faded. "You'll read how twisted in there." He pointed to the manuscript.

Starks pulled the memoir closer. "Which chapter?"

Paco grinned. "Nope. Don't want you skipping ahead. You got to start at the beginning and follow the thread."

"What do you plan to do with it?"

"I haven't decided."

"If the rest is as good as what I've read so far, you should publish it."

"I don't know. I'll give it some thought."

"What's there to think about? Maybe I could find a way to help."

"It's not that."

"What is it?"

"I don't know how long they'd—"

"What? They, who?"

"Just read it." Paco eased to his feet. "Think I'll get lunch then some fresh air and vitamin D."

Starks tapped the manuscript with a finger. "I'll finish this as soon as I can. Although, it looks like it may take a while."

"Looking forward to your thoughts." Paco shuffled, whistling, from the office.

Starks settled back and resumed reading, simultaneously impressed with the straightforward writing style, as much as how candid, raw, and revealing Paco's life story was. More than once, as he read the tiny print, he shuddered.

CHAPTER 24

tarks's time allotted for Paco's manuscript had not gone uninterrupted. Several inmates needed help on the computer. Others couldn't find the books they wanted to read. It had to be some of the lazier inmates who consistently put books wherever they felt like it, if they bothered to put them up at all.

By the time his shift ended at four, he'd read up to chapter nine. His four-to-seven replacement crossed the threshold to the library, nodding once at him from the other side of the window. Starks scooped up the manuscript and the uneaten sandwich, and hurried to his cell.

He and Paco were on friendly terms from the start, but never had conversations longer than a few minutes, and never about anything significant. Still, he'd considered Paco someone he could trust to leave in charge of the library whenever he had to step out to take care of something that couldn't wait. A service paid for with food and soft drinks from the commissary.

Based on what he'd read so far, he was eager to engage in lengthier discussions of substance with the man, who proved through his writing to be intelligent and witty and unvarnished in revealing the poverty and violence he'd been born into. Paco's childhood in such a dysfunctional home caused him to wonder how the man had eventually escaped, how he'd gotten himself through college. What or who it was that caused him to throw away all he'd worked for. And, what it was he wanted Starks to know about Sands.

Starks positioned his thin pillow against the wall and read with the manuscript on propped knees. He came to a passage about an argument Paco's parents had when he was six years old. It turned into a brawl, leaving both parents bruised and bleeding. It was the words they'd said to each other, and Paco's now-adult insightful comments about how some people crush love until it no longer resembles anything worth saving, that reminded him of how he'd spoken to and about Kayla when enraged, a rage that had lasted several years, only abating recently. He'd never struck her, but it had come close a few times. When he'd been drunk, waiting for her to stagger in during the middle of the night, also drunk. Suspecting she was cheating on him. Learning later that his suspicions were justified, but more egregious than even he had anticipated.

They hadn't spoken since her last visit, despite the news that she was dying.

He brought the large library book to his bunk, opened it, and took out the cell phone. Thought about all the things he should say to her, needed to say. Like how sorry he was. About everything. Imagined how their conversation might go, or rather, how he wished it would. Dialed the area code and stopped. Switched the phone off. He wanted this to go right.

He turned the phone back on and dialed the house number. Sweat beaded at his hairline.

Kayla answered. Said hello. Said it again, and a third time.

With hands shaking uncontrollably, Starks pressed the off-button, put the phone in the book and the book back on his desk.

The illusion of unlimited time was no longer a luxury.

He had to face this.

Before time ran out.

CHAPTER 25

A faint, narrow rectangle of first light crossed Starks's blanket. The clock on his desk showed twenty-three minutes until lights-up. Above him, Jackson snored softly, like a man with no worries. Someone moved around in one of the cells on the same side of their corridor.

Jackson groaned. "You can have first dibs on the facilities. I'm not getting up till the last minute."

"Want me to wake you, if you go back to sleep?"

"That won't happen. Not with the lure of kitchen duty beckoning me."

Starks dropped to the floor and began his push-ups, ignoring his body's protests. After twenty reps with both hands pressed against the concrete, he switched to the one-handed version. Then sit-ups and lunges.

Ceiling lights came up. Barred doors opened. Jackson yawned loudly and dangled his legs over the side of his bunk. "Did you finish Paco's memoir?"

"Fell asleep."

"That bad?"

"That tired. Plus, it's long and with small print."

"How far did you get?"

"He's seventeen."

Jackson yawned again and scratched his crotch. "I remember seventeen."

"So do I."

"I was gawky as hell and doing magic shows for small change. What were you like at that age?"

Starks's lips formed into a half-smile. "Sure of myself. Cocky. Striving to make money and something of myself. Crazy about Kayla."

"So, not much different."

Starks started to speak then stopped. At the lavatory, he leaned over and splashed warm water on his face. When he straightened, his reflection in the mirror offered several physical contradictions to Jackson's statement.

He prepped his face with shaving cream. "I've decided to work the entire day."

"That's one way to keep out of trouble."

"One can hope."

Starks changed his clothes, tucking the fake thumbs into his pockets and the knitting needle into his shirt hem. He returned to his bunk and Paco's compelling story, while Jackson got ready.

"Catch you later, Starks."

"Uh-huh."

He read until the count, making mental notes of questions he wanted to ask Paco.

Starks took the manuscript with him to the library, certain there would be time to read more. He made a quick stop for packaged cinnamon rolls from the commissary. One for him, two for Paco.

The usual inmates who went to the library as soon as it opened were there, minus one. No Paco.

He continued into the office. "Morning, Sam."

"Thought you were working the afternoon shift."

"Decided there was nowhere else I wanted to be."

"What scheme are you working now?"

"No scheme. You're welcome to stay or take the day off."

Sam shook his head. "You kill me."

"You're not on my list." Starks placed the manuscript on the desk. He met Sam's gaze. "What?"

"Too many damn people in here got too many damn people on too many damn lists."

"It happens."

Sam stared at Starks a moment then stood. "I'm going to get my butt out of here and figure out what to do with all this free time you've given me. By the way, we're expecting a shipment today." He started for the door.

"One more thing."

Sam looked over his shoulder and waited.

"Let them know I'm working. Don't want to get a Tier One for not being at my cell at eleven and three."

"I'll do that. Wouldn't want you to get into any trouble."

"Appreciate it."

"Man like you does everything he can to avoid trouble."

Starks narrowed his eyes. "There a point you want to make?"

"I'd be wasting my breath." Sam lightly punched the door jamb as he passed it.

Starks took a seat behind the desk and positioned the manuscript in front of him. He turned to the next page to read, opened the cellophane wrapper on one of the rolls and took a bite. He'd barely finished one chapter when the familiar squeak of the handcart crossed the entrance threshold. Through the window he watched an inmate wheel three large boxes toward the office. He noted the page number and put the manuscript into the top drawer on the right.

The first box was filled with magazines to be cataloged on the computer then filed properly in the reading room, which took all morning. Periodically, he'd check to see if Paco had arrived. By noon, there was still no sign of him. No one was there he cared to leave in charge, so he ate the rolls and continued to unpack the remaining boxes containing books rejected by their owners for whatever reason.

Four o'clock. Paco hadn't so much as popped in to find out how far he'd read. He supposed eight hours a day, seven days a week for five years, and in the same chair, warranted a change of scenery.

Starks's replacement arrived ten minutes late. He instructed him as to what was left to do, retrieved the manuscript, and returned to his cell.

At 4:47, Jackson stopped at the cell entrance. "Even dragons need to eat. Some of the guys are waiting at the end of the corridor. Act like the leader they think you are."

"The old adage is true. Misery loves company." Starks put the manuscript at the foot of his mattress then folded his blanket neatly, using it to cover the memoir.

Eleven pairs of eyes fixed on him as he walked up the corridor. His crew had expectations.

What he wanted to tell them was, even if they expected that anything could happen, it was never preparation enough.

CHAPTER 26

On line, Starks scoped out the chow hall, focused on Seth, whose head hovered low over his breakfast tray. Seth shoveled food into his mouth, scowling when the man on his right elbowed him and said something. Seth glared at Starks, whose expression remained a blanket of ambiguity, his interest fixed on seeing if he could estimate how many soldiers were Seth's. An impossible task. They could fill any number of tables. Maybe their numbers were so large, some of them had to eat during the other meal shift.

Only a few minor scuffles occurred. As usual, a result of one or more new inmates unaware that seating was not first-come, first-sit.

He reached his table, relieved to see Blackie seated among his crew. One down, who knew how many others to go.

Starks ate what he could tolerate. Declined his crew's invitation to join them in the yard. Back in his cell, Paco's life story held his attention so firmly, Roberts had to tap his nightstick twice on the barred door.

"Starks. Visitor."

"Who?"

"Jeffrey Davis."

"Give me a minute."

Roberts nodded and waited a few yards from the entrance.

Starks positioned his blanket over the manuscript and joined Roberts. "Everything still good with the payments? They're being made on time?"

Roberts twirled his nightstick. "So far."

They turned right at the end of the corridor, making a left at the next hallway. Laughter drew Starks's gaze to a cluster of inmates heading for the yard. Seth, with about fifteen or so others trailing him.

Starks and Roberts made another right. "You don't need to walk me all the way."

Roberts shrugged and headed off in the opposite direction.

Starks made the five-minute trek to the visitors' room in under three minutes. It was easy to locate Jeffrey, who stood out like a bronze God of Cool amid yellow-clad inmates and beige vinyl tables and chairs. His friend's selection of a table positioned in a corner at the back wall, had to be deliberate. A hoped-for signal he had something needed ready to transfer to Starks.

Smiling, Jeffrey stood, got a better look at Starks and shook his head.

Starks threaded his way through tables and bodies, holding his breath to block the assault of body odors and cheap colognes. They managed a quick man-hug, without reproof from guards.

Jeffrey waited for Starks to sit then took the chair next to him. "Another fight? Did you win?"

"I'm here, aren't I?"

Jeffrey glanced around the room. "That's a fact." He shifted his focus back to Starks and gave him a once-over. "You've got some muscle definition going on. Few pounds lighter, too."

"Weights, floor work, some jiu jitsu." At Jeffrey's puzzled expression, he added, "An expert is training me. Used to win competitions before he came here."

"No shit? Looks good on you, bro. Okay. Business first. I got the powders from Mason. Had to use the fake-thumbs trick again. You know the drill."

Jeffrey surreptitiously loosened the Latex appendages from his thumbs and palmed them. Out came the handkerchief for the pretended attention to his nose, then down to the ground went the white square with the thumbs inside the fold.

Starks retrieved the handkerchief, which he placed on the table. Hands in his lap, he slid the fakes over his thumbs and pressed the edges until they blended with his skin. "You said you had something else to tell me."

Jeffrey cracked his knuckles.

Starks's smile faded. "Crap. Is it Kayla?"

Jeffrey shook his head. "She's maintaining. But that's not it."

"I wish she'd change her mind about treatment. Any extra time she can get seems worth whatever discomfort it might cause."

"She's afraid of how the effects might scare the kids, more than they are now."

"Talk to her. Convince her to at least see or talk with Garrett Hall. He knows his stuff. If he can't personally help her, I'm sure he'd refer her to someone who can."

"I'll suggest it, but you know what she's like when her mind's made up." Jeffrey stared at his joined hands resting on the table. "You should call her."

"I tried."

"You couldn't reach her? I understood she never leaves the house."

"Froze when I heard her voice."

"That's not like you."

"I was afraid of what might come out of my mouth. Or that I'd break down. She needs me to be strong, the way I was when we were together."

"Bro, what she needs is for you to be real."

Starks pursed his lips and nodded. "I'll call her. Soon. What about Nathan and Kaitlin?"

"Your kids are doing as well as anyone has a right to expect. I saw them Wednesday evening. Wanted to check on how things were going, see if they needed anything, above what I'm taking care of."

"I'll never be able to thank you enough for looking after my family."

"They asked if they could come with me next time I visited you. I told them I'd see what's what. Didn't want to tell them I was coming today." Jeffrey cracked his knuckles again.

"Spit it out."

Jeffrey bowed his head. "I'm trying to figure out how to say it."

CHAPTER 27

Jeffrey wiped his palms on his pants and nodded once. "Kayla had called me about Blake's behavior. Said she didn't have the strength to control him. That the nanny's hands were already full with helping her and minding the other two. They'd both tried talking to him. He said he understood, but his behavior got worse, not better. She asked me to go to the house and talk to him, since for once, he was there.

"It was a Saturday afternoon. He'd invited one of his friends over to hang out by the pool. I told her not to tell him I was coming to the house. Better to show up and confront him, not give him a chance to bug out of there."

"Smart thinking."

"Maybe." Jeffrey cleared his throat. "I parked in front and walked around the side of the house. Made sure I didn't make any sound that would alert him."

"You're taking your time getting to the point."

"Yeah. All right. I didn't see them. Then I noticed the door to the pool house was partially open. Went to a window and looked in. Found Blake and his friend. Kissing." Jeffrey looked at Starks. "His friend wasn't a girl."

The news hit like a blow. For a moment Starks sat still and breathless. He eased forward and rested his forearms on the table, hands clasped. "What did you do?"

"I tapped on the window. I'll never forget the shock on those boys' faces. I went inside and told the other boy it was time for him to leave. He did. At warp speed."

"What did Blake say?"

"Nothing. Just sat there looking terrified. I asked him what that was about. He pleaded with me not to tell you. Said you wouldn't understand."

"He's right. I don't. You were here last time he visited. You remember how pissed off he was that Kayla didn't approve of his girlfriend. The one he was so 'in love' with that he intended to marry her as soon as it was legal."

"I asked him about that. He said when they got around to their first kiss, it felt weird. Like he was kissing his sister."

"She wasn't the right girl."

"That's what I told him. He didn't seem to go for that, so I asked him how it felt to kiss his friend."

Starks's features were pinched. "And?"

"He clammed up. Couldn't get so much as a nod or head shake after that." Jeffrey sat back. His shoulders lifted then dropped.

"Did you tell Kayla?"

"Figured she has enough to deal with."

"Good. Don't."

"How do you want me to handle this?"

Starks raked his fingers back and forth across his forehead. "Hell if I know. He's my boy. I love him no matter what. But I never expected this." Only, he reminded himself, Blake wasn't his biological child. Did it matter? If he and Kayla had been one of those couples who'd had to adopt in order to have a family, he'd be facing the same situation. He'd yet to tell Jeffrey the truth about Blake. He'd told Demory and Gabe. Why not Jeffrey? Because he didn't want it to slip out accidentally. To anyone.

What was he thinking? Jeffrey had always kept his secrets. He opened his mouth to speak then clamped it shut.

"What were you going to say?"

"That as unexpected as this is for me to wrap my mind around, imagine my mother's reaction, if she finds out. If it turns out that he's gay, that is, instead of this being some one-time adolescent exploration. We never discussed homosexuality in our family, so I don't know what she'd say."

"She's old-school."

"Close-minded and stubborn."

"Proud."

"Pride hasn't always worked to our advantage in my family." Starks's body slumped in the chair.

"What do you want me to do about Blake?"

"For now, about the kissing, nothing. He's already consumed by confusion, with all that's going on. Besides, I don't know what I feel about it, much less what to say. About his other behaviors, tell him we talked. Tell him I said he'd better straighten up and help with his mother, brother, and sister."

"Or what?"

"Or I'll have you bring him here so I can get real with him. Give him a show-and-tell about what happens to people who screw up their lives."

"He's been here, has seen what's what."

Starks patted his scarred abdomen. "He hasn't seen these."

CHAPTER 28

Starks reached his cell in time for the eleven o'clock count, with only seconds to spare. Thoughts tumbled in his mind. He was in unfamiliar territory.

After the count, he paced in his cell, a different kind of panic shooting through him. What if it turned out to be true? What the hell did he know about raising a gay son? A predilection so opposite his own. He needed to be better informed. Only one person could do that.

The barbershop was empty, except for Steve, who sat with a fashion magazine outstretched in front of him. He tilted his head one way then the other and said to the model on the runway, "Sorry, sister, but that is *not* a good look on you."

Starks rapped on the open door.

Steve looked up. His smile faltered. "Your poor face!"

"Matches the rest of me."

"Tell me who did this. I'll give him, or them, the worst haircut they ever got."

"Appreciate the thought, but no way. Not going to get you into trouble."

"You're right, of course. I'd either look worse than you do or be unable to sit for weeks."

Starks cringed. "How about a trim and some advice?"

Steve bounced from the chair and gestured for Starks to sit. "Lucky you. I can provide both." He secured a paper cape around Starks's neck. "I'm *so* relieved you said 'trim.' I would have been a puddle if you'd said to shave your hair off again."

"Once was enough."

"Such thick, wavy locks." Steve retrieved a pair of scissors he kept in a locked drawer. He ran a comb through Starks's hair, paused and said, "I'm sorry about Kane."

The few people who'd offered condolences had said, *Sorry about your son*. Hearing his name confirmed that Kane had been real, not a figment of his imagination. Starks made eye-contact with Steve's reflected image and nodded.

"You know, Starks, if you want to talk about him, I'm a good listener. They say it's healing to do that. I should know." Steve made the first snip.

"It's another son I want to talk about. I need advice."

"I've only been Daddy to a Pekinese, but I'll do my best."

"My son might be gay. He's only fourteen. What the hell does he know at that age?"

Steve halted, scissors poised to cut. "What did *you* know, when you were that age?"

"I knew I liked girls."

"*Bing*-o!"

"You can't repeat any of this."

Steve crossed his heart and waited.

"He was caught kissing a boy."

"Unh-hunh. Did he like it?"

"He's not talking."

"Is he afraid of what you might say? Is he afraid of you?"

"He never was before. At least, not more than what's normal between parent and child. I need you to be honest with me about what it's like. I know it can't have been easy to come out. You did come out, didn't you?"

"When I was twenty-three. Like a bud in bloom."

"How did your family take it?"

"Some accepted it. A few said they'd always suspected."

"What about your father?"

"Too much humiliation for him. Such a prominent businessman. An *esteemed* member of the community."

"He rejected you?"

Steve checked his reflection, patted his thinning hair on top. "Oh yes. After he tried to beat the gayness out of me. I was in the hospital for a week."

Starks's face paled. "I'm sorry. I can't imagine doing that to any of my kids. Only time I touched them was to hug them."

"It was the same for my father. Until it wasn't. I'd always thought love ran deeper than that, especially for one's child. All any of us want is to be accepted for who we are. After all, it wasn't as though I chose it. Never talked to him or any of my family again. Saw his obituary in the paper. I avoided his funeral, but I cried like a baby for weeks and weeks. Then I came up with a way to cope."

"Which was?"

Steve shrugged. "Had rousing sex with a beautiful man I picked up, and then downed a bottle of sleeping pills. The next morning, he left to get breakfast sandwiches and a paper for us. When he came back, he tried to wake me and couldn't. That was the first time I tried to kill myself. The second time failed as well." He cocked his head. "From what I hear, you know what *that's* like."

Starks rubbed the older scar on his right wrist and said nothing.

"*Anyway*, I figured since I hadn't succeeded, there must be some purpose to my being alive." Steve waved his hand holding the scissors and looked around the room. "Some purpose."

"Sounds like hell."

"Some might say I exchanged one for another."

"I'm trying to get a sense of what my son might be feeling now. Confused, for one."

Steve raised the scissors and began to snip at an unhurried, contemplative pace. "People around you have expectations about who you are and how you should be. Like a box with your name on it that you're supposed to fit into neatly, so they can feel safe inside their own boxes. I heard derogatory comments about my kind while growing up. Not a lot, just often enough to let me know there was something wrong with *those people*.

"I was confused when I started crushing on boys in my class. I didn't dare show it.

"By the time I was in high school, I knew. I carried on a pretense. You know. Asked girls to dances and out on dates. I was terrified of drawing attention. Believed I was flawed beyond redemption."

"Were you ever with a woman?"

"Honey, I tried. And failed. Depression settled in like a hen on her eggs. I felt alone. Desperate. Then I learned about a gay bar a few towns away. Finally, I didn't have to be lonely. To say I flourished is an understatement. But I kept my doings hidden. Until my boyfriend insisted I come out and move with him to Manhattan so we could be free." He rested a hand on Starks's shoulder. "If your son is gay, please love him for who he is. It'll make life less tragic for both of you."

"No offense to you, but I pray he isn't. I don't want him going through the hell you did."

"Is it his hell you're worried about or yours?"

Starks made eye contact with Steve's reflected image. "Both, if I'm honest."

"You have to deal with your own feelings, but you can make it so it isn't as difficult for him as it was for me."

Starks shook his head. "I'm old-fashioned enough to believe a man should be with a woman."

"I think you mean *conditioned.*" Steve propped his hands on his hips. "What if society forced you to suppress those feelings and be with men only? Would you conform? Could you?"

Starks rubbed his face. "Point taken."

"I hope so. Because if your son discovers his key fits a different lock, he'll need you to be there for him. When a son knows his father loves and accepts him ..." Steve sniffled and crossed the room for a tissue.

"There's a lot to think about."

"Better if you feel rather than think. Now, let's finish your trim. Unless there's more you want to ask."

"Not at the moment. But if I need to talk again ..."

"You know where to find me."

They were silent until Steve removed the cape. While Steve brushed hair from his neck, Starks said, "What happened to the boyfriend who wanted you to move to Manhattan with him?"

"He's the one I told you about when you forced me to shave your hair off."

Starks nodded and exited, shaking inside at the possibility that Blake could end up imprisoned for life, like Steve, or dead, like Steve's cheating lover.

In teaching him to be strong, his grandfather had forgotten to tell him that events had a tendency to reveal exactly how fragile life could be and often was.

Especially when you weren't expecting it.

CHAPTER 29

Back in his cell, Starks removed his shirt and used a wet paper towel to wipe away the tiny hairs that had fallen past where Steve's brush could reach.

His stomach roiled at the thought of Blake perhaps having to face similar experiences. Rejection from some. Beatings. Being berated. Maybe worse.

Blake needed guidance more than ever now, and here he was, getting ready for a fight that might take him out of his son's life. What would Blake do then? Jeffrey considered Blake, Nathan, and Kaitlin as his nephews and niece. But that role was far removed from one of a parent. Plus, Jeffrey kept busy with the business and handling all the various payments, et cetera, he sent his way. Nor did he want to burden Kayla with this. He could get Jeffrey to bring Blake to Sands more often, but that wasn't the kind of readily available support the boy might need.

That left one person, who'd known and loved Blake since before he was born.

Another shiver ran through him. He had to do it. It couldn't be helped.

He took the phone and book to his bunk, dialed his mother's number, and said, "It's me," when she answered.

"Whenever you call me so soon after the last time, it's never good."

"There's something I need you to do."

"If I can do it, I will. If I can't, I'll find someone who can."

"I'm afraid you're the only one. And I need you to keep it confidential."

"Now what?"

Starks took in a deep breath and let it out. "I'm not certain, but it's possible Blake may be gay." Silence filled the space between them. "Mom?"

"Are you on drugs?"

"I'm serious."

"That's it. I'm getting him the hell away from that crazy, messed up house. Away from that vile woman who's confused my grandson with all her screwing other men in your bed."

"There was only one man she took home."

"Whatever. Nobody's going to tell me my grandson is gay. Screw that."

"But if he is—"

"Then he got it from her side of the family. No one in our family is gay."

"That we know of."

"No one. Period. Nor would we have allowed it. As soon as we hang up, I'm going over there. I'll straighten Blake out, and tell Kayla what I think about how she's mixed up my grandson."

"I forbid you to do any such thing."

"Why the hell do you call me to give me bad news then demand I do nothing? Why call me at all?"

"If I weren't here, I wouldn't bother you."

"Whose fault is that?"

Starks groaned. "I'm not even certain this is a real situation. I don't think Blake knows either. Kayla doesn't, and I want it to stay that way. All I want you to do is offer your love and support, without any conversation or judgment about this, so he doesn't feel abandoned. Can you do that? Because if you can't, you might as well stay away from him. I don't want to humiliate him more than he already is. And, I don't want him made to feel like a freak, because of your intolerant attitude."

"My attitude? As for tolerance, it seems to me that I'm asked to tolerate a lot more than I should have to. And to keep quiet about it."

"If I can't trust you, there's nothing left. Do you understand that?"

After a pause, Lynn said, "I'll do as you ask."

"But you don't have to like it."

Lynn sniffed. "Some things never change."

"Mom … thanks."

"Huhn."

Starks turned the phone off and cradled it to his chest. The thing about involving his mother was that he never knew if he'd done the only thing he could or made a massive mistake that would leave teeth marks on his ass. That depended on what she actually did. Her intentions were good, most of the time. But how often her good intentions wreaked havoc in their lives were too numerous to count. His grandfather had been able to rein her in. When Ryan spoke, Lynn listened and obeyed. However, he doubted his grandfather would have been understanding about any of this.

For thirty-nine years, he'd believed everything his grandfather and uncles had told him was true about life and love. Those beliefs had influenced every decision he'd ever made.

How disquieting it was to now question so much of what had been his compass. Jackson would tell him it was life showing him who's boss. There were any number of inmates who wanted to show him the same thing.

What else was life planning to dump on him, to prove them right?

CHAPTER 30

Sunday morning, Seth and five of his gang sauntered into the chow hall. They cut in front of inmates on line for breakfast trays, confident no one would confront them.

Starks kept watch, reminding himself he needed a plan, preferably one that might prevent a full-on gang confrontation. He also needed to know how many men were aligned with him, were willing to put their lives on the line for him, as much as for their own benefit. That was information any general would need, before devising a feasible strategy.

After breakfast, most of Starks's crew headed to the yard for a basketball game. It took cajoling, but Starks finally agreed to play. This time, despite remaining soreness in his torso and limbs, his movements across the dirt-packed court were sharp, quick, accurate. New members lauded him, as though scoring points with the orange ball proved his ability to win in other matters. Crew members not playing occupied the bleachers, cheered, occasionally shouted rude comments made in jest, and sometimes not.

Starks got the ball from Pete, adroitly dodging attempts from other players to get it away from him. He drove up dust as he dribbled the ball and jogged toward the net. Scored then mused about how seldom it was for any of them to have moments like this, when they could, if only for a while, forget where they were.

In his imagination, he was with Jeffrey on the asphalt court in their neighborhood park, where they and several of their friends played this game. He recalled clear images of ducks skidding across the water's surface of the lake yards away, landing, paddling yellow-orange webbed feet. Recalled how when someone overshot the net, they'd all rush into the water to retrieve the ball and cool off during those July and August days, laughing as the ducks quacked their displeasure at being disturbed.

Starks leaped, slammed the ball through the hoop. Grinned at the inmates' whoops and returned the high-fives. His eyes flicked right when he saw Jackson enter the yard. His smile faded in response to the set features of Jackson's face, and the manner in which he carried himself as he continued toward the bleachers. The expression Jackson wore was all too familiar.

He started toward Jackson, slowly at first, hesitant to hear what his cellmate had to say, then broke into a jog. "What's happened?"

"It's Paco, man. Some guys just found him in the gym. Strung up."

Starks bent over at the waist and propped his hands on his thighs, his breaths shallow.

Jackson kicked a dirt clod. "That's not the worst of it."

Starks straightened and aimed his eyes skyward. "What could possibly be worse?"

"Someone carved your name into his chest. Whoever did it, didn't wait until he was dead to cut into him."

"Sonofabitch." Anger pushed in on him. "Come with me."

"Where we going?"

"Just walk, Jackson."

They started for the building. Starks's crew yelled for him to get back in the game. He ignored them.

Starks entered the cell first, cursed and kicked his chair.

Jackson looked around the room. "What?"

Starks grabbed the folded blanket at the foot of his bed and flung it to the opposite end. "Damn it."

"Again, what?"

"It's gone. Paco's manuscript. Now I get his motivation for killing him."

"I don't follow. What motivation? Who?" Jackson pulled his chair from under his desk and sank into it.

"Seth. Who else? Paco told me he included something about how twisted it really is in here. When I asked if he planned to publish it, his response indicated someone might block him. He wouldn't say more.

Said to read it. That I'd see what was what. He had something on Seth, bad enough for that bastard to do this to him. Bet on it. "

"You get to that part yet?"

"I was getting close. I should have ignored him and skipped ahead."

"What are you going to do about—?"

They were interrupted by CO Roberts. "Starks, Spencer wants to see you."

Starks sneered. "Of course he does." He faced Jackson. "I'll see you when I see you. But just in case, wait here, at least until lunchtime."

He and Roberts kept silent until they turned right out of the corridor. Starks said, "No shackles and just you. Should I take that as a good sign?"

"I wondered about that. Spencer likes to make a show of you, whenever there's an opportunity."

"Guess I'll see what kind of entertainment, at my expense, he's in the mood for this time."

Three corridors and two electronic doors later, they reached the investigative council room. Roberts put his hand on the doorknob. "Here we go."

"The question is, Where will I be going when he's done?"

CHAPTER 31

Roberts shut the door behind them then took his position in front of it. Starks strode directly to the chair bolted to the floor, centered a yard in front of the long table located at the far end of the room. Tony Spencer sat ramrod-straight in his usual chair, his eyes trained on Starks.

Starks said, "You're alone today. And, since when do you guys do your thing on weekends?"

Spencer removed his glasses and cleaned the lenses with his tie. "New policy. We work weekends and rotate who's here." He slipped the glasses back onto the bridge of his nose.

Starks shifted to the edge of the chair. "For your information, I was fond of Paco. I believe it was mutual. I'd never hurt him."

"I know it wasn't you."

Starks cocked his head. "That's different."

Spencer's complexion flushed red. He pointed his finger at Starks. "So far, I haven't been able to pin you with any of the deaths related to you since you got here. I know you're guilty, or at least involved. But I also know you don't autograph your work."

Starks started to proclaim he was guiltless of the other deaths, but they'd already done that dance a number of times. To go there now would trigger Spencer. "So, why are you talking to me?"

"Since it was your name used, maybe you can tell me who did it."

Starks exhaled hard. "I'd like to know that, myself. He was an old man. Any sign he put up a defense?"

"You can forget about me giving you details."

"He wasn't strong, but neither was he feeble. He'd have put up a fight. Did you look for anyone with fresh injuries?"

"I just said no details. There's something else, off-topic but equally disturbing, I want to discuss with you."

"You've lost me."

"I've been here long enough to smell when a war's brewing."

"What war?"

"Don't screw with me, Starks."

"Wouldn't dream of it."

Spencer picked up his pen and aimed it at Starks. "I want it stopped. Now. I'm not going to have another damn battle in my prison. Hasn't been one for five years. I don't intend to allow another one. Takes too damn long to recover. Too many damn people to answer to."

"I'll put the word out, if you think it'll help. Maybe whoever is involved will call off whatever he's planning."

Spencer leaped up and slammed a palm against the table. "I'm telling *you* to your face. And, you can shove that clueless expression up your ass. Someone killed Kane. I didn't believe you then that you didn't know who it was, and I still don't. In all this," he scowled and waved his hand, "deep mound of manure, you're in the middle of it. Because you always are.

"Tell me who killed your son. Tell me who you think killed Paco. Tell me what the hell is about to go down. I can help you. Let me. So this thing doesn't blow the walls off this place."

"If I hear anything, learn anything, I'll get word to you."

Spencer's hands knotted into fists as he glared at Starks. He shook his head. "Roberts, get him the hell out of my sight. If he wants to leave in a body bag, there's nothing I can do about it. I just wonder how many others he's going to take with him. And, if it'll even bother him."

Roberts opened the door as Starks reached it. They didn't speak until they were yards from the council room.

"What *is* being planned, Starks? How bad is it going to be?"

Starks kept his face forward. "I can honestly say I have no idea what the plan is."

They reached the corridor of C Block. Roberts put a hand on Starks's arm. "Will you give me a heads-up when you do? Some of us have a wife and kids we have to look after."

"As soon as there's something you need to know, I'll tell you."

Roberts nodded and headed back the way he came.

Ethan rounded a corner and stopped, grinning when Starks motioned for him to join him.

Starks kept his voice low. "You heard about Paco?"

"Yes. I'm most displeased."

"I liked him, too."

Ethan huffed. "It's not that. I'm displeased that someone's trying to one-up my creativity."

Starks's expression was grave. "As surreptitiously as possible, confirm it was Seth who did this, and—"

Ethan's surprise registered on his face. "What's the connection between Seth and Paco?"

"Me." Starks explained what he suspected. "Get back to me as soon as you know something."

"Can I torture people for information?"

"I said to be surreptitious."

"Just eager to feed a need."

"Practice a little patience. Please. Now beat it. We're starting to draw stares."

Ethan picked an invisible something from the top of Starks's head and began to talk to *it* as he trotted away.

Starks continued on to his cell. Spencer had stated what he'd tried not to focus on. How many of the people relying on him, wouldn't survive the storm when it broke?

CHAPTER 32

Jackson sprang up in his bunk when Starks entered the cell. "I was sure Spencer would stick your ass in the Hole again."

"That was my thought, as well."

"What'd he say?"

Starks turned his chair around and sat with his forearms resting on the back. "Wanted to know if I knew who did Paco, and ordered me to stop the war before it has a chance to start. Said he can smell one brewing."

"He's sharper than I gave him credit for. What'd you say?"

"That I didn't know anything about either situation."

"Bet that went over well."

Starks's brow creased. "Whatever Paco included about Seth in the memoir must have been significant." He pounded a fist against the back of his chair. "Why the hell did I listen to that old man? *Read the chapters in order.* I need that manuscript."

"I'd say the chances of getting it back are slim to nil."

Starks looked directly at Jackson. "You need to be extra cautious from now on. Same for the crew."

"You think Seth aims to pick us off one at a time, like tin ducks at one of those carnival booths? I thought you said he wouldn't do that."

"Maybe I was wrong. If you really want to make someone suffer—"

"Make those they care about suffer."

"We're not dealing with normal people, here."

"Psychopaths and sociopaths."

Starks nodded. "Speaking of which, I think it's time to accept Wolly's offer."

Jackson shifted to the edge of the bed and let his legs hang over the side. "That's like holding a match to a fuse. You do that, and some of our guys might bolt."

"Talk to them. Tell them I'll comp them."

"Supplying them with commissary won't make them feel better about standing with skinheads. Hell, they might side with Seth because of it."

"They're better off standing with Wolly's gang than against them."

"You have a point."

"Seth made a point with Paco, and by taking his memoir."

"Did you mark your place on the manuscript?"

"I never do. I remember the page number."

"Then whoever has their shorts up their ass about you reading it, doesn't know how far you got."

"Right." Starks turned to look at the currently empty cells across from him. "Inmates' things, mostly commissary, get trucked all the time. This is the first time anyone took anything of mine."

"Not even when you first got here?"

"Nope. Probably because I put Big Bo in the infirmary my first week in."

"I remember hearing about that."

"Lot of inmates thought I was insane."

Jackson chuckled. "I thought it showed you had promise."

"Stupid asshole made it a case of him or me."

Jackson leaped down and stood in front of the toilet. "Guess you arrived here with dragon mojo."

Starks stared out the window, while Jackson tended to his business.

Jackson pressed the handle down. "Guess we gotta hope your mojo doesn't go down the toilet. And us with it."

CHAPTER 33

"I don't want anyone or anything to go down the toilet," Starks said. "That's why I think it's prudent to talk to Wolly. Where can I find him?"

"Since Tommy was the one approached, ask him."

"Any idea where *he* might be?"

Jackson glanced at the clock. "Ten thirty on a Sunday morning? I'd say check the yard first. Like us, our crew members aren't the kind to attend services."

"Let's go."

"Scared to walk alone?"

"I might need back-up."

Jackson waited at the entrance. "You don't fool me. Want me to hold your hand?"

"You know where you can stick it."

"Not my kind of gig." Jackson saw Starks flinch. "What?"

"Nothing. Forget it."

They took the hallway turns needed and entered the yard. Tank and several of the crew lazed on the bleachers, Tommy among them. Starks stopped in front of Tommy. "Get word to Wolly that I want to speak with him."

To a man, the crew protested.

Tank said, "Could be more trouble than it's worth."

Starks looked at Tank then at the others. "We've already got trouble. I'm trying to make sure the odds are in our favor."

One of the new members jumped up and said, "I ain't standin' with no racist sonsabitches. They'd just as soon slice me, and you know it."

Tank hoisted his bulk from the bottom riser and stood next to Starks. "Sit down and shut it. You too damn new to the crew to know what's what. Starks takes care of his own. He never led us wrong yet. And he ain't gonna start now. He don't do nothin' unless he got a good reason. Ain't that right, Starks?" He faced Starks. Reticence struggled with something else in his eyes.

Starks took the something else to be loyalty competing with hesitation. He nodded at Tank then faced the inmate. "Tommy?"

"You want to talk to him, him and meats are over there. In the corner." Tommy gestured with his chin. "Can't miss 'em. They all look like a bunch of used lightbulbs."

Starks faced the designated direction. Twelve or so inmates with shaved heads clustered in the southwest corner of the yard. "I'll be back."

Tank said, "*Watch* your back."

Starks cut across the yard. With each step, he questioned the wisdom of what he was about to do. He was ten yards away when one of them noticed him and said something to the shortest inmate among them. All turned to watch his approach.

He scanned their faces, taking in the sharp-planed features, shaved eyebrows, muscles that received a great deal of attention to keep them honed. Each of them had the same three black letters tattooed vertically on their left forearms.

The shortest man stepped forward. "Wondered when you'd decide."

Starks pronounced his name as Wally.

"It's Wolly, spelled and pronounced like Molly. Not Wally."

It sounded the same to Starks's ears. "Got it. Never came across it before."

"It's short for Wolfrick." He grinned. "Means wolf ruler." Wolly's gang whooped. He held up a hand to silence them. "Let's hear what the man has to say."

"I want to discuss an arrangement."

Wolly grinned. "You can do more than that." He shifted his gaze to the door. "Ten more are coming our way. It's not all of us, but it's enough for the meeting I called. Stick around."

"How many more of you are there?"

"About another dozen. And more looking to get in all the time." Wolly turned back to Starks. "Like you, we're the ones to give the orders. We know who's who, when it comes to masters and servants."

Starks kept his expression impassive and questioned whether he could stomach what he was about to do.

He listened to their justifications for supremacy. Strained to seem unaffected by labels used for anyone who didn't meet their criteria as worthy of being classified fully human.

After their ten-or-so-minute parody of righteousness, and echo-chambers of self-aggrandizement, which had felt interminable to Starks, Wolly said, "Say it."

The gang all but shouted, "White revolution is the only solution."

Wolly turned to Starks. "We teaming up, or what?"

"I'd like to speak with you alone." When the gang mumbled their displeasure, he added, "Leader to leader."

They went to the fence line about forty feet away from the gang. Starks rested against the stiff wire mesh. "The tattoos you all wear—WAR—does it mean you're always up for a fight or something else?"

Wolly pointed to each letter in turn. "White American Resistance."

"Got it. I'm interested in having you align with me, but I have a problem with a few things."

"Like?"

"Like the fact you're all adamant that you aren't to mingle with other races."

"We can give them orders and put them in their proper place, but we don't mate with them or sit with them."

"I'm not a racist, evident by how my crew includes anyone worthy of joining."

"Your *crew* is made up of whichever dregs you could get." Ethan emitted a high-pitched squeal and skipped toward the bleachers. Wolly followed him with his eyes. "As I said. Bunch of rejects no one else wants."

"I could argue so many points with you, but it wouldn't … Nevermind. My question is, if we align, can race be put aside? Will your soldiers defend mine in a battle? Or even before it happens?"

Wolly glanced toward the bleachers and sneered. "Better put a bell around all the Uncle Toms' necks, or a ring in their noses, so we can tell who's who." He grinned at Starks. "Wouldn't want any accidents."

"My men are the one thing a leader needs from his soldiers—loyal."

"Whatever."

"I have another question."

"Let's hear it."

"Your people seem to approve of the merger, even though they know who's in my crew. Why?"

"Should be obvious."

"It isn't."

"It's the dragon, man."

"Still don't follow."

"Our primo leader. The White Brotherhood? The KKK? Created and perpetuated toward ultimate victory by the Grand Dragon."

Starks worked his jaw and looked away. After a few moments he said, "Seeing that this is a life-or-death situation—"

"For you and your mongrels, maybe."

"If this thing escalates the way I think it will, no one will be left out. We might as well join forces so we have a better chance of winning."

"Even so, we could do with an advantage."

"I have one."

"Oh, yeah. The secret weapon people whisper about. What is it?"

"It's effective. Look at me. What man my size could survive this long, with everyone who's been after my hide? Yet, I'm running things."

"Not everything."

"Pretty close."

Wolly kicked the fence. "Here's what me and the others decided. Our merger, as you call it, has to be temporary."

"You were that sure I'd agree?"

"What choice did you have? Look, soon as the war is over, we part ways. Maybe we do a little business from time to time, but we're not ever going to eat next to any Uncle—"

"I get the picture. And I'm fine with that arrangement."

Wolly held out his hand. "Shake on it."

Starks glanced at the bleachers. Kept his eyes on Tank, who watched him. His hand clasped Wolly's. Tank shook his head and shrugged.

"All right, Wolly. We watch your backs, you watch ours. When the fight comes, we all do whatever it takes."

"Wanna place a bet on who's left standing when it's over?" When Starks didn't readily answer, he said, "Thought not." He returned to his gang and raised a fist in the air. Another whoop, louder than before, sounded from them.

Starks pivoted and wrapped his fingers around the mesh. He stared unseeing at the wall and waited for the bile in his throat to stop burning.

Jeffrey—half White, half Black—was worth more than the whole damn bunch of the self-righteous racists, whose sole motivation to fight at his side was the color of his enemies' skin, not for justice.

Could he go any lower?

CHAPTER 34

E than ran in circles around the bleachers. Other crew members talked among themselves, while keeping an eye on what was going on near them. Starks studied their faces. Some looked tough enough. Most looked like so many at Sands—wary. He could count on his original crew. That meant he needed to engender loyalty in new members. And that meant that at some point, he'd have to talk to Brunson about additional phones. However, it was too soon for that. How many of his crew would survive, and how many of those would remain with him after the war, was an unknown factor. That is, assuming he made it through the fight alive. Whatever it took, he had to survive.

Jackson hopped off the bleachers and started in his direction. He stood next to Starks, eyes fixed on the skinheads. "So, you made a deal with the devil."

"Not the first time. Likely, not the last."

"How's it feel?"

"Hours in a sauna *might* make me feel clean again." Starks glanced back at his crew. "Any of the new guys ask about phones since you explained the business to them?"

"Yeah. Told them I'd talk to you."

"Get them in on any of your other deals, if you want them involved. But let them know nothing will happen about the phones until this Seth business is resolved."

Jackson scratched his chin, his nails rasped across stubble. "Makes sense. No point in spending money that doesn't need to be spent. I'll involve them just enough, so they don't feel cheated.

"Back to the matter of the moment. Personally, I think your decision about Wolly sucks. When the fight comes, they'll go after those of us who aren't lily-white and say it was a mistake. They won't sit next to us, but it doesn't bother them to get our blood on them, as long as it means there will be fewer of us."

"I need as many hands as I can get."

"That's some of that enemy of my enemy is my friend shit, right?"

"Only until I don't need them." Starks checked the time on the digital clock above the double doors. "Any of them try anything, we take care of them after the fight.

"Fifteen minutes to the count. Get the guys moving. I'll see you at the cell."

Jackson flipped his chair around. "So, what's the grand plan with Wolly?"

Starks repeated the agreed-upon terms. "Better have everyone in the crew get the same dragon head tattooed on the back of their right hand. You, included. I want the skinheads to know who to protect rather than kill."

Jackson nodded. "I'll set it up."

"While you're at it, set it up with Tat Man. Tell him he knows I'm good for it. Give him a list of names and have him check their IDs before he does any work. No name on the list, no dragon head."

"Smart."

"I have my moments."

Jackson slapped his thighs. "Time for lunch."

"You go ahead."

"I know it's crap, but you gotta eat."

"I'll get something from the commissary."

Jackson walked to the cell entrance. "What if the guys have questions about Wolly and et cetera?"

"Tell them what I told you. About Wolly and the tats. I need to make a call." Starks took the large book to his bunk. "Anyone out there?"

"All heading where I'm going."

"Let me know if there are any dissenters we need to be concerned about."

Jackson saluted. "Will do."

Starks turned the cell phone on and stared at it.

Now was as good a time as any to call Kayla. To tell her the things he needed to say. To tell her how he felt. To get it done, while the block was empty.

He dropped the phone into the recess and put the book away.

What was happening to him?

Some morphing process had taken over. Had done so without his permission. By the time Sands spit him out, who and what would he be?

And, would he be able to live with himself?

CHAPTER 35

The next week went by more routinely than anticipated. Although it was something of a relief, it also left Starks feeling more anxious than usual. It was too quiet, especially considering what stirred beneath the surface.

He left the task of interviewing new recruits to Jackson. It wasn't as simple a matter as he'd hoped. Only some inmates were eager to get on his team. *Team*—as though what was going on was a sport. He supposed that for the worst of them inside the oppressive environment, their very existence was a blood sport. A way to keep sharp skills they'd learned on the streets. A way to feel important, as opposed to how insignificant they likely had felt outside these walls. The only redeeming aspect was when Jackson told him recruiting was proving equally challenging for Seth, if the rumors were true. Many were unwilling to get embroiled in a battle that wasn't theirs.

That, Starks imagined, was a factor in the matter going quiet, in some measure, but also due to more watchful observance by guards. They knew what was coming, just not when.

Starks worked his shift every day, Monday through Friday, arriving at the library a few minutes early. It took until that fifth day for the shock of seeing another inmate seated where Paco should have been, to cease startling him like an electric jolt. Sadness replaced shock, followed by cold anger.

The second week after Paco's death—execution was more accurate—he realized he'd forgotten about his scheduled times with Demory. What the hell did it matter? Most of the time, it seemed the sessions were more for the benefit of the counselor than for him. He erased any guilt about not so much as notifying Demory that he wasn't going to show up.

Better to miss the appointments. Demory would have wanted to talk about his feelings. How he felt about Paco's death, as well as the other deaths that shadowed him. He had too many other things on his mind. He'd go back when and if he felt like it.

Two weeks since Paco's presence on this earth had been erased. Two weeks of memories of conversations and gestures and facial expressions still sharp in his mind. These memories would fade in time. Life would find a way to begin to fill that void with other thoughts and concerns, until he'd have to remind himself to remember the details. He'd been through it before. Too often. Too recently.

On Saturday morning, as he lay awake in bed before first light, these thoughts and the thought that he'd been wrong about a number of things pressed against him like an enormous wave bent on knocking him down and dragging him under.

Wolly's gang believed they could mistreat anyone unlike them. If it turned out that Blake was gay, his son would face similarly prejudiced individuals the remainder of his life, possibly even to the point of threats on his life. Possibly actions taken by a person or persons too insecure about who they were to let others be who they were. People were born into their skin color. They had no choice about it. It was the same for sexual preference. People were who they were. There were choices they could make in life, but not about that. Choose to alter behaviors, yes. Alter the facts, no.

He'd decided long ago that prejudice was etched into a person's psyche from birth. That a person could learn to adjust this, but most people generally never chose to leave the sheep-like mentality they were raised with. The other sheep in their flock would fight them if they tried. Or disown them. Or worse.

However, when a person realized that what he'd always believed was wrong, he had to face it and do something about it.

His grandfather and uncles had taught him how to treat women. That he was to get married and have a family. That he was to provide for his family, as well as take care of his needs. That, as a proper man, he was to have more sexual needs than his wife could or should attend to. He'd listened to them when they'd advised him. He'd listened to them when they didn't know he was anywhere near. Heard them discuss the minute intimate details of their escapades, usually described in coarse terminology. Their banter had informed, as well as formed him.

In this way, he thought, he was no different than Wolly or anyone who'd been fed a steady diet of beliefs that oppressed or harmed others. They felt compelled to believe they were right. Because to be wrong about something so significant was too much to fathom or bear. The cost of discovering they'd been wrong might be too dear.

After all the conversations he'd had with Demory, this new realization came about from seeing himself reflected in the mirrors of people he'd always detested and believed he had nothing in common with.

Starks swung his legs over the side of the bed. His chest heaved with the revelation. A revelation is only as good as what you do with it, he told himself.

At eight o'clock, he stood outside his cell for the count. At eight twenty, he joined Jackson and most of his crew in the chow hall. At nine o'clock, he sat on his bunk with the large book on his lap and the cell phone in his hand. At ten after nine, his fingers hit the familiar numbers on the keypad.

"Kayla, it's me."

CHAPTER 36

S tarks pressed the phone against his ear. Waited for Kayla to slam the receiver down, unsure whether he wished she would do that more than he wished she wouldn't.

After a few moments, she said, "What do you want, Starks?"

He released the breath he'd been holding. "I want to apologize for how I treated you last time you came to see me." When she said nothing, he continued. "And for every time before that, all the way back to the beginning. I made life easy for you in material matters, but not in emotional ones."

"Do you mean that? Or is it because Jeffrey told you I'm dying and it seems the polite thing to do? Maybe to ease your conscience?"

"I'd like to think it's because I care about you."

"But you aren't sure."

Starks ran a hand through his hair. "It's just a figure of speech, Kayla. This isn't easy for me to face or talk about."

"Funny how reality can shift your thinking about what's easy and what's hard."

She'd always been one to challenge him, to point out his flaws, whether real or how she perceived him. He sucked in a deep breath and let it go, in an effort to release how easily she could still trigger him. "Did Jeffrey tell you to contact Garrett Hall?"

"He did."

"And?"

"I'm considering it."

"Kayla, I want you to have the best doctors. I really think—"

"Jeffrey said he told you Blake was acting out."

Starks shook his head. For now, he'd allow her avoidance of the topic. "Is he still doing that?"

"He's calmed down somewhat, but I don't know how long it'll last. He fidgets. As though being in the house is like being in prison." Kayla paused. "Sorry. It's just a figure of speech."

"Touché."

"Still …"

"I blame myself for not being there. I abandoned my family. We both did, in our own ways. Our kids are paying the price. We're all paying. However, with everything you're dealing with, the last damn thing you need is Blake giving you grief."

"Starks, I need you to listen to me. I don't know how long I have left."

"That's why I want you to contact Garrett and let him—"

"Please. For once, just listen."

"It's impossible to imagine life for our children without you there for them."

"That's what I want to talk to you about."

"I don't want you to worry. They'll be all right. I'll make sure they're well cared for."

"Please. Stop. I need to say something to you, and you're not making it simple, not that there's anything simple about it."

Starks sat up straight. "I'll shut up."

"You've hated me for a long time."

"Kayla—"

"What I'm going to tell you is likely the nail in the coffin, if you'll pardon my phrasing."

"I'm not amused."

"There's nothing left for me to lose. Actually, that's not true. That's what's so painful. I still have a lot to lose." Kayla exhaled a ragged breath. "As the saying goes, better one sure whack than a thousand small cuts.

"Blake is not your biological son. But he's yours in every way that matters. I learned this the first time they typed his blood. I lied and told you he was Type O, like us. I let you believe the lie all this time."

"I know."

Kayla's sharp intake of breath sent her into a spasm of coughing.

"Are you okay? Kayla!" He waited for her to be able to speak again.

Her voice more frail than before, she said, "How did you find out?"

"That doesn't matter."

"How long have you known?"

"For a while."

"You never said anything."

"Honestly, I didn't know if you knew. Whether you did or didn't, I didn't want Blake to find out. That meant keeping my mouth shut. I'm still firm about that, more so now than ever. He might go completely off the rails if he learns the truth now. He may find out one day, but this isn't that day."

"You knew? When I was at Sands?"

"Yes."

"That explains why you acted the way you did."

"It ripped my heart out, Kayla."

"I'm sorry." She began to cry.

As Starks waited for Kayla to compose herself, he listened to footsteps in the corridor. He lowered the phone, positioning it inside the book, returning it to his ear after an inmate walked past and down to the last cell on the left.

"Starks?"

"I'm here."

"How do you feel about this? More importantly, how do you feel about Blake?"

"At first it wasn't easy. Paternal affection for the child I'd loved and raised, competed with rage for what you'd stolen from me, and from him."

"What about now?"

"About Blake? I've realized I can't cut that love off. There are times, out of habit, when I forget. Then the truth punches me in the gut. But it's getting better."

"And about me?"

"I'm working on it."

"That's all I deserve."

"Kayla." Starks hesitated. Part of him wanted to leave it alone. Part of him needed to know. "Who's the father?"

"You are."

"I deserve a straight answer."

"Yes. You do. I don't know."

Fury crept up his spine, moving like a needle into his brain. "At this point in time, how many men you've been with no longer matters."

"But it does."

"I wish I could be more magnanimous, but—"

"Today is not that day. The betrayal was too great."

His words came out harsher than he'd intended. "As I said, I'm working on it."

"You're keeping what you really think and feel in because I'm dying."

"Consider it part of my apology."

"The kids are stirring. I need to go."

"Give them a kiss from me."

"Starks."

"Yes?"

"Thank you."

"I don't know how to respond to that."

Kayla stayed quiet a moment then said, "Then just say goodbye."

Starks's throat constricted. His voice paper-thin, he said, "I don't know how to do that."

Kayla, weeping, ended the call.

Starks put the phone and book away and returned to his bed. He buried his face in the pillow, muffling his own wracking sobs.

Footsteps, a number of them, tramped toward his cell. He dried his face with his shirtsleeve. Rested his right hand on the base of the needle in his hem, ready for a possible attack.

Tank and four new members of his crew bustled into his cell.

Starks willed himself to relax. "What's up?"

Each man thrust his right hand out, displaying dark-inked dragons on light skin and white-inked dragons on dark.

"Good. Tank, see to it that the rest of them get theirs. You guys go do whatever. Tank, you come with me."

The crew members left, strutting more than walking to the end of the corridor.

Tank said, "Where we going?"

"I need to take care of Tat Man."

"What's he gettin' for doin' all this?"

"Not enough."

CHAPTER 37

The following Thursday, Starks eyed the digits on the monitor clock, watching until they flipped to show it was noon. He glanced left, where ordinarily, Paco would be head-down over the computer keyboard, tapping out, letter by letter, the things he wanted someone to know about him from before his time in prison, as well as since he'd begun his residency at Sands for life. And death. He would have asked the old guy to keep an eye on things. Would have run to the commissary to pick up something for lunch. Paco had known the drill: in exchange for the service, Starks would have brought him a ham sandwich, chips, and a soft drink.

His food stock had run out, and he'd failed to replenish it. From now on, he'd have to plan ahead, so he always had something to bring with him to work. This time, he let his stomach rumble its request, followed by its demand for food.

Since Saturday, he'd replayed segments of his conversation with Kayla. They'd only scraped the surface of what had driven them apart. So much had gone unsaid. Unspoken words swirled around in his mind nearly every waking moment. At some point, he'd have to tell her everything he felt about her, and for her. He'd have to extend the same courtesy. Perhaps even tell her about Kyle and Kane. Let her convict him of his sins, just as he'd convicted her. The slate needed to be clean between them. For Kayla, it was because death would claim her soon. For him, because the same was a possibility in his sphere every moment. But he wasn't ready to face that level of disclosure or honesty or shame as yet.

By two o'clock, Starks decided to keep his four thirty appointment with Demory. At five till four, Sam showed up and stood in the office doorway.

Starks glanced at Sam then back at the monitor. He finished entering information into the computer. "You here to check out a book?"

"I'm here because your replacement has a tummy ache."

"At least I don't have to worry about him arriving late as usual. I've got something to take care of."

"When don't you?"

Starks snickered, hit the Enter key, then stood. "There's not much left. Shouldn't take you but about a half hour to finish the entries."

"Did you micromanage your staff?"

Starks grinned. "Didn't need to."

"Get outta here. Go take care of whatever."

Starks exited to the right out of the library, and then left at the next corridor, speeding up as he neared the commissary. He tossed a dozen sandwiches, sweet rolls, and an equal number of bags of chips onto the counter, which the inmate on duty dropped into a paper bag. Starks grinned. "Prison must be the only place where you're not asked if you want paper or plastic."

"Some guy pisses off another guy, the first guy could smother the other guy with a plastic bag. Can't do that with paper. Plus, you run out of toilet paper, you can use the paper ones to—"

"I've got the picture."

Starks scooped up the bag and walked quickly in the direction of Demory's office. He was taking a chance. Demory might have given his appointment time to someone else.

It took a few minutes to assure the guard at the first barrier, that he did, indeed, have an appointment. He paused in front of the office door and peered in through the glass portion. Watched as Demory extracted a folder from one of his filing cabinets. Starks knocked. Demory turned, saw him, shook his head and gestured for Starks to enter.

Demory slapped the folder onto his desk and plunked into his chair. "Your amnesia clear up?"

"Apologies." Starks lowered himself into the chair, placing the bag on his lap. His stomach gurgled. "I missed lunch. Mind if I eat?"

"Have at it."

Starks held up a sandwich. "Interested?"

"Nah, I'm good."

"Chips?" He held up a bag.

"Are you stalling?"

"Being polite."

"Now you're polite. After letting me sit here two Thursdays in a row, waiting for nothing." He tapped the folder. "Pulled your file every Thursday, just in case. Guess it's true that the third time is a charm."

"Want me to leave?"

Demory scratched his neck. "You can give it, but you can't take it, even when you're in the wrong."

Starks studied the limp slice of what was supposed to be roast beef, took a bite and chewed.

Demory sat back, keeping unblinking eyes on Starks. "You wouldn't have changed your mind about showing up for my benefit, so what's on your mind?"

Starks took another bite, chewing slowly. "I talked to Kayla."

"How'd that go?"

"Better than I had a right to expect. Less got said than needed to be, but we cleared a few cobwebs." Starks shrugged. "It's a start." He put the remainder of his sandwich back in its container.

"And?"

"You know there are skinheads here?"

Demory nodded. "Not that any of them will ever sit their butts in that chair. What does that have to do with Kayla?"

"I had the occasion to talk with some of them the other day. It sickened me to listen to their warped beliefs. But it made me think about how beliefs get indoctrinated into people. Into all of us. We're born. Then we find ourselves immersed in someone else's philosophy, maybe for generations. We may not even give ourselves the opportunity to prove the philosophy true or false, because we don't see the need."

"Insightful. But, again, this relates to Kayla how?"

"I've told you about my grandfather and uncles. Cheating on their wives was as natural to them as it is for some people to be taught to hate or fear people of color or those with sexual predilections different from theirs. And never question it." He considered discussing Blake, but what was the point? It's not like he had proof the boy was gay.

"Where's all this coming from?"

"I wondered what might have happened had I grown up in a family where the men held marriage vows as sacred. I'd like to think that even if Kayla had picked up her beliefs about men and sex from her tramp of a mother, my love, my being faithful to her, might have dissolved those beliefs that led to her behaviors. We'd be together now, instead of in our separate hells."

"You surprise me, Starks."

"I'm surprising myself."

"Are you saying you've decided to forgive her? That you finally believe you can?"

"What she's done still hurts. But I also get that it's in the past. Although, some of it is still current. I also know that a day will come when I'll ask how I allowed myself to waste time I'll never get back."

"We're never free, as long as we blame others for our problems, or our actions."

Starks shifted his gaze from Demory's face and aimed it at the small window. "I think something may be wrong with me. You know? Because of all the anger I've worn like a second skin."

"Listening to you, I'd say you're discovering you're as human as the rest of us. Maybe that's the issue. Maybe that realization is stunning to you after years of …"

Starks shifted his gaze back to Demory and grinned. "After years of thinking I crapped gold nuggets?"

Demory smiled. "Something like that." He edged forward in his chair. "You're right. We come into life as a blank page. Some families write poetry on that page. Others put uninspired graffiti on it, crude and jumbled repetitions copied from their own page. And we don't know the difference. Unless we take the blinders off one day. Or life rips them off for us. It doesn't matter how they come off, just that they do."

Starks stayed silent.

Demory leaned back. "What else is swimming around inside your head?"

"Not much more than that."

"Here I was, thinking we were making real progress. Denial won't help."

"What am I denying?"

"It's not every day someone finds out his name was carved into another man's flesh."

"I don't want to talk about that."

"You need to. You need to talk about all of your losses. Starks, it's been one thing after another for you since the day you crossed the threshold of this place. We can't deal with something until we're willing to look at it, to see it for what it is and how it affects us. How it impacts our life. Or how we allow it to."

Demory was right, in a way. Yet, in his experience, talking about matters made him feel weaker rather than stronger. Action led to results sooner than any amount of gabbing ever could. Starks picked up the bag of food and stood. "You need to take a vacation. A long one."

Demory threw his hands up. "What did I do this time to piss you off?"

"I'm not angry with you. I'm giving you an important piece of advice."

"I've only just gotten back."

"A war is coming, Doc. I don't know how bad it will be or exactly when it'll erupt. I don't know how contained it will stay. I don't know who in the administration will be safe and who won't. It shouldn't affect you, but it might. You have a son and daughter to think about."

"You have three children to think about."

"That's what I'm doing."

"Can't you stop it?"

"It's not up to me."

"I can get you put into isolation. Say you're suicidal again. It'll keep you out of harm's way."

Starks shook his head. "Someone determined enough could get to me while I was in there." He flashed the extra scar on his right wrist. "And if not then, they'd be waiting for me when I got out. No way in hell will I spend the rest of my time here in solitary." He nodded once and headed for the door. "One more thing. You don't repeat what I just told you. To anyone. Prison officials already know something is brewing. But you say anything … if you mention my name, you might as well kill me yourself." Starks opened the door.

"Hang on."

Starks looked back and waited.

"Aren't you afraid?"

"What do you think?"

He closed the door behind him.

Afraid? The counselor didn't know half of what scared him.

CHAPTER 38

Starks changed his mind about his destination. Paper bag in hand, he made the necessary turns that took him to the workroom. There was a difference between talking things out with Demory, who lived in a bubble and whose mind would always slant one way, and talking with someone who lived inside the beast. Perspective mattered. And Gabe's was the one he needed more. All he had to do was make it a point not to piss the old guy off again. He knocked on the door and waited.

Moments later the door opened. Gabe glanced at the bag. "You come bearing gifts?"

"It's my commissary stock. You going to let me in?"

Gabe shouldered the door open, threw the bolt once Starks was inside.

Starks put the bag on the small table and reached into it. "You're welcome to some of this. I've got ham, beef, turkey—"

"I'm covered." Gabe waved toward the bag. "Eat if you want to."

"I'll wait." Starks took a seat at the table.

Gabe sat across from him. "What's on your mind this time? Not that I lack any clues about what that might be."

"Since you tend to know what's going on, any definite info about who killed Paco? And why?"

Gabe studied Starks's face then leaned back in his chair, eyes cast upward. "The grapevine about that turned out to be drier than I'd like. But I have my suspicions." He looked straight at Starks.

Starks's expression registered his disappointment. "Who and what do you suspect?"

"You first."

"Seth. In part, to get at me because he knew Paco and I were friendly. Not friends, mind you. Friendly was enough of a reason for an animal like him. Otherwise, why put my name on Paco's chest? It was his message to me."

"Not enough facts to back up your theory, but it sounds logical."

"I also think it has something to do with Paco's memoir. He'd asked me to read it. Wanted my input."

"What makes you think the memoir has anything to do with Seth?"

"The second I got the news about Paco, I went to my cell. The manuscript was gone."

Gabe waved a hand. "It's a waste of energy to think about it anymore."

"I don't agree."

"Here's something we can agree on. You need to plan how you're gonna deal with Seth."

"I'm still recruiting. I want make sure my numbers match, if not surpass, his. Any scoop about what he's planning?"

"Beyond kicking your ass into the next life, no."

"The grapevine really is dry."

Gabe shrugged and kept his gaze on Starks.

Starks rested his forearms on the table and linked his fingers. "You never know about a person. All this time, I considered Paco to be simple. Not simple-minded, but never as intelligent as he proved himself to be on paper. He had a hard start in life."

"A lotta people do."

"He fought to better himself. Did do better. Then he ended up here."

Gabe studied his chipped nails then focused on Starks. "You finished reading it?"

Starks shook his head. "There was something in there he wanted me to read. Something about corrupt goings-on in here. I wish to hell I'd jumped ahead. Then I'd know what he had on Seth.

"Put your feelers out. I want it back. I'll pay."

Gabe snorted. "You can keep your money or whatever. If someone wanted that memoir to disappear, it's flushed or ash by now."

"You're probably right." Starks slammed his fist on the table. "Damn it. All that hard work. All that history."

"History belongs to the ones who take it over."

"It isn't right."

"Life is what we make it."

"You're giving me platitudes?"

"Facts of life. Here's another fact of life. So far, you got nothin' but numbers regarding the war that's coming. How many of those guys can your life depend on?"

"Most of them. One in particular."

Gabe's eyebrows shot up. "Who's that?"

"Ethan."

"The nut-job who stutters?" Gabe threw back his head and laughed. "You're worse off than I thought. Might as well scratch you off my Christmas card list now."

"Ethan *is* insane."

"Like I said."

"The kind of insane that can be useful." Starks shared the details of Crazy D's murder. "You can imagine my surprise when Ethan gave me the specifics and never stuttered once. I'd wondered about him. Watched him make a clever move on two inmates in the chow hall. No one but me saw what he did. The inmates didn't have a clue. Just knew they were pissing blood for some unknown reason."

"I must be getting old. The kid fooled me." Gabe glanced at the clock on the wall and stood. "If I hear anything about anything, I'll get word to you. You need to get going. Almost time for the count."

"Sure you don't want a sandwich?"

"Trust me."

Starks grabbed the paper bag and went to the door. He pulled the bolt to the side.

"Starks."

"Yeah?"

"Never underestimate your enemy."

"I try not to."

"*Try* will get you killed."

"Looking at someone in here the wrong way can do that."

Gabe sighed and shook his head. "The thing about stupid people is they never know they're stupid."

"You think I'm stupid?"

"I think you're not as smart as you think you are."

"What's the matter with you lately?"

"The same thing that's the matter with me every day. Now, go."

Starks increased his pace, so as not to be late.

Gabe's hotline seemed to be cooler than usual. Usually, the mafia don knew as much as he did, or more, which explained his sour mood.

Starks finished his half-eaten sandwich as he waited for the count, wishing some flash of inspiration would come to him as to how to win all the battles being waged around him and inside him.

Gone were the days when winning was guaranteed.

He had to find a way to change this. Outcome was everything.

CHAPTER 39

The count ended at 6:13. Jackson leaned against the cell door. "What are your plans for the evening?"

"Maybe I'll read. Take my mind off things for a while. What about you?"

"Checking out possible recruits."

"I have to give it to you, you're dedicated."

"I like the idea of keeping my blood inside my body and my bones intact."

"I hear you."

"I also like the idea of keeping my face pretty."

"Your ass."

"That too."

Starks pulled a book from his small stack. "Happy scouting."

"Instead of reading, why don't you come up with a plan that's foolproof."

"You're the brains. I'm the muscle."

"Since when?"

"Jackson," Starks held his forefinger a half inch above his thumb, "you're this close to getting tedious."

"Fine. Let me do all the heavy lifting."

"I'm doing my share."

"Finances and fights."

"You have a problem with me?"

Jackson rubbed his face. "Nah. I have a problem with what's about to come down on our heads."

"Then go do something about it."

"Enjoy your friggin' book."

Starks sighed as Jackson stomped away. Jackson was right, of course, but he felt trapped. There was no way to avoid the war. Too many people wanted it to happen. On both sides. Anything to relieve the tedium. Even the anticipation was worth the price of admission for some inmates.

He took the book to his bunk, opened it, and let his eyes skim the words. Had to start over several times, each time losing his concentration within seconds. He glanced out the window. The light outside had shifted while he'd been lost in thought. He glanced at the clock—7:12.

The alarm blared. Starks tossed the book onto his mattress and hurried to the door. Over the intercom, a voice ordered all inmates to return to their cells immediately.

He stood at the entrance, waiting for Jackson who, a minute or so later, came puffing around the corner and down the corridor.

"What now?" Starks asked.

"No idea. Gotta be bad, though."

A second announcement gave inmates five minutes to be inside their cells.

Inmates sped around the corner and into their six by eight enclosures.

Cell doors slid closed and locked. Every inmate in Starks's block stood with their hands clutching the bars, waiting and watching. The volume of confused voices echoed in the corridor.

Minutes ticked by before Roberts and Jakes arrived. They began their inspection of inmates in the first cell on the right. Cell by cell, inmates stripped down to their briefs and turned in a slow circle. The only sounds were the orders from the corrections officers.

Roberts and Jakes reached Starks and Jackson, who did as instructed.

"Starks, you're lucky," Roberts said. "Only injuries on you are old ones."

"What's happened?"

"One of Seth's men—Buster—you know him?"

"No. What about him?"

"He missed the count, so we had to look for him."

"And?"

"Found him."

Jakes snorted. "That's one way to put it."

Starks slipped his pants on. "What's another way?"

Jakes grimaced. "We found him, just not all in one place."

Jackson gripped the bars. "You sayin' you found him in pieces?"

"Yep."

"Shit."

"One piece is still missing."

Starks swallowed hard. "Which one?"

"His head. Not looking forward to finding it, but we have to keep looking."

Jackson whistled low. "You checked the dryers?"

"First place we looked, smartass. Before you ask, it wasn't in any of the washers, either. It's not like there's a lotta options for where to hide a head."

Jackson shuddered. "This shit freaks me out. We have someone in here who's into some nasty shit."

"Or a copycat," Starks said.

Jakes leaned in. "If this isn't a copycat, I'm going to start thinking someone in here either has a head fetish or is starting a collection. But where the hell would he hide it?"

Starks looked from Jakes to Roberts. "Am I going to be called in for this, as well?"

Roberts answered. "Don't know. But I'll tell Spencer that your shock was real, and that you're unmarked."

"Damn straight."

"We need to finish the block. Later."

Starks eased onto his bunk and buried his face in his hands.

Jackson pulled out his chair and plunked into it. "We need to find out who's doing this. Since he's going after people who have it in for you, we need to recruit him. Then never get on his bad side."

"I suppose that makes a modicum of sense."

The last thing Starks wanted to admit was his suspicion about who had done this.

Especially because he believed he was right.

CHAPTER 40

Starks grabbed a roll for breakfast and a sandwich for lunch, before leaving for his shift in the library. Nearly there and lost in thought, he jumped when someone whispered his name close to his ear. Had it been anyone but Ethan, or another member of his crew, he could have been attacked far too easily.

Ethan grinned and said, "Seth shouldn't have put your name on Paco."

"He shouldn't have touched that old man. Period."

"You liked him that much?"

"More than I realized."

"I wonder what that feels like."

Starks stared at Ethan for the length of several heartbeats. "Where's Buster's head?"

Ethan winked and dashed away, arms flailing, talking to himself about butterflies trying to nest in his hair.

Starks shuddered and continued to the library, wondering if Gabe had guessed who'd done Buster. For a moment, he wondered if he'd made a mistake by revealing Ethan's true nature. However, Gabe *had* kept his mouth shut. Otherwise, Ethan wouldn't be free to run away from dangerous butterflies.

Throughout the day, Starks stayed watchful, believing Spencer would haul him in for questioning. Spencer left him alone. At the six o'clock count, Starks confirmed with Roberts that the head was still missing.

After a sleepless night and an inedible breakfast Saturday morning, Starks joined his crew in the yard for a game on the dirt court. He played the first thirty minutes then had one of his crew take his place, stating he wanted everyone to have a turn. The fact was, his mind wasn't on the game. He'd missed twice as many hoops as he'd made, drawing curious and disapproving stares from new members.

Corrections Officer Jakes approached him. "Visitor, Starks."

"Who is it?"

"Tall and luscious Emma Guyson."

Starks blew out a breath and nodded. "Escort me to the visitors' room."

"Sure." Grinning, Jakes said, "I'll even take your place, if you want me to."

"Why would I do that?"

"You don't look happy to see her. Just a glimpse of her made my johnson happy."

"I prefer not to think about your johnson."

"Just sayin'. Didn't mean anything."

"It's not you. Nevermind. Let's go."

They walked in silence to where visitors eagerly, and sometimes not so eagerly, waited for a loved one. A few of the people were loud, uninhibited about their words and volume. Most spoke in hushed tones, as though in an effort to counter the others' behaviors.

As always, Emma radiated her beauty like a rose in a cactus garden. Even months past summertime, her shoulder-length hair was more platinum blond than usual from the sun. Or the salon. Didn't matter. She looked luscious. Tawny skin made her eyes—the same shade of blue as her attire—more noticeable than usual. She stood slowly when she saw Starks at the entrance. Instead of a leg-revealing dress, as she'd worn for previous visits, she had on second-skin slacks and a matching halter top that emphasized her physical attributes. All eyes fixed on her.

Every man's wet dream waited to see him, drove for two hours to be with him, and he hadn't given her a first, much less second, thought in weeks. Make that months.

Starks plastered his best smile on and maneuvered his way to her through the tables and chairs. This time, she didn't fling her arms around his neck or kiss him on the lips. Instead, she air-kissed his cheek then returned to her chair.

Starks sat in the chair next to her. "You're breathtakingly beautiful."

"Too bad that's not enough."

"For what?"

"You said you'd do better about keeping in touch. You haven't. Not a word."

"I'm sorry, baby. There's been a lot going on in here."

"Not only here."

Starks grew still. "What do you mean?"

"I bumped into Jeffrey. He told me about Kayla."

Starks's shoulders sagged. "Oh."

"That's why you haven't called or asked to see me."

"That's not the reason."

"Last time I was here, I asked you to be honest with me about us. If you want to end our relationship, do it. Don't let me hope for something that will never happen."

"Kayla has nothing to do with us."

"You'd be a monster, if her condition didn't affect you or influence you in some way. Your first love, and all that."

"It affects me, but not in the way you think. You're building this into something that doesn't exist."

"You still love her. Don't try to deny it. We're past that point. All I ask is that you be honest with me."

Starks cupped her hand in his. "I care because she's the mother of my children, but it's you I love."

"You make it difficult for me to believe that."

"You said difficult, not impossible." He smiled. "So, there's still hope on my side of the equation."

Emma didn't return his smile. "I don't believe you'll ever love me as much as you've loved her. Still love her. Despite what you say."

Starks fought his urge to recoil as tears welled in Emma's eyes. He stroked the back of her hand. "You don't like it when I tell you my intention is to protect you from my problems, but that's the truth. I love you. I want the best for you. That's the main reason I haven't gotten in touch."

Emma slid her hand from his and placed it in her lap. "You're sending mixed signals. That makes me wonder if what you really want is for me to break it off, so you don't have to carry any guilt about doing it yourself."

"Give me your hand back. Please."

Emma brushed tears from her cheeks and placed her hand in his.

"Emma, baby, I'm more than sure about my love for you. What I'm not sure about is what my incarceration is doing to you. Sometimes, I think it's unfair not to let you go. But the thought nearly paralyzes me. I'm not indecisive. I'm terrified of losing you. Kayla's caused conflicted feelings in me for a host of reasons. But I've never felt conflicted about you. You have to believe that."

Emma studied his face for a few moments. "Here's what I'm beginning to believe. I believe you want to be with Kayla. That if you got out of here today, you'd be at the house with her, not with me. I believe that since Kayla won't live much longer, it's convenient to have me waiting on the side, so I can fill the void when she's gone."

Starks released her hand. "I can't believe you said that."

"How long it takes for her presence in your heart and mind to really be gone, at least enough for someone else to be allowed in, is another matter."

Emma scraped her chair back and stood. "I've said what I came here to say. You said what I wanted to hear you say, but I'm not convinced. Because I still love you, I'll give you one last chance. But don't think I'll wait too much longer for you to prove I mean more to you than a replacement for Kayla. If I can even take her place in your heart." She started to walk away.

Losing wasn't his way. Starks leaped up and grabbed her by the arm. "Kayla, don't leave me."

Pain etched on Emma's face. "Did you hear what you said?"

"I asked you not to leave me."

"No, you didn't." She pulled her arm free and hurried from the room.

He'd made the number-one mistake a man should never make.

Starks sunk into his chair. Maybe it wasn't fair to stay in a relationship with her. Maybe it was time to let her get on with her life, since he was certain he was here for the duration of his sentence, at the very least. She'd been right that he'd be with Kayla, had he been able to get out. Emma was on target about that, and about keeping her available for whenever, despite how much he wished it weren't so.

When he'd fallen in love with Kayla at first sight, in ninth grade, the quality of their love, or at least his side of it, had an innocent, trusting aspect to it. Reality, with its betrayals, deception, and pain, had tainted his perspective regarding love. Had ended his ability to trust any woman. If any woman could be trusted, it was likely Emma, so completely opposite Kayla in every way. Still, he was never going down that path again. Make the sounds of love they want to hear, finance them, take them to bed, but never trust them. It was too costly.

She was also right about the fact that he gave little thought to her. She was wrong about him not being a monster. Time spent continually trying to stay alive was gradually changing him into one.

It wasn't fair to Emma. Even if they were together one day in the future, he wouldn't be the man she'd fallen in love with. All of these issues needed to be added to the long list of things to ponder.

He returned to the yard. He needed something to take his mind off of everything and everyone.

Starks motioned for Pete, who called a time-out and sprinted over. "Sit out and let me in the game."

"Only if you play better than you were playing before."

"Watch me. Scoring is my middle name."

CHAPTER 41

Starks and most of his crew entered the chow hall at lunchtime. Animated voices diminished to quiet murmurs. Inmates cast glances at Starks then quickly looked away. Aside from threatening glares from Seth and his soldiers, it was relatively calm in the room, but the tension was palpable.

Starks rapped on the table and sat. "Why are so many of these guys giving me looks?"

Tank answered. "They think you did Buster."

His crew members kept their faces toward him, waiting. Starks pressed his lips into a tight line. "I didn't have anything to do with it."

Blackie, who sat across from him, said, "You'd swear on the Bible?"

"And mean it. I didn't even know him."

One man new to the crew said, "What about Crazy D? That was you, right?"

Starks speared a clump of mystery meat. "Innocent."

The inmate snickered. "Until proven guilty?"

"Until hell freezes." Starks dropped his fork and looked up and down both sides of the table. "What's with everyone?"

Blackie scooped hash onto his fork. "Speaking for myself, I want to be sure I didn't hook up with a psychopath."

Tank huffed. "Listen, you numb-nuts, one thing you gotta get and stick in your empty heads is that Starks strikes back, not first. How many times I gotta say that?"

The new guy snorted. "Some of us don't know what to think. Word is, Starks did 'em both."

Starks tossed his fork onto his tray, rapped on the table and stood. "What happened to Buster and Crazy D is as much a mystery to me as it is to any of you."

The inmate said, "That Trevor kid also a mystery?"

Tank rested a hand on Starks's arm. "Ignore these assholes."

"Right now, I'd prefer a sandwich in the company of someone who has full faith in me."

"Who's that?"

"Myself."

Shortly after eight thirty that evening, Jackson returned from working the dinner shift. At nine, the lights dimmed. Starks and Jackson lay in their bunks.

Jackson yawned. "You still awake?"

Starks turned onto his side, his face to the wall. "How long have you known me?"

"Did you have Trevor killed?"

"What have you heard?"

"That you had him wasted."

Mention of Trevor at lunch had annoyed him. Now, Starks smiled. "And?"

"Some of the guys think that ramped up your rep."

"I'm okay with that."

"They think you're some kind of chill-assed killer who believes mercy is how you say thanks in French."

"You said some of the guys. What about the others?"

"They're not as impressed. Said Trevor was just a kid, and didn't deserve to die just because he ran his mouth faster than his brain. That anyone who offs kids needs to be punished. The vote is split in that group about whether you've lost your marbles or your morality. My word, not theirs. But the sentiment's the same."

"Ironic, considering who's willing to criticize me. People think what they think."

"Personally, I don't think you did it. But that's me. Since you're not offering anything, what do you want me to tell the crew?"

"Tell them there was a problem, and I took care of it."

"Makes me nervous when you talk like that."

Starks flipped onto his back. "What's there for you to be nervous about? It's me they're talking about."

"Because the last damn thing we need is for any actual or potential recruits to turn on you."

"We don't want anyone who can't be loyal. Nor do we want anyone who's too chicken-shit to realize what's what here and stand up to anyone who'd go after them."

"That's the point. They think you'd go after them if they did something you didn't like."

Starks sat up and gazed out the narrow window. "I'm not like Sanchez. Sounds like someone's stirring people up for no reason. People who know me ought to know I only go after those who go after me."

"I'll see what I can do to reassure the doubters."

"Including you?"

"You don't have to worry about me."

"I hope not."

Starks stared beyond the drizzle sticking to the glass. It was always one damn thing or another. Whatever he did, someone was going to approve and someone else was going to get pissed off. Jackson had a right to be concerned. This result wasn't one he'd anticipated, but he should have.

This Trevor matter couldn't be helped. Gabe had gone after him about the kid. He couldn't have that. The old man's opinion of him mattered too much.

"Jackson."

"Yeah?"

"I can't let people get away with shit. If they don't want trouble with me, they shouldn't start what they don't want me to finish."

"That oughta make the crew feel better."

"I can't be overly concerned about how they feel."

"Maybe I'll keep *that* to myself."

After a moment, Starks said, "Emphasize my better qualities."

"Will do. Maybe you should remind me what they are."

"Screw you."

"When I'm into dragons, you'll be the first one I call."

Starks folded his pillow in half and punched it with his fist. "I'm drowning in comedians and killers."

"And, you ignore damn near every lifeline thrown to you."

Starks chose not to respond. Partial truths were useful only to a point. No matter how many men he surrounded himself with, when it came down to it, he was on his own.

CHAPTER 42

Inmates lined up for the eight o'clock count. Minutes later, Roberts moved into position in front of Starks. "Brunson said to tell you it's three, plus five. You know what he's talking about?"

"Tell him I'm on it."

Roberts shrugged and moved to the next cell, followed by Simmons.

After the count, Starks placed his call to Jeffrey, gave him the amount, learned there was nothing new to report about his family, and ended the call.

Time to reap the reward for his efforts.

On the way to his destination, he caught up with Roberts. "Tell Brunson it's this Saturday, same place, four thirty."

"Sure thing. I'd ask, but if you wanted me to know, you'd tell me."

"As I said before, you're the smartest one in the bunch."

Roberts continued straight ahead. Starks veered right.

He thumped his fist against the workroom door. When nothing happened, he pounded harder. The bolt clanked open and the door was flung wide. Gabe strode stoop-shouldered to the table and took his usual seat. Starks entered, securing the door behind him, then sat across from Gabe. "Are you in a better mood today?"

"Take my moods or leave 'em."

"That answers my question."

"What do you want?"

"Did you hear about Trevor?"

"I heard."

"You were right. He needed to be taken care of. Can't let even a young pissant like him get away with anything."

"So, big-time head man that you are, you handled it."

"Had to." Starks shrugged nonchalantly.

Gabe studied his fingernails. "I hope you handle your dick better than you handled that punk."

"What's that supposed to mean?"

"When are you gonna learn that I know everything what goes on in this place?"

"Not everything."

"You're worse off than I thought. Not only can't you stomach doing what needs to be done, when it needs to be done, you come up with some pansy-ass solution and lie about it. And you expect me to fall for it."

"All right. So you know the truth. I'm not into killing kids, especially after my nineteen-year-old son died in my arms. So I'm not like you."

"You should be so lucky."

Starks jabbed the tabletop with his finger. "I do only what I have to, because people keep trying to kill me."

"That's the kind of big-boy arena this is. Maybe what you need is a playpen and your diapers changed. Maybe one of them wet-nurses."

"Always with the insults. I'd ask what's up with you, but I have it figured out."

"You got nothin' figured out."

"You grew up in a crime family. It was a business, rather than an anomaly. You took over for your father, like it was nothing. Because it's in your blood. It's not in mine. I never wanted any of this shit."

"Too late now."

"Who's your informant, or is it informants?"

Gabe guffawed. "Seriously?"

"Why don't you use your connections to find out what happened to Paco's manuscript."

"Like I give a shit. Not my business."

"Everything else is."

"Only the important stuff."

"What happened to Paco isn't important enough for you?"

"I don't give two shits about that old man or anyone else in this place."

"That include me?"

Gabe shrugged.

Starks's chair clattered to the floor as he leaped up. He made no attempt to hide his disgust. "To think I admired and respected you. When you got your degree in psychology, which behavioral abnormality did you diagnose yourself as having? Or is it more than one?"

Gabe narrowed his eyes. "You sure you want to go there, slick?"

"Why aren't you ever in the yard or the chow hall? Or the showers? Why do you have privileges others don't?"

"The first two questions? None of your damn business. The third question? Same reason you do." Gabe ran his thumb back and forth over his fingers. "Green is for go. And that's what you need to do." He stood and picked up a mallet. "Before I relocate your ass into that empty skull of yours, and then crack it open with this hammer. Who the hell do you think you are, talking to me like that?"

This wasn't going at all as Starks had intended. Getting on Gabe's bad side was stupid and dangerous. "I don't know what to say to you anymore."

"Say goodbye."

Starks righted the chair then slunk to the door. He turned. "This place does something to you."

"Wait until you've been here a few years."

"What I'm trying to say is, I'm sorry. You deserve more respect than I gave you."

"Your problem is, you think we're equals. You couldn't be more wrong."

"Maybe I should come back when we're both in better frames of mind. That okay with you?"

"All the same to me. If nothin' else, you're a diversion."

Starks hurried down the hallway. He'd tried to fool Gabe. To win his approval. And he knew why. The old man's resemblance to his grandfather was all in his mind.

What the hell had he been thinking? People like Gabe didn't approve of others. Didn't care about others. They used people like toilet paper. Kept them around until they served their purpose then flushed them, believing—knowing—there were always more where they came from.

Loyalty meant servitude to Gabe, until a person's usefulness ran out. It meant something else entirely to him.

In fact, it meant everything.

Otherwise, there was nothing left of value in life.

So, what was the mental twinge in his mind about?

Jackson was on his way to his kitchen shift minutes after the barred doors slid open. Still in bed, Starks touched the frosted window glass. The season had changed overnight. He did his usual workout, followed by a sink-bath. Thermal underwear went on before his scrub set. The heat wouldn't be turned on at Sands, until the outside temperature went down to forty-two degrees.

Starks ate a sweet roll and waited for the first count of the day, his mood as dark as the sky outside.

He was never getting out. Kayla would die, and they wouldn't allow him to attend her funeral. His children would be taken care of—Jeffrey would see to that, but they'd be lost without him, just as he was lost without them.

The air became too thin to breathe. Starks fell back on his bed, gulping breaths as his pulse raced. Minutes later, he dried his eyes on his shirtsleeve.

For the last three years, he'd lost more than he'd won. It was intolerable.

Also intolerable was the idea that Gabe had a point. Since he was forced to remain here, he had to become more like Gabe. Had to compartmentalize who and what to care about, who to consider expendable. Behaviors and decisions he otherwise would consider aberrations had to become second nature.

Who was he kidding? He was already off to a good start.

Still, having to lose the last vestige of who he'd been before prison, sickened him.

Like Gabe, when it came down to it, he'd always have to choose himself. Every man in this godforsaken place would do the same.

CHAPTER 43

Starks entered the library and stopped short. For a brief moment, he thought it was Paco seated at the first computer. The similarities threw him off, but he soon realized the white-haired man was twenty pounds heavier and a few inches shorter.

The error twisted in his gut as he walked toward the small office. He should have chosen Paco to confide in, to seek guidance from. Instead, he'd chosen Gabe. The blatant reason for his choice being that Gabe was a big shot and Paco wasn't. Gabe had power within these walls. Paco didn't.

Were Gabe to write a memoir, it would never possess the sensitive wisdom of lessons learned the hard way, as Paco's had. Instead, it would be filled with braggadocio and sensationalized brutality proclaimed as necessary in order to win and be top man. Your basic survival-of-the-fittest story.

Starks caught his reflection in the window that fronted the darkened interior of the office. That critical description could just as easily be applied to him the longer he remained at Sands. The burden of truth sank its weight onto his shoulders.

Screw it. It was what it was.

He switched on the light and turned on the computer, pulling the sticky note left by Sam from the monitor. Delivered boxes had been stacked to the right of the desk. It would be another full day. A small favor, indeed. Staying occupied was what he needed. Too busy to think or feel or regret.

At 3:37, Starks carried the last stack of books to be shelved into the main room, placing them on the table behind him. Two inmates seated a few feet away spoke in low voices.

One of them said, "I never seen a shrink. What's it like?"

"I don't know about that Demory guy. It's like he wants me to say killing my girlfriend was the wrong thing to do. I told her what would happen if she ever gave me a plate of beans for dinner again. Was I supposed to go back on my word?"

Starks checked the time. He'd deliberately missed his four thirty appointments on Thursdays because he'd chosen to believe Demory had taken his advice and stayed clear of Sands.

This lie held no comfort for him, because the truth was that he hadn't given the counselor another thought, his mind too crowded with other matters. Like self-preservation. Although, Kayla would call it something else.

His replacement arrived several minutes after four. Starks avoided the man's anticipated lame excuse for tardiness and marched toward Demory's office. After getting past the barriers, he flung open the door without knocking or waiting for an invitation to enter. "What the hell are you doing here?"

Demory slammed a file drawer shut. "It's me who should be asking you that. You miss appointments with complete disregard for my time. There are any number of inmates who'd be willing to take your place. Instead, I sit here waiting for someone who doesn't exercise the common courtesy of telling me he has no intention of showing up. So, why did you? Why are you gracing me with your *serene* presence now?"

"I thought you'd listened. Would play it safe and stay away. Go get a position somewhere else, someplace it's unlikely anyone will stick a shank into your protruding gut."

"You're saying you're here because of your fondness for me?"

Starks paced then dropped into the chair in front of Demory's desk. "I'm trying to save your ass."

"Ditto." Demory flopped into his chair and took several deep breaths. "I haven't left for one reason. I'm needed. Maybe you don't need me, but others here do. Men who want to prepare themselves for the day they get released. They don't want to leave as the same men who came here. Most don't know how to accomplish that. They come to me to help them. You come to me to bitch about your life, and usually end up bitching at me."

Starks rubbed his face hard and leaned forward. "I don't bitch about my life."

"That's your opinion."

"Parker filed an appeal."

Demory's eyebrows flew up. "But, that's good news, Starks. He knows his way around legal matters. You'll be out in no time."

"Appeal denied."

"Well, damn."

"He says he's going to try again, but it's not going to happen. I know it in my gut."

"It's important to keep a thread of hope at all times."

Starks picked at a cuticle. "I'm stuck here, until my sentence is done. If I last that long."

Demory picked up his pen and doodled on his tablet. "Okay. Say that's how it goes. Having to stay here, I mean. Will you keep going the way you are or will you choose to be a better man than the one you are now?" He leaned forward and fixed his gaze on Starks. "Whether it's sooner or later, you'll get out of here. You'll have to integrate back into society's norms. There may be some lessons you learned in here that serve you on the outside, but some you need to leave behind. Need to forget you ever learned them."

"Yeah, well, while I'm here, I have to do what I have to do. It's survival of the fittest, Doc."

"I'm so tired of hearing that excuse."

"It's not an excuse. If I'm perceived as weak, I'll be a bigger target than I already am. And I'm a target with every breath I take. You still don't get that, because you don't live it. You live on the periphery. I need to be like the phoenix and rise from the ashes every time one or more of these assholes burn me. Before you give me any guff about that, let me remind you that I don't choose my enemies, they choose me. Then I have to deal with them."

Starks got up. "It's not too late for you to get out. Save your butt, Demory. I'll feel a lot better if you do. Allow me to get something right."

"If I do, it won't be by next week. Will you show up for your session?"

"If my heart's still pumping, maybe I will. Maybe then, you'll tell me you came to your senses."

"Ditto."

CHAPTER 44

Light from halogen fixtures in the yard, filtered through snowflakes stuck to the narrow windowpane. Starks sat up in his still-dark cell. He touched the glass, shivered, and wrapped the thin blanket around his shoulders. The weather had turned frigid overnight.

Where was the damn heat?

He stripped and, teeth chattering, put on his thermal underwear, followed by scrubs, adding two pairs of socks over the ones he had on. He returned to his bunk and peered past the lacy crystals. At least for the moment, the ground had more frost than snow covering it. That would change soon. Probably before noon.

He stayed curled under his blanket until the lights brightened at six.

Jackson groaned. "I hate being so damn close to the damn overhead light. It's Saturday, damn it. Can't they give us a damn break on weekends? And, where's the damn heat?"

"It's snowing. Looks like it might get heavy in a couple hours."

"Great. We can build a snowman. Bring it inside so it won't melt."

"Doing my routine will warm us up." Starks stood and prodded Jackson's back. "C'mon."

"Screw that. I'm not moving till they," he shouted, "turn the damn heat on."

Inmates in their corridor echoed shared sentiments.

Jackson drew his knees to his chest and dragged the blanket over his head. "Always wanted backup singers for my magic act."

Starks started with stretches until his muscles were warm enough to move with more ease. He added extra reps, finishing an hour later.

Perspiration dampened his clothing. Despite this, he abandoned the idea of stripping and washing off at the tiny sink.

At eight o'clock, every inmate lined up for the count. Simmons and the rookie, Stone, stood at the end of the corridor, waiting for everyone to settle down before taking the tally and handing out mail. Starks hadn't seen Stone for a while. Roberts' doing, he supposed. Simmons was on his payroll. Stone was someone he could live without. The guy was too eager to punish someone. Anyone.

Simmons raised his hands. "Quiet. The heater's not working."

"No shit," someone shouted.

Inmates yelled and cursed at the guards. CO Stone, hand trembling, drew his Taser. Simmons said something to him. Stone clipped the Taser back onto his belt, his face unable to disguise his fear.

Simmons hollered for everyone to settle down. Aside from bouncing in place and rubbing their arms, they did.

"We've called for a repairman. He'll be here Monday." At the outpouring of displeasure, Simmons raised his hands again. "Wear extra clothes. Exercise. Stay in bed, unless you have a work shift or scheduled program. Bitching won't make repairs happen any sooner. You're not the only ones freezing their balls off."

An inmate shouted, "Yeah, but you get to leave."

"You assholes want your mail or not?"

Just as there was a code of silence regarding violence among inmates, there was a code about mail, understood as a lifeline for inmates who received it. Those who seldom or never got mail demonstrated respect for those who did. The grumbling continued, but muted.

When it was their turn, Starks nodded at Simmons, but stayed quiet. The last thing he wanted to do was give away his arrangement with Simmons in front of Stone, who leaked attitude toward him from every pore.

Afterwards, back in their cell, Starks waved a packaged sweet roll at Jackson. "Going to the chow hall, or would you like to dine here with me?"

"Chow hall. You should come. Maybe the oatmeal mucus will be warmer than it usually is."

"I'll pass."

"Suit yourself."

Starks ate the roll and chased it with a ham sandwich. He took a book with him to his bunk, pulled the blanket up to his chin, and mostly paid attention to the biography he'd borrowed the prior week, but hadn't started.

At 9:51, Simmons rapped on the cell bars. "Visitor, Starks. Dr. Garrett Hall. He's got his black bag with him. You called for a doctor? I thought you liked the new guy."

Starks sat up. "I didn't. And I do."

"You got a pain somewhere?"

Starks slid his feet into his shoes, tossed the book onto the bed and stood. "How many inmates in here now?"

"Nine hundred, thirty-seven."

"I've got nine hundred, thirty-six pains in my ass."

"This is me, laughing."

"This is me, walking."

"This is me, walking with you."

"I can get to the visitors' room by myself."

"The doc requested a private room. For consultation."

Starks preceded Simmons out of the cell, and wondered what was up with Garrett Hall.

CHAPTER 45

Simmons led Starks to the same small, windowless room where he and Parker usually met. Starks closed the door and reached out to take the hand extended to him.

Garrett Hall gripped his hand. "You let your hair grow back. I like it better than the shaved head."

"Made Steve, the barber, pretty happy. He cried when I had him shave it off."

Starks gestured toward the chair across the small table and took a seat.

Garrett sat forward in his chair. "How are you feeling? Anymore health problems since I saw you last?"

Starks shook his head. "So far, so good. I didn't know doctors made prison calls for patients they treated at a hospital."

"They don't. This was the easiest way to bypass the long vetting process for approval. I'll check you, of course, but I'm here for a different reason. One only you can understand better than anyone else."

"You look like crap. What's going on?"

"That's primarily why I came. To discuss my situation with you. Get your input. It'll take a while to tell you everything."

Starks slouched back in his chair. "I've got fourteen years to listen, unless Parker can work some magic to get me out sooner."

A little over an hour later, Starks sat knees-up on his bunk, his gaze fixed out the window. Larger, thicker flakes blew in all directions. An inch or so of pristine white covered the usually brown ground and capped the few guard towers in his field of vision. He wondered if the guards used small electric heaters or dressed for arctic temperatures.

Anyplace else, snowfall would render the landscape stunning. The only thing in common with the world outside was the quiet. Inmates were subdued, either a result of a mostly universal effect snow had on people, or because they were too cold to do anything more active.

The measured, temporary serenity eluded Starks. He hadn't expected what he'd heard from Garrett. Hadn't expected to smell alcohol on his friend's breath so early in the day. Hadn't expected to learn that Garrett had put a gun in his mouth and pulled the trigger, only to realize he hadn't chambered a round. Had done this because his wife, Chelsea, was cheating on him with some no-name author.

Garrett had flung the author's book onto the table, back cover showing the smiling face of the cocoa-complexioned Luke Thompson, who was giving Chelsea a good time in the sack.

Garrett admitted to having driven to Thompson's house late at night, gun loaded and ready, his intention to kill the man. Had he carried out his plan, Garrett could be in line to freeze his balls off at Sands in winter and sweat them off in summer, possibly for life.

Their situations had enough parallels to cause his long-time friend to seek him out for advice. How odd it had felt to say things to Garrett that others, especially Demory, had said to him. Things he'd resented and rejected. Now he had a better understanding of their motivation: To save him from himself. That's why he'd said what he had to Garrett. Why he'd risked, and received, Garrett's resistance and resentment. Even down to being accused of taking Chelsea's side, just as he'd accused Demory so many times regarding Kayla.

How much he believed, and didn't, of what he'd told Garrett rankled him. He'd laid it on thick, in an effort to get Garrett not to act as stupidly as he had about Ozy Hessinger and end up incarcerated. Yet, he didn't go as far as he might have. He'd nudged Garrett to reconcile with Chelsea. Maybe he would. Or maybe Garrett would cling to his anger and pain about her betrayal, as he had about Kayla's.

Another thing Demory mentioned often was what was needed to heal. Forgiveness, of course. As though doing it was as easy as saying the word. As it was, healing took the time it took. If healing rested on forgiveness as the first rung on that ladder, it could take a very long time—for him, as well as for Garrett.

It had unsettled him when his friend reflected far too many of his own attitudes and behaviors. Especially when he'd insisted Garrett needed to look at what he'd done to Chelsea that led her to cheat on him, as Kayla had done to him in retaliation.

Garrett had said nothing about Kayla's condition, which likely meant she hadn't reached out to him for help or guidance. Kayla always did what she wanted to do. Perhaps she'd contacted someone else, some doctor beyond the several she'd already consulted.

Someone he hadn't partied with.

He could have asked Garrett to call Kayla, or to see her at the house, but the man had enough going on. Maybe it was for the best. Professional or not, he might not have felt charitable toward Kayla, all things considered.

Kayla was suffering and dying, without his being there to support her. That was his fault.

There was no denying it. Garrett had held up a mirror, one displaying a truly ugly reflection. That should inspire him to make some of those changes Demory hoped he would, and insisted he must.

But how could he change for the better when nearly everyone around him wanted to force the worst that lived inside him to the surface?

The only thing that lifted him slightly from his dark mood was the possibility that Garrett would succeed where he had failed.

CHAPTER 46

J ackson interrupted Starks's thoughts. "Brought you something."

Starks wrinkled his nose. "What's that smell?"

Jackson drew out his right hand, which he'd tucked inside his inadequate coat. Atop a folded dishcloth was a bowl with something steaming in it. "Bean soup. Guess they didn't want a riot by feeding us anything cold. Heated it until it boiled so it wouldn't freeze on the way. Brought a couple packets of salt and pepper. Might help it go down better."

"Playing mother?"

"You didn't show up for lunch. Figured you were moping in here."

"I don't mope."

"Right. You're in here contemplating the mysteries of the universe." Jackson placed the bowl and condiments on Starks's desk. "It may taste as bad as it stinks, but at least it's hot. However, in my opinion, only a sadist would provide bean soup to prisoners trapped inside during a snowstorm."

Starks uncurled his legs and picked up the bowl. "Thanks."

"You have to eat it now so I can take the bowl back. Don't want anyone thinking I wait on you."

"Did you bring a spoon?"

"Some people are so hard to please."

Starks brought the bowl to his mouth and took a swallow. He added two packets of salt and worked on the soup.

Jackson jabbered on about recruits not being the best or brightest. That this was one of those times when brawn mattered more than brains.

Starks drained the bowl and grimaced. "Be good if we could get the two in one."

"Roll of the dice, man."

Starks rinsed the bowl and handed it to Jackson.

Jackson tucked it inside his coat. "You stayin' in this cell all day?"

"Unless I have a good reason to leave it."

Jackson shrugged. "Suit yourself. Stay frosty."

"You're a riot."

"One of the many reasons you keep me around."

Starks picked up the book, but left it closed. The natural light outside grew darker, causing halogen lights to spring on, their illumination all but invisible behind what had become an impenetrable blizzard. He hoped Garrett had made it back safely before the storm had begun in earnest.

Starks flinched and cursed when someone said his name. "Damn it, Ethan. You have to stop sneaking up on me like that."

Ethan laughed. "You need to stop letting your attention drift. However, I doubt any of these clods would or could employ the finesse it takes to creep up on someone."

Starks pointed to Jackson's chair. "First time you've come to my cell. Must mean you have something."

Ethan pulled the chair out and turned it to face Starks's desk. "In case I need to spontaneously return to my pretense."

"Your cellmate must enjoy your company."

"He's hard of hearing. When I catch him looking at me, I move my mouth as though speaking, but make no sound. That trained him to ignore me as much as possible. Plus, he stays away until it's time to be locked in. I do just enough to keep up the charade, but mostly leave him alone. He's not a target."

"Speaking of targets, what did you find out?"

Ethan polished the trimmed nails of his right hand on his pants before inspecting them. "There's ever so much treachery in this place."

"That's not news."

"So many traitors, so few really sharp knives."

Starks grimaced. "And?"

In a sing-song voice, he said, "You're not going to like it."

"Also not news."

"But, I dare say, you aren't expecting this revelation." Ethan forced his expression into a sad frown. "I discovered who violated the privacy of your cell and stole Paco's memoir, ripping those profound words from your view."

"And?"

"Sam."

Starks went completely still. "Carson?"

"The very one."

Starks stared at Ethan for several silent moments. "How certain are you?"

"As certain about that as I am about where Buster's head is, which is likely a Popsicle by now in this frozen wasteland."

"I can't believe it."

"More like you don't want to. Anything else I can do for you?"

"Not at the moment. Unless you get anything about where the manuscript is now."

Ethan placed Jackson's chair back under the desk. He dropped to one knee and clasped his hands at his chest. "Please, please, please give me the green light on Seth. Something to break the monotony of this dull existence."

Starks struggled to keep his expression blank. "I'll think about it. One more thing. Keep this information about Sam between us."

Ethan jutted his chin out. "You needn't tell me what I already know. I don't want to blow my cover. Ah, well, the show must go on." He checked the corridor then skipped away, singing, "Row, row, row your boat …"

Starks ran a hand through his hair.

Sam. A traitor.

The Sam he trusted.

The only person, other than Jackson, who'd known Paco had given the manuscript to him.

He flung the book with all the force he could muster. The book plunked into the toilet. Starks cursed, fished the book from the bowl, and tossed it into the small plastic trash can.

Gabe was right. He couldn't trust anyone, even those he felt certain it was safe to.

His hand went to his chest, as though the instinctive gesture might keep the ache from exploding out of him.

CHAPTER 47

The blizzard persisted. The temperature dropped low enough inside to frost people's breath. By four that afternoon, the only inmates not hunkered in their bunks were those completing their shifts in the kitchen for the evening meal. More bean soup. But no one missed the meal, including Starks. Everyone looked as though they'd put on weight, padded with every article of clothing owned, topped with the prison-issued coat squeezed on over the layers.

The six o'clock count that evening was understandably subdued. Jackson returned a few minutes after seven, vaulted into his bunk, and pulled the blanket over his curled up form.

Starks debated whether or not to tell Jackson about Sam, but chose to wait. First, he wanted to hear what Sam had to say. Besides, it was possible Ethan had gotten it wrong. He wanted that to be true, but knew it wasn't.

He spent Sunday in his bunk, planning how to approach Sam regarding his perfidy. Contemplated how screwed up life had become, compared to what he'd planned when he was a teen dreaming of a bliss-filled life with Kayla.

The blizzard downgraded to light snow by the afternoon, but there was no going out. Like others, he'd checked the doors that led to the yard. Rather than late afternoon light or sky in the small square windows positioned at eye level, there was solid white.

Someone needed to dig them out, before sunlight melted the snow drift enough to turn it into solid ice once nighttime temperatures dropped. The someone would have to be a guard or a person hired from outside. No way would they hand over shovels to inmates who'd been cooped up and freezing for two days.

Monday morning at first count, Simmons and Stone, looking weary after being trapped at Sands, announced repairmen were working on the heater. Cheers erupted. Simmons and Stone avoided any attempt to get them to settle down.

Starks's shift was to be a half-day, starting at one. As soon as the numbers on his clock showed as 12:43, he started for the library.

News of imminent heat caused hopeful inmates to resume their usual activities, including filling seats at the computers and at reading tables. Sam glanced up as Starks made his way toward the office. He waved. Starks, unsmiling, nodded.

Sam leaned back in the chair. "Hell of a couple of days."

"You could say that. Had a lot of time to think." Starks lowered himself into the chair in front of the desk.

"You're looking grim. Couldn't find any good thoughts to mull over, while you froze your ass off?"

"Betrayal has that effect."

Sam rested his elbows on the desktop. "Shit. Who betrayed you now?"

Starks locked his gaze on him. "Funny you should ask. Only, it's not at all humorous. Betrayal's a bitch, but it's always worse when it's someone you never would have expected. Wouldn't you agree?"

Sam swallowed hard. "Yeah."

"Why did you do it?"

"Me? I didn't do anything. What are you going on about?" Sam ran a shaky hand over his hair then dropped it into his lap.

"Paco's memoir. No point denying you took it from my cell. I want it back."

Sam leaped up. "You got it all wrong."

"Sit. Down. Just tell me why."

"Shit." Sam cradled his head in his hands. "Had to."

"Again, why?"

"Ordered to."

"By who?"

"I can't tell you."

"Don't make me hurt you, Sam."

Sam balled his hands into fists. "Yeah. You'd hurt me. Or you'd get one or more members of your gang to do it. You might even watch. I know about the shit you and they get into."

"Everybody knows about that. Start talking."

"I talk, I die."

"You don't talk, that may happen anyway."

"I'd rather it be you than …"

"Than who?"

Sam shook his head. "You might off me, but you wouldn't harm my family."

Starks absorbed what had been said. "And Seth would. You sure that's not just a threat to control you?"

Sam's eyes widened. After a moment's hesitation, he muttered, "I've already said too much."

"Where's the manuscript?"

"I don't know."

"Sam."

Sweat beaded on Sam's forehead. "I swear I don't. I handed it over and was out of it."

"I'll protect you."

"Maybe you mean that, Starks, but you and I both know that don't mean shit in here."

Starks slapped his hands against his knees and stood.

Sam stood as well. "What are you gonna do?"

"For now, nothing. I'm going to continue showing up for my shifts. Neither one of us is to mention our talk to anyone. I'd ask for your word on that, but we know how much that's worth. However if I hear you opened your mouth …"

"Yeah, I know. You'll close it permanently."

"I still may."

CHAPTER 48

The yard remained inaccessible. That left Starks with his cell to return to after his shift ended or communal space within the gray walls, which pressed in on him even more so than usual. So far, he'd avoided the gym, where Paco had been hanged. If he continued avoiding spaces where any violence had occurred, eventually he'd end up on the roof. And even that area wasn't a given.

He stood inside the doorway, scoping out the gym and the people in it. Ethan swirled dumbbells over his head in the far right corner. Felipe and several Los Hermanos occupied the mat and the bench press. He nodded at Felipe then joined him.

"You want a match, amigo?"

"Not today." An uncontrollable reflex caused Starks to look toward the ceiling then quickly away.

Felipe tapped him on the arm and indicated he was to follow. They moved a few yards away from the mat and out of earshot. "It's one thing to return to where an enemy got what he deserved. It's different when it was a friend who didn't."

Starks frowned. "Or a son."

"Never let anyone who's with you, or against you, know this is how you feel."

"Or I'll be like a fish lured to a hook."

"They'll catch you, gut and fillet you, and serve you to their amigos for dinner."

Starks made eye contact with Felipe. "How have you managed to keep a measure of humanity?"

"I think what you mean is, How have I managed to keep it secret."

"However you want to put it."

"You're the only one who knows any different."

"My lips are locked."

"Your humanity may have diminished since you came to this place, but the seed is still in here." Felipe tapped his own chest. "You wouldn't be taking care of my family, if it wasn't."

"What if I did that to get you on my side?"

Felipe grinned. "I'm smart enough to know that was part of it. But there are less expensive ways. Now, since you're here, let me throw your ass around on the mat for a while."

"Maybe next time."

"You have something better to do?"

"Not better, just something to take care of."

"Up to you." Felipe returned to his gang, fussing about the sloppy performance of the men practicing on the mat.

Starks faced where Ethan watched him from the corner. Ethan winked at him. Starks gave an imperceptible nod toward the door. He walked into the hallway and waited.

Ethan joined him. In a low voice he said, "Please tell me you have a special assignment for me."

"I talked to Sam."

"I've come up with something brilliant for him."

"Leave him alone. Seth used him. Threatened his family, if he didn't follow orders, and if he talked. He was willing to risk my killing him to save them. Can't hold that against him."

"I could."

"Suppress that inclination. I'm not concerned about Sam. The bigger concern is Seth. Only thing I want you to focus on is how I can get that manuscript back."

"Then I can enjoy myself?"

"First things first."

"Anything else?"

"That's it."

"Then, here I go. Off to see the wizard." Ethan dashed forward, stopped, spun in circles, and disappeared down the hallway to the right.

Starks made his way to the commissary, to stock up on more cardboard sandwiches and junk food. Sam stood in front of the sweet rolls, debating his selection. Starks sidled up next to him.

Sam glanced to his left and started to back away.

"Relax. If I was going to do anything to you, it wouldn't be in here. Since you are here, I might as well tell you that I've given your situation thought."

"Where'd that take you?"

"Did you mention our conversation to whoever has your pecker in a vice?"

"No."

Starks narrowed his eyes. "Is that the truth?"

Sam glanced around then made a small cross over his heart. "I swear on my grandchildren."

"Keep it that way. What you did sickens me, but what was done to you is more egregious. You can understand why I'd resent anyone going after a man's family."

Sam's shoulders and face relaxed. "It's more than I deserve."

"Probably. Just know this. If you tell anyone about our conversations, especially Seth, all deals are off. Are we clear?"

"Like my departed mother's windows."

Sam's attention shifted, his eyes grew wide. Starks aimed his gaze in the same direction. Seth and two of his soldiers watched them from the far side of the room. Seth's bead was on Sam, who swallowed hard. It was all the confirmation Starks needed.

He turned back to Sam, waved his arm in an arc and said, "Get whatever you want. My treat."

Sam whispered, "What the hell? You trying to get me and my family killed?"

"As far as anyone knows, we get along just fine. Now smile and say 'Thanks' with enthusiasm. Like I, your good buddy, am being generous. Because I am."

Sam pasted a broad smile on and did as instructed. They walked to the counter together.

Starks told the attendant, "Bag our stuff separately, but I'm putting his stuff on my tab." He grinned and slapped Sam on the back. "Treating my boss today."

Sam nodded at Starks. "Again, thanks."

"See you tomorrow."

Sam grabbed his bag and rushed out, passing Seth with a quick nod.

The attendant said, "You do that often?"

"Only when I'm in the mood. He's one of the good guys."

"I'm one of the good guys."

Starks studied the man for a few seconds then keyed in ten dollars on his account. "There's ten for you. Spend it wisely."

"Thanks, man. I've been needing—"

Starks picked up his bag, said, "No need to tell me," and started for the door, ignoring Seth's poisonous glare. He turned right and continued toward his cell. He'd accomplished several significant things in under twenty minutes.

They were some of those small comforts Jackson always spoke about, but he'd take them.

CHAPTER 49

Starks arrived a few minutes early for his eight thirty shift. Books to be re-shelved littered two of the long tables. He turned on the office light and the computer. Got busy filing the books back where they belonged and organizing those shelved in the wrong place. Sam arrived at twelve forty-five to take over, his demeanor that of a man chased by hornets.

Starks stood in the doorway. "Something new happen?"

Sam, head down, jumped. "No. Why?"

"You look like you're waiting to make the walk."

"Got grief about the commissary."

"What kind of grief?"

"Wanted to know why you did it."

"What'd you say?"

"That you've done it before. Lots of times."

"I haven't."

"Not with me, maybe. But everyone knows you've done it for guys in your gang."

"It's a crew, not a gang."

"Whatever. Anyway, I said I couldn't suddenly tell you to stick it. You'd get suspicious."

"The response?"

"Said I was smart to play it like nothing is going on."

"Guess that means I need to keep it up."

"Sorry."

Starks shook his head once. "Money's the cheapest way to pay."

"I am sorry, Starks. About all of it."

"I almost believe you. See you tomorrow."

By Thursday, snow in the yard had melted enough for inmates to return to fresh, though frigid, air and sunshine. Patches of ground retained sheets of ice thick enough for the men to skate across a distance of ten or so feet.

After breakfast, Starks sat on the bleachers, watching a number of his crew doing just that. For several moments, he didn't see hardened criminals who would slit a man's throat to save their own skin or to steal someone's money or possessions. He saw them as children, smaller in size—some skinny, others tubby—playing with boys from the neighborhood. Young enough not to feel the cold in their bones. Young enough to play on the ice until streetlights came on and their mothers called them inside for a hot dinner. Young enough to go to bed that night with full stomachs—most of them, he hoped—tucked in by one or both parents or some other adult who genuinely cared about their well-being.

Chapters he'd read in Paco's memoir impeded his desire about this. The reality a number of inmates had experienced was akin to Paco's or worse.

Although his father had abandoned him and his mother when he was three, his grandfather and a host of uncles and aunts treated him and his cousins as their own children. The men may have cheated on their wives, but no child within their family ever went hungry or unclothed or undisciplined or unloved. Every scraped knee had a big deal made over it, until the child turned eight and was told to buck up. He'd been provided with examples of the benefits of hard work and family nurturing, even if not overtly affectionate.

The probable examples some of these men had been exposed to as children made him shudder. Demory would say they could unlearn what they'd learned. But, would they want to? His grandfather had told him to be the opposite of those who refused to change until it became unbearable not to. That, if he wanted to win or remain unscathed, he had to be one or more steps ahead of any potential crisis.

Once again, his own hypocrisy reared. He'd had it better than most of these guys growing up, yet here he was, trying to figure out what had gone wrong in *their* lives.

There seemed to be a temporary reprieve from violence. A result, he supposed, of the heat working and the yard being accessible again. But a different kind of heat was building. It was evident in the chow hall at every meal, as well as in the yard and corridors. Like a pressure cooker with a flame turned too high beneath it.

It was only a matter of time before the lid blew off.

CHAPTER 50

Mid-morning on Sunday, Starks positioned the large book against his bent legs. Cell phone in hand, he keyed in five digits of his mother's home number then stopped. A while back, Roberts had suggested he occasionally use the phones provided for prisoners so no one got suspicious. Too risky. His presence at the shared phones would start the rumor mill whirring. Nor did it appeal to him to wait in a line. The last thing he wanted was for anyone's ears to aim in his direction like satellite dishes. If anyone got curious about his absence at the phones, screw 'em.

Lynn Starks answered. He said, "It's me. Have you been in contact with my family?"

"I went to the house yesterday. Thought I'd see if Kayla would let me take the kids out for a while."

"Did she?"

"Yes. I think it was a relief for all of them. I told her I'll do that more often."

"How does she look?"

"How do you think?"

Starks wanted details then changed his mind. Kayla's ragged appearance, when she'd come to Sands several months back, lingered well enough in his mind. Easy to imagine how she must look now.

Lynn continued. "I took them to the mall to do some shopping. That gave me a chance to pull Blake to the side."

Starks clenched his hand around the phone. "What did you say to him?"

"Don't get wound up before you know what's what. I went along with what you insisted. However, I did ask him if he knew how ill his mother was. He said he did. I told him there's a possibility that he and his brother and sister might have to live with me at some point."

"What did he say?"

"He shrugged and nodded. I still detest Kayla for what's she done to all of us, but I suppose it's best for my grandchildren if I keep my mouth shut about it. At least until they're old enough to understand more."

"I appreciate how you handled that. As far as ever discussing what really happened, I prefer nothing be said by any of us, unless specifically asked. That includes any member of the family. Can we agree on that?"

"My grandchildren deserve to know the truth about their mother."

"When they're older, and when they ask. And it needs to be facts unembellished by emotion."

"How do you expect me to separate what I feel from the truth? *You* don't."

"If you can't do that, it's best you leave any explanations to me. They're having to watch her suffer and die. That's enough pain for them, don't you think?"

Lynn sniffed. "Whoever said life was easy?"

"Not easy is one thing, brutal is another."

"Always with the criticism. You'd think I'd never done anything right in my life. Not with you, not with my grandchildren. Your comments feel pretty damn brutal to me."

Starks cupped his forehead in his hand. "When I was a child, what would you have done to protect me?"

"Anything. And I did. More times than you know."

"Then maybe you understand where I'm coming from."

"I can't believe you think I'd do anything to hurt my grandchildren."

"Perhaps not deliberately. But in your trying to defend me, they'd choose to hate you over hating their mother. Facts are one thing. Your making disparaging remarks about the mother they lost—are losing—is another."

"Maybe I should take a vow of silence when I'm around them. Maybe that will satisfy you."

Starks flinched when she slammed the receiver into the cradle. He listened to the dial tone for a few seconds then called back.

Lynn answered. He controlled his tone and said, "I need you to help me out, here. I need you to be a soft place for my kids to land. You can be prickly, and you know it." He heard her sniffle. "You've got real strength, Mom. Sometimes it's misplaced, but they'll need someone strong for them. That's my role, but I can't fill it for a long time. Will you do this for them, and for me?"

After a pause, Lynn said, "I'll do my best."

"That's all I'm asking."

Awkward silence stretched between them. In typical families, he'd tell his mother he loved her and would wait for her to say the same to him. Their family had never been typical.

"Tell everyone I said hello. Mom?"

"What?"

"Thanks."

She blew her nose loudly before hanging up the phone.

Starks stared unseeing into the cell across from his.

There was always some damn obstacle to deal with.

CHAPTER 51

J ackson stretched and yawned. "The last thing I want to do is get out of bed."

Starks opened his eyes then closed them again. "Damn it, Jackson, I was sleeping. Didn't drop off until sometime after four."

"Don't I know it. Your nighttime habits suck."

"Your snoring should be illegal. Get it checked or something."

"Why don't you get a sleeping pill and shove it up your ass."

Starks turned on his side, punched his thin pillow, which he'd folded in half, and attempted to go back to sleep. "Lately, you're bitchy when you wake up."

"That leaves the other twenty-three hours and fifty-nine minutes for your moods." Jackson leaped to the floor. "Shit, it's cold. Word is there's another blizzard kicking in Wednesday afternoon and into Thursday. That's going to mess up some Thanksgiving plans. Good thing we don't have to worry about that."

"Just what we don't need."

"I need thick wool socks and bigger shoes."

"I know where I'm going to put a sock if you don't shut it."

Jackson wet his toothbrush under the tap. "What's got you PMS-ing now?"

"You're not a family man. You wouldn't understand."

Jackson paused his brushing and said, "Call them. You haven't seen your kids in a while. Get someone to bring them here. Put you in a better mood."

The overhead lights brightened, the cell doors clanged open.

Starks clamped his eyes shut. "It takes two visits to see all three."

Jackson rinsed his mouth and toothbrush. "Get someone to bring them in two shifts. Maybe the rule is you can't have more than three visitors at a time, but I don't recall one that says you can't see more than three visitors in one day."

"I'll think about it."

Jackson dressed in silence. On his way out, he said, "Time to congeal powdered eggs. I'd tell you to lighten up, but what's the point?"

Starks dropped his sock-clad feet to the floor and stayed seated on the edge of his bed. It might help to see his children. It had been months. The last time, he'd been healing from the knife wound to his wrist. Kaitlin had been sympathetic, as well as fascinated by what and who she saw. Blake had been surly, upset that his mother didn't like his girlfriend. With this latest development, Blake might possibly be concerned about his family not liking his boyfriend. As though there weren't enough disconcerting matters going on in their lives at present.

Starks started his routine but lost count so many times, he gave up. He brought the large book with the phone to his bed and dialed Jeffrey's cell phone number. "It's me."

"Bro, are the worms even moving yet?"

"Sorry. I wasn't thinking about the time. Is it true there's going to be another blizzard?"

"Yeah. It's screwing up a lot of holiday plans."

"Including mine. I was going to ask you to bring two of my kids to see me. My mother could bring the other one earlier or later."

"It'll have to be the following weekend."

"Do me a favor and make sure Kayla and the kids have everything they need before the storm hits."

"Already on my schedule to take care of this afternoon. Snow's supposed to start tomorrow during the day, so I'm closing the offices at noon today. Everybody's excited about getting an extra day and a half added to their holiday weekend. Hasn't stopped them from bitching about having to shovel snow. Saw lots of food-shopping lists being made, as well, now that their travel plans are screwed."

"If Kayla has an emergency and can't get out—"

"I'd find a way. In fact, I considered camping out in the guest bedroom until streets are cleared."

"I'd relax some if you would. How is she?"

"Relieved the experts were wrong about having only two months left. I think she's living on pure will. Although, existing is probably more accurate."

"She always was stubborn."

"It's more than that. Time with the kids seems to be keeping her alive. At least for now."

"That's worth something. Just hate that it took this to get her to spend time with them, instead of … Nevermind."

"I'd planned to get out there to see you, but with the weather—"

"I'd rather you stay close to Kayla and the kids. They need you more than I do."

"Anything else I can do for you?"

"You have paper and pen?"

"Yeah. Let me sit up and turn on the lamp. Okay, go."

"Here's what I want you to get everyone for Christmas, from me and some from Santa."

"Santa's not in the picture anymore."

"Since when?"

Jeffrey hesitated. "Last Christmas."

Starks took a moment to let this reality sink in then gave Jeffrey the list. He ended the call and put the phone away.

Last Christmas. He'd been in the local jail, waiting for his trial. Parker had taken care of his kids' gifts but said nothing about it being the end of Santa for his young daughter. Kaitlin was growing up too fast. They all were. He was stuck in a time warp, while his children moved forward in their lives. Without him.

Despite all his screwing around with other women, he'd stayed home for holidays. Made a huge deal of it for the kids, especially when they were small.

He'd long believed treasures were what he could purchase with money he'd worked his ass off for, objects that allowed him to display how well he was doing, how superior he was to most men. Only now was he beginning to understand that some things had a price and others were priceless. Like lost years. Like memories being made in his absence, relegated to photographs and retold stories long after events.

Like the privilege of being a husband and father.

The price being paid for his selfishness and pride was one he'd never anticipated. And, it was flaying him one strip at a time.

CHAPTER 52

Thanksgiving Day brought a whiteout from the blizzard and fistfights among frustrated inmates prevented from spending time with family. Everyone's fuses ran shorter than usual. Prison phone banks stayed congested with men using the few minutes allowed for each call to check on the safety of their loved ones, or to connect in some meaningful way with those closest to them.

Those in the know, caused Starks's cell phone business to boom, using all the minutes left on the phones, days before he'd be able to get Brunson to buy more. New members in his crew complained about not being in on the action. His explanation that their inclusion was temporarily on hold resulted in several of them telling him to go screw himself and to forget their names. He kept to himself that he'd never bothered to learn them.

"This is not good," Jackson said.

"Nothing I can do about it, at least not for a while." Starks stretched out on his bunk and propped his crossed arms behind his head.

"You better think of something. They believed they'd be making money and kicking Seth's ass by now. What's the hold-up on going after him?"

"He's got to make the first move."

"Since when?"

"The penalty for self-defense is less. They may not appreciate that fact now, but they will."

"Your reputation is hanging on by a thread with some of these guys."

"I'm not going to make the first move."

"Keep stalling, and you won't make the last one either."

"Where's Starks? Where the hell is he? I have to find him. Now."

Starks, squatting over a box of books delivered an hour earlier, stood at the sound of the stressed voice. He hurried to the door of the office and said, "Tommy." He motioned for his crew member to join him then closed the door. "What's the matter?"

"Someone went after Ethan."

"Shit." Starks dragged a hand through his hair. "Dead?"

Tommy shook his head. "I don't think so. But he's in the infirmary. Only just got the word he'd been attacked. Knew you'd want to know."

"Watch the library while I check on him."

"What am I watching for?"

Starks shoved Tommy into the main room. "Make sure no one steals or destroys anything."

He'd tempt fate if he went unarmed, but he'd never get past the metal detector at the entrance to the infirmary. Not with the needle in his hem. He tore a piece of duct tape from the roll on a shelf and taped the needle under the desk. As he passed Tommy, he said, "I'll be back as soon as I can."

Heart thumping, Starks speed-walked into the corridor, making the turns leading to the infirmary. He sailed through the metal detector and skidded to a stop. Ethan lay stretched out on an examination table.

Marc Stewart, the former military doctor who'd replaced the egregiously inept Dr. Troy, gently prodded Ethan's ribs and abdomen, while asking questions about pain or tenderness. Ethan uttered his stuttered answers in a quiet but clear voice.

Tightness in Starks's chest eased from a ten to an eight. From his viewpoint, Ethan's face looked okay. Any injuries must have been inflicted to his torso, and was why, he assumed, Stewart focused his attention on that area.

Stewart glanced at Starks. "He was asking for you."

Starks started toward the exam table. "How is he, Doc?"

Ethan winced and turned his head to look at Starks.

Although the injuries were nowhere near as destructive as what had happened to Kane, bile rose in Starks's throat. Blood covered the left side of Ethan's face. Swelling nearly closed his left eye. His cheek was split to the bone and also starting to swell.

Stewart straightened up and pointed to a chair. "Maybe you'd better sit."

"I'm fine. What about him?"

"Fortunately, he looks worse than he is. No broken or cracked ribs." He smiled at Ethan. "This young man's got six-pack abs." He returned his focus to Starks. "Slightly bruised internal organs. Bed rest for a couple days will take care of that. He'll need stitches for that gash. And ice for the swelling. What kind of animals go after someone like him?" Stewart looked down at Ethan. He rested a hand on his shoulder. "Sorry. I don't mean to talk as though you're not in the room."

Starks inched closer. "Will you keep him here?"

"At least overnight." Stewart looked directly at Ethan. "Then I'll see how you're doing."

"S-S-Starks? W-w-will y-you s-s-stay w-with me?"

Starks looked at Stewart. "Can you arrange that? I think he'd be better off if I stay with him."

"I'll take care of it. I've still got to clean him up and sew the cut. Go get whatever you need. By the time you get back, I'll have him fixed up."

Ethan grabbed Starks's wrist. "D-d-don't g-go."

Starks said, "As long as you feed and water both of us, there's nothing I need."

Stewart nodded. "All right, young man, let's get you sewn up."

"S-s-scar?"

"Yes. Sorry about that. One advantage is you'll look like you might be dangerous. Maybe then you'll be left alone." Stewart smiled at Ethan, patted him on the shoulder then left to retrieve what was needed.

Ethan grinned at Starks, grimacing with the effort.

Twenty minutes later, Ethan lay in one of the patient beds in the back room. An I.V. dripped saline into his left arm.

Starks stood on the side of the bed opposite the pole holding the drip bag. "Who did this to you?"

Ethan glanced at the large window on the top half of the wall adjoining the two rooms. He kept his voice low. "No idea. I was taking a shower. Got soap in my eyes and turned my face to the water. Something dark slipped over my head and the throttling began."

"Did you recognize any voices?"

"They were careful. Never even whispered anything."

"Any idea how many of them?"

"At least three. Maybe four."

"You provoked anyone lately?"

"No more than usual. Whenever I see I'm about to push too far, I back off. My goal is simply to maintain misguidance."

"I'm sure it's a message from Seth. However, I'm not entirely certain how to interpret it. It's not like him to allow his victims to live, especially not ones under my protection or that I like."

Ethan's eyes flicked toward the glass window. Starks followed his glance. Stewart got whatever it was he was looking for and returned to the other side of the room.

Ethan said, "My best guess is, it was a shot over the bow."

"For what purpose?"

"Maybe Seth hopes to trigger you into full-on engagement. Likely wants to get the war over and done. I'm sure he figures you'll attribute this to him and kick into gear."

"He's going to be disappointed."

"Why?"

"A number of reasons. One specific reason being, you're one of my best soldiers. Unless I'm forced to, I'm not going into battle without you at my side."

Ethan laughed and gripped his side. "Promise me one thing."

"What's that?"

"When the time comes, you hold him while I gut him."

"We'll see."

"What's to see?"

"Depends on how much time we have."

"I work fast."

Stewart crossed the front room and came to the door. "Starks, if the bed next to Ethan is vacant tonight, you can bunk there."

"Appreciate it."

Starks turned back to Ethan. "You need to get some rest. Sleep, if you can. I'll be right here." He borrowed an extra chair from the main room and positioned it next to the bed.

Ethan yawned. The sedative Stewart had given him had started to kick in.

Starks rested his head back and closed his eyes. Unless a horde stormed the infirmary, they were both safe for the night. And, if such an unlikely threat occurred, he was certain his weapon remained where he'd hidden it, in the bathroom to his right.

He reminded himself that, should he need to defend himself and Ethan, a plethora of tools of destruction surrounded him.

Starks nodded off within seconds.

CHAPTER 53

B y mid-December, tension among inmates, and guards, ran high—in the chow hall, in the corridors—anywhere the men's paths crossed. Fistfights erupted. Threats punctured silence and psyches. An undercurrent of murmurings filled every space with a hum of disquiet and discontent. The warden threatened to revoke privileges, if inmates didn't settle down. The threat worked in some measure, but mostly on the surface.

CO Brunson finally managed to purchase more minutes for the illegal cell phones, tripled at Starks's request. For the holidays, he'd explained. Starks reduced the charge inmates paid to use the phones by half for the same reason. That appeased only some of the men who knew about his private enterprise.

Cross-legged on his bed, Starks watched light snow start to fall on the other side of his narrow window, grateful Jeffrey kept up payments to the guys who cleared the driveway and doorways at his former house. He took the large book to his bunk and dialed his mother's home number. "Everyone doing okay in this weather?"

"I'm sick of seeing white. Can't even hear the Christmas song without wanting to break something. What about you?"

"Doesn't affect me as much." The lie was safer, for both of them.

"I intended to bring Nathan and Kaitlin to see you this Saturday, and Blake the following Saturday, but they're afraid to leave Kayla."

Starks sat erect. "Is she worse?"

"Not especially. Although, she's had a couple of bad spells. Scared everyone, including me. The kids refuse to leave her for any reason now."

"It's probably better if they don't come here."

"What do you mean?"

"The holidays, and being stuck inside, have some of these guys wound tight. Brawls keep breaking out in the visitors' room. Guards call it the winter black-and-blues syndrome. I don't want my children exposed to anything like that or to be put in harm's way."

"Then I'll come with your aunt and cousin."

"Don't."

"No one's going to stop me from seeing my son."

"If you do, I'll refuse the visit. Wait until after the holidays. Let tempers here cool down."

"Are you in danger?"

"I'm careful to avoid confrontations."

"Since when?"

"I need to go. Give my love to my family. All of them."

He didn't need to hang up, but if he continued to talk, he'd be tempted to say things to his mother he preferred to keep from her. Like the fact that the brawls had increased in frequency, especially with one snow or ice storm following the last—there would be little reprieve from their confinement for months. Like the fact that delaying their visits until after the holidays, was a sacrifice he firmly believed he had to make. That the thought of any spontaneous attack, which might cause him to leave this life without ever seeing his children or family again, woke him soaked with sweat every night.

And the fact that he felt more alone now than any previous time in his life.

He desperately wanted to see his family, especially because if emotions continued to ramp up inside Sands, the war might break out and escalate in ways none of them were prepared for. As it was, he didn't know why Seth was waiting to engage, other than to torment him and his men. He was determined to play defense rather than offense, despite several crew members' occasional protests. Anything to avoid his sentence being upped to life. If he survived.

Feeling both noble and deprived, Starks let the holidays grind past him without even one phone call to any of them. Hearing their voices would crush him. Only phone calls to Jeffrey for updates were made, and even those were scarce.

Because of his imprudent actions, two Christmases for his family had been marred. But it wouldn't stop there. Every holiday, from now until who knew when, would never hold the same anticipation and joy for his children they'd once known. He'd stolen their innocence and the lives they deserved. Kayla's passing would steal what little joy remained.

It was a relief, of sorts, to leave the old year behind and begin a new one. He recognized this as the illusion it was—nothing would improve. There were no knew goals to set. No dreams or visions to motivate him, other than survival. No appeal or new trial that might set him free to look forward to.

He wondered if Emma had sat by the phone for the holidays, or if she'd given up on him completely. He wouldn't blame her if she had. The only person he'd called to wish a happy new year to was Jeffrey, who didn't pick up, no matter how many times he called. At first, this terrified him. He tamped down that emotion by assuring himself that his mother or some other family member, or Parker, would have reached out to him if anything was amiss. In a way, hearing nothing was a relief as well. There was only so much anguish a person could keep contained.

The effort was exhausting.

As was waiting for the inevitable ax to aim for his neck.

CHAPTER 54

Mid-January, during a reprieve from winter storms, Jeffrey waited in the visitors' room, hands linked atop the table. Starks paused at the entrance, sighted Jeffrey seated at the preferred spot in the corner. Dark circles and bags framed his friend's eyes, which were bloodshot. His clothes were rumpled, as though he'd slept in them.

Starks's mouth went dry. This was it. Had to be.

He placed a hand on the door jamb to steady himself. Started forward on uncooperative legs. He halted and forced his lungs to take a few deep breaths.

Jeffrey glanced up, spotted Starks and stood. Understanding registered in his expression and he shook his head, mouthed the words, *Not Kayla*.

Relief flooded through Starks, but it didn't last. If it wasn't about Kayla, what then?

He reached the corner, shook Jeffrey's hand, and studied his friend's face.

Jeffrey said, "Your family is fine."

Starks collapsed into the chair next to Jeffrey's, resting a hand on his chest. "My heart's about to jump out. If they're all right, what is it?"

Jeffrey cracked his knuckles.

Starks inched forward on his chair. "Just say it."

"I was out of the country for three weeks. Sorry I couldn't get word to you beforehand. I made sure everything was set up for Kayla and the kids before I left. Checked in with them every day. Got back yesterday and saw the newspapers. Read everything I could get my hands on."

"Get it over with."

"Garrett's dead, bro."

Starks stared in disbelief at Jeffrey then slammed his fist against the table. Held up his hands and said sorry to the approaching guard. He lowered his voice and leaned forward. "Damn it. The sonofabitch killed himself. I was certain he'd gotten past that."

Jeffrey's expression reflected his shock. "What are you talking about?"

Starks scrubbed his face with his hands then dropped them to the table. "Garrett was here. Couple weeks before Thanksgiving. He had a situation with Chelsea similar to mine with Kayla, just not as extreme. Wanted to talk about it. Said he started to go after the guy, but changed his mind. Also told me about his failed suicide attempt. He left me thinking he was going home to reconcile with Chelsea. Stupid, selfish sonofabitch."

"You got it all wrong, bro. Garrett didn't kill himself."

"What the hell happened?"

"First, police thought it was suicide by accident. He'd started a note to Chelsea, but didn't get past the first few words. Then they switched to just an accident. He was driving too fast and too drunk during a storm."

"What was he thinking?"

"They believe it was because of his brother."

"What does any of this have to do with Richard?"

"Richard died the day before. Some freak accident in Garrett's parents' house."

Starks slumped back. "No wonder Garrett was distraught. First Chelsea, and then Richard. They didn't act like they were close, but Garrett was protective as hell when it came to his family. The Halls must be losing their minds."

"Especially now. Turns out Garrett's brake line had been cut. Couldn't stop if he'd wanted to. However you look at it, he was murdered."

Starks's lips curled in contempt. "Chelsea. That bitch."

Jeffrey shook his head. "The boyfriend."

"Thompson."

"You know about him?"

"Garrett brought the guy's novel. Showed me Thompson's photo on the back cover."

"That must have messed him up bad."

"Did that bitch get Thompson to kill Garrett?"

"Thompson swore Chelsea knew nothing about it. Said it was all him. That he did it to protect her."

"From what?"

"Said Garrett physically abused her. Claimed he even tried to rape her."

Starks's face flamed red. "Bullshit. He's lying. Only person he's protecting is himself."

"Ask him when he gets here."

"He's coming to Sands?"

"Soon as they arrange the transfer. He confessed. Plus, police had irrefutable evidence, so the legal stuff went at warp speed."

"I'll ask him. Bet on it. Just before I settle that debt with him."

"Bro, Garrett was our buddy, but he wouldn't want you to do anything that makes your situation worse than it is."

"Thompson's going to find out exactly how bad it can get. It'll be worth whatever it leads to for me. I'm damn sick and tired of people killing those I care for."

"What are you talking about?"

"Skullars. Paco. Kane."

"Who?"

Starks leaned in and lowered his voice even more. "I'm about to tell you some things you can never repeat to anyone."

"Got it."

Starks talked without interruption, ignoring the repulsion and shock expressed on Jeffrey's face.

He'd expected to feel better—feel *something*—after having done so.

He did.

Rage lit a fire in every cell of his being.

CHAPTER 55

On the way back to his cell, Starks caught up with CO Roberts. They walked at a slow pace in the corridor that led to the yard. "I heard Luke Thompson's coming here."

Roberts glanced at Starks then continued to monitor inmates. "You know him?"

"Only about him. When is he arriving?"

"Tuesday. The guy he did in—something Hall—"

"Garrett."

"Hold up." Roberts halted his steps and faced Starks full-on. "Wasn't he your doctor?"

"Correct."

"Shit, Starks. Is this going to be a problem?"

"Not for me." Starks headed off in the opposite direction.

"Starks. Damn it."

Starks shrugged, made a left turn, and continued to his cell.

Jackson was stretched out on his bed. He glanced at Starks and said, "What's got you looking so satisfied?"

"The imminent potential for justice to be served."

Jackson clapped his hands, sat up and dangled his legs over the side of the top bunk. "You finally decided to launch the attack on Seth. When is it going down? Give me the details."

"It's not about Seth. I told you, I want him to make the first move. This is about something else." Starks pulled out his chair and explained.

Jackson hopped down and walked to the end of the cell. He leaned against the open cell door, giving the impression of someone paying attention to what was going on. "You really piss me off sometimes."

"What now?"

"You're gonna go after Thompson, land your ass in the SHU for shit knows how long, and screw up everything."

"I'm smarter than that."

"You like to think so."

"What do you want me to do? Shake Thompson's hand and say, 'Shit happens. Let bygones, et cetera.'?"

"At least wait until this Seth matter is settled."

"I might be dead."

"Then, problem solved."

Starks's face flooded with anger. "He killed my friend."

"And Seth killed Kane and Paco. Crazy D killed Skullars. You killed Big Bo and had Sanchez kill Weasel because he tried to help Big Bo kill you. You had Felipe kill Sanchez, and maybe you arranged for Crazy D and Buster to be taken out, as well."

"What's your point?"

"Screw it. Like talking to a friggin' brick wall."

"You like being one of the bricks getting compensated to hold it up."

"It's looking more and more like it's going to fall down and bury us under it." Jackson shook his head and walked away.

Starks cursed and punched the wall.

Starks's shift was a half day on Tuesday. He'd thought about taking the entire day off so he could be available to give Luke Thompson a *proper welcome*, but changed his mind. Let Thompson get settled in. Give him a couple weeks. Every new inmate arrived and remained skittish, wary, at least at first. In the meantime, he could find subtler ways to intimidate the guy, ones that wouldn't get him into trouble.

He'd had Jackson put the word out that he had it in for Thompson. If Seth knew Starks had a grudge to settle with Thompson, he'd, more than likely, warn his gang to leave the guy alone or try to recruit him. Seth was only interested in destroying people Starks cared about.

He also privately warned Ethan away. Dealing with Thompson was to be his privilege, alone.

Several minutes before the eleven o'clock count, Starks got word that Thompson had arrived and would be sharing a cell with Chris Cage one block over. Starks didn't know much about Cage, other than that he worked in the mailroom and kept mostly to himself. But like so many of the inmates, Cage knew who the Dragon was. Cage would warn Thompson, which would work in his favor. He wanted Thompson looking over his shoulder so often, and not find Starks there, that he stopped looking. Let Thompson get used to feeling fairly safe. Then strike. Thompson would get the dose of poison delivered by the knitting needle he deserved.

The intercom hissed and a nasal voice announced it was time for the count. Starks strained to tamp down his excitement. Minutes from now, he'd see that bastard, Thompson, for the first time. He'd make his presence known then back off. Until the moment was right.

The count ended. Starks moved at pace to the end of the corridor, turned right, and stopped at the mouth of D Block. He spotted Thompson, leaning against his cell door. Too bad he had to kill the sonofabitch. Thompson had several inches over his five-nine, probably twenty or so pounds on his one eighty, and all muscle. Under different circumstances, he'd recruit him.

He waited for Thompson to look his way. Fought the urge to rush forward. Thompson said something to Cage, who was inside the cell. Starks sneered in satisfaction when Thompson's expression revealed he understood trouble was in the wind. And who the trouble was.

Thompson retreated into the cell. Starks returned to his own. Each footstep brought back scenes of his attack on Ozy Hessinger. The remorse he'd felt about Ozy's young children watching in horror, as he beat their father into a coma. Kayla's betrayal with Ozy still stirred those primitive emotions inside him. Garrett had felt the same way when he'd learned Chelsea was spreading her legs for Thompson, and then had claimed to love him enough to leave Garrett.

Jackson had a point, and it was one he'd considered before: how could brutality ever end, if no one put a stop to it?

Still, like him, Thompson had to pay for what he'd done. He'd suffer excruciating pain, but only until some doctor shot him full of morphine. The bastard would likely die while knocked out. He wouldn't know what hit him. Only who.

CHAPTER 56

Starks had three problems. The first was Sands guards, who were aware of his enmity toward Luke Thompson, so watched him more closely than usual. He didn't hold Roberts' responsible. Word traveled fast among inmates as well as guards. The only guards Roberts would have mentioned anything to would have been the ones on Starks's payroll, and they knew better than to interfere, that is, as long as his actions weren't so obvious they couldn't afford to look the other way.

The second problem created an unanticipated dilemma. It had taken mere days for inmates to learn Thompson possessed skills as a writer. A steady stream of men flowed in and out of Thompson's cell, from after the first count until just before lights-out. The report he got was that Thompson had gone to the chow hall only once, the first day he'd arrived. Afterwards, he didn't have to worry about meals. Inmates who needed his services comped him with commissary for helping them with their continuing education papers, letters to loved ones, lawyers, and hate mail. Thompson used the library computers, but made certain it was never when Starks was there. Somebody kept the author informed about his work schedule. That was fine with him. It fit his plan.

The third problem was that he'd entrapped himself between the proverbial rock and hard place. He'd made his animosity known, and would be the first person anyone looked at.

When he ended Thompson, it had to be in a way that could never be pinned to him. Otherwise, inmates would turn on him. Tricky, though not insurmountable. But it meant the poisoned needle was out.

He'd have to devise a different plan for Thompson.

Easy enough to do.

Shift over, Starks was yards from his cell when Jackson called his name from behind. He halted and waited for Jackson to catch up to him.

"I checked the library first, but you'd already buzzed out of there. The crew is waiting for us on the bleachers."

"I thought it was snowing."

"A few flakes. It's practically a heatwave. Get your coat and let's go."

"What do they want?"

"No idea. Tank said to find you and bring you to them."

Starks shrugged into his coat and pulled a thin knit cap over his hair. "Let's find out what's on their minds."

They pushed through the double doors. Two or so inches of snow covered the ground anywhere footsteps hadn't disturbed it. Wolly and his gang shivered in their usual corner, wearing bravado rather than any cover on their shaved heads. Starks gave Wolly a subtle nod, which was returned in kind.

Starks and Jackson reached the bleachers, their shoes and socks damp and getting damper by the second. Tank, Pete, Stinky, and Tommy were on the lowest riser. About thirty others huddled against the wind to the right or behind them. Ethan had the top riser to himself. The rest of his crew were either not interested or didn't care to freeze their balls off in the blistering cold. It seemed, to Starks at least, someone had called an impromptu meeting, without his consent.

He stomped snow from his feet and nodded at the inmates. "What's up?"

Pete nudged Tank. Tank swatted snow from his hair. "Some of the guys been talking. Saying we oughta have enough numbers now to take Seth out. They gettin' tired of waitin'. Wanna know when we gonna hit him."

One new guy said, "Yeah. What we waitin' for?"

"We're waiting for Seth to strike first." Protests erupted from the crew. Starks held up his hands in a gesture to indicate they were to settle down. It took longer than expected.

Tank lumbered to his feet and faced them. "Shut it, assholes. Let's hear what the man's gotta say." He returned to his seat and nodded once at Starks.

"Guards have their radar tuned to high. I'm sure you've noticed. They're watching us with more attention than usual, especially me. If we start the attack, we'll be the ones punished more harshly. If we defend ourselves, we'll get off with a lesser punishment, if we get any at all."

A new member leaned forward. "How do you know that?"

"Experience. We'll get grilled, but likely not receive anything as bad as Seth and his guys, whichever ones survive. With any luck, some or all of their survivors will get transferred to Red Onion."

The same new member said, "Red what?"

"Where the worst of the worst get transferred to. You don't want to go there."

"Seth and them gonna see us as a bunch of pussies. You know it was them that went after Ethan. Can't blame them. The little shit is annoying. Any of us could be next."

Ethan blew a raspberry at the inmate then tried to catch snowflakes on his tongue.

Starks said, "We'll show them how wrong their assessment of us is." His statement seemed to please half the men. Half was better than nothing. "Memorize as many of their faces as you can. Carry concealed. Travel in numbers. Stay watchful. If you even suspect it's about to go down, find me, Jackson or Tank so we can rally. When the time comes, we have to fight smarter and harder."

Ethan said, "K-k-kick b-b-balls."

Pete turned around. "That's kick ass."

Ethan grinned. "That t-too."

Starks shook new snow from the tops of his shoes. "Everybody on board? Anyone have a problem with me or the plan?"

Tank rose and glared at the crew. "You got a problem with Starks, you got a problem with me."

Starks nodded at Tank and started for the door.

Jackson jogged to Starks's side. "They're fired up."

"Everyone's nerves are stretched taut. I wish the bastard would get this over with. One way or the other."

"It's the *other* that has me staining my briefs. It's like a big friggin' neon question mark hanging over our heads."

"As long as it isn't a period."

CHAPTER 57

Starks came close to refusing the visit. What the hell did she want with him? It had been nearly two years since he'd seen Chelsea Hall. He almost didn't recognize her. Forty or so pounds lighter, but still not as slender as Garrett had preferred his women. She'd pinned her auburn hair up, obviously more for convenience than style. He waited at the entrance. Her gaze flicked around the room, akin to the inability not to look when going past an accident. Her light eyes landed on him. Her pale complexion lost even more color. He found Chelsea's discomfort particularly satisfying.

Starks wound his way to the table in the middle of the room. "I can't believe you had the nerve to show up here." He pulled out the chair across from her and plunked into it. "What the hell do you want? Didn't cause enough destruction yet?"

Chelsea chewed her bottom lip for a moment then said, "So, you know about Garrett. I wasn't certain."

"About Garrett. About Thompson. Why'd you ask to see me? Or are you seeing me *and* your love toy today? Two for one, right? Like when you were screwing him and your husband?"

Chelsea twisted her linked fingers back and forth. "I'm not ever going to visit Luke."

"I'm supposed to believe that?"

"I'm wrecked about Garrett."

"Not the most appropriate word choice."

Tears welled in Chelsea's eyes. "You don't understand."

"Who would understand better than I do what it's like to find out your wife is opening her legs to someone else? That she believes she loves some new guy who showed up just to have a good time, and with no concern about the lives he destroys."

"Maybe I shouldn't have come." Chelsea turned tear-filled eyes to Starks. "But I had to."

"Let me guess. You want to give me your side of the story. Why not. Should be amusing."

"That's not why I'm here. I came to ask you to go easy on Luke. In fact, anything you can do to keep him safe will be appreciated."

Starks's jaw tightened. "Did Thompson scramble your brain when he screwed you?"

Color flooded from Chelsea's neck to her face. "He thought he was protecting me."

"Garrett never hurt anyone, especially not a woman."

"He changed."

"Bullshit."

Chelsea, eyes pleading, shook her head. "Garrett's cheating ceased to be *recreational*. He was at it all the time. Every night and on weekends. Like an addict or something."

Starks blanked his expression and said nothing.

"I caught him with Penelope."

"Your best friend?"

Chelsea nodded.

Starks's laughter drew attention from everyone in the room. "That's one way to retaliate."

"It wasn't retaliation. He didn't know about Luke then. But once he did, he went into a rage and struck me. He destroyed that expensive grandfather clock he had to have."

"I always liked that clock."

"Then he tried to rape me."

"More likely, you weren't in the mood, because you'd been getting it from Thompson. Or maybe you hadn't had time to clear the deck, if you know what I mean."

Chelsea wiped tears from her face. "You don't want to believe it, but Garrett meant to rape me. He was vile. He didn't succeed, but he still beat me. The things he said to me …

"When Garrett realized what he was doing, he was so ashamed. He ran from the house and drove away like a crazed man, which, at that time, he was.

"Luke became concerned when he couldn't reach me. He came to the house to check on me. Saw my face and arms. And the destroyed clock. I made him promise not to confront Garrett. I told him Garrett was appalled at what he'd done, and that I was certain he'd never do it again."

"Thompson should have believed you."

Chelsea stared at her hands. "Luke was afraid for my life."

"Garrett had come to his senses and would've made up for it."

"Luke was afraid because of what Garrett did to Richard."

Starks sat with controlled stillness. "What are you saying?"

"Penelope tricked Garrett into believing Richard and I were having an affair, which we weren't. She wanted Garrett. She was willing to do anything to get him. Garrett believed her. He was furious. He attacked Richard at the Halls' house. During the fight, Richard hit his head on the marble hearth."

"It's a damn lie. You're making this up to convince me to leave Thompson alone."

Chelsea stared dull-eyed at Starks. "It was their sister, Chloe, who told me what happened. Their parents witnessed the fight. But they didn't want the truth known. Even Richard's wife doesn't know what really happened. Garrett didn't mean to kill Richard, but he did. Luke was terrified that in one of Garrett's drunken rages he'd do the same to me. I didn't learn what Luke did, or why, until after he was arrested."

"He murdered Garrett. He had no right to be judge, jury, and executioner."

"No, he didn't. But we want to protect the people we love. You know that as well as I do."

Starks ran his fingers back and forth across his forehead in response to her reminding him what a hypocrite he could be. "Maybe that was part of Thompson's motivation, but you're a fool if you think it wasn't to get you, along with Garrett's money, for himself."

Chelsea's chin quivered. "Garrett pleaded with me to take him back. That was right before Penelope's lie. The next day, I called to tell him yes, but the damage had been done. I discovered later that Garrett had learned the truth, but it was too late. A few hours after I heard Garrett had died, I ended the relationship with Luke. Everyone was being hurt by all Garrett and I had done, especially our daughter. It had to stop. As for Garrett's money, there is none."

"Now you're really milking it. Garrett was flush. Plus, he had more than enough life insurance."

"As I said, he'd changed. He'd sold the policy and put the money into his struggling practice. Struggling because he stopped showing up for work. He'd also been suspended at the hospital, without pay, for drinking on the job. I had no idea about any of this, or that nothing was going into the account. Not until the past due notices arrived. The bank took the house. I had to sell everything to pay bills he hadn't paid for months. I'm living at my parents' house, while my daughter, who rightfully hates me, lives with a friend."

Starks stared unblinking at her. "So Garrett actually did decide to work it out with you. To give your marriage another chance."

Chelsea lowered her eyes. Tears streaked her cheeks. "Yes."

"Knowing this, you still want me to protect lover boy."

Chelsea's eyes locked with his. "He thought he was saving me. He's a good man."

"Sure. I'll take care of him."

"Do you mean it, Starks?"

"I'll see to it personally."

Chelsea moved to the chair next to Starks's and rested her hands over his clenched ones. "That's all I ask. I know it won't be easy for you."

His smile was tight. "It'll be my pleasure."

Starks slipped his hands from hers and stood. "I have to go now."

He left without saying more.

His talk with Garrett had made a difference.

Penelope was a tramp. Always had been. She was, in large part, to blame for Garrett and Chelsea not getting back together, but the truth of her deception had been outed. Had Thompson not interfered, his friend would be alive and getting his life straightened out. Garrett might have accomplished with Chelsea what he hadn't been able to with Kayla.

Starks's hands balled into fists as he stormed through the corridors. He'd definitely take care of Luke Thompson. The question was, which part of the bastard's body would he start with?

CHAPTER 58

Starks grabbed his coat and cap, and made his way to the yard. Fresh air was needed to clear his mind after listening to Chelsea Hall's drivel. What had happened to Garrett was her fault. All of it. What did it matter whether or not she'd known what Thompson had planned? The end result was the same.

He reached the fence and kept his back to the nearly empty grounds. The truth was, he was equally guilty. He'd advised Garrett not to go after Thompson. Didn't want his friend to end up here. He should have kept his mouth shut. As a medical professional, Garrett might have found a way to end Thompson and get away with it.

It was up to him to settle the score on Garrett's behalf. Thompson wouldn't be allowed to get away with what he'd done.

He pivoted and leaned against the fence, arms folded. A good number of his crew sat on the bleachers. Others slipped on the frosted ground in a four-against-four basketball game with the Hermanos. His bond with Felipe had all to do with two such diverse gangs getting along rather than competing. At least that much was going well.

Several inmates, laughing and talking loudly, entered the yard. Luke Thompson trailed the procession then dropped back, obviously not part of the group. He was on his own.

Thompson's presence surprised Starks, since the man never seemed free of inmates clamoring for his services.

Then, it was as though every frustration gnawing at Starks collided. He bolted across the yard, grabbed Thompson by the neck and shoved him against the prison wall. He exchanged his hand for his forearm and pressed hard against Luke's neck. "You know who I am?"

Luke, struggling to breathe, nodded.

"You screwed my friend's wife then killed him."

"I'm sorry."

"Not sorry enough. Not yet."

Luke's eyes swept frantically around the yard.

This wasn't the time or place to settle things the way he wanted to. Starks dropped his arm to his side. "If you're thinking about yelling for help, there's something you need to know. Any inmate who tattles breaks the code. Any inmate who breaks the code regrets it, if he lives that long. And it often isn't even the inmate he tattled on, who takes retribution."

"Get away from me."

"Make me. C'mon." Starks released him and backed up. He motioned with his hands. "Go ahead. Take your best shot."

Luke's body tensed in readiness. His attention shifted to the right.

Starks looked that way as well. Tank, Stinky, Pete, Tommy, and several others walked toward them.

Starks faced forward. "You're going to wish you'd kept your prick out of where it didn't belong."

"We didn't mean to fall in love. It just happened."

"Don't give me that love crap."

"I do love her. I would have died for her."

"The opportunity still exists."

"When I realized what Garrett might do to her—"

"I've already heard all that bullshit. They'd decided to get back together. That's why you murdered Garrett."

"I swear I had no idea. Had Chelsea told me, yes, I may have tried to convince her otherwise, but I would have respected her decision."

Starks's crew formed a semi-circle behind him. He sneered. "More bullshit. You didn't respect the sanctity of their marriage."

Luke narrowed his eyes. "Neither did he. The same goes for you, from what I've heard."

Starks slammed his fist into Luke's jaw. Luke's head snapped back and hit the solid wall.

Starks leaned in. "You don't destroy lives and people the way you did and not pay for it."

Luke rubbed his head. He checked his hand. No blood. "I'm here, aren't I?"

Starks adjusted the collar of Luke's coat. "Right where I want you." He gave a hard pat to Luke's cheek.

Tank moved forward. "Anything you want us to handle, here?"

Starks shook his head. "We're good. For now. Let's get back to the game."

Starks and Tank sat next to each other on the lowest riser.

Tank said, "What was that about?"

"It's personal."

"I got that. What'd he do to you?"

"What's the score?"

"Must've done something."

"He did something he shouldn't have."

"That's all of us, man."

"Tank."

"Twelve to two."

"Who's winning?"

"We are."

Starks rested his back against the riser behind him.

He desperately needed a big win.

CHAPTER 59

Tank shuffled into the laundry room. Seth stood with his back against one of the dryers. He moved forward and told two inmates assigned to laundry duty to beat it. Dodging Tank, they scarpered from the room.

The long folding table groaned as Seth sat atop it. "How easy do you think it'll be?"

Tank moved forward and positioned himself next to Seth. He leaned his backside against the table. "Don't worry. I'll get him here. You gonna pay the guard to look elsewhere?"

Seth picked at something stuck between his front teeth. "That, or get some of my men to create a diversion."

"Paying 'em works better."

"Depends on the guard."

"I figured out some of the guards Starks has in his pocket, but not all of 'em."

"You could ask him. He trusts you."

"Not the kind of thing you supposed to ask the leader."

Seth hocked and spit on the floor. "Leader, my ass." He grinned and punched Tank's arm. "Guess you'll be takin' over, once Starks is out of the way."

"Nah. I ain't no leader. I'm a follows-orders guy."

"Jackson?"

"Jackson wants to be a hotshot, but even he knows he ain't no Starks." Tank glanced around the rectangular space. "Shouldn't be a problem, if you clear the room and take care of him fast."

"It'll be fast."

"Wasn't sure if you wanted to play with him some before finishing him."

"Much as I'd get off doing that, that's not what this is about. No Starks, no war." Seth squinted his eyes. "Or am I wrong about that?"

"Some of these bozos wouldn't mind, but I'm with you. Long as nobody knows for sure who did him, nobody will know who to go after."

Seth scowled. "I'm smart enough to figure that out myself."

"Just sayin'." Tank stepped away from the table. "When you want this to go down?"

"Tomorrow morning."

"You not afraid of doing this on a Sunday?"

"Fewer people moving around on Sunday. Why you think the last big hits been on a Sunday? You superstitious or something?"

"What time?"

"I'll find out who's walkin' this corridor tomorrow and see if he can be bought. Just in case, I'll use a diversion as backup. Gotta time it just right. Get Starks here by five after nine. Any problem doin' that?"

"Nah. I know how to handle him." Tank started for the door.

Seth slid off the table. "Don't screw this up."

Tank looked back. "Can't afford to."

"None of us can."

CHAPTER 60

Tank placed his breakfast tray next to Starks's, rapped on the table and plunked onto the bench. He brought his nose close to Starks, sniffed, and screwed up his face. "Still washing your clothes in the sink. Man, you so used to the stink, you can't smell it."

"You're saying I stink?"

Tank stirred the glop of something brown on his tray. "Didn't say you. Said your clothes. They ripe. Time to go back to the room, Starks."

Starks used a paper napkin to wipe off the hard roll some careless person in the kitchen had dropped into his soupy fake eggs. "You know why I can't. I'll pay one of the workers to do my clothes. That way I won't offend your delicate sense of smell."

"People talkin'."

"Not my problem."

"About to be." Tank shoveled the brown stuff into his mouth. "They sayin' if you can't face a room, how you gonna face the devil when he strikes? Some of these guys know you been tough in the past. Not what they seen lately. They say you gettin' weak. Won't stand with no one who can't do the job."

"Have any of them left?"

"They talkin' about it. More they talk, more others listen. I'll go with you, man. I'll get some of the others to go too. Nobody gonna mess with you. Not with us standin' guard. You get to feelin' anxious or something, suck it up and deal with it later. Don't let no one know you lost your nerve."

Starks stabbed the roll with his fork. "I haven't lost my nerve."

"Then you gotta prove it. Otherwise, Seth and his soldiers show up for the fight, it'll be you, me, and a couple guys getting our guts spilled."

"Fine. We'll go after breakfast."

"Got something I gotta do first. Meet you at your cell at nine."

"What do you have to do?"

"Eliminate some of this fine food. Goes in, goes right out."

"Do I need to hear this while I'm eating?"

"Dragon asks, I answer."

Starks rapped on the table and stood. "Lost my appetite. I'll be ready at nine."

"Yeah. Me too."

CHAPTER 61

Starks scooped up the box he used for dirty laundry and exited his cell ahead of Tank. "Where are the others?"

"Told them to check out the room. They see any problems, they'll stop us on the way. No need to get into trouble, if we don't have to."

"You always have my back."

"If you're taken care of, I'm taken care of."

"Were you serious about some of the men doubting me?"

"You don't come from the streets like most of us. I get where you comin' from, but you can't expect some of these pricks to do that. One little thing be off, they walk off."

"Temperamental bunch."

"Cautious. All it take is to get burned once."

They turned into the corridor that led to their destination. Sweat beaded on Starks's forehead. His mostly empty stomach roiled.

"Man, you just turned green. Get it together."

"You're right." Starks put the box down. He wiped his forehead on his sleeve and took several deep breaths. "I'm fine."

Tank grinned. "That's more like it."

"I'm guessing that since the crew didn't come looking for us, we're good to go."

"Yeah. We good to go."

Starks and Tank crossed the threshold of the laundry room. Starks went directly to one of the front-load washers. He positioned the door so the glass reflected the room and people behind him. Despite Tank's recon efforts, he kept his eyes fixed on the reflection. Wondered where the crew members Tank had sent ahead were. Had they somehow missed them in one of the corridors?

Starks loaded one item at a time and let his eyes dart from the inmate digging through clothes in an open dryer, to the three who kept their backs to him and their heads down as they folded clothes on the long metal table. His movements slowed when the man at the dryer turned around. Seth.

Starks continued to add clothes into the washer. Whispering, he said, "Tank."

"Yeah?"

"We've been set up."

"Nah, man. You been set up."

Tank lunged for him. Starks dodged and scurried for the exit. His hand reached for the needle in his shirt hem. Before he could remove the weapon, Tank tackled him, pinning him to the floor under his bulk. Air whooshed out of Starks.

Starks used a new move Felipe had taught him. It worked well enough to shift Tank off of him, but didn't free him from hands that lifted him from the dingy floor and held him vice-like.

One of the men stuffed a sock into Starks's mouth. Tank's fists flew fast, hard, hitting their mark with practiced precision.

Stark's bottom lip split open. Then the skin next to his left eye. A hard punch landed to his solar plexus, doubling him over, gasping for air.

Tank glanced back at Seth, who stood grinning two yards away. "I thought you said this was gonna be fast."

Seth drew a butcher knife from under a pile of clothes. "Always someone spoilin' my fun. Hold him so I can finish him. There's something has to be done first.

"Tank, pull his pants down. I'm gonna send this dragon into his next life as a girl."

Starks struggled to break free. He choked on the sock, felt bile burn his throat. Eyes wild, he attempted to kick his way out, but the third man grabbed his legs and held fast to them.

Seth hummed and danced as he slowly moved closer, waving the knife back and forth.

From their left, someone said, "No, really. The Oxford comma does matter."

All eyes turned toward the entrance. Chris Cage and Luke Thompson stared, mouths open, at the scene before them.

Luke spoke first. "Looks like we've interrupted something."

Seth pointed the knife at them. "Get the hell out or join the fun. Your choice."

"There's only one choice." Luke tossed his laundry to the floor and raised his fists. "Chris, I hope you know how to fight."

Cage backed out of the room and took off running down the corridor.

Seth laughed. "Looks like only one of you has shit for brains."

"Let Starks go."

"Somebody grab that asshole and hold him, while I finish Starks." Seth aimed the knife at Luke. "You gonna have to wait your turn, cupcake."

Luke rushed Seth like a linebacker. Seth slashed out with the knife. The blade sliced into Luke's arm, near his shoulder. One deft kick sent the knife skittering across the concrete surface.

Seth threw a punch. Luke ducked and dropped to the floor. With force, his foot slammed into Seth's right kneecap. Seth collapsed into the fetal position, yowling and cradling his knee to his chest.

Luke leaped to his feet and moved like a matador when Tank hurtled toward him. Hands on his hips, he faced Starks. "Are you going to let me have all the fun?"

Starks swung his legs up high, using momentum to flip over the heads of the men restraining him. Practiced kicks sent them careening in different directions. He yanked the sock from his mouth, and in the brief pause, watched Tank swing his fists at Luke, who bobbed and weaved, landing punches to the larger man's face and torso. Tank puffed from exertion and frustration.

A fist connected with Starks's jaw on the right side. He sent his foot into the man's soft middle.

Tank, panting, collapsed to the floor.

Luke joined Starks, grinned and said, "Guess Tank's more of a sprinter than a marathoner."

Fists and feet flew in all directions.

Roberts, Jakes, and Stone skidded into the room, Tasers drawn and ready.

Roberts said, "Shit," then tasered Seth's man nearest him. The man dropped and lay twitching on the concrete. A urine stain spread across the front of his pants.

The other two backed up, hands behind their heads. Seth remained where he'd fallen, rocking on the blood-splattered floor. Tank stayed down, still gulping air.

Starks and Luke placed their hands behind their heads, as well.

Luke said, "Officer, if you look under the table, toward the end, you'll find a long knife. Should be easy to get fingerprints off of it."

Roberts glanced at the bloody gash in Luke's upper arm, walked to the end of the table and squatted down. "Yep." He grabbed a clean washcloth and picked the knife up by the blade, near the handle. "Not much blood on it."

"Someone's party," Starks said, "got crashed." He gave one subtle nod of his head at Luke, who returned the gesture.

Stone had a death-grip on his Taser. "What's the protocol for this shit?"

Roberts shook his head. "Investigative council has to decide what to do with them."

Stone motioned with his Taser. "Let's go, assholes. Single file. Keep a two-foot distance between you." He moved toward Tank and kicked his thigh. "You. Let's go."

Jakes pressed a button on his radio. "We need a gurney in the laundry room."

The receiver said, "I'll get one there ASAP."

"No hurry. Soon as you can get to it." Jakes turned to Roberts. "I'll stay here with Seth and the twitcher on the floor. They won't give me any trouble."

Starks winked at Jakes as he exited the room.

John Bentley sat alone at the investigative council table. "You guys and your damn code of silence give me piles. Whichever one of you brought the knife to the fight is going to get it the worst. I can promise you that. But you're all going to spend time in the SHU."

Luke leaned toward Starks. "What's the shoe?"

"S-H-U. Not s-h-o-e. Secure housing unit."

"Solitary?"

"You got it."

Bentley slammed his hand against the table. "You don't talk when I want you to and yammer when you ought to keep your damn mouths shut." He stood. "Put them in the Hole then get me their files."

Roberts said, "For how long?"

"When the rest of the council is in tomorrow, we'll decide."

"Some of them need medical attention."

"Put them in solitary then bring them one at a time to the infirmary. In shackles."

"Ten-four."

The inmates walked single-file. Roberts led the way. Stone stayed at the end of the line, Taser in hand. Luke shuffled behind Starks.

Starks glanced back. He kept his voice just above a whisper. "You could've kicked my butt in the yard."

"Wouldn't have been smart, considering I was outnumbered."

"You let me think you were a pushover."

"I figured if I did anything to you, your gang would talk to me by hand."

"You saved my ass in there."

"The way you handled yourself, I was probably more of a distraction than anything else."

Stone shouted, "Shut it or get zapped."

Starks ignored his throbbing face and aching torso. Thompson was playing down what he'd done, but he *had* saved him. He could have run, especially after realizing the odds. Especially after he'd been threatened in the yard. The guy had risked his life for someone who didn't deserve it.

If Thompson was willing to do that for a relative stranger who had it in for him … If he genuinely loved Chelsea, what would he have done for her if he believed the threat against her was real?

Starks cursed under his breath. Gray areas always made him uneasy.

CHAPTER 62

I t had been a long night for Starks. He'd sat in semi-darkness on the concrete rectangle that doubled as a seat and mattress-less bed, his mind whirling with dark and confusing thoughts. Few places on his body were uninjured, but none of those pains compared to the profound ache of Tank's betrayal. Had the man been disloyal from the start? Or had Seth recently convinced him to switch sides? It was like Mike, the Weasel, all over again but without the two-month coma that followed the stab wounds.

Added to this was the matter of Luke Thompson. It was no insignificant favor Thompson had done for him. How could he justify taking the life of the man who'd risked his own to save his?

Overwhelm and numbed senses competed inside Starks. Yet, even amid chaos and despair, stunning clarity arrived. The seed of a plan followed during the long hours, more a result of desperation than creativity.

Starks glanced right, intent on checking the light outside, momentarily forgetting cells in the Hole were windowless.

What did it matter? Time had stopped, at least temporarily.

Moments after he had this thought, the single overhead bulb brightened, shifting deep gray that encased him in a lighter shade.

Starks lowered his stiff and throbbing legs until his feet touched the concrete below. With effort, he slowly stood and lumbered to the sink. Repeatedly, he splashed frigid water on his face, careful to avoid the bandaged, stitched cut under his left eye. He shut the tap off just as the steel door unlatched.

CO Roberts stepped in. "You're probably tired of hearing this, but you look like crap."

"Some things never get old, especially when you're still alive to experience them. Isn't it early to take me to the council, or did you drop by to say hello?"

"You're clear to go back to your cell."

"I was certain Spencer would leave me in here for a month of nutraloaf."

"Seth's prints were on the knife handle. Thompson's blood was on the blade. It isn't often we get evidence delivered gift-wrapped to us, but when we do, fair is fair."

"So what was the point of leaving me in here overnight?"

"Bentley thought you could use a night off."

Starks nodded. "What about Thompson? He getting out?"

"Yep."

Starks followed Roberts out of the cell. The CO stepped to the door to the right and opened it. "You're clear, Thompson. Let's go."

"What about Starks?"

"He's right outside. You're both cleared."

Luke walked out and nodded at Starks. "You look like crap."

Starks gave Roberts a pained half-smile then said to Luke, "I've looked worse. How's the arm?"

"It'll heal."

Roberts closed both doors but left them unlocked. "Let's get you guys out of here."

Starks and Thompson walked side by side and ahead of Roberts, as he escorted them through the several electronic doors that fed them back into general population.

Starks turned to Roberts. "What about Seth and the others?"

"They're in for a while longer."

Luke winked at Starks. "What about Seth's knee? It looked to me as though he injured it."

"He'll limp for a while, but he's fine. Doc is keeping him in the infirmary another night. Then it's the Hole for him, for an extended stay."

Starks tensed and faced straight ahead. "Where's Tank?"

"Only so many cells available in your section. He and two of the others are in another one. Someone else is letting him out."

They reached the last electronic door. Roberts motioned to the monitoring guard. The door slid open. "See if you can stay out of trouble for at least five minutes."

"Not always up to me." Starks gestured with his head for Luke to follow him.

They traveled several yards in silence. Starks glanced at Luke then returned his gaze forward. "You know why I'm in here?"

"If I recall correctly, you beat your wife's lover into a coma. At least he recovered."

"It was self-defense." Starks sighed. "Whatever. Truth is, a part of me wanted him to die because of what he did to me and my family. It took coming here for me to finally get that he didn't destroy it. I did that. All he did was entertain himself with the wreckage."

"When I found out my first wife was cheating on me, rather than go after the guy, I cheated on her. The problem with making that kind of choice once is that it's too easy to make it again."

"Been there, done that." Starks glanced at Luke. "Garrett wanted to kill you. Bet you didn't know."

Luke's shock registered on his face. "No, I didn't."

"Even went to your house one night with a gun loaded and ready."

"What stopped him?"

Starks shrugged. "Whatever it was, I'm grateful."

"Can't be easy for you to say that, all things considered."

"I was all set to avenge Garrett's death. Ready and eager to slice and dice you."

"You made that plain. Although, thankfully, not quite so graphic."

"Why'd you risk your life for me?"

"It was the right thing to do."

"I don't get it."

"It wasn't a fair fight."

Starks nodded. "More of them."

"That and the knife."

"Still, letting them take care of me would have solved your problem. At least, the one with me. Had the tables been turned, how do you know I wouldn't have let them finish you off? Maybe even helped?"

"Your choices have nothing to do with mine. I have to live with myself. I've already stained my life with blood that I had no right to spill."

"Well, I can't kill you now."

Luke grinned. "Don't expect me to be disappointed."

Starks shook his head. "I'm left with conflicted feelings."

They reached D Block. "This is my stop," Luke said. He locked his eyes with Starks's. "I get why you feel that way. Human nature tells us to protect those we love. When we can't do that, we seek to avenge whatever happened to them."

"Chelsea said you were a good man. She's right. Your true character is like a neon sign over your head. That could prove dangerous for you in here."

Luke's eyes opened wide. "You spoke with her? About me?"

"She came to see me."

"When?"

"Recently."

Luke's arms hung flaccid at his side. "She didn't ask to see me."

"Sorry, Thompson. Said she has no intention of ever visiting you."

Luke grabbed Starks's arm. "How'd she look? Is she okay?"

"Not at her best, which is understandable. She's been through the wringer."

"Every bit of it my fault. Hurting her is the last thing I ever intended." Tears filled his eyes.

"I was wrong."

"About what?"

"You did love her."

"Present tense."

Starks extended his hand. Luke shook it then strode, shoulders bowed forward, toward his cell.

He waited until Luke disappeared into his six by eight concrete cubicle then started for his cell. He'd gone after Ozy Hessinger out of overblown pride. Luke had gone after Garrett out of genuine love for Chelsea, and fear for her life. Thompson's motives were misguided but noble. His had been selfish and territorial.

The contrast between them gnawed at him.

It wasn't an emotion he could entertain. His gauge had hit the Full mark the previous morning.

CHAPTER 63

Starks sat cross-legged on his bed, gazing out the narrow window. Thick snowflakes drifted to the ground. He paid little attention. Footsteps behind him interrupted his thoughts. He swiveled to face the entrance. Jackson. Back from his lunch shift. Starks positioned himself on the edge of the bed.

Jackson yanked his grease-stained scrub shirt over his head and reached for a clean shirt from his shelf. "You're out of the Hole a lot sooner than I thought you'd be. You look like shit, man."

"As I've heard a number of times."

Jackson dropped the clean shirt over his head, pulled his chair out and lowered into it. "I've been waiting to get the straight scoop from you. Only buzz I got was from Cage. Said he and Thompson got to the laundry room and saw just enough to send him running for guards."

"He ran. Thompson stayed."

"He fight for you or against you?"

"For."

"Surprising, but at least that upped the odds. Four to three, from what Cage said."

"His math is wrong."

"I'm not following?"

"It was five against two. Tank ambushed me. Sided with Seth. I have him—Tank, that is—to thank for my face and damn near every sore spot. Thompson prevented Seth from carving me up and turning me into a eunuch."

Jackson sat motionless. "I'd say you're shittin' me, but you wouldn't. Not about this." He ran a hand back and forth over his shaved head. "Tank. Damn. I can't hardly believe it."

"I had a lot less time to wrap my mind around it."

"What are you gonna do? What the hell are *we* gonna do?"

"Understandable that you're upset."

Jackson leaped up. "Upset? Upset? Man, don't you get it? You're the draw, but Tank's been the glue. What's gonna hold us together now? We're gonna get slaughtered."

Starks kept his gaze fixed on Jackson but said nothing.

"What are we gonna do, Starks? With Tank pulling for the other side, we're screwed. Say something, damn it. Tell me your brilliant plan to deal with this."

Starks remained quiet.

"Don't go all silent on me. I'm shittin' spiked bricks here. Why aren't you?"

"I'm thinking."

Jackson threw his arms up. "Great." He flopped into his chair. "Let's hear it."

"Interesting what having time alone to think leads you to."

"And?"

"I've finally realized what it is they want from me."

"You lost me."

"They want me to become one of them."

"What's that supposed to mean?"

"It's time I accommodate them."

"What the hell are you going on about?"

"Call a meeting. Get a message to the crew."

"How soon?"

"Yesterday."

"I'd appreciate you being more specific."

"One o'clock. The bleachers."

"It's snowing."

"Just do it."

Jackson grabbed his coat and cap. He paused at the entrance and saluted. "Dragon's got a plan. I can see it in his eyes." He bounded from the cell.

Yes, he had a plan, but it was nothing Jackson would have ever imagined.

Starks retrieved the book and cell phone, checked the corridor then positioned himself on his bed. Part of his plan required the expertise of a private detective who knew how to keep his mouth shut.

He dialed Jim Rogers' number. "It's me. Are you where you can write things down?"

"As it happens, I am. And hello to you too."

"No time for niceties. I've got a list and instructions. Ready?"

"Whenever you are."

"I'm more ready than anyone's expecting."

CHAPTER 64

S now fell heavy and wet. Starks ignored the discomfort demonstrated by his crew, who sat shivering on the wooden bleachers.

Tommy blew on his hands then rubbed them together. "Tank's late. Start without him. We'll catch him up."

"He ain't late," Pete said. "He ain't coming."

"Why not? They let him out same time as Starks."

Pete shook his head. "Stupid bastard slugged the guard what was letting him out the Hole. He's stuck in there, till they decide when he can get out. Shouldn't have been in there. You either, Starks. All the man was doing was protecting you. Might as well start talking so we can get back inside. My balls done shriveled to peanuts."

Starks paced back and forth for several moments. He stopped when he reached the center point. "I made it clear that loyalty is imperative for anyone to remain in my crew. Not just for my sake but for yours." He scanned their faces. "What I'd hoped to create and build was a system where we looked out for each other. Protected each other. Stood together. No matter what. It seems, instead, that I find myself with a nest of traitors in the mix. Now it's a matter of knowing who's with us and who isn't."

Tommy's face flushed red. "What the hell?"

Starks went into detail about what had happened in the laundry room. When he stopped talking, the crew members erupted in shouts, curses, denials, and more questions than he was willing to answer.

Tommy sat motionless, shock evident on his face. "Sonofabitch." He jumped from the second riser to the ground. "Sonofabitch! Tank's going down. Soon as he gets out, that mother's going down."

Starks let them carry on long enough for him to listen to and observe each man as they talked and shouted among themselves.

Wind whipped hair and coats. The sky darkened. Thick flakes and ice crystals pelted them. Starks pulled his coat collar closed and hollered for their attention. "Settle down. That's all I had to say for now. You're free to leave."

The men bounded from the bleachers, Jackson included, with Ethan trailing behind. Starks stayed where he was.

"Ethan."

Ethan jogged back. "Yes?"

"Know how you've been wanting a special assignment?"

Ethan's grin stretched wide.

"Your wish is about to be granted."

"You understand?" Starks asked.

Ethan nodded. "I'd bow in homage, but that would be obvious to guards who tower above us."

Starks glanced toward Jackson, who waited and shivered at the double doors. "Your gash healed nicely. The doc did a good job with the stitching."

"We nearly have matching scars."

"Go on inside. And remember what I said."

Ethan tapped his head. "Steel trap when it comes to memory." He ran in a few circles, arms out like an airplane, then dashed past Jackson and into the prison.

Jackson slapped his hands together and bounced in place as Starks approached. "I'm freezing out here."

"You should have gone in."

"What was that about?"

"Doesn't concern you."

"Really pisses me off when you do that."

"I wanted to make sure he's okay. His attack was severe."

"Right. Want to sell me a bridge in Brooklyn while you're at it?" Jackson stomped his feet to remove snow. "That little speech of yours?"

"What about it?"

"It put everyone on edge."

"That's where they need to be."

"Man, Tank didn't just screw you over. He screwed all of us. That doesn't mean anyone else, much less everyone else in the crew, is guilty."

"Time will tell."

"What's with you lately?"

"Same ol', same ol'."

"Bullshit. It's one thing if you act frosty with some of them, but this is me, your faithful right hand."

Starks didn't respond.

"Look, man, prison's filled with assholes lookin' out for themselves first and last. You gotta expect some of them are gonna stick with you, and that some would betray their own mamas to save themselves."

"Exactly." Starks opened the door and entered ahead of Jackson.

"Wait up, man. Starks!"

But Starks was done talking. For now.

He hadn't touched his dinner tray and had skipped breakfast. It had been too painful to eat. But now, with his plan shifting into first gear, his appetite compelled him to eat through any discomfort.

He reached the commissary and grabbed the usual from the shelves. His tongue gently pressed against two teeth loosened by Tank's fist. He tossed several cup-a-soups into his paper bag. Previous experience had taught him that if he left a loose tooth alone, time would strengthen it in place, as long as its roots held.

That's what was happening to him. Betrayals were a fact of life, and he'd had more than his share for one lifetime. Sure, they'd knocked him on his ass, but either he could curl up and die a little each day or grow stronger where he was. He might die inside Sands, but it wouldn't be because he'd folded up and invited it.

From now on, this was his party. All he needed was confirmation of which names to put on his guest list.

CHAPTER 65

The overhead lights flickered from dim to bright. Cell doors made the usual racket as they opened. Jackson slid from his bunk to the floor. Starks lay still, eyes closed. He wasn't in the mood for a Q&A session, which he knew was coming.

Jackson smoothed shaving cream onto his face. "I know you're awake."

"Is that a result of mentalism?"

"More like knowing you, after sharing a cell for about half a year, give or take. You wouldn't talk last night. Figured you might be in a better frame of mind after a good night's tossing and turning."

"Your keen wit has me laughing on the inside."

Jackson dragged the razor down his cheek. "You've got something cooking with Ethan."

"I told you what that was about."

"Now it's me you don't trust?"

"Drop it."

"Screw you, man."

"I'm done getting screwed."

"Maybe so. But I'm concerned about you doing it to yourself."

Jackson rinsed his face and got dressed. "I'm going now. But anytime you want to talk to a real friend—"

"I know who to call."

After Jackson left, Starks launched into his morning routine, which turned into an abbreviated workout. His body refused to do more than the minimum.

He waited for the first count of the day to end, and inmates to clear out for the chow hall, before calling Michael Parker.

"Any update?"

Parker sighed. "Let's go with no news is good news."

"You haven't made any progress at all?"

"It's more a matter of some obstacles that have to be overcome."

"What you're saying is, it isn't going well."

"More like I'm trying not to say it. I don't want you to get upset. I'm still—"

"I'm not upset. I'm not even angry."

"That's disconcerting. What's wrong?"

"It is what it is."

"You used to say it gave you a hot rash to hear someone use that phrase. That what is can be changed, and you were the man to change it."

"That second part still holds."

"What's going on, Starks?"

"I'm finally getting a true grasp on the situation. That's all. Thanks for all you've done."

"Damn it. Please tell me you're not going to do something stupid."

"Wouldn't dream of it. I'll check back with you another time."

Starks shut the phone off before Parker could pry further. There was nothing his attorney could say that would change the course he was on. The fact of the matter was clear, and he needed to resign himself to it.

After his shift, Starks searched for and found Ethan in the yard, seated alone on the top riser. Half the number of inmates usually outside, milled about, keeping their distance from the bleachers. Starks climbed up and sat next to Ethan. "You aren't afraid of being out here without some of the crew?"

"As you can see, people tend to give me a wide berth. Besides, you should talk."

"Point taken. When it's time, will you be ready?"

"Naturally."

"When I'm ready, I'll give you the powders. Are you clear about how to use them?"

"All the details have taken root in my brain."

"Any word about when Tank's getting out?"

"Seems he continues to cause problems so they'll keep him isolated a while longer. He's afraid."

"Too bad he wasn't that smart sooner." Starks stood and stretched. "I'm arranging a practice session with Felipe in the gym. Six-twenty. I want you there. I want you engaged in the practice. Figure out how to be your usual self *and* participate, without causing suspicion."

"No problemo."

Starks dropped from the bleachers, ignoring the jolt, and started for the double doors. Jackson pushed open the door to Starks's left as Starks opened the other. Starks pulled him to the side. "I thought I'd find the guys out here before dinner, but they're elsewhere."

"Looking for company? Or something else on your mind?"

"Get everyone to the gym for six-twenty. Make that about ten minutes before. I want to observe their skills while they practice moves and perhaps learn a few new ones, especially the newer members. They haven't had the opportunity to get trained. I want them to know at least some basics, before the shit hits the fan. Or in the event someone else plans another ambush."

"I'll get the word out. You eating in the chow hall?"

"That's the plan."

"Where you headed now?"

"Need to set up a few things."

Starks entered the building and stopped when Jackson followed him. "I thought you were going to the yard for a reason."

"Was looking for some of the guys. Since they're not outside, and now that I have a mission to accomplish, I'll get that taken care of. Need to hustle so I catch as many as I can. The rest can be told at dinner."

The gym topped Starks's list of places where he might find Felipe. His hunch proved accurate. His cohort-in-crime occupied the bench press. Starks started across the room. Felipe's spotter saw him and said something. Felipe placed the weighted bar onto the hooks and sat up.

"I heard rumors, amigo. How close they are to the facts?" He shrugged. "Only you can tell me."

Starks glanced at the spotter then at Felipe. Felipe said something in Spanish. The man walked away.

Starks sat on the bench. He filled Felipe in on the details then made his request. When Felipe nodded, Starks said, "Good thing you prepped me."

"Only for what you got yourself out of."

"And even then it was because I had help."

"What are you going to do about Tank?"

"Nothing I can do, at least, not until he can't hide anymore."

"Stupid mother."

"So, we're definitely good for later?"

"You realize you may be arming some of the enemy."

"I have my reasons."

Starks did one of those complicated handshakes with Felipe and left. There was one more stop he needed to make.

CHAPTER 66

Starks made it to D Block with minutes to spare before it would be time to make his appearance in the chow hall. Had he not known which cell was Luke's, the four inmates lined against the wall, waiting their turn, would have made it evident. He nodded as he passed them then rapped on the barred steel door.

Luke pulled his attention from the form he was helping an inmate with, saw who it was, and smiled. "Your bruises are turning green. That's a good sign."

"I need to talk to you for a minute."

"Give me a second."

Luke pointed to a line on the form and said to the inmate, "After you finish filling out those answers, sign here, and you're done."

The inmate stood, form in hand, thanked Luke and moved head-down past Starks. Starks said to the waiting inmates, "I need to borrow Luke for an hour or two. You won't mind coming back later, right?"

A few of the men complained. Others said it was no problem. Starks watched from the door until they'd disappeared around the corner.

Luke stood, stretched, and yawned. "What's up?"

"The enemy of my enemy is my friend."

"That would be me, I suppose."

Starks rested back against the wall, arms crossed at his chest. "I owe you."

"That's not how I roll."

"Let me put it this way. Because you saved my bacon, you now have a target on your back."

Luke's smile faltered. "I'm listening."

"Whether you want to or not, you'll be safer if you stick with me and my crew. What's left of it."

"Wouldn't I be safer if I minded my own business?"

"Not how it rolls in here."

"That sucks."

"You're in danger now, whether you're with me or not. Better to be with me. Smarter too."

Luke shook his head and blew out a breath. "What do I have to do?"

"Come with me to the chow hall. I'll introduce you to whoever is there. At ten after six, we hit the gym for training with one of my associates."

"What kind of training?"

"Martial arts. Although, looks to me like you've trained some already."

"Couldn't always afford it, so had to drop out."

"That won't be a problem here. I have an arrangement." Starks glanced at the clock on the desk. "Time to go."

Fourteen or so of Starks's men were ahead of them at the front of the line.

Luke leaned forward. "I already know one penalty for being with you."

"What's that?"

"Having to eat in here."

Starks chuckled. "I don't do it often. When I need to talk with most of my guys, it's convenient. We can meet on the bleachers only so often before it looks conspiratorial."

They inched their way up the line, retrieved trays pushed through the slot, and headed for the usual table. Starks glanced at Felipe as he passed the Hermanos' table.

They rapped on the table. Luke slid in first, leaving the end of the bench for Starks, opposite Ethan.

"Crew, this is Luke Thompson."

Ethan grinned. "S-s-saved S-S-Starks."

Luke covered his surprise quickly and said, "What's your name?"

"E-Ethan."

"How old are you?"

"Old enough."

Luke smiled. "Good answer."

"I l-like b-butterflies."

Starks kicked Ethan under the table. Ethan tucked his head down and shoveled food into his mouth.

Jackson, who sat next to Ethan, shifted over a few inches. "Everything is set up for the gym," he told Starks.

Blackie, seated on Jackson's left, said, "Should be fun."

Starks chewed a tough piece of roast something, swallowed and said, "We're not doing it for fun."

"I just meant—"

Starks waved him off and leaned forward. He tapped the end of his fork on the table and waited for his crew to look at him. "I want everyone focused when we're in there. No screwing around."

A guard strutted up to the table. "You ladies gonna gab instead of eat?" He glared at them for a few moments then continued his rounds.

Several minutes later, Starks rapped and stood. "Soon as the six o'clock count is over, meet me in the gym. Practice starts at six twenty. Sharp. Warm-up begins ten minutes earlier. Be on time."

Starks led the crew members present through stretches. He'd wait for the others to arrive then initiate his plan. A total of thirty-four crew members were there by a quarter after.

Fate, or fortune, would have it that the skinheads nearly doubled his number of soldiers. Add the Hermanos, who were also actively recruiting, and the number doubled again. That eased his concern but only slightly. His final crew count would remain unconfirmed, at least for another several minutes, followed by however long it took to do what needed to be done.

He exercised them in place, working them to a soaking sweat. Several protested. He told them it would loosen their muscles; that he didn't want them pulling anything. He joined them, for the most part, but primarily walked around them as he did countdowns.

Felipe and nine Hermanos strolled in. Starks told his men to keep at it. He joined Felipe, who wore a quizzical expression.

"Warm up is one thing, amigo, but isn't this overdoing it? They won't be worth shit if you wear them out before they start."

"I have my reasons."

Felipe shrugged. "Ready when you are."

Starks removed his scrub and thermal shirts. "All right. Let's get to the mat."

The rest of his crew stripped to bare-chested and took their positions around the practice area.

Felipe stood in the center of the mat. "I'm going to show you a few simple moves, after I give you a demonstration with one of my men."

One of the new members said, "Why not with Starks?"

Felipe fixed his focus on the inmate. "I know what Starks can do. Besides, he already demonstrated his skills in the laundry room."

"We wanna see him in action."

Felipe's smile stopped at his lips. "Maybe you'd like me to demonstrate the move where I put my foot up your ass, all the way up to my knee."

Several of the men snickered. One of them said, "That's one way to shut his mouth, since he talks out his ass."

The inmate's face burned red. He balled his hands into fists. "Keep it up, asshole. I'll shut you down for good."

Felipe moved like a flash of light. The inmate lay on his back with Felipe's knee to his throat. "Amigo, you need to learn to channel that aggression the right way. *Comprendo?*"

"Yeah."

"Good. After my demonstration, I'll spar with you first."

Starks moved around the mat as his crew practiced moves. A half hour later, they took turns sparring with Felipe or some of the Hermanos, and then with each other, as Starks observed.

Ethan made a show of concentrating, more often looking awkward than smooth. It was a convincing act. The mouthy inmate released a string of obscenities when Ethan flipped him. Ethan clapped his hands. "L-look what I did, S-Starks."

Starks kept his smile to himself. As his crew practiced, he moved at snail's-pace around the large padded square.

Watching.
Observing.
Memorizing.

CHAPTER 67

"What have you got?" Starks listened attentively to Jim Rogers, his lips pressed tightly together. A little over a quarter hour passed as research results were conveyed. "Well, crap."

"Bad news?"

"Yes, but expected, at least in some measure."

"Anything else I can do for you?"

"I'll let you know. Thanks, buddy."

"Anytime."

"Tell Jeffrey I approved the expense."

"Already did."

Starks hit the off button and cradled the phone to his chest. Everything made sense now. The dots connected, showing him the bigger picture. All he needed was the stones to follow through.

Thompson would never play God and decide who lived and who didn't.

Thompson wasn't him. Thompson had gotten only a small taste of what life was like inside. Had only one scar. So far.

Starks mulled his justifications over in his mind. There was no getting around what had to be done. No way to escape it.

What if, despite what he'd learned, he was wrong? What if he launched his plan then discovered his error too late? There would be no going back. No way to make up for what he'd done. If there really was a God, he could forget ever being forgiven and cleansed of his sins. Not after this.

Turn the other cheek at Sands, and you were dead.

As Thompson would say, the choice sucked.

It was time. Any hesitation could cost him. From between the pages of a book, he removed the cellophane wrapper he'd cleaned and dried, added the appropriate amount of each of the powders directly onto the wrapper, which he folded until he could hide the tiny square unseen in the palm of his hand.

Now to locate Ethan.

Starks found him heading outside. "Hold up."

"What's doing?"

"Showtime." Starks looked around. Inmates came toward them, also heading for the yard, but still a ways back. "When I put my hand on the handle, put yours next to mine. I'll let what's in my hand drop from the top of the bar. You have to catch it in a way that it—"

"I'm not an amateur."

"Ready? Now."

They made the exchange with Ethan looking no more awkward than any other time.

"Remember my instructions about how to mix it?"

"If you don't stop nagging me, I'll use it on you."

"Fair enough."

Ethan slapped at something invisible in the air and dashed away from the door, back into a deeper recess of the prison.

Starks pushed the door open. Walked the perimeter of the yard. Waited for the thumping in his chest to slow to normal and the numbness in his limbs to subside. He shoved his hands into his coat pockets. Despite the frigid air, sweat trickled down his face, as though a high fever had just broken.

In a way, he thought, that's exactly what had happened.

CHAPTER 68

Starks adjusted books on the library shelf and fitted the novel into its proper place. He reached for another book to file away and halted with his hand halfway to the shelf. Jackson had called his name. He looked left, toward the entrance.

Jackson rushed forward, grabbed Starks by the arm and dragged him into the office. He closed the door and leaned panting against it.

Starks pulled his arm away. "What?"

"Two of our new guys were attacked."

"When?"

"About a half hour ago. I just heard about it."

"Bad?"

Jackson frowned at Starks. "That's the funny thing."

Starks gestured with a hand for Jackson to keep talking.

"No obvious bruises or cuts, but their symptoms are a lot like when you use the poison."

Starks stared at Jackson with an unreadable expression. He patted his pockets. "The thumbs are where they belong."

"What the hell's going on?"

Starks sat half-on, half-off the desk. "What's the word on Tank?"

"Still in lock-up. And before you ask, Seth's still locked up."

"I get why Seth's still in the Hole. But it's been a little over two weeks. No way they know what Tank's role was. What's he doing, establishing squatter's rights? "

"They'll boot him out. Eventually. That's not our immediate problem. Who the hell went after our guys?"

"Damn if I know."

"That's all you have to say?"

"Be careful."

Jackson crossed his arms at his chest. "Be straight with me, man. Is this your doing?"

Starks locked his eyes on Jackson. "Use that brain you're so proud of."

Jackson's body slumped. "You're right. I don't know what I was thinking. After all our efforts to build our numbers, the last thing you'd do is take out your own men."

"That's more like it. Anything else?"

Jackson shook his head.

"Let me know if you hear anything, especially about how they're doing." Starks walked around the desk and lowered into the chair.

Jackson placed his hands palms-down on the desk. "What are you going to do?"

"Give the matter some thought."

"That's all you do lately."

"What do you expect me to do?"

Jackson shrugged. "I don't know. Act like you're friggin' bothered, maybe?"

"Believe me, I'm bothered."

"I've seen you bothered. This is not it."

"All right. This is me flummoxed. Better?"

"You're not yourself."

"You're not my mother."

Jackson opened the door. He glanced at Starks and shook his head.

Starks kicked back in the chair and propped his feet on the desk. He crossed his ankles and rested his chin on his steepled fingers. He remained in that position, until his replacement arrived a half hour later.

Starks returned to his cell.

Jackson, seated at his desk, looked up. "Any brilliant thoughts come to you?"

"Yes. Let's go to the chow hall at five."

"That's the fabulous result of your contemplation?"

Starks leaned against the door, his focus on the corridor. "I want to take the temperature of the room."

CHAPTER 69

A quarter after eight the next evening, Jackson returned from his dinner shift. He stripped to his underwear and used a wet washcloth to wipe off sweat and food splatters from his skin.

Starks lay on his bunk, arms folded behind his head. "I went by the infirmary earlier to check on our guys."

Jackson rinsed his washcloth and hung it over the back of his chair to dry. "They doing any better?"

Starks shrugged. "The doc said he initially thought it was an especially serious case of food poisoning, but no one else got sick."

"I told you, this shit is suspicious."

"He told me there were drugs in their system, like a cocktail. They showed up in both of their blood test results."

Jackson eased into his chair. "So someone maybe put something in the drugs. Maybe got them to ingest it another way."

"Whatever it was, it was undetectable in the basic test. Stewart sent them to the hospital. They're better equipped for diagnostics there."

"Did you get to talk to them?"

"Doc had them knocked out on morphine. All I was allowed to do was look at them through the window."

"When they get back, they can tell us what happened. Bet they give up doing that shit after this."

"You never know. They ever buy from you?"

"All I do is tell people who to see then take a percentage."

"Maybe we ought to make it a rule that none of the crew uses."

"That'll go over big. They'll either tell you where to stick it or smile, agree, and do it anyway."

"If someone's dicking around with the stuff …"

Starks and Jackson chatted off and on until the lights dimmed at nine. At ten, guards made their rounds, aiming flashlights at beds to make certain every inmate was where he belonged.

A beam landed on Starks's face and remained there. He sat up, eyes squinting and hand held out to block the beam. "What's the deal?"

"It's Roberts. Come to the door."

Starks tossed the blanket aside and shuffled over in his socks. "What's up?"

"Both your guys died an hour or so ago, about a half hour apart."

"Damn it. Any further info about what happened?"

"Doc Stewart requested—make that insisted on—forensic autopsies."

"Maybe something will show."

"You know anything about this?"

"Only what I've heard."

Roberts nodded. "Watch your back."

"I'm watching on all sides."

Roberts continued to the next cell. Starks pivoted. Jackson was propped up on one elbow, eyes fixed on him.

Starks shivered and returned to his bed, pulling the blanket over him.

"Shit, Starks. What are we going to do about this?"

"See about replacing them."

Jackson flopped back on his mattress. "Don't go all sentimental or anything."

"I can't afford sentiment."

"And here I thought you could afford anything."

"Knock it off."

Starks sat up and pressed his shoulder against the wall, near the window, blanket wrapped around him. The glow of the halogen lamps highlighted thick, low clouds clotting the sky. He picked at a cuticle until the skin tore, flinched, and lay back. The final time he checked the clock it was almost five.

He punched his pillow and turned onto his side, feeling certain Gabe Bianchi had never lost a night's sleep.

CHAPTER 70

The next week went by in relative quiet tinged with inmates' anxiety, evident in how they jumped at sounds or how they continually monitored others, including those whose proximity they'd previously considered safe. Starks split his time between library shifts, working out with Felipe and some of the Hermanos in the gym, the yard when the weather allowed, and his cell.

Rumors passed in hushed voices about Seth, Tank, the two dead crew members, the impending war, and the belief that there was a psychopath on the loose, one more insane than usual. Lots of questions, lots of speculations. When asked, Starks either shrugged or said he didn't know any more than they did.

Mid-morning on Friday, Starks and most of his crew were outside, some on the bleachers, others playing basketball in the muck created by dirt and snow melting from the most recent minor storm.

The alarm blared. Starks turned his attention to CO Jakes, who stood alert at the fence line directly across from him, his radio pressed to his ear. The announcement followed, ordering all inmates to return to their cells. Jakes made eye contact with Starks and motioned for him to join him.

Crew members next to Starks leaped from the bleachers and hustled toward the building, hesitant to merge too closely with other nervous inmates attempting to squeeze through the two doors. Starks maneuvered his way through them to where Jakes waited.

"What is it this time?" Starks asked.

"More of your guys are having the same symptoms as the last two."

Starks shifted his eyes left and stared beyond the fence. "Names?"

"Pete, Max, and Wayne."

Starks gave a nearly imperceptible nod of his head.

"Spencer and the others want to see you."

"Let's get this over with."

"Start for the door, but go slow. Better to wait till all these guys are inside."

They wound their way through corridors, stopping at the open doorway of the investigative council room. Spencer was in the middle chair, as usual, with Bentley on his right, Kratz to his left. All eyes fixed on Starks as he entered the room and eased into the chair reserved for inmates.

Spencer rubbed the deep furrow between his eyebrows. "This makes five. All yours."

"It's not me."

Spencer waved a hand. "That's obvious."

"How are they?"

"In morphine land. Waiting for three ambulances to arrive to take them to Grace."

"From personal experience, I know it's a good hospital."

"Maybe getting them there earlier will make a difference this time."

Starks propped his elbows on his knees and stared at his linked hands.

"Here's what I think," Spencer said. "Someone's after you. And whoever it is—"

"Is whittling away at my associates."

"Any idea who and how?"

Starks shook his head.

Spencer pulled a roll of antacids from his shirt pocket and popped two into his mouth. He chewed, swallowed then said, "And of course, no one's talking." He rubbed his belly. "We conferred while we waited for you. Maybe the best place for you, for a while, is in isolation."

Starks's head jerked up. "No."

"Look, Starks—"

"If the plan is for these attacks to continue, my being in isolation won't stop whoever is doing this, and it'll make me crazy. Plus, we all know that, even in the Hole, there's no guarantee of my safety."

Kratz slumped back in his chair and flicked his pen back and forth. "It burns me to admit it, but Starks is right."

Bentley inched forward in his chair and craned his head to look at the other two. "Maybe a transfer?"

Starks's spine snapped straight. "Absolutely not."

"Why not?"

"Better the devil you know, and all that."

Spencer picked up his pen and tossed it back onto his tablet. "From the first, I said you have a death wish."

"On the contrary," Starks said. "This is where my son was. I want to be where Kane was."

"Damn it, Starks, I'm trying to keep you from ending up like him."

"No isolation. No transfer."

"Shit." Spencer grimaced and silenced a belch. "It's your head."

"Exactly. Maybe I can discover something, if I'm free to move around. While I'm sitting here, what are you doing?"

"Everyone's cells are getting searched."

"Maybe something will turn up. Anything else?"

"Not from you. Not at this time. I wish you'd reconsider."

Starks stood. "I'm always considering my options."

"One option you can forget arguing about, is to have guards keep a closer watch on you."

"I can live with that."

"You hope."

Starks nodded once at the council members and joined Jakes at the door.

They covered several yards before Jakes said, "We'll all do the best we can to keep you safe."

"I know. But it can't be so obvious that inmates see it as preference. That'll piss some of them off faster than you can spit."

"Can't be helped."

"Are we still in lockdown?"

"Let me check." Jakes used his radio, making sense of garbled words mixed with static. "They need another ten or so minutes to complete the search."

"Probably won't look good for me to show up at my cell just yet."

"Where do you want to go?"

"Anywhere. Once the doors open, I'll go back."

"Might as well stay here. It's as good a place as any. Then I'll take you back."

Twenty minutes later, the grind of doors sliding open echoed through the corridors.

Jakes said, "At least it's not a long walk."

"It's longer than you think."

CHAPTER 71

"Where the hell have you been?" Jackson leaped from his bunk and stood with his fists planted on his hips. "At first I thought it was you lying in the infirmary. Then I got word it wasn't."

"As you can see, I'm all right."

"No one and nothing is all right. Shit, man. Barely knew Wayne or Max. But Pete." He kicked the bottom bunk frame.

"I was getting grilled by the council."

"They trying to stick this to you?"

"They think I'm a target. Offered solitary or another residence."

"You take 'em up on either one?"

"Won't solve my problems."

"Maybe you ought to reconsider."

"Forget it."

Jackson kicked his chair. "Man, I was in here shittin' bricks, wondering if you had anything hidden I didn't know about."

Starks's eyes flicked toward the large book. "The cell phones?"

"Safe. Roberts searched our cell."

"Did he find my phones?"

"Nah. I don't know what they're looking for, but they don't think it would fit inside a book."

Starks rinsed his face with cold water. He ripped a paper towel segment from the roll and said, "Where do you keep your phone?"

"Kitchen."

"Smart."

Jackson pointed at his head. "No grass growing here."

"Let's hope some of the others were as clever."

"I thought about that. Especially when I saw how thorough their search was. No telling what all they found."

The attacks continued. By the fifth week, fifteen of Starks's crew had suffered a similar demise. Lockdowns and searches brought no results, other than finding more contraband each time.

Guards' tempers frayed. Inmates whose drugs or alcohol had been confiscated, either bothered Dr. Stewart for something to ease the pain or got into fistfights over the smallest matters. Other inmates watched everyone, especially Starks, as though he might disappear with a poof before their eyes. According to the gossip mill, most were convinced his heartbeat had a time limit.

Several of Starks's crew attempted to stick with him, eyes darting about continually, postures tense and alert for potential attacks. Despite their efforts, Starks didn't trust them. Not completely. A lesson hard learned wasn't easily forgotten.

Two more of his crew suffered the same fate. All hell broke loose. Inmates went into lockdown yet again. This time the search included full body-cavity exploration. All except Starks, who, instead, spent those times with the investigative council, yet again stating he had no information and refusing any protection other than guards' observance.

After the search, Starks returned to his cell. Jackson sat in his chair, fuming. "Sonsabitches. When I find out who's doing this, I'll kill him myself."

Starks remained silent. He sat on the edge of his bed. Got up. Went to the sink to wash his hands.

"What'd the council say?"

Starks dried his hands on his shirt. "The usual. Did I know anything. Did I want to go into isolation or to another place."

"I can't help wondering when it's gonna be my turn. Don't you wonder the same thing?"

"Won't do me any good to dwell on it."

"That fake calm you're wearing is about to come off."

Starks arched an eyebrow and waited.

"Seth's out of the SHU, and he ain't happy about it."

"Interesting."

"My ass. This shit has been going on while he was locked away. What the hell you think is gonna happen now that he's back in general population?"

"I imagine we'll find out."

"You don't fool me."

Starks kept his expression blank. "I wouldn't try."

"It wouldn't work."

"I'll keep that in mind."

CHAPTER 72

S tarks and Jackson got their trays and joined crew members at the table. Voices stayed low as questions and best-guess answers permeated their conversations. Starks kept his responses restricted to nods, head shakes, or shrugs. Let his crew think whatever they wanted about his reticent manner.

The already somber room grew quiet. All heads turned to face the entrance. A limping Seth and several of his soldiers got into the line. As though a spell broke, murmuring resumed. Starks's gaze remained fixed on Seth.

Seth's eyes raked the room as he moved forward, until they landed on Starks. He sneered and said something to his men. They snickered, but Seth looked away first. However, not fast enough to hide his fear.

Starks rapped on the table and got up. "Lost my appetite."

Jackson glanced up at him. "Been doin' that a lot lately." When Starks didn't reply, he said, "I'll go with you." He raised his fist.

Starks stopped him. "It's fine. Finish eating. Seth's not stupid enough to try something so soon."

Jackson started to protest.

Ethan rapped and stood. "I w-want to g-go with you."

"See, Jackson? I'm protected."

"Yeah. Gotta watch out for crazed butterflies."

Starks, followed by Ethan, dumped his tray. They exited into the hallway.

Ethan glanced back and whispered, "Too crowded. Let's go somewhere more private."

"My cell's closest."

Ethan turned Starks's chair around and sat, legs splayed in front of him.

Starks leaned against the opposite wall, nearer to the door, listening for footsteps. "I got concerned when I heard about the cavity search. Afraid maybe you hid the packet of powders where you thought they wouldn't look."

"I'm smarter than that."

"Where did you hide them?"

"In the library. No way would they think to go through every book, magazine or newspaper."

"I've never seen you in there."

"I make it a point never to go while you're working."

"Why's that?"

"So they don't connect the dots. You'd be surprised at the stash I've found tucked away in there."

"I touch that stuff all the time."

"Not everything."

"What have you found?"

"Shanks of all sizes and sharpness. Drugs. Condoms."

"What did you do with them?"

"Put some of it to good use, quite recently." He winked. "Moved all the others. Only I know where everything is hidden now." He laughed. "It's amusing to watch inmates search for their hidden stash. Such panicked expressions. I've nearly peed myself a number of times."

"All this time working in there, I never came across anything like that."

"They choose obscure materials and locations. Most consider me of little to no consequence in the grand scheme of life, so don't even consider that I may be watching them as they hide or retrieve their items."

"Where have you hidden the stuff?"

"I think, for now at least, I'll keep that to myself." He studied his hands then focused on Starks. "It wasn't just Seth who got released. They forced Tank out of his cage this afternoon." Ethan grinned and wiggled his eyebrows. "I think it's time we set a play date with ol' Tank."

"Any preference for when?"

"The sooner the better. Don't you agree?"

Footsteps echoed in the corridor. Starks moved closer to the door, kept his gaze on an inmate, until he entered the second cell on the opposite side. "You know I'll be blamed for anything that happens to Tank. The crew won't hesitate to pin it on me."

"Not if it's done right, which it will be, just as all the other times. There's something else to consider."

"Such as?"

"Think about it." Ethan shifted forward. "Some of your crew will suspect Seth. It's not beyond the realm of possibility that he or his men believe Tank botched the job. Your crew may also look at each other, as the one or ones who sought retribution. There are also inmates who, at the very least, respect you and may hold a grudge. Rumor mill, remember?"

"I want to talk to him, just before you do whatever."

Ethan puckered his lips. "That's a bit trickier. Guards are practically sticking to you like Velcro."

"It's imperative."

"Never fear. I'll devise a foolproof way for that to happen." Ethan stood and bowed. At the cell entrance he turned. "I'll brief you on the arrangements, as soon as I have them firmed up."

"I'll be ready."

Starks stood in the doorway until Ethan turned right and disappeared from view. He made his way to Luke's cell. He'd kept his distance from him during these weeks, believing if he didn't make their association obvious, Thompson would be left alone. Inmates needed to believe Thompson had acted as he had in the laundry room, not on behalf of close ties with Starks but out of decency. It didn't guarantee trouble wouldn't look for and find the author, but it wouldn't be because of Starks. Not if he could help it. He owed the guy that much and more.

About a dozen or so inmates, hands gripping various items, stood in a line against the wall. One less thing to worry as much about. As long as men relied on Luke, as long as they waited to see him every day, it was doubtful anyone would dare bother him, much less harm him. Not if they wanted to live.

Uneasiness tweaked Starks. By the time he was a yard from the cell entrance, he understood what it was about. Inmates' regard for Thompson resulted from the fact that he served through significance, whereas his own concern had been self-serving, no matter how he dressed it.

Starks stopped at the cell entrance. "Thompson. I'd like a minute."

"Can you give me about five? I'm almost done here."

Starks said to the other inmate, "How about you step out. This won't take long."

The inmate nodded and hurriedly retreated.

Luke remained seated. "What's up?"

Starks moved to stand next to him, kept his voice quiet. "Tank got out of the Hole this afternoon. I haven't see him yet. He's probably laying low. The thing is, I don't know who all is siding with him."

"You're telling me to be cautious."

Starks nodded. "And I have a question. Was what you did a one-time deal or are you willing to stand with me again?"

"I thought we already covered this."

"People have a way of changing their minds around here."

"I'm no boy scout, but right is right."

"Good enough."

"What's going to happen to Tank?"

"Your guess is as good as mine."

Luke frowned. "Is it your intention to go after him?"

"I'd be asking for it if I did."

"True."

"However, if the opportunity presents itself, I would like to find out why he betrayed me."

"Do you think he ordered the hits on your guys?"

"It wouldn't surprise me to learn he was, in some way, responsible. I don't know that he'll be willing to talk, but it pays to ask, right?"

"Can't hurt."

Starks kept his retort to himself. "Stay extra sharp. As long as you have a crowd outside your door, you should be okay. However, if you feel something is off, get in touch with me."

"Thanks for the heads-up."

"Later."

Starks started back toward his cell. Now, it was a matter of waiting on Ethan. He doubted the wait would be long. Ethan enjoyed his work far too much.

CHAPTER 73

Starks emerged from his bed in slow motion, after yet another sleepless night. He stood in front of the tiny mirror, expelling a sigh in response to the dark circles and bags under his eyes. After his awkward teens, his reflection had pleased him. Who was he kidding? He'd been arrogance personified. These days he used the mirror before him solely for the purpose of shaving. And sometimes, to verify he still existed. Too often he felt more and more like a shell a stiff wind might scatter. How much of who he'd once been still resided inside him, was anyone's guess.

He followed his morning routine, and after the count joined the stream of inmates heading for the chow hall. Ethan slid up behind him and whispered his name in his ear.

Starks lurched forward. "Stop doing that."

"Stop making yourself such an easy target. Listen up. At five after nine, be near the shower room corridor, but not in it."

"Why?"

"To fulfill your wish." Ethan moved closer and pretended to talk to himself as near to Starks's ear as possible. "When you hear the diversion and see the guards running toward it, give me three minutes. Then make haste to the laundry room."

"Isn't that taking too big a chance?"

"That makes it all the more fun."

"For you maybe."

Through gritted teeth Ethan said, "Just be there. Leave the rest to me."

On the way to the table, Starks scoped the room. No Seth. And, no Tank. He sat facing the entrance. Still no appearance of the man who'd shattered something inside him. Throughout breakfast, Starks forced food past the constriction in his throat. Across from him, Ethan ate as though at a picnic. They left the hall at the same time. Ethan bounced off to the right.

Starks waited and paced in his cell as the minutes clicked by. He should have forced details from Ethan. Instead, he was forced to fly blind. At ten till nine, he left the cell, keeping his speed at stroll-pace. He glanced behind him. His eyes locked onto CO Stone, twenty feet back and following him.

Starks maintained his pace as though he had nowhere to go but wanted to walk for the sake of moving. He glanced up at the hall clock when he neared the place where he was supposed to wait—9:04—and kept walking. Ethan's diversion had better work, because Stone was sticking to him.

Sweat trailed from Starks's scalp, down the side of his face. He swiped at it with the sleeve of his thermal top, swallowed several times, imagined biting into a lemon, so his mouth moistened. He needed to be able to speak. He wanted answers.

At precisely five after nine, shouts erupted around the corner to his left. He stopped and looked back, eyebrows raised.

Stone had his radio pressed to his ear. He pointed at Starks and yelled, "Get to your cell and stay there." Starks nodded once and started toward Stone. Stone took off running. Starks reversed his steps.

He watched the clock. Three minutes. It might as well be three hours.

Scuffling feet, grunts, and muffled screams came from the hall to his right. Starks inched forward and peeked around the corner. Ethan exited the shower room, followed by four men wearing shaved heads and rubber gloves, as they dragged Tank with them. Duct tape covered Tank's mouth. Shirtless, his pants hung around his knees. He stumbled as he shuffled forward unwillingly.

Starks turned his eyes to the clock. He chewed his bottom lip as one digit shifted to the next number in line, scrubbed his shirt sleeve over his forehead and face. Wiped his palms on his pants. At eight after, he ran full-speed into the laundry room.

Wolly slammed his fist into Tank's jaw. Tank struggled against the duct tape securing him to a metal folding chair then went limp.

Ethan rested casually on the table. His head swiveled left as Starks stepped fully into the room. "Right on time." He faced the four men. "Ease up so Starks can talk to him."

Tank raised his head and looked at Starks through one swelling eye and one bulging in terror.

Wolly's grin was malevolent. "He's all yours."

Tank thrashed in the chair. Wolly's fist connected with Tank's head, just behind his temple. Tank slumped back, but his eyes stayed on Starks.

Starks stopped a yard from the chair that held Tank. "I want answers. The tape will be removed. If you scream, it won't go well for you. Do you understand?"

Tank nodded.

"Peel the tape back."

Wolly yanked the tape away, pulling skin from Tank's lip with it. He left the tape dangling from Tank's cheek. Blood smeared and dripped from the adhesive side.

Starks moved closer. "I made clear what would happen to anyone who betrayed me or the crew. You had to know it would come to this. Why'd you do it?"

Tank coughed, spit blood onto the floor and rasped, "No choice."

"Were you Seth's man from the start?"

Tank looked stunned for a moment then began to moan and shake his head.

"Look at me."

Tank turned his face away. Wolly nodded at one of his men, who moved behind Tank. He grabbed Tank's head with both hands and forced him to face forward.

Starks moved forward until he stood a foot and half from the chair. "Last chance to tell me everything. Make it fast."

Sweat streamed down Tank's face. It mixed with his blood before dripping onto his heaving chest. "Can't."

"Damn it, Tank. I trusted you more than any of the others."

Ethan said, "I take exception to that statement."

Starks ignored him, kept his attention trained on Tank. "Maybe that was the plan all along."

Tank began to sob. "No choice. Had to."

"Shit. Then you leave me no choice." Starks turned to Ethan. "Make it quick."

Tank opened his mouth to scream. Wolly slapped the tape into place before breaking Tank's nose with his fist.

Ethan slid from the table. "Want me to remove his tattoo? He doesn't deserve to wear it."

"Leave it. Removing it might draw more suspicion my way than there already will be. Don't dawdle. Clean up and get out." Starks glanced over his shoulder. "Wolly, not a word about Ethan. Not even to the rest of your gang. Any of you blows his cover, you'll deal with me."

"We're good," Wolly said. "We respect the Dragon's secret weapon."

The sounds of death being inflicted chased Starks from the room. His feet and legs struggled to move him forward until his need to get away took over. An avalanche of emotion gripped him.

It was like a scene from a war movie played in his mind. But he'd never been a soldier sent to the battlefield. Never had to dive into a rain-soaked trench to escape bullets, surrounded by enemies intent on wiping him out with little or no regard for his life, gripped by fear of losing everyone he'd ever loved—and being lost, being forced to fight and kill, or die, all for a greater purpose.

Soldiers' circumstances differed from his own, but similarities existed in shared terror and soul-wrenching anguish. The battles true soldiers found themselves ascribed to engage in raged around them while, at the same time, were fought within them. They fought to win, only to reach the understanding that sometimes winning was inseparable from losing.

Then it became a question of how to restore what was lost, if that was even possible.

Some losses were too great.

Some wounds too profound to heal.

Which, he wondered, was worse—to lose one's life or one's soul?

Starks broke into a run. He skidded to a stop at the intersection and wiped tears and sweat from his face before turning the corner.

Punctured. That was the word that fit the emotion he couldn't shake.

Starks half-walked, half-ran to his block. He was alone. All cells were empty. He pounded his fist against the upper bunk.

Seth had much to pay for. And he needed to pay sooner rather than later.

CHAPTER 74

Frigid tap water stung his skin, but Starks scrubbed his face and hands as though the water or pain it caused might cleanse him. He hadn't touched Tank, but his former crew member's blood covered him like a web he couldn't remove.

Get a grip, he told himself. It was imperative that he appear unaware of anything other than a disturbance he'd avoided.

He dried his face, changed his sodden shirt, and took position on his bed, open book propped against his thighs, waiting for the alarm to blast notice of Tank's execution.

He chewed on a cuticle, worried that Ethan and the others had lingered too long in the laundry room. Or hadn't cleaned up quickly enough. Or cleaned up too quickly and had left some smidgen of evidence. Ethan, if alone, could manage to cover his tracks. More than just him involved added a disquieting measure of unpredictability.

Starks's eyes repeatedly shifted from the unread book to the clock, ears straining for the alarm so he could get this part of it over with. Muscles taut, he jumped when the alarm whined, followed by the order giving inmates five minutes to be in their cells. He sat on the edge of his bed, book gripped in his hands.

Footsteps clattered into the block corridor.

Jackson sped into the cell. "What the hell is going on in this place?"

"I don't know."

"I'm starting to hear that damn alarm in my sleep. I wake up sweating, heart thumping out of my damn chest."

The doors slid shut. The piercing alarm ceased, leaving the silence that followed equally unnerving.

Starks and Jackson did as every other inmate in the block and stood, hands wrapped around the bars, waiting for whatever was to come. New footfalls entered the corridor. Two guards, from what Starks could judge by listening. Within seconds, he didn't have to guess. Roberts and Stone stood in front of the cell.

The corners of Roberts' mouth sagged. "Starks."

"I swear I didn't do anything."

"I know. Somebody did Tank."

Stone smirked and said, "Butchered is more like it."

Jackson sucked in air and faced Starks. "Damn it, Starks."

Inmates uttered Tank's name, passing it from cell to cell. Stone shouted for them to shut it.

Starks's skin grew moist with sweat. He rushed to the toilet, vomiting until there was nothing left inside. He rinsed his mouth and face with cold water, avoided facing his reflection in the small mirror. The last thing he'd wanted was to humiliate himself or seem weak in front of inmates focused on his cell. On him. However, his reaction might work in his favor. Everyone, including guards, knew how close he was—had been—to Tank. He glanced at Jackson, whose expression stayed locked in shock. "Council wants to see me, right?"

Roberts nodded and opened the cell door, locking it after Starks stepped through. Inmates' stared, transfixed, as he walked ahead of the guards.

Starks stayed silent, not solely because Stone was there, but because he wanted to think about what he might have to say. There were only so many who knew about Tank's betrayal. His crew knew. Seth and his men knew. Wolly and those he'd selected for the task. Guards on his payroll had been deliberately left out of the loop.

The full council waited at the table. Starks took his seat, lowered his head and shook it slowly from side to side.

Spencer spoke first. "Another one of your men."

"I hope like hell it's the last one."

"Still no idea about who might be doing this?"

Starks's chin quivered. "Tank was someone I liked and trusted." His head dropped into his hands, his shoulders shook with sobs he barely kept quiet.

Spencer remained silent a few moments then said, "We figure Tank was attacked and killed about fifteen, maybe twenty minutes ago, at most. We have to ask—where were you at that time?"

"My cell." Starks pointed behind him with his thumb. "Something was going on. Officer Stone was several yards behind me. He ordered me to get to my cell. I did."

Spencer looked past Starks. "Stone?"

"Yessir, that's what happened."

Starks's word choice—*ordered*—was deliberate. A marionette like Stone would respond to that better than *told, said* or *suggested.* He'd made Stone sound in charge. Stone wouldn't want anyone to question the fact of his authority, least of all himself.

Spencer stared at Starks over his glasses. "My offers still stand."

"I haven't taken them off the table."

"How many more attacks like this will it take before you decide?"

Roberts' and Stone's radios crackled. They listened.

Spencer glanced from one guard to the other. "Well?"

"Search is complete," Roberts said.

"And?"

"Nothing found, and no indication of who to pin it on."

Spencer cursed and rested his forehead in his hand. "Beats me to hell and back." He held his thumb and forefinger millimeters apart. "I'm this close to keeping people locked in round the clock, until this shit settles down."

Starks sat up. "That would only make things worse."

"It's also not feasible. But the warden and board are climbing up my ass about these attacks."

"They can't go on forever. Either someone will make a mistake or they'll feel they've accomplished what they set out to do."

Spencer aimed his pen at Starks. "I don't have to tell you what that might be."

"No."

"Get your gang to—"

"Crew."

Spencer waved a hand. "Whatever. Get them to stay in groups from now on, especially around you, as much as possible. I'll keep the guards as close as they can manage."

"I will, and thanks."

Spencer sighed and slumped back in his chair. "Return Starks to his cell."

Starks eased to his feet. "Are you keeping us locked in for a while?"

"Maybe another thirty minutes. Maybe longer. Give them all something to think about. Piss enough of these guys off, they might say something."

"If they're not talking, as freaked as they are now, I wouldn't hold your breath."

Spencer popped two antacids into his mouth and gestured to the guards to leave with Starks.

CHAPTER 75

Sweat soaked Jackson's shirt down the middle, front and back. He waited until the guards locked the door and left. "Was it you?"

"I swear it wasn't."

Jackson, breathing hard, glared at Starks. "Shit." His shoulders drooped. "Everybody's going to think it was."

"They might. But why not Seth? Or someone else who knew what Tank did?"

Jackson swiped moisture from his forehead. "Yeah, I guess so. I'm losing my mind here."

"That's not helpful to me or to you. You need to keep your wits."

"My wits get flushed down the toilet every time I think about what's going on. Keep wondering when it's going to be my turn. I'm watching everybody. *Everybody's* watching everybody. No one knows who to trust anymore."

"I know the feeling."

Jackson moved to the door and grasped two of the bars. "How long they keeping us in?"

"Not sure. You in a hurry to get out?"

Jackson turned and rested against the bars. "Not particularly. But we had to turn everything off in the kitchen."

"Worried the food will be ruined?"

"*Now* you have a sense of humor?"

"Why don't you land somewhere. See if you can calm down while you wait."

"Who the hell can calm down?" Jackson shuffled to his chair. "What'd you tell the council this time?"

"I told the truth, without breaking code, of course."

Jackson bounced his feet up and down. "I can't believe Tank. You tried to warn me. I was so damn proud of picking someone like him. Thought I knew better than you. Some friggin' mentalist I am."

"He fooled all of us, so don't carry that guilt too far. By the way, any idea what his real name is? Was?"

Jackson grew still and directed his gaze toward the ceiling. "I saw or heard it once. What the hell was it? Oh yeah. Percy Morris. Why are you asking that now?"

"Just curious. Even though he betrayed me, it seems only right to know who he really was."

"All he deserves is an unmarked grave."

The locks clanked and the doors ground open. Jackson slapped his thighs. "Didn't expect them to let us out that fast. Back to the ovens."

As soon as Jackson left, Starks retrieved the phone and dialed Jim Rogers' number. "It's me. I need intel on Percy Morris, nicknamed Tank."

"And he is?"

"Inmate."

"How thorough?"

"Does he have family, children, et cetera. Whatever you can find in a brief amount of time."

"I got computer programs that can practically tell me what size underwear he wears. Anything else?"

"Not at this time."

"Give me a couple hours. I'm on the road. Soon as I'm back at my office, I'll look it up."

"I'll call you around three thirty, as long as nothing stops me."

"Who or what might do that?"

"You never know."

"Shit. Okay. Talk to you whenever."

Starks shut off the phone. There was no way to escape the inevitable escalation. Because it had to escalate. Seth might be limping around, but he'd know who was behind Tank's demise. If Seth's plan to strike wasn't already formed, he was working on it with his soldiers now.

Starks stared at the phone still in his hand. There were things he needed to settle before anything else happened.

CHAPTER 76

First things first, Starks told himself. Best to get the legal stuff out of the way. He punched in Parker's cell phone number.

Parker answered on the second ring and said tentatively, "Starks?"

"Yes. I wanted to—"

"How timely. You saved me a trip, at least for now."

"What are you talking about? Has something happened?"

"No disrespect meant, or at least not much, but Judge Solomon, the sonofabitch, had a heart attack."

Starks sat up straight. "He's incapacitated?"

"He's dead. A new judge replaces him next week. I know him, he's fair-minded. If everything goes the way I believe it will, based on the new evidence, he'll either grant you a new trial or waive the trial and grant your freedom. Of course, that may take weeks. Even a month or so. But at least we're moving in the right direction. I feel it in my bones. You'll be getting out not too long from now."

A vortex opened and threatened to swallow Starks. "I'm having trouble taking this in. I thought for certain I'd be—"

"I know. I hated your believing that. But now you have a chance. More than a chance if I have anything to do with it."

"What's the next step?"

"I get my team to wrap up the new appeal. Then I'll go over it with a fine-tooth comb and submit it to the court."

"I don't know what to say."

Parker laughed. "This news should improve your mood."

"Yeah."

"Sorry, Starks, I have to run. I was just leaving for an appointment when you called. You'll be hearing from me."

"Parker? Thanks."

"Hang in there. This nightmare will be over soon."

Starks's hand holding the phone lay limp on the thin mattress. Every decision he'd made recently had been based on the knowledge—the firm belief—that he wasn't going anywhere until his full sentence was served, if then. Now he found himself in so deep there was no way out.

Wrong. He still could take Spencer up on his offer. But it would have to be isolation, not a transfer. No way would he go someplace where he'd have to start from scratch. Who knew what kind of shit he'd face with new people. No way would he put himself through that again. Not to mention he had no idea how far away a transfer would send him. Maybe even out of state. As he'd told Spencer, better the devil you know. Isolation for a month or longer wouldn't be easy. But it would be easier than before. Protective isolation meant no nutraloaf as punishment. An hour a day outside, if the weather was good. Protected showers. The amenities sucked, but they'd let him have books to read this time. Maybe even a radio.

But no cell phone. He'd have to use the regular phones and have a guard stand by. They might even put him in one of the camera-monitored cells, as an extra precaution. A guaranteed end to even the limited privacy he had now.

He cursed under his breath. Sure, he could find a way to tolerate the inconveniences. What he couldn't tolerate was abandoning the relatively innocent crew members to their inevitable fate. He'd gotten them into this situation. Plus, he still owed Seth, for Kane's sake. And Paco's. If he hid away, after all the shit he'd started, and more importantly, that others had started in his regard, he might get out alive, but he'd have to live with himself. Doing so would be hard enough as it was.

No way could he stop now. No way would he turn coward after facing all he had. Some would think choosing solitary was wise, others would despise him. They'd know he'd left them to finish what he'd started.

Besides, as he'd told Spencer, not even isolation could stop someone who wanted to kill him bad enough. So many people stood in line eager to do just that, they'd probably fight each other to see who won the privilege. Word would get out as to why he was in the Hole. That would motivate a few people even more. He had no doubt they had the means.

He'd see this through. Or die trying.

The seed had germinated long enough, accompanied by the constant niggling about how Tank hadn't answered him under threat of death or, rather, had.

CHAPTER 77

Ten till noon. There were things Starks needed to do. He debated whether or not to skip his shift that started at one. No. Nor was waiting an option. He'd take his phone with him. There were calls to make, aside from the later one to Jim. The office would provide enough privacy. He'd just have to keep watch through the window.

He checked the corridor then mixed the powders into paste, which he spread on the needle. Once the paste dried and the needle was hidden in his hem, Starks tucked the phone into his underwear, put the book back in its place on his desk, and grabbed two sandwiches from his stash. He'd be an hour early, but he needed more time on his side and as much privacy as he could garner.

As he walked, he glanced around warily, mentally took stock of who was left that he felt certain he could trust. Luke, for one. Ethan, for another, as long as he never got on the wrong side of him. Felipe and the Hermanos, yes. Wolly and his bunch—check. He hoped he was right about these people.

Jackson? Jackson seemed balanced on the brink of panic, so was moved into the questionable column. It wasn't that he thought Jackson would deliberately betray him, but Jackson wasn't as strong as he preferred to believe. Someone could get to him, and he'd crack under the pressure.

The word *betray* brought him back to Tank. Others had betrayed him since he'd arrived here, but not since Kayla had anyone shredded his faith in a person as she had, until Tank. It rankled him that he couldn't risk completely trusting any of his remaining crew members, but he had to act as though he did. For all he knew, some of them remained loyal to him, despite their fears about recent events. Anyone still loyal to him wouldn't begrudge what he'd had to do about Tank. Maybe that was nothing more than wishful thinking. However, several had expressed a desire to handle Tank themselves. He likely wouldn't know for certain who the loyal ones were, not until the fight began.

Starks marched across the library threshold, straight to the office where Sam sat with his eyes aimed at the computer monitor. "I'm starting early."

Sam leaned back in the chair. "It saddens me to think how we used to say hello and shoot the shit."

"Not my fault."

Sam sighed and nodded. "Yeah. I suppose that, as usual, you have something going on and want me out of the way."

"And with no reports to anyone. Or—"

"Or I take up space in a body bag. Got it. Sorry about Tank, and all the others. Any idea who's behind it?"

"Maybe I should ask you."

"Every damn thing is screwed up in this place." Sam pushed back on the desk and stood. "You feel safe enough in here?"

Starks gestured to the window. "Security glass. And, I'm going to close the door and lock it. Someone would need a rocket launcher to get in."

Sam came around the desk. "If I could go back in time …"

"We're stuck with where we are and who we are."

Starks locked the door then checked the window, punched in Parker's cell phone number again and fixed his eyes on the main room. He got voicemail, which he'd expected. And preferred. He didn't want to hear Parker's response when he said what was needed.

"Parker, shit happens here. I don't want you to worry, but if anything does happen to me, I want you to launch a major investigation into Sands and some of the key players, especially major inmates. There's corruption going on. I know this from a reliable source. I'm not able to give you more details now. Maybe later. But you're good at what you do. So is Rogers. Involve him as needed. There are some real assholes here but some good men as well. At the very least, they deserve an investigation done on their behalf. I'm sure everything will be fine.

You'll do your thing. I'll get out. And then I'll help you with the investigation. It has to be done. Thanks, buddy. Later."

He ended the call then called back. "One more thing. Just as a precaution, prepare papers that state, in the event of Kayla's death, and or mine, my mother is awarded custody of our kids. I don't know if Kayla's taken care of that as yet or not. Maybe check with her. Get this done ASAP, and have Jeffrey sign. Giving him my power of attorney was one of your better ideas. Let him put it to good use."

The next call could be more complex, but not the most difficult one he had to make. He'd save that one for last. He dialed his mother's number.

"Who is this?" she barked into the phone.

Starks smiled. "Hi, Mom."

"I don't like it when there's no caller ID. How are you, son?"

"Well enough, I suppose. You and the family? All okay?"

"I never thought I'd live long enough to say that Kayla and I are getting along. We still don't like each other much, but she needs help from someone in the family, and I'm it. As soon as she told her family how ill she is, they disappeared. I'm filling that void as best I can."

"They always did put themselves first. Thanks for helping her and the kids. I appreciate it more than you know."

"I may harbor a grudge, but I'm not heartless."

"No one would ever say that about you. Feisty, yes, but not heartless. Listen, I asked Michael Parker to prepare the papers for you to get custody of the children. Just in case that needs to happen. Call him tomorrow to make sure he follows through as soon as possible."

"I will. I know it isn't easy for you, but it's the right thing to do."

He wanted to tell her Parker's news, but he wouldn't. It would be cruel to raise her hopes only to, perhaps, have them crushed if he didn't make it out of Sands. "Thanks again. For everything. Please give my best to the family, and … I love you."

"That's it. What's wrong?"

He spoke past the lump in his throat. "I just thought it was time I told you."

"Well."

He heard her sniffle, pictured her fishing for the tissue tucked into her sleeve.

"Well." She blew her nose. "I love you, son."

"Gotta go. I'll call again soon."

He ended the call before she could say anything else. Maybe this was somewhere in the realm of what it was like for those who knew they had little time left to say what they felt. Or to make their goodbyes. Like Kayla. If it felt this way to say a limited version to a parent, when a person's demise was still an unknown, it had to be hell to say the real thing to a child. He wondered if Kayla had had such a conversation yet. Or, perhaps, was waiting for when she knew the time was getting closer.

There were more calls to make, but he needed a moment. He turned the phone off, placed it out of sight, and cupped his head in his hands.

CHAPTER 78

Starks made his call to Jeffrey a quick one. His lifelong friend was another person he couldn't bear to say, possibly, a final goodbye to. He posed his reason for calling as a thank you for looking after his family, including his mother, both emotionally and financially. Told Jeffrey to make sure Jim Rogers got a huge bonus for all his help. Made him promise to keep the private investigator in business. When Jeffrey asked if everything was okay, Starks assured him it was. Told him he occasionally needed to know everyone was being looked after since he wasn't there to do it. Old habits and all, he assured him.

Starks glanced at the clock. Way too early to call Jim, and he wasn't ready to make the last call on his list. Not yet.

He got up and walked to the window, checking to make sure nothing was amiss. Satisfied, he returned to the chair and ran through scenarios in his mind, those upcoming as well as ones past. Periodically, he looked at the time.

At three twenty-five, he checked the main room again, then drummed his fingers on the desk as he watched the countdown on the monitor clock. At precisely three thirty, he called Jim Rogers, listening intently as Rogers' words seared into his brain. There were times when confirmation was a bitch. Not that he hadn't believed he'd already figured things out for himself. But hearing it in absolutes was another matter.

He waited for four o'clock to come around, waited for his replacement to show up. When the man crossed the threshold, Starks put the chair back in its place and left, ignoring the man's complaints about having so much work to do and his query as to what the hell he'd been doing all this time.

Starks returned to his cell, rechecked Jackson's work schedule taped to the wall. He was scheduled to work the lunch and dinner shifts. At five, when everyone in his block headed to the chow hall, he'd make the call he dreaded most.

He took a seat at his desk and pulled the envelope containing the comb from where he kept his small treasure hidden. Recalled brown eyes so like Nathan's fixed on him, watching him. Pleading with him for acceptance.

If it was the last thing he did, he'd exact payback for what had been done to his son.

CHAPTER 79

Six minutes after five. Starks stood at the door and trained his ears to listen for any sound in the otherwise silent block. He needed an hour, but that was a luxury he didn't have. Some of the inmates would return to their cells not long after they ate dinner. Most wouldn't return until several minutes before the six o'clock count. His call had to be finished before then.

On his bed, large book in place, he dialed Kayla's number. "It's me."

"I thought you'd call before now."

"There were many times I almost did. How are you and the kids?"

"I'm still here." Kayla's attempt at laughing caused a coughing spasm. Before Starks could ask, she said, "I'm okay.

"The kids missed you for the holidays but were afraid to leave me. They watch me like a ticking bomb, which is what I am. But they thought you'd at least call. We all did."

Starks blinked away tears filling his eyes. "It wasn't easy, but I thought it was necessary. Too hard. You know?"

"I *sort* of get that. Still, they wanted to talk to you. We all did."

"Are they with you now?"

"I told them to do something while I took a nap."

"That means I disturbed you."

"No, I'm glad you called. It's what I tell them so I can have some alone time."

"My time is limited, but—"

"I know what *that's* like."

"Damn it, Kayla."

"My attempt at humor, again."

"Maybe hold off on that for a few minutes."

"You sound serious."

"I don't know if you did anything legal about the kids yet, but I took it upon myself to ask Parker to draft custody papers listing my mother as their legal guardian after … Just in case."

"Leave it to you to handle what I put off."

"You're not upset with me?"

"I'm a lot more particular these days about what I allow to upset me. There was a time when I would have fought to keep our children out of her reach, but she's descended on all of us like an angel in disguise, with a tiny mustache I'm aching to wax."

Starks laughed. "She told me she's been helping out."

"Blake stopped misbehaving, once she started showing up more often. She's moving in with us this weekend."

"I spoke with her a bit after noon today and she didn't say anything about that."

"She must have decided after your call."

"You're okay with it?"

"It'll be different, but it's giving me a needed sense of peace. Plus, Nanny Anita is being pulled in too many directions. It'll make it easier on all of us to have Lynn here." Kayla hesitated. "Starks, do you ever think about when we were first together, after high school I mean?"

"Sometimes. We were broke, struggling. Dining on Ramen noodles by candlelight, night after night."

"One candle at a time. We couldn't afford more. We were in love then."

"One of us was."

"About that—I lied."

Starks's spine stiffened. "What do you mean?"

"I did love you. But I was terrified of feeling so consumed by it. I was afraid you'd hurt me."

Starks expelled a hard breath. "You were right."

"It wasn't all you did. You put up with me and my spending habits. So often, I felt guilty about what you went through then, but I believed if I … Nevermind. My point is that you promised to give me the world, and you did."

"Then why did you cheat on me?"

"Fear. Insecurity. Eventually, a sense of justification, once I knew you were cheating on me."

"I'm still arrogant enough to want to blame you for everything. Ozy. Blake. Speaking against me in court."

"Of course. The loyalty issue."

"It matters." He scrubbed his hand through his hair. "To be clear, I'm not referring to your escapades with men. I'm talking about being there for the person who's been there for you, no matter what. Then you picked Ozy over me, our marriage, even our children."

"I didn't pick Ozy. Not really. I chose illusion over truth. He made me feel appreciated when you didn't. Then he dropped the facade and acted like the bastard he was. It didn't take long before I discovered the true level of destruction I'd caused. Didn't know how to repair it, either. Couldn't let on, could I? Had to act as though everything was just the way I wanted it. Do you want to know why I cheated those last few years? The real reason?"

"More than what you just said?"

"I believed that if I made you jealous enough, angry enough, you'd straighten up and go back to making me your priority."

"Instead, I failed you again."

"And I hurt you back. Revenge exacts an awful price."

Starks aimed his eyes at the ceiling. "Sometimes, it's the only way."

"Are we still talking about us?"

"There are some things I need to tell you. It won't be easy for either of us."

"Maybe I don't want to know."

"I can't let you believe that you were the only one who … This is harder than I imagined. You're probably going to hate me. But I can't not tell you."

"How about this? How about if I say I forgive you, even before you say another word?"

Starks shook his head. "You've changed."

"Impending death does that to a person."

He shuddered at her words. Her imminent death was changing her for the better. His was not. The difference, he reminded himself, was that they were confronting very different enemies.

"Starks?"

"I'm still here."

"Take a deep breath and just say whatever it is."

He told her about Kyle first then Kane. When he finished, he let out a breath and shook his arms, which felt numb. He heard Kayla weeping softly. "I'm sorry to hurt you like this, especially now, but I needed to come clean with you."

"I'm not crying for myself. I'm crying about how many people we've hurt. I'm crying because you lost two sons and had to live with it in silence. Because you couldn't share your loss and pain with me. I'm crying about how this is going to end, when it could have been, should have been, different."

Numerous footsteps and voices moved closer to the block entrance. He was out of time. "I have to go. But I want you to know how much I care about you. From the first time I saw you, until now. And even after—"

"Let's stop. I don't think I can hear anymore. At least, not right now. I need to rest. Call again soon."

"Kayla …"

"Me, too."

He listened to the dial tone for several seconds before shutting the phone off. Wondered if this was the last time to hear her voice. Tightness in his chest deepened. He placed his hand over the spot, as though that might keep his heart and pain contained.

He'd thought he'd feel cleansed, lighter, after making his confession. He didn't. But there were no more secrets unrevealed between them. At least not ones she needed to know. She'd forgiven him. They'd both learned the hard lesson that regret came with tendrils that wrapped around a person's heart and mind, and squeezed the life out of them. The difference was, Kayla would be released from those thoughts and feelings far sooner than either of them wanted. He'd be the one left to carry them alone.

Unless someone put him out of his misery before death put Kayla out of hers. If it happened that way, she'd have the burden of regret thrust upon her. He'd do everything possible to prevent that from happening.

Tears streamed from his eyes. He put the phone and book away and went to the sink. The brittle-cold water offered some relief. He glanced in the mirror as he dried his face and neck. The tears he'd just washed away might be the last ones he ever had the chance to shed.

Tell yourself another one, Dragon Man.

CHAPTER 80

He'd give himself a brief reprieve then do what had to be done. It was intolerable to delay any longer than that. Starks waited until lights-out to tell Jackson to call a meeting.

Jackson lay in bed, in the dimly lit cell. "Got it. Four-oh-five, on the bleachers. What's the meeting about?"

"I'd rather say it just once."

"You really piss me off sometimes."

"At least it's just sometimes."

"I was being generous."

"Any rumors flying around?"

"Plenty. Although, short on actual facts. That is, if you're talking about Seth retaliating anytime soon."

"You read my mind."

"Used to could. Now there's a wall up. What's with that?"

"Go to sleep, Jackson."

"You still need me, you know."

"I need you to shut up."

"Fine. This is me shutting up." Jackson rolled onto his side, punched his pillow then rolled back. "There was a time—"

"Still waiting for silence."

Jackson punched his pillow again, mumbled obscenities, then was snoring in under a minute.

Anyone who said life was fair was wrong. Starks pulled the blanket up to his chin and waited for the sleep he knew wouldn't come.

After the count at eight, Starks made a quick call to Jim Rogers.

"More people to dig up dirt on?"

"No," Starks said. "This request is different, unusual. Matthew Demory's a counselor here."

"I remember."

"Locate his house."

"And do what?"

"Tomorrow night, disable his car. Nothing too serious."

"I can remove his distributor cap. He won't be able to go anywhere without it."

"Can he get another one easily?"

"Depends."

"Better flatten two of his tires, as well."

"You got a beef with him?"

"Just the opposite."

"Wanna tell me why I'm hindering this guy's mobility?"

"Not really. Contact Jeffrey to—"

"I'll add it to my tab. Just, one day, tell me what all this is about."

"If I can, I will. Later."

If there was a later.

CHAPTER 81

Starks grabbed a sweet roll and a sandwich before heading to his eight thirty shift. During the morning, he ran as much of his plan as he could predict, over in his mind repeatedly, as he shelved books and created busywork to keep his fear from causing him to change his mind.

Sam showed up at one o'clock. Starks nodded at him, but said nothing before exiting. It took restraint, but he managed to walk out casually, acting as though it was a day like any other.

He found Felipe in the gym, pulled him to the far side of the room and spoke in muted tones. The Hermanos continued working out but kept their gazes fixed on the two men. Felipe did the complicated handshake with Starks and returned to the mat.

Starks hurried toward the yard. At the windows on the double doors, he stopped to confirm Wolly and the skinheads were in their corner. He pushed open one of the double doors and walked straight, without looking anywhere but directly at Wolly. He repeated the same process as he had with Felipe, with one exception. He made it clear, before giving them the news, that they weren't to give any indication as to what he told them. No shouts. No cheers. No high-fives.

Two tasks accomplished, he returned to his cell, trailed by Roberts, who was making his rounds. He should tell Roberts what was going on, but that would defeat his purpose. Everything had to appear a certain way. One small cog out of place, even a nervous twitch, and the whole plan could shift against him.

Back in his cell, Starks wet a washcloth and wiped down his sweat-drenched face, chest, and arms. And waited for four o'clock.

Waited to assess the reaction he'd receive.

Starks took his position on the top riser, next to Ethan. Jackson sat next to Starks. Luke was absent, by Starks's preference. He'd talk with him separately. The remnant of the crew, those still willing to show up, took seats on the bleachers, heads turned toward Starks.

"Face forward. Pretend to watch the game, but listen carefully to me."

One of the newer members said, "Why we watchin' a bunch of spics?"

"You, whatever your name is, you're out. Anyone else who cares to make similar comments about people ready to defend us, can join him."

The inmate faced Starks. "Shit, man, why you being like that?"

"I said leave. Do you need assistance?" Starks's gaze remained on the man. "One more thing. If you value your balls, after you leave, you'll keep your mouth clamped."

The inmate cursed and muttered to himself as he stomped off.

Starks waited a few seconds then began to speak. "It's time. Tomorrow morning, here in the yard. My plan is to draw Seth into the yard by nine thirty. Some of his soldiers will be with him, of course, but likely not all of them, since he won't be expecting what we're going to give him."

He waited for the crew to settle down. "With all the recent searches, some of you may be missing shanks. If you've replaced yours or can, turn and look at me." Six out of twenty looked back. "Jackson, can you supply them?"

"I can maybe get ten, maybe thirteen."

"Get them to the library by eight forty-five tomorrow."

"How the hell do you expect me to do that?"

"Can you do it or not?"

"Shit. I'll find a way."

Starks leaned toward Ethan and whispered, "Be in the library by eight thirty. You need to unpack a few things." He waited for Ethan to indicate he understood.

Jackson cleared his throat. "I thought you said we were going to wait for Seth to make the first move."

"I've decided his attack on me was the first move. I'm not going to wait for another one or for him to go after any more of you." The lie produced the reaction he needed to see. "However, it needs to look as though it was his move."

"How," Jackson asked, "do you plan to accomplish that?"

"Ethan, how would you feel about being bait?"

A few heads swiveled to look at him and Ethan then turned quickly back.

Ethan laughed and clapped his hands.

Starks said, "Just after nine thirty, once Seth is out here, Ethan's going to annoy him or one of the others. Get them to go after him. That's our signal to launch our attack."

"That'll work," Jackson said.

"And," Starks said, "any of you so much as thinks of betraying me or the crew by blabbing to anyone, or so much as talks about this where anyone can overhear you, you will regret it beyond what you can imagine. I hope you're all clear on that. Understand something. This isn't just for me. This is for all of us. There's a cancer in this prison, and it's time to remove it. Whether we like it or not, the task falls on us." Starks leaped off the back of the bleachers and came around to the front. As he did this he said, "Eight forty-five. Library. Anyone not there will pay the price. Any questions, now's the time."

He faced them and waited. Comments of "We're with you," and the like spilled forth.

Starks gave them a few more instructions then left without looking back. How many of them might be lying was anyone's guess. But he could only go with what he had.

Back in his cell, Starks used his thumbnail to loosen the screws on the base of the toilet. He wedged an envelope underneath, and used it to remove the two replacement shanks Jackson had hidden there after the others had been lost in a fight. He grabbed Jackson's roll of duct tape and wrapped one end of each shank with enough tape to protect the user's hand, but thin enough to still be hidden without making much of a bulge. He hid one shank in the thick book, the other in the back of his waistband.

He made his way to D Block, booted the *client* out of Luke's cell, telling him he needed a couple of minutes.

Luke slouched back in his chair. "What's up?"

Speaking low, Starks said, "Rumor has it there's going to be an attack on one of my crew tomorrow morning. Around nine thirty. In the yard."

Luke narrowed his eyes. "That's pretty precise."

Starks shrugged. "I just hope it's accurate information."

"Why would you hope that?"

"Because, if it's true, maybe this time I can stop it."

Luke leaned forward. "You think it's Seth, intending to kill another one of your men. Am I right?"

"I think it's a possibility. If the information is good, we need to be there to stop it."

"We?"

Starks glanced back to make sure no one was watching. He removed the shank from his waistband and held it out for Luke to take.

Luke held up his hands in rejection. "What's that for?"

"I've asked my crew to be in the yard around that time, just in case we're needed. I'm not going to ask the same of you, even though I did before. I'm going to leave it up to you. At the very least, you should have a way to defend yourself in the event someone comes after you. Guilt by association matters in here. Some guy could come in here, acting innocent, and while you're not looking …" He placed the shank on the desk. "Hide it where no one can readily find it. Just make sure it's someplace where you can get to it if you need it."

"Thanks, I think."

"As I said, I leave it up to you whether or not to show tomorrow."

"I'll give it thought."

Starks pointed. "Hide that thing now, before I leave. And don't tell anyone what I've told you. If you talk, someone will definitely see to it that you never utter another word."

"I understood about the code the first time you told me."

Luke looked around his cell.

Starks shook his head. He grabbed the biggest book on Luke's shelf and opened it. "Put it in here."

Luke placed the knife on the open page. Starks closed the book and replaced it, covering it with others. "Watch your back."

"You do the same."

Starks nodded at the men waiting on line outside the cell. He turned left at the corridor entrance then left again into his own block.

Jackson was waiting for him, pacing back and forth. "All the talking and worrying about it, and now it's really going to happen."

"Like any medical procedure, you fret about it, about what might happen, and then it's over. You're relieved and chastise yourself for being so anxious."

Jackson sat on the edge of his chair, clasping and unclasping his hands. "I've got a bad feeling."

"It's scary shit."

"More specifically, I'm scared tomorrow's gonna be the last time I see you."

"I'm touched."

"Yeah, in the head."

"What about the shanks?"

"I'll come through." Jackson nodded toward the toilet. "Forgot about the two under there."

"I didn't. I took one for myself and gave the other to someone."

"You should've asked me. Did it cross your mind that I might need one?"

"You've got a kitchen filled with possibilities, and friends in low places who work in there with you. Each one of them can get their hands on something."

"Guess I'm feeling antsy about the short damn notice."

"Better if everyone worries about it for as little time as possible, including you. You've been unusually skittish lately."

"I'm way past skittish. Because I live with a man with a damn dragon tattoo who thinks he's invincible."

Starks glared at Jackson. "I never said I was."

"But ain't it lucky how you keep making it through whatever shit gets thrown at you."

"That's one way to put it."

"No other damn way to put it."

"What the hell do you want me to do?"

Jackson looked directly at Starks. "Beat the odds again."

CHAPTER 82

Seated on the top riser, Starks periodically glanced at the double doors. Some of his crew sat with him. Others had taken their designated positions around the yard, several closer to the doors, where Seth and his men tended to congregate. Despite the cold, a sheen of sweat covered Starks's forehead. He and his men, Wolly's gang, and those aligned with Felipe were the only ones not wearing the thin coats provided by the prison. Yet, none of them shivered in the brisk wind and light snow, at least not as a result of the weather.

Wolly and his men occupied their usual corner, doing a good job of acting the way they normally did. Felipe and some of his men stood at the fence line, directly across from Starks, pretending to watch and cheer the Hermanos and another Hispanic gang aligned with Starks, play basketball.

If all had gone well, one of Felipe's men had gotten word to Seth, via one of his soldiers, that he knew Starks's plan and would tell Seth in the yard. That if he was a few minutes late, wait for him. That, at the latest, he'd show by nine forty-five.

Starks's jaw tightened as both doors opened and Seth and eight of his men strutted toward their spot in the southernmost part of the yard. Seth caught him staring and sneered before Starks looked away. Starks focused on Felipe, who was to give the signal.

A bead of sweat trickled down the left side of Starks's face. He left it there. His palms remained dry, as should those of his crew. All of them had powdered their palms, as instructed.

Felipe gave the first signal. Ethan had entered the yard and approached Seth. Starks kept his eyes on Felipe, with occasional glances to his left. His heart thumped against his ribs. He sucked in deep breaths, willing himself to remain still until it was time.

Seth's men began to move into a circle around their leader. Starks aimed his head forward. Felipe gave the second and final signal. Starks looked left, able to see some of what was going down through a gap in the inmates. One of Seth's men had Ethan's arms pinned behind his back. Seth's first punch landed on Ethan's jaw. As though walking on sand, Starks trod down the risers. His crew followed him. He hoped Ethan held on as punch after punch was delivered to his slender torso.

Felipe and the others walked with measured steps toward the southern section. Starks checked to make sure his other crew members did the same.

One of Seth's men said something. Seth took his focus from Ethan. His malicious grin spread wider. He spoke to the man, who turned and ran inside the building.

The man yanked open one door and bolted inside. Luke exited the other door, surveyed the scene and spotted Starks watching him from amid the approaching throng. He gave one nod of his head, which Starks answered in kind.

The sun hung low in the eastern sky. The prison blocked direct sunlight over the shadowed section where Seth stood but shined in tower guards' eyes, all according to Starks's plan.

He reached the halfway point in the yard. The attack on Ethan halted as all eyes shifted to Starks. Ethan, still in the grip of the man restraining him, hung like a rag doll. Blood dripped from his mouth, nose, and cuts to his face.

The double doors burst open. More of Seth's soldiers poured into the yard. Seth moved one flap of his coat to the side, reached behind him and laughed as he pulled a long knife from his waistband. His sneer stretched into a toothy yellowed smile. The remainder of his men drew shanks from wherever they'd hidden them on their person. The man dropped Ethan, who lay still on the ground, and pulled his own weapon out.

Starks and the others continued forward.

Ethan moved slug-like over dirt and snow toward where the skinheads waited. One of them lifted him to his feet.

Starks and the others were mere yards from Seth. They withdrew their own weapons. Starks smiled with satisfaction as realization struck Seth. This showdown had been planned.

Seth limped forward a few feet. Starks stopped and stayed where he was.

Seth grinned and said, "Maybe you want I should call a truce."

"Maybe not."

"Then maybe you need to look behind you."

Starks glanced over his shoulder. Three dozen or so inmates flanked his people. Felipe looked back as well. Made eye contact with Starks and winked.

Starks turned back to Seth. "Any last words?"

"Yeah. Time to kiss your ugly ass goodbye."

CHAPTER 83

Seth and his men launched forward. Shanks cut through air and skin and muscle. Fists and feet made contact. Red splattered and mixed with snow and mud beneath their feet. Starks fought off three of Seth's men—he was determined to reach Seth. So determined, he removed the prepped needle from his hem and used it on one of the men. In the chaos, the needle flew from his hand.

Rifle cracks split the air as tower guards fired rubber bullets into the crowd. Some of the men went down but only temporarily. Too much adrenaline flowed for the stings to stop them.

The alarm blasted, covering most of the screams. The call of Red Dot blared from the outdoor speaker. Other guards spewed into the yard through the double doors. Aware they were outnumbered, guards clustered on the sidelines where they conferred among themselves.

Seth wobbled on his unstable leg but stayed upright, slashing at anyone who came near him.

Movement to Starks's right drew his gaze. Ethan crawled until he was behind Seth, whose attention was directed at his nearest attacker. Ethan winked at Starks, sat back, and, with force, slammed his foot into the back of Seth's injured knee. Seth bellowed, hit the ground, and clutched his knee to his chest.

Like players guarding the star quarterback, Felipe and several Hermanos cleared the way for Starks. Using their bodies, they shielded him from view as he approached Seth, who screamed and writhed in the muck.

Ethan pulled an icepick from his waistband and thrust it between Seth's collar bone and upper arm. He pressed down with his weight, pinning Seth's arm to the ground.

Seth flailed and sent his free fist into Ethan's face. Ethan shook off the blow, grabbed Seth's free arm, wrenched it with full force, dislocating the shoulder. With a small leap, he landed on Seth's legs.

Starks grabbed Seth by his hair. "You're one lucky bastard."

Seth spit blood onto Starks's face.

Starks left the red spittle where it landed. "Know why you're lucky?"

Seth, eyes bulging, screeched obscenities.

"You're going to get off a lot easier than Kane did. I don't have the luxury of time to give you more of what you deserve." Starks drew back his hand holding the shank.

Ethan said, "Let me do it."

"Why should I?"

"I'll do a faster, better job."

Starks gazed into the insanity in Ethan's eyes. Ethan didn't care how many souls he stripped from people's bodies. Maybe he didn't possess the capacity to care. Starks, however, did, and the thought disgusted him. Turning the task over wouldn't save him. Still, he cursed silently as he handed his shank to Ethan, who was right. Time was running out.

Seth laughed. "Big man. Too chicken-shit to take care of his own business. Gonna run to a corner and puke your chicken-shit guts out? Like your bastard kid?"

Starks's lips formed a straight line. "Do it."

Ethan dragged the sharp edge across Seth's neck. Warm blood spurted onto Starks's face, arms, and clothing. He looked away as the murderer of his son strangled on his blood. He wanted this over. Done with. Behind him.

Someone yanked Starks onto his back. Kicks landed on his torso and head. He struggled to shield his face and head as best he could.

Pepper spray sent inmates and guards into coughing fits. Eyes and noses streamed. Several inmates hit the ground, twitching as Tasers sent jolts of electricity into them. Others shrieked, cursed, and fell to the ground as rubber bullets were fired at close range.

Starks lay unmoving in the mixture of red, brown, and white, barely aware the war had ceased.

A guard near him said, "We're gonna have to hose 'em all down before we bring 'em inside."

Roberts squatted next to Starks and felt for a pulse. "First, we have to figure out who's still breathing." He stood and shouted, "All right. Let's do some triage here and get some of these men to the infirmary."

"Maybe we should get Doc Stewart out here, instead. Then we can call the meat wagon for the ones what ain't going nowhere but in the ground."

"Whatever it takes," Roberts said. "However, you and I are going to carry this one to the infirmary. He's still got a pulse."

Starks opened his eyes into slits as hands took hold under his arms and at his ankles. Roberts had his ankles. Eye contact was made. Roberts, his lips compressed, shook his head.

Starks closed his eyes, shut everything out. The war was over.

For all but one.

CHAPTER 84

S tarks shifted uncomfortably in the unforgiving chair. Stewart had kept him in the infirmary five days, releasing him after dinner the prior evening. Now the investigative council wanted their turn with him. Each man stared at him, at the bruises staining his skin, at bandages covering stitched cuts he hadn't felt when inflicted. Gingerly, he rubbed his taped ribs and waited.

After several moments of silence, Spencer, red-faced, shook his head. "Was it worth it?"

"You'll have to give me more information than that so I can answer." Starks grimaced as he attempted to find a position he could tolerate longer than a few seconds. Shackles around his ankles clanked against the metal chair legs.

"After all this carnage, you're still a smart-ass. Lucky for you, a tower guard reported Seth went after that guy who's not quite right. Ethan …" He searched through the files in front of him. "Last name—"

"I know who you mean."

"You should, since it seems he's one of yours."

"Someone like him needs people to look out for him."

"Yeah, and because of that, you got your war."

"I never wanted it, and I didn't start it."

"That second part is the only thing saving your ass from being shipped to Red Onion. Never saw so many damn weapons." He glared at CO Jakes, who stood at attention in front of the door. "And after all the damn searches that supposedly found every last one of them. What the hell is going on in this damn prison?"

Starks stifled a grin. "Not my area. I'm just on the receiving end."

"I've got a last nerve twitching, here."

"Understood. How long do you plan to keep us locked in our cells?"

Spencer shoved the stack of files forward a few inches. He yanked his handkerchief from his jacket pocket and swiped it across his damp forehead. "I'm opening them today. Anyone still has a bloodlust, let them kill each other off, for all I care."

"Even I know you don't mean that."

Spencer slammed his hand against the table. "The hell I don't." Kratz leaned over and whispered something. Spencer pursed his lips and nodded. "Of course, no one still alive is talking. I saved you for last. Not that I believed for one damn second you'd give me anything to work with. Ought to feed the whole damn bunch of you nutraloaf for a month. Too damn expensive. As it is, I'm suspending phone and visitation privileges for a month."

"Starting from the day of the incident or now?"

"Damn it. That's all you have to say?" When Starks didn't respond, Spencer said, "Retroactive." He waved to Jakes and Stone and said, "Get him back to his cell. Then go ahead and open the animals' cages before they start another damn riot. Warden's all over my ass, as it is."

Starks suppressed a groan as he raised slowly from the chair. He shuffled to the door and waited for the guards to open it.

Spencer called out, "Jakes. Take the damn shackles off. His wrist is bleeding."

Starks turned to thank Spencer but stopped the words from leaving his mouth. Spencer had his face buried in his hands.

Jakes removed the shackles and said, "Want to stop by the infirmary first?"

"I've seen enough of that place."

He'd rest a few days then take care of finishing this business once and for all.

CHAPTER 85

"Knock, knock." Luke entered the cell, pulled out Jackson's chair and lowered carefully into it. "It's good to be able to get out and walk around again."

Starks, prone on his bed, sat up with a groan. "You're healing okay?"

"Considering the beating I took. At least I gave as good as I got. Didn't need nearly as many stitches as you. You look like hell."

"You'd think I'd tire of hearing that by now."

Luke studied the kitchen schedule taped to the wall. "Sorry about Jackson. Did he have any family?"

"He never mentioned any."

"Must be why they buried him in the prison graveyard."

"It's a couple miles from here. I don't know exactly where."

Luke placed his gaze above Starks's head. "There are a good number of beds empty now."

"Won't be long before they fill them again." Starks rubbed his ribs. "Thanks for showing up."

"I wasn't going to."

"What changed your mind?"

"You were looking out for me. I had to return the favor. Only, it was worse than I expected." Luke rested back, frowning as he rubbed a sore area on his chest. "Word is, it was Ethan they went after."

"They knew it would trigger me."

"I also heard you planned it."

Starks huffed. "People, for whatever reason, love to attach my name to every bad thing that happens here. I'm used to it."

"At least Ethan made it. Poor kid. Any idea who slit Seth's throat?"

"I was too busy fighting my own battles."

"Right." Luke got up and put the chair back under the desk. He glanced at Jackson's shift schedule again than at the window. "I read an epic poem in high school about a leader who blundered big-time. He led his men into a no-win situation, but his men didn't know that. They trusted him. Fought with all they had in them and followed him to their death."

Starks kept his expression impassive. "What's your point?"

Luke faced Starks. "No point. It just came to mind. That's all. Catch you later."

Starks remained seated on the edge of his bed, unmoving, as the weight of Luke's words pressed him further down, to a place with no up.

CHAPTER 86

Despite the absence of Jackson's snoring, or perhaps because of it, Starks lay awake. For over a year, he'd been put into one situation after another, all with the potential of being a no-win. But as Jackson had stated, he'd continued to make it out, damaged but alive. Demory, were he sitting in front of him, would remind him of what he'd said, what seemed like eons ago: physical wounds heal far easier than emotional ones.

What the hell was he supposed to do? Give in? Give up?

Still, Luke's and Demory's words ate at him.

The counselor had tried everything but having him hauled physically to his office to see him. He'd flatly refused. He'd done Demory a favor by deterring his arrival at Sands that day. Even if he didn't know it was Starks's doing, he should be grateful he'd been kept away. And he should leave well enough alone.

Unable to find comfort in body or mind, Starks paced in the dark cell, pausing occasionally to lean on Jackson's former bed. He stared through the narrow pane of glass, into the empty yard. It was snowing again, as it had later the day of the fight. The white covering the ground had remained pristine that day, as no inmates had been allowed out. It had covered the blood, watered it down once the sun came out, causing evidence of their brutality to be absorbed into the soil.

He moved to the barred door and stared into the dimly lit corridor. Inmates were unusually quiet since the fight, some still recovering from their wounds. Some recovering from various surgeries that required they be locked in rooms in the mental ward at Grace Hospital.

Wolly was healing in his cell. Eleven skinheads had died.

Felipe and his men fared better, but still received wounds; though, none were life-threatening. Nothing remarkable about that. Felipe had trained his men well. So far, thirty-six inmates had died, either during the attack or not long after. Ten had been in his crew.

Now that they were free to move about, he should call a meeting, but he'd never arranged one before. Jackson had always handled that detail as well as so many others. Jackson had been a pain in his ass a lot of times, but only now did he realize how often and in what measure he'd relied on him.

Who could he possibly move into that position?

Had everything not gone off the rails, he would have arranged it so that Tank took over for Jackson—his duties, and even his bunk.

So much waste.

He desperately needed to get away from the oppressive atmosphere, away from these men and their attitudes, ignorance, and vile body odors. Needed to get away from floor-to-ceiling gray. Away from the ghosts; though, he doubted they'd stay within these walls, once he managed to get out.

He needed to get to Kayla before it was too late. And to his children. Before they wanted nothing more to do with him.

He needed green grass and trees and flowers and air that didn't choke a person.

Starks's pulse raced, his head throbbed. His breaths came in shallow gasps. He collapsed onto his mattress and pounded it with his fists. Ignored the pain. Ignored healing skin on the back of his hands that re-opened and bled.

I have to get out.

Starks gulped air. Told himself to get a grip.

There was still one score left to settle, and it had to be done before he went anywhere.

CHAPTER 87

The question in Starks's mind was, Should he act as though all was normal for a couple of days, and *then* handle the last detail? Should he, instead, handle it immediately? He believed, or wanted to, that he still had the element of surprise in his favor.

One person could settle this for him.

The library was open, one privilege the warden and council didn't dare revoke. He spotted Sam at the desk in the office and strode quickly toward the small room. He closed the door behind him.

Sam's face paled at Starks's clouded expression. "Is it my turn?"

It took Starks a moment to realize what was meant. "What I want from you are truthful answers."

Sam shook his head violently. "I told you, I can't talk."

"What if I make it so you can?"

"It'll never happen. I'll be a tool till I die."

Starks eased into the extra chair and stretched his legs out in front of him, ankles crossed. "Gabe Bianchi."

Sam remained silent, but his expression barely covered that the name had struck.

Starks steepled his fingers and stared at a point on the ceiling. "I asked myself who in this place could terrify so many guys who were, as a rule, considered too dangerous for polite society. I played with a few names. Tossed what I knew about them around in my head, but none of them really fit. Until I dropped Gabe's name into the top slot."

Sam swallowed hard, he checked the main room through the window. "Anyone gets wind of this conversation, we're both dead. And so are our families."

"Only if you're the windbag." Starks sat up and leaned forward. "The sonofabitch needs to be taken care of, in a permanent way."

Sam's eyebrows arched. "You're gonna try to kill Bianchi?"

Starks shook his head. "No. I'm going to succeed in killing him."

"Man, if I could believe that …"

"Believe it. He's got to be stopped. For that to happen more efficiently, I need some information. So, I want you to start talking."

"Crap." Sam rubbed his hands up and down his face. "There's only so much I can tell you. What is it you need to know?"

"First, why did Gabe want Paco's memoir destroyed? Did Paco have anything specific in there about him?"

"Paco wasn't no fool. Specifics would've gotten him killed a lot sooner. But that didn't stop him from dropping enough hints to create suspicion. Left clues for anyone smart enough to recognize them and look into things."

"How do you know this?"

Sam cracked his knuckles and avoided looking at Starks. "Skimmed through the Sands chapters before I deleted it from the computer."

"Damn it, Sam." He took a moment to control his anger. "Does Gabe know you read some of it?"

"Still got my nuts, don't I?"

"What happened to the hard copy?"

"Gabe got it. And don't ask me what he did with it, 'cause I don't know."

"Why didn't he simply force Paco to hand it over or destroy it? Why did Paco have to die?"

"Because that stupid old man gave it to you to read. Only someone in here with the right brains could've connected the dots. He figured you'd see what he was hinting at and do something about it."

"So Paco died because you told Gabe."

"It was him or me and my family if I didn't. Gabe would've found out somehow. Bastard always finds out. Makes me sick at my stomach every damn day, what happened to Paco 'cause of me."

"I figure Gabe has some guards in his pocket, but how is it that he gets the extraordinary privileges he does, including getting away with the shit he does?"

Sam checked the window. He wiped sweat from his upper lip. "Warden's on his payroll. I don't know for how much, just that it's enough to keep him looking anywhere but at Bianchi. And when Bianchi tells him not to look, he don't look."

"That clarifies some things. Since Gabe knew Paco was writing his memoir, why'd he allow him to complete it?"

"Said he wanted to read it. If it had gone differently, maybe he would've told Paco what to take out. Instead …"

"Paco gave it to me."

"Yeah."

"And that's why Gabe had my name carved into Paco's chest before hanging him."

"Yeah. Said he wanted to leave a clear message. Said it was one of those killing two birds with one stone kind of things. A message to Paco and everyone else, especially you. No one knew how much you'd read in it." Sam shifted in his chair. He chewed a fingernail off and spit it out. "Something else you need to know."

"I'm listening."

"Bianchi ordered the hit on Kane. Seth and the others did it 'cause they were ordered to. When the master orders you to do something, you do it. Or you're next, after your family I mean."

Starks went still. "There was no way, at that time, he knew Kane was my son."

"He didn't. Made that sick bastard friggin' giddy when he found out."

"Why Kane?"

"Cats torture mice before biting their heads off."

Starks took in what he'd heard. "I'm the mouse."

"Yeah. Only a matter of time before it's your turn. He still finds watchin' you twist entertaining." Sam studied Starks. "What are you thinking?"

"That the main question in my mind has been answered. However, I have one more question for you. What do you know about the black arrow?"

Sam's surprise was evident. "You know about that?"

"I'm waiting."

"I know I hate that it points to my ass."

"Not the info I'm looking for."

Starks listened intently for the next several minutes. When Sam finished, Starks stood up. "This conversation had better go nowhere."

"I swear on my family's lives."

Starks flung open the door.

Sam jumped up. "What are you gonna do now?"

"Take care of a few details and schedule an appointment."

Wolly, accompanied by eight of his men, walked past the library entrance seconds before Starks exited. "Wolly, hold up."

Bruises on Wolly's face and arms had faded to a dull yellowish-green. He bounced on his toes. "If you got another battle planned, we're ready. We'll pay back some of those mothers we missed."

Briefly, Starks considered using the skinheads for his final task. He decided against this. He needed those whose loyalty went beyond their warped biases. Those who couldn't be bought so cheaply. "I appreciate all you and your men did."

"Any chance to go after ni—"

Starks held up a hand. "Don't. Don't ever use that slur in my presence."

The skinheads muttered their protests. Without looking at them, Wolly held up a hand to silence them. "Man, I don't get you."

"There's a lot you don't get."

"You gonna give me that bleeding heart crap about everybody being equal? Forget it, man. The facts speak for themselves."

"In my experience, prejudiced people seldom concern themselves with facts. The only way you can convince yourself to hate a person because of the color of his skin, or any other lame excuse, is to fool yourself into believing they're not human."

"And the only way you can convince yourself they're not animals is to put blinders on. That way, you only see what you want to see, instead of what's staring you in the face."

"That example is as skewed as your logic."

Wolly looked momentarily confused. Then his expression shifted. "Yeah, well, what kind of excuse you wanna give for Tank and Seth? Huh?"

"My issue with them had nothing to do with race, and you know it."

"Call it whatever lets you sleep at night."

"One thing I've learned is that people's closed minds won't open until they see that what most of us have in common is greater than our differences."

"Whatever. Stick to your delusion. I'll stick to the truth."

"We discussed our different opinions before we agreed to join forces. We also agreed to part ways, once the war was over." Starks held out his hand. "Guess we do that by agreeing to disagree."

Wolly stared at Starks's extended hand then shook it. "You'll be back."

"Don't count on it."

He watched them strut away.

Only one more score to settle.

Definitely better sooner rather than later.

CHAPTER 88

S tarks glanced behind him then rapped on the workroom door. It took several seconds before he heard the bolt thrown and the door opened. "Okay if I come in?"

Gabe shrugged, waved him in then pushed the bolt back into place. "That was some brouhaha last week. Looks like you're healing well enough."

Starks waited for Gabe to take a seat at the small table then sat across from him. "Sorry you missed it?"

"Nah. I'm too old for that physical shit."

"Maybe so. But I think your avoidance is for a different reason. I think you're someone who prefers to fly under the radar. That way, your signature is never on your work and never obvious to anyone not in the know."

Gabe slouched back in the chair and narrowed his eyes. "Wanna tell me what you're getting at or do you wanna dance around the maypole some more?"

Starks's lips twisted into a wry smile. "Of course. You like to get to the point, don't you? Like it delivered straight. Like an arrow."

Gabe crossed his arms and watched Starks through half-closed lids. "Well, well. You're finally getting interesting."

"I admit a certain measure of humiliation. And deference. All my talk to my crew about the importance of loyalty. And my threats if they betrayed me or the men." Starks laughed without amusement. "Kindergarten stuff, compared to you."

"Looks like you're smarter than I credited you."

"I only threatened their lives. You threatened their families, as well as their own necks."

Gabe shrugged. "When you work with animals, you gotta remind 'em who the biggest animal in the kingdom is. Gotta be vicious so they don't ever forget who they're dealing with."

"That's why your black arrow is twice as big as theirs, I suppose."

Gabe snickered. "Caught on, did you?"

"Paco. And Tank and those other guys so eager to be part of my crew. Thankfully, not all of them. No wonder you knew nearly every damn thing I was doing."

"You still surprised me from time to time."

"Because I didn't tell everyone my business."

"As I said, slightly smarter than I gave you credit. How'd you find out about the arrows?"

"I didn't realize until later that I'd seen one on Paco's back in the showers. I figured if he had one, it was possible others did as well. That made me suspicious. Came up with a reason for my crew to go shirtless and not question it."

Gabe nodded. "Got what you were looking for. Then you killed 'em, or had 'em killed, is more like it. Bet it bunches up your tighty-whites to have that in common with me."

"Frankly, yes. But there are differences. Donny Mortelli. Stefano Rossi."

Gabe's eyebrows shot up. "You have been busy."

"I've got a good private investigator on my team."

"What's his name? I'd like to give him some business."

"Bet you made it a point to tell every one of your recruits about those two men, about the *family practice*." Starks sneered. "Like father, like son."

Gabe shrugged. "Why reinvent the wheel when what you got rolls just fine?" He laughed and massaged his chin. "I was thirteen when the old man took me to watch their families receive the packages. Delivered 'en by courier. Wished we could've been inside when they opened the gift-wrapped boxes. Found their loved ones' heads inside, with a bow tied around them. But we heard the screams all the way outside. Afterwards, we went to Antonio's Bistro for stuffed manicotti and octopus salad.

"A week later, the old man snuffed out every member of the two families he could trace. 'Don't just eliminate 'em,' he told me. 'Get rid of their spawn as well.'" Gabe jabbed his forefinger against the tabletop. "That's why people in the business kissed my old man's ass and acted like it was a privilege. Hell, it was a privilege. Don't come across someone as powerful as him every day."

"Until you."

"Yeah." Gabe grinned. "Only here, it was more effective to reverse the order. Threaten to off the family first. Even you should be able to see the logic."

"Some of those your father killed were children."

Gabe shrugged. "All the same to me."

"You never tried to recruit me. Why is that?"

"Feeling left out?" When Starks didn't answer, Gabe continued. "I needed shit-for-brains street thugs who thought they were hot shit or guys ready to piss their pants out of fear of what I'd do to 'em. Monkeys I could bend however I wanted. That black arrow meant when I gave an order in this place, it got followed. When I gave a command for someone in here to off somebody, it got done or they took the person's place. You think you'd have signed on for that?"

"You knew better."

Gabe pointed at Starks. "Exactly."

Starks kept his voice calm. "Why did you order Kane's death?"

"Figured that out as well, huh? You got a busy mind. Maybe too busy." Gabe's shoulders lifted then dropped. "You were becoming competition. And you stood a good chance of being stiff competition. I just wanted you to be a stiff." Gabe chuckled then dropped the smile. "I'm top of the food chain inside. No way in hell am I gonna share that place or move over for some pissant wannabe." He leaned forward. "Am I making myself clear here?"

"Perfectly."

CHAPTER 89

tarks got up and walked back and forth slowly. "Your depravity isn't reserved for people unrelated to you, is it?" He faced Gabe. "You admitted you murdered your wife, and why. For all I know, you lied about her cheating and her plot against you. Maybe you killed her because you were in a bad mood. Maybe she overcooked your eggs that morning or your pasta went a minute past al dente. You also dropped a significant hint that it was you who killed your son. Your one and only child. How could you do that?"

Gabe waved a hand in a dismissive manner. "He really pissed me off. Said he didn't like the business. Refused to train to take over one day. What a pussy. Lost his lunch first time I took him out. You know all about that kind of thing, don't you? Said I was disgusting, called me warped, twisted. Proved to me where his loyalty wasn't."

"He was your flesh and blood."

Gabe slammed his hand against the tabletop. "He was a waste of space. An expensive one. A friggin' hazard waiting to happen. Hardest part was trying to work up a few tears at the funeral. Couldn't do it. Nodded all solemn-like anytime someone patted me and called me stoic."

"You're one sick bastard."

"That from a damn hypocrite. You claim one thing, while wiping blood off your hands. And, don't fool yourself. It's a lotta blood."

"You didn't give me a choice. Once I figured out what was going on, I knew it was only a matter of time. At the very least, the war would've started and I would've been ambushed by your guys. However, there's one big difference between how we operate, what our motivations are. I didn't kill your guys solely for my protection. I realized one of them might succeed. Then anyone else in your sights was a potential victim, especially anyone who'd had my back. No matter what was going on with me, the branches had to be pruned."

"You messed up my plans."

"Can't say I'll lose sleep over it."

"From what I hear, you're always losing sleep about something. Lost any sleep over Tank? How'd it feel to execute someone you trusted with your life?"

"I regret it. Especially once I realized you held the lives of his wife and children over his head. He'd already lost one daughter. Of course, you wouldn't understand how that feels. You're incapable of any emotion that isn't destructive or evil."

"Like I told you, you're not equipped to be at the top. Me? I get off on this shit."

"That's because you're psychotic."

Gabe's face and neck turned florid. "I don't like when people call me that. Makes me lose my temper."

"That's *your* hypocrisy slapping your two faces."

Gabe balled his hands into fists. "Start counting your days, you pathetic prick."

Starks rested back against the long worktable behind him. "The ironic thing is, I did all I did because I believed I had to. Had I realized I'd be getting out soon, I would've done everything differently. Well, most things. Some events I had no control over. I was forced to act. You saw to that."

"What's this bullshit about you getting out?"

"Heard from my attorney. Yep. It won't be long now."

Gabe slid from his chair. He walked to the worktable a couple of yards behind him, picked up a hammer and screwdriver then turned around.

Starks smiled and edged toward the door. "Want me to leave so you can get back to work?"

"You can forget leaving Sands." Gabe's eyes bulged, his lips formed into a sneer. "You can forget getting out of this room. You'll simply disappear. I'm expert at that. The smaller the pieces, the better they flush." Gabe licked dry lips and started forward.

Starks rushed to the door. He pivoted and said, "This is for Kane." He threw the bolt and opened the door wide. Ethan, Felipe, and seven of Felipe's strongest soldiers stepped inside.

Felipe said, "You can go now, amigo. We got this."

Starks exited the room and stood outside the door until he heard the bolt latch.

At the start of the muffled sounds behind the steel door, he walked away.

CHAPTER 90

Two hours later, as agreed, Felipe joined Starks on the bleachers. A light snow drifted to the ground from low, pallid clouds. An occasional breeze sent the white flakes bouncing through the air. Starks pulled his coat collar up and huddled in the cold. "I wonder how long before the alarm sounds."

"Could be five minutes. Could be five days. Maybe longer."

"Why the discrepancy?"

"Amigo, that Ethan guy is mucho loco. A friggin' genius but not right in the head."

"I'm damn lucky Gabe didn't stick a black arrow on *his* back. I wouldn't be sitting here now."

"Maybe, maybe not. Seems he's loyal to you. And, he's clever as shit."

"Want to explain that last part?"

"Couple reasons. First, Gabe knew something about Ethan we didn't." Felipe made eye contact with Starks. "Something you knew but didn't share."

"He made it clear I wasn't supposed to."

"Yeah. Except it seems you shared it with Gabe. Ethan wasn't happy about that. Then he saw the terror in that old man's eyes. That's when he got into it. He said if we valued our genitals and our tongues, we'd take his secret to our graves. Said he was your secret weapon."

"One of them. You said there were a couple reasons."

"After we finished with Gabe, we sanitized ourselves, right?" Starks nodded. "Ethan had us leave the room so he could bolt the door."

"Shit. He's still in there?"

"Let me finish. The workroom is in one of the first sections built. It's a lot older."

"And?"

"You ever notice ceiling tiles in there and the hall that leads to it?"

"No."

"Ethan did. He used the worktable by the door, and I don't know what else, to reach the ceiling panel above the door. He climbed over the friggin' wall. Dropped from the sky, man." Felipe laughed. "Had us lift him so he could put the panel back in place. They're going to need a blowtorch to get that door open. Now it's just a matter of when someone gets curious enough to look."

Starks shook his head. "I never would have thought of that."

"Guess whoever built the place all those years back, believed a drop-ceiling that high wasn't a problem. We're lucky they didn't fix that when they made additions. Anyplace else, we would've needed a different escape plan."

"Short of starting a fire, no way to get him to leave the room. Plus, the workroom has to be the most private spot at Sands. No cameras in the room or hallway leading to it—Gabe's idea, I bet—and a lavatory and chemicals to clean traces. What about your clothes?"

"Ethan said he bagged them and tossed them on top ceiling panels. Unless someone knows where to look, those clothes won't be found until they demolish the building."

"When Gabe *is* found, there's going to be a number of unhappy people inside and outside these walls."

"I can live with that."

Starks stared up at the clouds. "So can I."

CHAPTER 91

The next morning, after the count and as prearranged, Felipe and several Hermanos met Starks at the entrance to C Block. They walked together, stayed on line for their trays together, separating when it was time to sit at their respective tables.

Starks's steps slowed as he noted how many seating gaps were interspersed throughout the room. Wolly's table looked like one of those large cartons missing several eggs. From the enemies' side, starting back to when he'd arrived, absent were Sanchez, Lawson, Big Bo, Crazy D, Seth, Tank, Stinky, Pete, Big-Boy—those last four, prior members of Big Bo's gang. All gone, along with numerous others. He would never include Paco with their ilk. Paco belonged with Kane and Skullars. And Jackson and Tommy.

His own table seemed nearly empty. Relief welled in his chest at the sight of Ethan, Luke, Blackie, Mike, and a few others who hadn't been marked with a black arrow and never would be. Each man watched him make his way toward them.

Starks rapped on the table and sat next to Luke. He should express his gratitude to them, not just for their courage but for so many other reasons. There was a lot he should say, but the words wouldn't come.

What could people say to each other after fighting their way through hell and back, and after losing so much? How does a person talk around unseen wounds he doesn't want to admit to? Maybe the fact they'd each shown up at the same table was enough.

Starks cleared his throat. Felt their eyes focus on him. He looked at each one. His throat constricted and his eyes grew moist. He nodded once then pretended to wrestle with his food.

Luke elbowed him lightly.

Starks looked up.

"You did what you had to," Luke said. At Starks's stunned expression, he added, "No way to avoid that fight. Seth had done enough damage. I overheard some details I hadn't known. Had it been my son …" He stabbed a chunk of powdered egg onto his fork.

Overwhelm crashed down on Starks. He had to get out of the chow hall. Needed to get away from them. Get away from the various pretenses running in his mind at one time that threatened to collide. He rapped on the table and stood. "Need to get to the library."

His shift didn't start until one. He dumped his tray and walked at a fast clip toward his cell, turned left into his corridor and jogged the rest of the way.

Breathing hard, Starks paced inside the small space. One thought kept at him: he might actually get released from Sands in the near future but the effects of his time inside would never leave him.

CHAPTER 92

The library became a refuge of sorts. A place where Starks could escape into tasks, could even create needless ones, convincing himself of their significance. Anything to avoid the racket in his mind. Four days had passed since Gabe had taken his last breath, and still nothing. No alarm. No lockdown. No cell and strip-searches of inmates.

No way to know whether or not Gabe had ever informed the warden about his visits to the workroom or who the warden may have told. When the news broke, would the warden tell the council to look at him first? He'd lie, of course. But that might not save him, especially if the warden was pissed about losing the money he'd been so willing to take. Depending on how much it had been, perhaps he could pick up the payments. Get the warden on his side. At least until he was set free.

It was almost noon when Sam, face flushed, zoomed into the library. "Office. Now. I have something to tell you."

Starks followed Sam, wondering what had the man flustered this time.

Sam collapsed into the chair behind the desk. "Better close the door."

Starks did so then took a seat in the extra chair and waited.

"You don't have to worry about ending Bianchi." Sam laughed. "Sonofabitch killed himself. Just heard about it. Man, I feel like singing that song from that movie. You know, Ding-dong, the wacko's dead."

Starks went still for several moments. "Tell me exactly what you heard."

"Seems this morning some gizmo broke on the warden's fancy leather chair. He had a guard wheel it to Bianchi's inner sanctum. This guard, Powell—you know him? No? Anyways, he knocks and gets no answer. So he pounds on the door, right? Still no answer. Puts his ear to the door and hears nothin'."

"Any chance I can get you to cut to the chase?"

"Sure. So they call in a specialist with a blowtorch, to crack the door like an egg. The air inside leaks out and smacks him and the guard in the face."

Starks gripped the chair arms. "Sam."

"Some of the place is torn up. Bianchi's slumped in a chair in a back corner, rotting. They think maybe for days. Locked up tight as a tick in his lair."

"Why do they believe it's suicide?"

"Thought it'd be obvious. The door was *bolted*. Anyways, there's a hammer and screwdriver on the floor on either side of him. First thing, they checked fingerprints—Bianchi's, and only Bianchi's. Man, I wanted you to nail the sonofabitch in the worst way." Sam laughed again. "Bastard must've finally gone all the way crazy and saved you the trouble. That's good news, right?"

"Stunning."

"I thought you'd be happier."

"Still taking it in."

"Man, I feel reborn."

"Any idea how many more inmates have arrows?"

Sam shook his head. "Gabe kept that info to himself. Sure, every now and then, like in the showers, I'd see some guy and know he'd gotten hooked, but that's all."

"Anyone I should know about?"

"The few I knew about got removed in the yard. You shouldn't worry about that. Anyone with arrows are the muscle, not the brains."

Starks nodded, wiped his palms on his pants and stood. "Thanks for telling me.

"I'm gonna sleep like a baby tonight."

"I'm going to go finish my shift."

Starks returned to what he'd been doing. It hadn't gone the way he'd expected. It had gone better. His only concern was that once Gabe's former minions found themselves without their leader—those who'd relished their assignments—they'd look for someone to aim their radar at, someone to hold responsible. He doubted they'd believe the suicide story.

It was one more thing to sweat about.

About a half hour later, he heard his name called. He looked around and spotted Felipe standing outside the entrance. Felipe gave him a half smile and a quick nod before walking away.

Perhaps his luck truly was changing. Unless it was another trick the universe had chosen to play on him.

CHAPTER 93

The following Monday, Starks sat at the office desk, cataloging new magazines into the computer. Roberts knocked on the door. Starks pulled his attention from the monitor. "What's up?"

"Your attorney's here."

Starks's pulse quickened. "Does he look upset? Happy?"

"Didn't see him. C'mon. I'll walk you to the room."

Starks rushed to finish the entry then closed the program. He wasn't ready to mention anything about what he hoped Parker's appearance was about so stayed silent. Roberts wasn't talkative, either. He wondered if that should concern him, then decided to let it go. If Roberts didn't bring up the workroom incident, he certainly wouldn't. No reason to give even those on his payroll reason to connect him to Gabe.

Parker could be waiting to see him for any number of reasons, but only one he prayed it wasn't.

As soon as the door closed behind him, he said, "Is it Kayla?"

Parker, his hand extended, said, "Relax. I'm not bringing you bad news."

Starks's shoulders loosened. He shook Parker's hand then sat in the chair nearest the door.

Parker took his seat across from Starks. His somber expression split into a broad smile. "We did it."

"I'm getting out?"

"You'll be walking around in your Ferragamos soon."

"I don't understand. I thought you said there'd be a new trial."

"There was always a chance. I filed a writ of habeas corpus and an affidavit. That got me a court date. I brought Margaret Hessinger with me as my sole witness. I'd had a private talk with Judge Montrose beforehand and told him about the situation with Kayla, how dire it is. I also told him about all you've been through since you arrived here. Stated as a matter of fact that, based on Margaret's admission, or, rather, lack of one, you'd been placed in a maximum security prison when it should have been a less dangerous facility and a shorter sentence. Montrose owed me for something way back, so I used that to expedite the matter. Not to worry. Everything is completely legal and aboveboard."

"He agreed. Just like that?"

"He asked Margaret a few questions about the knife—why she lied about it at your trial, why she waited so long to come forward about it. She answered his questions, and told him Ozy finally admitted his intention to incapacitate then neuter you. Montrose came down just hard enough on her to make his point. Said the conviction was in some ways valid but in other ways not, because of Margaret's perjury and obstruction of justice. Therefore, the sentence was inappropriate. He amended it to time served. Because of her children, he fined Margaret a hefty sum, rather than jail time, which I paid and added to your billing."

"No argument from me."

"You're not as animated as I'd expected."

"I'm trying to take it all in. When do I leave?"

"Tomorrow."

Starks's mouth dropped open. "Seriously?"

Parker chuckled. "Montrose was easily persuaded, and he has pull. Anyone you want me to tell about your release?" He grinned. "Or should I tell everybody?"

"For now, no one but Jeffrey. And tell him to keep it to himself. Does the prison have to transport me or can he pick me up when I get out?"

"Jeffrey can do it. I'll firm up the details with the warden on my way out."

"No!"

Parker studied Starks for a moment. "That's an extraordinary reaction. I'm obligated to—"

"You'll have to trust me on this."

"An explanation would be better."

"Later. I promise. It's imperative they don't find out I'm leaving, not until Jeffrey shows up to drive me away from this place."

"I'm sorry, Starks. That's not how it works. I gave the paperwork to the warden's assistant when I arrived."

Starks blew out a hard breath. "It is what it is."

"I wish you'd help me to understand."

Starks shook his head.

Parker pushed his chair back and stood. "Anything else you want to talk about? Anything I can do for you in the interim?"

"Nothing I can think of. If anything comes to mind, I'll call you." Starks walked around the table and clasped Parker's hand. "I don't know how to thank you."

Parker rested his other hand on Starks's shoulder. "Remember that when you get my bill."

Starks smiled. "Expect a bonus."

"Getting you free is bonus enough."

They exited the room at the same time. Roberts waited in the hallway. Parker went one way, Starks and Roberts went in the opposite direction.

"Everything okay, Starks?"

He should tell Roberts so he and the others could provide additional protection. But fear of word getting around stopped him. Fear of how Roberts and the other guards on his payroll might react to their funder leaving them. Fear that one of them might talk. Fear of jinxing himself. "Just needed to address some personal matters. At least things here are quiet for now."

"Yeah. We'll see how long that lasts."

They reached Starks's section. Roberts signaled for the door to be opened. "Catch you later."

CHAPTER 94

Tomorrow would come both soon and not soon enough. There were details, significant ones, Starks needed to attend to. He moved quickly through the corridors to the gym, where he found Felipe and several Hermanos working out with weights. He caught Felipe's attention and motioned for him to join him.

Felipe grabbed a towel and wiped his face as he walked toward Starks. "Why do you look so jumpy? Something happen?"

"I have business to discuss with you."

"I'm listening."

"Not here. I'd rather talk on the bleachers. Can you interrupt what you're doing and go with me now?"

"No problemo. I'll tell my guys."

"Actually, it's probably a good idea to bring them. But, I want to talk to you alone."

"Give me a second."

Felipe returned to his men, spoke in low tones. They nodded and moved toward where Starks waited. The nine men exited the gym and made their way into the yard.

Starks climbed to the top riser. Felipe joined him, as the Hermanos stood in a cluster several yards to their left.

Felipe, elbows resting on his knees, said, "Is this good business or bad?"

"Depends on how you look at it, I suppose. I'm getting out of here."

Felipe laughed. "You've gone loco, amigo. No one breaks out of Sands."

Starks explained the shift in his circumstances.

Felipe said nothing for a few moments. "Mañana. Lucky S.O.B."

"I'm thinking it's a good idea not to spread that news."

Felipe nodded. "Probably right."

"There are a couple of things I have to set up before I leave. For instance, I'd appreciate it if you'd have the backs of what's left of my crew."

"I'll see to it. Anything else?"

"Watch my back until I'm out of here."

"Done."

"Last thing. Tell me your parents' address. As soon as I get somewhat organized, I'll visit them and make sure they still have what they need."

Felipe gave him the information. "What are you going to tell them?"

"That their son is a model prisoner and an example of integrity." Starks faced Felipe. "That you saved my life and the lives of other inmates, and I owe you."

"You don't owe me."

"That's a matter of opinion."

Felipe nodded and looked straight ahead. "Never did get my dragon tattoo."

"Don't. Someone like you doesn't need to wear any label but his own."

"What's the first thing you're going to do when you get out?"

"Your guess is as good as mine about that."

"I wouldn't need to guess. I'd find me a beautiful woman and a couple bottles of Tequila."

"Sounds like a plan."

"The simple pleasures, amigo. You want to stay happy, keep everything simple."

"My life has never been simple."

CHAPTER 95

S tarks and his crew moved together in the line for lunch trays. As they moved forward, he said, "From now on, we sit at Felipe's table.

Luke was the one to break the stunned silence. "Why would we do that?"

"Our numbers have significantly decreased, as you're well aware."

"I thought the threat was over."

"Thompson, you're one of the few guys who gets to live in a bubble in this place. The threat is never over."

"But—"

"Sit with us or sit alone. Your choice. I hope you play it smart."

Starks and his crew took their places at the Hermanos' table. Everyone noticed, including the guards. Without broadcasting any announcement, the forged alignment had been made clear. Starks's men would be as safe as he could make them.

Several times, he came close to revealing his impending release to his crew. Each time, he stopped himself. The fewer people who knew the better. They'd find out tomorrow. Maybe they'd feel abandoned. Or betrayed. But then they'd realize he'd done what he could to look after them in his absence.

Between bites, he studied their faces. Flashbacks flooded his mind. Other memories filled him as well. As much as he wanted to rap on the table and leave, go somewhere where he could be alone, it would be imprudent to do so. Just like waiting for tomorrow to come, he'd wait on the group.

With the exception of times for the counts, Starks stayed with Felipe and the others. He deliberately made it into his cell seconds before the barred doors groaned shut and the lights dimmed at nine.

His last night in Sands. In this cell. Sometime tomorrow, he'd take an actual shower—alone—in a real bathroom. He'd stand under the stream until the water started to run cold. He'd eat real food again, drink fine wine and martinis again—three olives. Wear real clothes and leather shoes again. Would sleep in a real bed, with a mattress that cushioned his body, and between sheets with a thread count well over three hundred, his head nestled in a real pillow.

Where exactly would he be doing all these things? The question caused him to sit up in bed.

Maybe it was a good idea to spend the first night at Jeffrey's house. It seemed the logical way to ease back into his life.

He had a house where all his possessions, including his clothes, remained. But Emma lived there. Or maybe she'd moved. Last time they'd spoken, he didn't specifically tell her to stay there, nor had she mentioned any intention of moving out.

Starks glanced at the clock. Three minutes until guards started the ten o'clock rounds. He jumped out of bed, brought the book and phone back to his bunk, and dialed Jeffrey's number.

"It's me."

"Damn, bro! You're getting *out*. Parker's a friggin' miracle worker. I'll be there at eleven on the nose. I went shopping today. Got you new clothes and shoes. I hope I got the sizes right."

"As long as you didn't buy anything gray or beige, I'm sure it'll all be fine. I don't have but a few seconds to talk. Is Emma still living in my house?"

"Yeah."

"You're sure?"

"Made it a point to drive by every other day. Wanted to make certain it was still standing and occupied. Went by yesterday. Is her being there a problem?"

Starks heard a guard turn into the corridor. "Not with me. I have to go."

It was another option possibly still open to him.

He put the book away and returned to bed.

And, of course, there was his former home, where Kayla and his children were. Maybe his mother's house, where he could be alone that first night, since she was staying with Kayla and the kids.

These options were contingent on how he felt once he was out, as well as on others' reception of this fact. He couldn't afford to assume anything.

Nor was he certain what it would be like to spend his first night of freedom alone.

He hadn't been alone in over a year.

However, this would be his chance for a fresh start.

What it should be and would be might be a distance apart.

CHAPTER 96

At the sound of the doors clanking open, Starks, who'd fallen asleep sometime after four, jumped as though scalded. Once his breathing returned to normal, he launched into his morning routine. Now it was a matter of waiting. Shortly, he'd be counting minutes, not hours. Or years.

Most inmates would either be bagging their possessions or sitting next to the stuffed bag as they waited for a guard to escort them through the doors that led to freedom. He didn't want to draw that kind of attention. Still too much of a risk to clue anyone in.

He cleaned his body as thoroughly as he could at the small sink, then put on a fresh scrub set. Washed his hair using a plastic cup that needed to be filled numerous times to get all the shampoo out. He shaved, nicking himself a few times as he dragged the razor across his skin with hands that refused to stop shaking.

Starks returned to his bed, eyes focused on the cell entrance. His eyes darted to the book where he'd hidden the shank Felipe had given to him. Tucked it into the back of his waistband. Better to be prepared than not. It wasn't as convenient to hide as the knitting needle had been, but a person had to go with what was available. Nor was he able to poison the tip. The Latex thumbs kept in his pants pockets had been disposed of, along with his bloodied, ripped clothes.

Finally, the eight o'clock count was called. Once over, Starks joined Felipe and the others. Ate every bite of the crappy breakfast, for the sole reason of committing it to memory. One thing he never wanted to do, as he'd been wont to before Sands, was to ever again take anything about his life outside these walls for granted.

He went with the gang to the yard after breakfast. Ordinarily, it would be a way to pass the time until his shift started at one. Ordinarily, he'd inform Sam that he wouldn't be in. One way or another, Sam would discover that his resignation had been tendered permanently.

Starks declined to play basketball. But he cheered louder than he'd done before, checking the time every few minutes.

Felipe leaned in. "Amigo, stop fidgeting."

"Why is it as excruciating to wait for something you want to happen as it is for something you dread?"

"You sure you're supposed to be out by eleven?"

"I'm sure."

Felipe glanced at the clock over the double doors. "Less than fifteen minutes. How come no one's come to get you?"

"I don't know how this is supposed to go. You think I should have waited in my cell?"

"I think they'd find you wherever you are, or would have said something earlier."

Starks lurched to his feet and stared at the clock. "Damn it."

"Maybe it's nothing. Don't let it get to you."

"Too late."

"I shouldn't have said anything."

"No. You're right. Something is wrong. I have to find out what's going on."

"We need to go in for the count. Find out then."

Felipe leaped from the riser. He whistled and pointed to the clock. The Hermanos, along with Starks's diminished, soon-to-be-former crew, started toward the doors.

Starks waited just outside his cell for the eleven o'clock count. The announcement came over the intercom. He prayed it was the last time he ever had to hear those words.

Sweat beaded on his forehead.

CHAPTER 97

Roberts and Jakes started, as always, at the first cell opposite Starks's side of the corridor. Tucked under Roberts' arm was a bundle wrapped in brown paper. Starks's eyes trailed the guards, as though doing so might give him the information he craved. In what seemed an interminable amount of time, the guards reached him.

Roberts handed the package to him. "Stay in your cell after the count."

"What is this?"

"Your going-away clothes."

Jakes snorted. "You could've told us you were getting out."

Inmates to the left and right began to murmur among themselves, passing the news along. Starks didn't have to look to know inmates' eyes, up and down the corridor, were aimed at him. The energy coiling in their bodies was palpable as they waited for the count to be over so they could rush off to make the announcement to whomever might be interested. That worried him. Too many might be interested.

"I wanted to keep the news quiet," Starks said.

"Did a good job of it." Jakes moved to the next cell.

Roberts nodded. "Won't be the same."

"For me, especially."

"Soon as I finish at the last cell, I'll come back and escort you."

"Is my ride here?"

"He's been parked out front for a half hour, from what I heard. I'll be back in about two minutes."

Starks pivoted and stayed where he was. It was really happening. In two minutes, he'd start the walk he'd believed he'd likely never make. He brought the bundle to his bunk, tore the wrapper off, and stripped. Jeffrey's guess about sizes was a size too large, but who cared. He slipped his feet into silk wool socks, stepped into wool slacks with a crease he could cut himself on. The cashmere jacket went over the cashmere turtleneck sweater. Every item tasteful shades of charcoal brown. The Ferragamos were a little tight, but they'd walk him out of Sands.

"Where's your stuff? Most guys get everything ready the night before."

Starks turned and grinned at Roberts. "What do you think?" He gestured at his clothes.

"So this is what you look like." Roberts pulled papers stapled together from his shirt pocket.

"What's that?"

"Release forms. It's usually a more formal process, but the warden wanted it expedited." Roberts pulled a pen from his pocket and handed it to Starks. "Sign anywhere with a check mark."

Starks did as instructed.

Roberts put the forms back into his shirt pocket. "Okay, grab whatever you're taking with you, and let's go."

Starks handed the large book that held the two cell phones to Roberts. "Do me a favor. Give this to Felipe."

"Not that I blame you, but aren't you taking anything?"

"Just one." Starks pulled the envelope with Kane's comb inside from under the clock. He tucked it into an inside jacket pocket. "I'm ready."

CHAPTER 98

Starks walked alongside Roberts to the end of the corridor. Seven inmates he'd never seen before blocked their passage.

Roberts rested his hand on his radio. "Is there a problem?"

One of the inmates said, "Yeah. With him." He pointed at Starks.

"I don't even know you."

"Someone high up has a message for you."

"What's the message?"

"You're not goin' anywhere. At least, not alive."

Roberts reached for his radio. Two of the seven jumped him. The radio skittered across the corridor. The large book *thunked* as it hit the floor. One of the other inmates slammed his fist into Roberts' stomach, winding him. Two others moved in on Starks, pinning his arms behind his back.

"Careful. This is a new jacket," he said.

"It'll fit me just fine. I'll be sure not to cut it." The inmate slid a kitchen knife from his waistband.

"Someone having a party and didn't invite me?"

This had come from Felipe, who stood behind the inmates. He wasn't alone. Luke, Ethan, and a dozen or so Hermanos stood at the ready.

Starks grinned. "Nice of you to see me off."

"Couldn't let you leave without saying adios."

The inmate holding the knife said, "Beat it. This ain't your business."

Felipe moved forward. "Let me tell you how this is going to go down, amigo. Starks is going to walk out of here, accompanied by

Officer Roberts. And, you're going to let them." The others with him encircled the men.

The inmate glared at Felipe, worked his jaw as he clenched and unclenched his hand around the knife handle. He scanned the faces of the men ready to fight and sneered. "Let him go."

One of the inmates holding Roberts said, "Which one?"

"Both of them."

Roberts stumbled to his radio, wincing as he bent over to pick it up. Radio in hand, he instructed additional guards to get to C Block and to double-time it. He walked back to Starks, picking up the book on the way, and said to Felipe, "Keep these assholes corralled until the other guards get here."

Felipe smiled and said, "My pleasure."

"This is from Starks."

Felipe took the book and looked quizzically at Starks. "A parting gift?"

"You'll appreciate the subject matter." He adjusted his jacket and sweater then made eye contact with Felipe and the others, each in turn. "I'm at a loss as to what to say."

Luke stepped forward and extended his hand. "No need to say anything. Just promise you'll give us a thought now and then."

"Count on it."

The remainder of Starks's exit went without further incident. Until he reached the last hallway. A tall, slender man wearing glasses, his attention focused on a computer printout, stormed out of his office, yelling about a budget item. He crashed into Starks. The printout fell to the floor and fanned out. The man's expression revealed his shock.

Starks glanced at the brass plate screwed to the office door. He smoothed the lapels of the man's suit jacket. "Don't bother with any kind of special send-off. Just say goodbye." Starks walked off, leaving the warden red-faced and furious.

"What was that about?" Roberts asked.

"He understood."

Roberts halted when they reached the lobby. "This is where I leave off." He extended his hand. "It was good while it lasted, but don't come back. As for me, time to get back and make sure enthusiastic guards don't lock our rescuers up with the others."

Starks laughed and shook his hand. "Don't let the bastards get to you." He pushed the door open and drank in crisp air free of a wall topped with razor wire.

He spotted Jeffrey to his left, down the row of parked cars, leaning against Starks's transportation to the rest of his life. He jogged to where car and friend waited. "Nice ride. A Bentley, if I'm not mistaken."

Jeffrey grinned. "A good friend of mine took an extended vacation. Kept it in my garage for him. Thought it was time to give it a spin." Jeffrey held out the keys. "Want to test it? See if you might like one for yourself?"

Starks reached for the keys then pulled his hand back. "Maybe later. I'd prefer to enjoy the ride."

Jeffrey laughed and pulled Starks into a bear hug.

Once inside the car, Jeffrey started the engine. "Where to?"

"Home."

Jeffrey put the car in reverse. "Where exactly is that?"

"I'll let you know."

CHAPTER 99

J effrey pulled onto the two-lane blacktop. Starks released his breath and some of the tension in his limbs. He resisted looking back. He'd seen enough of Sands. Settling into the heated leather seat, his eyes took in trees waiting for new leaves to bud, evergreens taking up the slack until spring brought everything back to life, the sky which was clear and blue. He glanced at Jeffrey, whose mouth formed a perpetual grin as words came rapid-fire from him, words Starks barely paid attention to. At this moment, the visual feast called more loudly to him and had more to say.

Starks shut his eyes. Shut out everything—it was too much stimulation all at once. He tuned in to the feel of the car as Jeffrey took a curve then straightened out with the road.

Soon, he believed—or was it just hoped?—he'd adjust back into his life. Find his footing, as it were. It had been nearly a year and a half since he'd been outside Sands' walls or had done anything normal, usual. He was in the fortunate position of not needing to return to work immediately. He could take the time required to acclimate, to be with his children again so they could adjust to having him back in their lives as a father.

He would be available for however much time he had left with Kayla. Would look after her, forced to watch the disease consume her. Help Blake in his attempt to determine if he was gay or straight or bi. Figure out his own feelings about this.

There was the matter of the business in which he was no longer a major player. The question of Emma. His family's reaction to his return and what they might expect of him. People on the streets or in restaurants and other places in town, either commenting favorably to him, perhaps uncomfortably, about his release or avoiding him altogether from embarrassment as to what to say, or from fear. He'd be pointed at. Whispered about. Until he was no longer a novelty.

He'd left a dangerous, life-and-soul-sucking environment, but he wasn't returning to a life that would go easy on him. Instead, it would continue to make him pay, not just for his attack on Ozy but for all he'd done before and since. Life would also, more than likely, demand he earn anything good that came to him from this moment on. He'd have to be worthy. The end of feeling entitled, as Kayla had so often chided him.

"So, bro, what do you think about that?"

Starks opened his eyes. "What?"

"Your body's there, but where are you?"

"Sorry."

"Guess I'm motor-mouthing it. What do you want to do first when we get to Weston?

Starks sat erect and pointed up ahead. "Pull in there."

"Where?"

"Bob's Unbeatable Burgers."

"It's a roadside joint. If you're hungry, lets wait for a four-star restaurant. You're dressed for it."

Starks shook his head. "Maybe for dinner."

"It's your stomach."

Jeffrey slowed, put the blinker on, and eased the car to a stop on the shell-covered ground that crunched beneath the tires. He peered through the windshield at the tiny nondescript structure and its painted-white exterior dingy with age. Windows wrapped around three sides of the front. Rivulets wept lines through condensation on the glass. "You don't know how old what's on that griddle is."

"Doesn't matter."

"We'll have to eat in the car. No seats inside, and it's too damn cold to eat outside."

"One of those picnic tables will be fine."

"You're really slumming it, bro."

Starks opened the car door, stepped out and breathed deeply. "Smell that?"

Jeffrey slammed his door shut and sniffed. "I smell food that costs a whole lot less than an excellent steak."

Starks, arms extended, laughed. "It smells like freedom. Like life." He hurried to the door and held it open for Jeffrey.

Inside, Starks's stomach rumbled as he scanned the menu written in blue chalk on a green board.

Less than ten minutes later, Jeffrey shivered and cursed as he lowered onto the bench at the small table. Starks rapped on the wooden surface then sat.

Jeffrey warmed his hands on his coffee cup. "What's that about?"

"What's what about?" Starks unwrapped his burger loaded with everything.

"That knocking thing."

"Habit. I suppose it'll take a while to stop."

"Prison practice?"

"One of many." Starks took the first bite and moaned. Chewed a few times, swallowed, and took another large bite. Mouth full, he said, "I can't believe you didn't order anything. This is great."

"I'd rather risk salmonella from a better place than this. Whoa, bro. I'm eager to get back in the car, but you don't have to inhale your food."

"You don't understand."

"I guess not."

"Doesn't matter."

Starks studied Jeffrey, who frowned down at his steaming coffee. It would be like that for all of them. As difficult as it had been to adjust to prison, this adjustment might be equally challenging. Expectations in prison were few, distinct, limited in scope. Prior to his sentencing, he'd failed to notice how broad the canvas of regular life could be. Expectations from others—and there were so many others—would be greater on him. That is, once they figured out what it was they could reasonably expect of him, or unreasonably, as the case might be.

Starks chewed the last bite and crumpled the wrapper into a ball.

Jeffrey poured his untouched coffee onto the ground. "Good. Can we get out of here?" He slid his long legs from the bench and stood.

"How about treating me to one more? I'll eat it while you drive."

"As long as I don't have to freeze my butt off another minute." Jeffrey tossed the keys to Starks. "Get it warmed up."

Starks slouched against the leather seats. Blew on his hands as he watched Jeffrey drum his fingers against the Formica countertop. He'd always considered *simpler pleasures* a hackneyed phrase, an excuse given by those lacking ambition or too lazy to work any harder than necessary. He wondered if he'd spoiled his children past the ability to appreciate such things, as Felipe had advised. Wondered how his crew and the Hermanos were adapting to their new association.

He started the engine and waited in silence.

Several minutes later, Jeffrey climbed in and handed him the paper bag. "You really have changed."

Starks unwrapped the burger and took a huge bite. "Because I'm eating a second burger?"

"Because you're eating in your car. Used to be you wouldn't even carry anything cooked in it. Didn't want anything but the leather fragrance lingering."

"Needs must."

"Whatever the hell that means."

CHAPTER 100

N early two hours later, they passed the *Welcome to Weston* sign. Starks's stomach fluttered with nervous tension. Jaguars, Audis, Mercedes, and the like lined street sides. Elegantly dressed men and women paraded on sidewalks. He spied a woman admiring her reflection in a glass door before pushing it open. Recalled how often he'd done the same.

Boutique shops and businesses he'd dropped a bundle in, and people he didn't recognize, or did, zoomed into and out of view as Jeffrey gave him a quick main-street tour, pointing out changes that had taken place in his absence.

Jeffrey eased to a stop at a red light. "You decided where you want to go?"

"I'd like to stay at your house tonight."

"Won't your mom be pissed?"

"You and Parker are the only ones who know I'm out." His head snapped left. "You didn't tell anyone, did you?"

Jeffrey shook his head. "Parker made it clear."

"It's just that I need to decompress or something, before I jump into the deep end."

"Stay with me as long as you like. But you can't wait too long. People will see you. Hell, some of them will recognize this car."

Starks slid down in the seat. "Crap. Forget the tour. Get us to your house."

"Sonofabitch. Stay down."

"What is it?"

"More like who."

"Jeffrey."

"Ozy Hessinger. Strutting like he owns the damn sidewalk, the bastard."

Starks inched up in the seat. Ozy was heavier than the last time he'd seen him, he'd let his middle go to flab. His hairline had receded in an unflattering fashion. Memories poured in—of Ozy screwing Kayla any place where he could get his rocks off with her, of all the time he'd lost—so many losses—because of this pig.

Starks reached for the door handle.

Jeffrey grabbed his arm. "It's not worth it, bro. I'm not going to let you put yourself back at Sands. Not over that P.O.S."

Starks shook off Jeffrey's hand. Hot rage course through him. He opened the door and put one foot down.

"Damn it, Starks."

"Pull over and wait for me."

Starks shut the door and stepped onto the sidewalk. Ozy stood at the large front window of Weston Books, checking out new titles. Starks sidled up beside him. "Decided to switch to a safer hobby?"

Ozy glanced at Starks, sniffed, and returned his gaze to the books. "I beg your pardon?"

"You couldn't beg enough, you worthless sack of shit."

Ozy balled his hands into fists and faced Starks. "Who the hell do you think you are?"

"Give it a minute. It'll come to you."

Ozy's face drained of color. He started to back away.

Starks kept step with him.

"You keep away from me, Starks, or I swear I'll—"

"Relax. I'm not going to give you another second of my life."

"What do you want?"

"From you? Not a damn thing. On second thought, just one. You don't tell anyone you saw me or that I'm out."

Ozy threw his shoulders back. "Just the police. I'm going to get a restraining order put on your ass."

"Waste of time and money. But if you mention you saw me, I'll find you."

"That a threat?"

"A promise."

Starks walked to where Jeffrey idled at the curb a few yards ahead, and got into the Bentley. "It had to be done. Our paths were bound to cross at some point."

"Somehow I doubt you told him it was time to forgive and forget."

"I'll never forgive him, and I'll never forget. And if I start to, the mirror will remind me."

"You're freaking me out a little, bro." Jeffrey glanced at him then faced the windshield. "You're the same but different."

It was an understatement of grand proportions, and not anything he cared to discuss.

Jeffrey tucked the Bentley into the empty part of his three-car garage. The door slid closed behind them. Starks exhaled, grateful to be in what he hoped was a sanctuary, until at least the morning.

He followed Jeffrey through the entrance that led to the kitchen of the two-story house.

Jeffrey hung his keyring on a hook in the kitchen. "I'd tell you to put your stuff in the guest bedroom, but ..."

"I'm traveling light."

"It's a first, bro." Jeffrey opened the refrigerator, grabbed a beer and held it up. "Interested?"

"Oh, yeah."

Jeffrey grinned. "Now you're talking."

Starks walked to the sliding glass doors that opened to the land-scaped backyard. "Pool still heated?"

"You want to swim?"

"Later."

"Wanna look around?"

"I remember what it looks like here. You haven't changed any-thing."

Jeffrey started toward the adjoining den. "I'll get a fire going."

Starks trailed behind him and sunk into one corner of the plush sofa.

Jeffrey stacked wood in the grate, chucked in a starter cube and held a match to it. Within seconds, the wood caught. "I figured we'd go to your favorite restaurant tonight, but if you'd rather stay under the radar—"

"We can grill steaks."

"That calls for a trip to the store."

"Would you mind?"

Jeffrey took a pull on his beer. "Whatever you want. This is your day."

"I don't have any cash."

"Don't expect you to."

"I need some things."

Jeffrey grabbed a notepad and pen from a corner desk and handed them to Starks. "Make a list. Soon as I finish my beer, I'll head out."

Starks began to write, pausing occasionally to contemplate as he stared at the crackling fire.

Jeffrey plunked into the chair nearest the sofa. "What about the money in your Sands account? You get that back?"

Starks tapped the pen against his chin. "I'm going to get them to divvy it up and deposit it into a couple people's accounts."

"That's generous."

"Not nearly enough."

"What about all the extraneous payments? That's coming up on Wednesday."

"Make them. And have Jim's guy tell Roberts the payments will continue through the end of the year."

"Again, generous."

Starks shrugged. He ripped the top page from the notepad and handed it to Jeffrey. "That's everything I can think of for now."

Jeffrey scanned the list. "This will take about two hours, including food and beer shopping."

"Monday, I need to get my bank account matters in order. In the meantime—"

"I'll stop at the ATM while I'm out." Jeffrey folded the paper with the list and dropped it into his shirt pocket. "You'll be okay while I'm gone?"

"Better than okay."

"*Mi casa es su casa*, bro."

Starks walked to the sliding doors. "Think I'll go for that swim now."

"Trunks and towels are in the same place."

"Jeffrey."

"Yeah?" Jeffrey studied Starks's face. "No need to say anything, bro. Good to have you back."

Starks went to a front window and watched Jeffrey drive off. He used the land line to call Parker's cell phone.

Parker picked up on the first ring. "Jeffrey? Is everything okay?"

"It's Starks. I'm staying at Jeffrey's. Just for tonight. I think. At least while I figure some things out."

"Understood. Everything go okay at Sands? Any problems getting out?"

"Nothing out of the usual. Can you clear your schedule for ten o'clock tomorrow morning? I need to see you at your office."

"Tomorrow's Saturday."

"Same question."

"I'll be here."

Call ended, Starks went upstairs. He pulled one of Jeffrey's thick robes from the huge walk-in closet and a towel from the bathroom. In the guest bedroom, he stripped off his clothes and hung them in the walk-in closet.

He caught his reflection in the full-length mirror secured to the wall, his gaze drawn to the dozen pale purple-hued scars of various lengths on his torso and the several remaining bruises, shadows of a different kind of near-death experience. He was still in shape, in fact, better than when he'd gone in, despite the crap diet. But he'd never look at himself the same again. Starks put the robe on, grabbed the towel, and headed for the pool.

He stood at the edge of the deep end. The six-foot wooden fence and tall hedges provided enough privacy, more than he'd had in the last nearly sixteen months. If anyone saw him and got bothered about his swimming nude, screw 'em.

Starks dropped the robe to the tiles and dove in. Swam underwater to the shallow end. He raised his head out of the water, reveling in the contrast of warm and cold.

And wept without fear of discovery or any clear understanding of why he couldn't stop.

CHAPTER 101

Jeffrey slid several bags of various sizes onto the counter. "Considering how you scarfed the burgers, I got enough food to feed three for a week." He pointed. "Your stuff's in that bag." He opened the refrigerator and started to unload the groceries. "What's the tape recorder for? You making notes for a book about your experience?" He laughed. "I'd think you'd want to push those thoughts so far back they never surfaced again."

Starks's movements slowed. The image of Paco seated at the library computer, pecking at the keyboard with two fingers, played on the screen in his mind.

At Starks's silence, Jeffrey said, "You're gonna be okay, bro."

Starks looked at his friend and nodded. "Of course. I'm going to put this stuff in my room. Be right back."

"Hold up." Jeffrey pulled a plump white envelope from his inside jacket pocket. "You'll need some walking-around money, until you can get straightened out at the bank. There's two grand in there. If you need more, let me know."

Starks took the envelope and looked inside. His fingers flipped quickly over the hundreds, fifties, and twenties. "I'll have to remember how to spend that much."

"It'll come back to you. Faster than you think. It's a couple hours till dinner. What's the plan while we wait?"

"You don't have to babysit me. If there's something you need or want to do …"

"We got movies, sports channels—"

"Sounds good."

Starks started up the stairs. He hadn't anticipated how awkward his return might be. It should be easy to be with Jeffrey, to talk to him. Jeffrey, who knew more about him than his own mother.

The problem was, Jeffrey wanted—needed—him to be who he'd been before. They all would, in some measure. But the truth was, they'd be different in some ways from what he remembered, as well, even though they might not realize the subtle changes in themselves.

As Jeffrey had said about him, primarily the same, but different. There was no way around it. And they'd notice what was different about him. Hell, he barely recognized himself anymore.

The hours of his first day of freedom should have zipped by rather than dragged. It was a relief to tell Jeffrey he was tired and going to bed.

Jeffrey checked the time, eyebrows raised, and said, "Whatever works for you."

The absence of routine wasn't as easy or comfortable as he'd expected. How many times had he checked a clock to make certain he wasn't late for the count? Or watched the time to make sure he was where he belonged before the doors closed and locked at nine, leaving him in dim lighting until morning?

Starks stripped and climbed between the sheets, taking his position at the edge of the king-size bed. Smallness had become a habit. He scooted to the middle and flapped his arms and legs in the same way a child makes a snow angel.

He lay there, thinking about what he wanted to accomplish the next day. It was no use. He was nowhere near ready to sleep. For one thing, it was too quiet. With the light off, it was nearly pitch black in the room.

Like a tomb.

Starks switched on the bedside light. The recorder, tapes, and batteries were where he'd placed them, next to the lamp. He put the batteries in and inserted a tape. Did a voice-check.

Finger resting atop the record button, Starks organized his thoughts.

He pushed the button, heard the whir, and began to speak.

CHAPTER 102

He dropped his feet to the carpeted floor, wiggled his toes in the plush nap. Starks went to the window and peered out at first light. He put on the pajamas and slippers Jeffrey had bought for him and went downstairs to the workout room. The expensive treadmill, with its elaborate control board and video screen, offered no incentive. He opted for the weights, but did so after doing the routine he'd done every day for over a year.

An hour later, dripping sweat, he returned to his room, turned the water on in the shower as hot as he could stand it and got in. Jeffrey had a surprise waiting for him. On the small shelf, next to the cheap drugstore items he'd listed, were containers of his favorite Bvlgari shower gel and shampoo. He squirted a large dollop of green tea gel into his palm and worked the lather over his body, starting at his face. He reached the area between his legs, felt the initial stirring of a sensation he'd suppressed from the first moment he'd been arrested and locked in a city jail cell. It was a different kind of release, one that took far less time than his release from Sands.

Fifteen minutes later, a shaved and dressed Starks stood alone in the kitchen. He found the silence soothing but wanted to hear coffee brewing, wanted to inhale the aroma of fresh roasted beans. Another luxury he'd been without all these months. While waiting on the coffee, he pulled food items from the refrigerator and skillets from the rack suspended over the long granite-topped island.

Ten or so minutes later, Jeffrey padded into the kitchen, yawning, hair sticking up and out. "I smelled coffee and food. I thought you'd sleep in."

"Not something I did, even before."

"Bacon. Sausages. French toast. Omelet. Juice. Damn, bro." Jeffrey yawned again.

Starks pushed a steaming coffee mug toward Jeffrey. "I have an appointment with Parker at ten."

"I'll be awake by then."

"I'd like to go alone. In fact, there are several things I need to do. You won't mind?"

"Knock yourself out."

"I'd also like to use your car instead of mine."

"Keyring is where it always is. Car *and* house on it. Leave me the key for the Bentley, though. I don't plan to go anywhere, but you never know."

Breakfast, and the interval of time before Starks left at nine forty-five, passed more comfortably than the previous night. Jeffrey had never been much of a talker before nine on weekends. Weekdays were another matter.

Starks managed the small amount of conversation they had until Jeffrey returned upstairs, supposedly to shower and get ready for his day. In that interval, he used Jeffrey's laptop to research the seed of an idea buzzing in his mind.

Jeffrey was still upstairs by the time Starks was ready to leave. He went up to announce he was going and heard light snoring coming from Jeffrey's open door. Starks pivoted and headed for the garage. He adjusted the seat, which had accommodated Jeffrey's longer legs.

It was odd to drive again. Odd to negotiate his way around town. Thankfully, Parker's car was the only one in the lot. Starks parked and rang the buzzer.

Parker, dressed in slacks and casual jacket, unlocked the door. Smiling broadly as he ran his gaze over Starks, he said, "This is the Starks I know. How does it feel to be back?"

Starks was tempted to say he'd discovered there were walls other than those constructed with materials, but instead said, "It feels good." Why burden Parker with the tangled feelings rioting inside him.

Parker closed and locked the door. "What can I help you with?"

"Can we talk in your office?"

"Certainly."

Starks followed Parker down the long, carpeted hallway. Took a seat on the leather sofa in the spacious, well-appointed office.

Parker strolled to the small corner bar. He picked up a carafe. "Would you like coffee? I know it's early, but if you'd like something stronger …" He held up a bottle of brandy.

"How about both together in one cup?" He needed something to boost his courage for the task following this one.

Parker fixed their cups, placing them on the coffee table. He sat at the other end of the sofa and waited.

Starks sipped, sipped again. He put the cup down and retrieved three one-hour tapes from his jacket pocket, placing them on the coffee table. "A while back, I mentioned to you that if anything happened to me, I wanted you to investigate goings-on at Sands."

"I recall it clearly. You scared the hell out of me."

A small smile played on Starks's lips. "Lucky you. My experiences there scared the hell into me." At Parker's expression, he said, "It's not important, but these are." He tapped the tapes. "You'll need to get Jim involved, of course. Anything of significance regarding the corruption I discovered is on those tapes. If you have questions after you listen to them, I'll provide any answers or details you need."

"How bad is it?"

"Once the investigation is complete and charges are filed, Sands will need a new warden. And the warden will plead for his sentence to be served at a different prison, and likely in solitary confinement."

Parker whistled. "I'll arrange for Jim to listen to them with me."

"Good idea. He's as sharp as you are." Starks smiled. "In his own field."

"What about you? What are you going to do, now that you're out?"

"Get as much of my life in order as possible. Look after my family, especially Kayla."

"That's all well and good, but what about work? Do you want to return to Tandum? After all, you're the founder and the one who made it a successful enterprise. I'm sure the board would vote you back on."

"Maybe not. What I mean is, I don't want to return to the business."

Parker's eyebrows arched. "What do you intend to do? You're not one to do nothing."

"As I said, Sands will need a new warden. When the time's right, I intend to put my application in. In the meantime, I'll look after my family and life."

Parker placed his cup and saucer on the table, spilling the liquid as he did so. "You can't be serious. Besides, with your record, they'd never allow it."

"I think they will. I'll convince whomever."

"Why the hell would you ever want to return to that place, for any reason?"

"I saw what some of the men there possess. What they could be capable of, in a more productive manner I mean. Maybe I'm fooling myself, but I'd like to see what I can do to rebuild men who've been broken and damaged by a flawed system. And life. Some of them deserve that chance and more. I understand them." He chuckled. "How often are wardens or guards hired who've been on the other side? That's my advantage. And theirs."

"You're a mechanical engineer with zero qualifications for the job."

"Not true. I've got a degree, which is two degrees above the mini-mum that's required. I've more than proven my ability to operate a budget proficiently and manage people. And not just manage them, grow them. I've damn sure got experience with what inmates need and how they need to be treated. There are some educational courses required, like social work, the justice system, and institutional behavior and psychology. It'll likely be a year or so until Sands needs a new warden. It'll take that long to build a case against him. I'll have time to get done what needs to get done."

"What about Kayla? What about the kids?"

Starks linked his fingers and stared at them. "Unless a miracle happens, Kayla's own hell will be over not too long from now. Kids are mobile."

"Do you know how much wardens get paid?"

Starks grinned. "Less than eighty thousand a year."

"Who are you? And what have you done with Starks?"

CHAPTER 103

O n the way to his next destination, Starks detoured to Tandum Enterprises. He wanted one more look at the ten-story gleaming chrome and turquoise glass building he been so proud of. Cars filled half the parking lot. Likely, some of the employees were working on project proposals for new clients.

Starks slowed and pulled into the lot. All the hours and stress it took to turn his start-up company into an empire, and he had no desire to step inside its headquarters. Most of this stemmed from fear of humiliation, and he'd definitely reek with it in front of his former employees. They'd viewed him as someone just under a god. It was also a matter of being away from it for so long. The business, and what it required, no longer held any appeal.

So much of his former life lay behind him. What was ahead both frightened and exhilarated him.

He eased out of the lot and drove to a small florist in a strip mall at the outskirts of town, selected two dozen red roses then started for the house he'd bought and shared with Emma.

Starks pulled into the driveway. The garage door was closed. He tucked the box of roses into the crook of his left arm and got out of the car, quietly closing rather than slamming the door. Looking left and right, he walked to the stretch of small windows on the garage door and peeked in. Emma's car was there, parked at the center with no expectation of his car, or another man's, needing room next to hers.

Close to midnight, fifteen months ago, he'd left this house, with every intention to return in twenty or so minutes. Left a drowsy Emma, naked and warm in bed, with a promise to do more than spoon her as soon as he returned from his late-night drive. A drive he'd told her would calm his angst. A drive he never came back from. Until now.

He took slow steps as he attempted and failed to ignore the lurch of his stomach. What the hell was wrong with him? He'd always been confident, cocky, certain of his superiority. Doubt bore down on him, doubt that started to thread its way through his system as soon as he'd left Sands, ready to imprison him with invisible bars. This reunion had to work in his favor.

His house key was at Jeffrey's, on the same ring as the key for the Bentley, as was the key for the house he'd once shared with Kayla and his children. It didn't matter. For all he knew, Emma had changed the locks. He cursed as his trembling hand reached for the doorbell, relieved that the glass panes on the door were opaque.

After a few seconds, he heard heels clacking closer on the marble foyer floor. Emma had on those shoes she called mules. Such a peculiar name for footwear that had always motivated him to coax her out of her clothes. *Leave the shoes on.* That request, uttered as a command, had always made her laugh. Until what he did to her elicited sounds of pleasure.

The handle clicked, the door opened. Emma, wearing a quizzical expression, peered out at him. Her hand went to her chest. "Oh my God!"

Starks moved like a serpent and caught her with his free arm as she began to crumple to the floor. He positioned her in one of the foyer chairs that bookended an antique table they'd bought together. He placed the box of roses on the table and squatted in front of her.

"I should get you some water. Or whiskey. I'll be right back."

He ran to the bar in the den, filled a glass a third of the way with Scotch, downed it, refilled the glass then rushed back.

Emma downed the contents in one gulp. She remained where she was, staring at him with disbelief etched on her face.

Starks stood. "I wasn't sure what the best way was to do this. Should I have Parker call and tell you I was getting released? Should I call first? Should I show up? I decided on the element of surprise."

"I'm surprised." Her tone came out flat.

There was a question he needed to get out of the way. The answer had all to do with how the rest of his plan went. "Is your son home?"

"I dropped him off at school this morning. There's an event. Then he's doing a sleepover with one of his friends." Her sapphire eyes narrowed. "What the hell do you think you're doing by showing up here like this?"

"I had to see you."

"Why?"

"Because there's something I need to tell you." He glanced toward the den. "Let's sit where it's more comfortable."

"It's your house." She walked briskly ahead of him, her heels snapping against the cool marble. Her platinum blond hair hung loose past her shoulders, swaying right to left with each step. Her short pink shift draped her curves, revealing legs that used to love to wrap around him.

Starks grabbed the box filled with roses and swallowed hard as he watched the sharp, angry swish of her hips.

Emma dropped into one of the chairs near the crackling fire. She crossed her legs and arms and glared at him.

"These are for you." He reached for a large crystal vase from under the bar, filled it with water, and placed the roses inside.

Watching him, lips pursed, she said, "If you have something to say, say it."

Starks left the shelter of the bar and stood a few feet in front of her. "It's time you understand why I behaved as I did. You have no idea how it tormented me to leave you wondering."

Emma huffed. "Please don't try to convince me that it bothered you to toy with me."

"It was never my intention to toy with you. The first time you visited, I lied about how dangerous it was for me."

"It's dangerous for anyone who gets involved with you."

The truth of her words struck him. "I had time to think, to realize the only way my life could ever be what I'd always hoped, is if it's spent with you."

"Words I've heard before. No new material? How disappointing."

"One day I'll explain what happened to me in there. It's still too painful to talk about, but I can show you some of it. You already know what caused this." He lifted the bottom of his turtleneck sweater, raised it high enough to show her some of his scars. At her gasp, he added, "The others are hidden by my slacks."

Tears welled in Emma's eyes, the struggle within her obvious on her face.

He pulled up his right sleeve. Pointed to the newest scar. "This is from a knife. Used by a determined inmate while I was in solitary confinement."

"How—?"

"As I said, he was determined." Starks pointed to the older scar across his wrist. "This one was self-inflicted." Emma stared up at him with wide eyes. "There was another near-attempt. I stopped just short of carrying it out. Rather than losing all hope, I decided to get strong."

Emma's chin quivered as she fought back tears. She stretched her hand out a few inches then dropped it into her lap. "I need a moment to wrap my mind around all of this."

"How I behaved toward you was my poor attempt to protect you."

"I made myself clear about that."

"I never knew whether I'd survive from one day or moment to the next. There was also the fear that you wouldn't want me. Not after all the times you told me you thought my body was perfect. I'm damaged goods now. I wanted to be selfless enough to let you go but was desperate to keep you in my life. If, at the very least, you can forgive me, I'll have to let that be enough." He smoothed his sweater back into place. "What are you thinking?"

Emma wiped tears from her cheeks, leaped from the chair, and wrapped her arms around his neck, clinging to him for several moments. She lifted her head from his shoulder and placed her lips on his, starting with gentle kisses that deepened.

Starks felt the stirrings he'd had earlier in the shower. Gently, he pried her arms loose. "I need you, Emma. I need to see you. Touch you. Taste you. I need to bury myself deep inside you and never leave."

"I need to hear you say it."

"I love you. More than you know."

Emma stepped back a few feet. She reached behind her and undid the single button at the back of the shift. With a few shimmies of her body, the silky dress slithered to the floor. She stood naked in front of him, breathing harder as his unblinking eyes stayed focused on her. Slowly, she turned in a circle.

Were this an earlier time, he'd be all over her, confident in his abilities. But it had been so long. If he went too fast too soon, it would be over within seconds after he started. He couldn't fail at this. It was necessary to prove he was still the man who used to draw sighs and moans from her. There was only one thing to do.

"Leave the shoes on."

He took her by the hand and led her to the S-shaped chaise that curved upward where the sitter's knees were meant to rest. Emma lay on her back, arms stretched over her head. Starks's eyes traced every curve and mound. He moved to the end of the chaise, took hold of her ankles and drew her down, until her hips reached the elevated portion.

Starks slid his shoes off and stripped, leaving his clothes in a puddle, which he kicked to the side. He eased himself above her, started at her mouth and began to work his mouth and hands down her body, remembering what she liked. He took his time. Kept his satisfaction to himself each time she shivered or moaned.

Her body arched, impatient for him to reach his destination. He teased her with his fingers, lips, and tongue, deliberately stopping short of the tender target.

When she pleaded, he smiled.

He was back in control.

CHAPTER 104

They lay on the chaise, arms and legs entangled, perspiration worn as a sheen of satisfaction on their bodies.

Emma nuzzled Starks's neck. "Are you hungry?"

He lifted her chin with his hand, kissed the tip of her nose, and grinned. "I just ate. Twice."

She laughed and slapped him playfully on his backside. "You know what I mean."

"Actually, I'd like to take a shower." He placed his hand between her thighs and stroked. "With you."

Emma sat up. Her lips twitched. "I thought you just said you were full."

"Give me another ten minutes and I will be." He reached for her.

Emma, laughing, slid from the chaise. She started toward the hallway, stopped and looked over her shoulder. "Well?"

Starks bounded from the chaise, chasing a squealing Emma up the stairs. Inside the steaming shower, he took her again in a way that left him satisfied that his stake truly had been reclaimed.

Starks scanned the items of clothing on his side of the spare room he'd converted to a walk-in closet. He found what he wanted and began to dress.

Emma, still naked, came up behind him, draped her arms around his chest and said, "What are we going to do with the rest of the day? Not that I couldn't continue to do more of what we've been doing. It's been just as long for me, you know."

He turned, cupped and kissed her breasts. "Sad to say, but there are some things I have to take care of."

"Can I help?"

He kissed her. "Thanks for offering, but these are things only I can do." He selected shoes and slid his feet into them.

"What time will you be back? I can cook or we can order in."

"I'm not sure."

"Starks?" She chewed on her bottom lip.

"All I can tell you is, I'll return as soon as I can."

Emma yanked a silk robe from a hanger and slipped it on. "You didn't say when you got out."

"Yesterday."

"I see. How did you get back?"

"Jeffrey."

"Where did you sleep last night?"

Starks faced her. "Jeffrey's guest room."

"Where will you sleep tonight?"

Starks pulled her into his arms. "There are things I'm obligated to take care of, before we can fully be together. I need you to understand this."

Emma tried to pull away. "What you're not saying is that you need to take care of Kayla."

Starks held her tighter. "I have to check on her and be available for my children."

"I'll never see you."

"You will. My mother moved in there to help."

"But now that you're back—"

"I need her to stay."

"Even if she does, you'll probably sleep there."

"I may have to be there more than here, especially as the time nears for … Baby, you have my promise that we'll have time together. I need you. It's the only way for me to stay sane."

"How did *they* react when you showed up? Did you notify *them* ahead of time?"

"They don't know yet. Other than Jeffrey, you're the only one who knows. And Parker. I came to you first."

Emma pursed her lips into a pout and fiddled with the lapels of his jacket. "I suppose that counts for something."

"More than you know." He cupped her bottom with his hands and kissed her. "I need to get going. Don't wait around for me, if there's something you already had planned."

"Should I wait up?"

"I don't know. I'll call you as soon as I do." He smiled at her. "Walk me to the door?"

They returned downstairs with their arms draped around each other but in silence, for which Starks was grateful.

At the front door, he pulled her close again, caressed and kissed her in a way that let her know he'd be back. Just not when.

He stepped out and started toward the car.

"Starks?"

He faced her and waited.

"You do *really* love me, right?"

"With every inch of me."

Her expression made clear it wasn't the exact answer she wanted or needed, but it was the only one he could give her. For now.

CHAPTER 105

He'd forgotten to add sunglasses to the list he'd given to Jeffrey. Starks squinted and lowered the sun visor as he wended his way to the small mansion he'd built for Kayla and his children. He turned onto his former street, taking comfort at the sight of familiar elms, cedars, willows, and holly hedges filling yards that were several acres each. Children bundled against the cold rode bikes, played on swings and in treehouses designed by architects or chased each other around lawns pristinely maintained no matter the season. He rolled his window down an inch to better hear their joyous shouts and laughter. Wood fragrances wafted in from smoke pluming out of chimneys. Memories crashed down on him.

Tightness crept into his chest as he pondered what his own children's responses, or reactions, might be when they saw him. When they knew he was back. Blake, in particular.

He'd hide his external scars from them as long as possible. And would have to be attentive regarding internal scars that might surface.

These were not ordinary circumstances he returned to. His children were dealing with an illness they couldn't comprehend, as they watched their mother slip away from them in increments. A little less of who she'd previously been visible to them each day. What he might find on the other side of the front door, sent a nervous shudder through him.

He slowed the car to a crawl. Ignored stares from adults who happened to venture out of their cozy homes. Reminded himself that such an estimation—*cozy*—might be as much truth as fallacy. His own home had proven this.

The long, semi-circular driveway waited for him nine feet ahead on the right. Starks rested his foot on the brake to prepare to make the turn. He reached the end of the driveway. Kept the steering wheel straight and pressed on the accelerator.

His moist hands gripped the steering wheel. He wiped each hand in turn on his slacks. Rolled the window down all the way and gulped the chilly air. He drove around the neighborhood, drawing attention he didn't want. If he didn't go to the house now, he risked some nosy neighbor either calling the police or, worse, calling Kayla. That is, if anyone recognized him in Jeffrey's car. Any one of those possibilities was too great.

Starks drove back to his desired street, pulled into the driveway and parked in front of the house. Whoever came to the door would see Jeffrey's car through the glass side panels. They'd believe it was their close friend showing up to offer his help again.

He rested his finger on the doorbell and hesitated. He'd threatened Ozy, promised to harm him if he spoke to anyone about having seen him. Even if Ozy had ignored him, it was unlikely he'd contacted Kayla. Once he'd gotten what he wanted from her, once he'd destroyed their family, the man had no further use for her.

Jealousy began to seep into Starks's thought, to muddy his already muddled emotions. He shook it off. These feelings had no place or purpose once he crossed the threshold before him. Unless Kayla brought up the painful topic, not one word about that time would come from him. No one on the other side of that door, including him, needed to revisit an event that had ripped their lives apart.

This moment was one he'd dreaded as much as anticipated. A moment of unvarnished truth, as it were, when he, like a phoenix, could rise from the ashes of his former life and start anew.

There was one potential glitch in that story—memory. Did the phoenix's memory of its prior life disappear with its incineration or did the mythical bird retain all memories from that recent incarnation? If the latter, was this nature's way of allowing the winged creature the opportunity to learn from its mistakes?

Which option was the better one?

Another moment of truth—the choice was his alone.

This was an opportunity he didn't deserve but had been granted. The burden of how it went rested on him.

Starks rang the bell and waited, wondering whose face he'd see first. He didn't wait long.

His mother opened the door, continuing to wipe wet hands on the apron tied around her waist.

Lynn Starks took a few seconds to realize who it was that stood before her. Her eyes grew wide. Her lips parted, ready to release a scream.

Starks rushed in and clamped a hand over her mouth. He gently pulled her outside and closed the door.

Weeping and laughing, Lynn flung her arms around Starks. "My son. My baby." She cupped his face in her hands. "Is this real? I don't understand."

"I'll explain another time."

"Did you get out this morning?" She glanced at Jeffrey's car. "Did Jeffrey bring you back to me? Where is that little so-and-so? Why didn't he tell me you were coming home to us?"

"I promise to tell you everything but later. How is it in there?" He tilted his head toward the house.

"We're managing. It'll be better now that you're back with us."

"I hope so. At least that's my intention."

Lynn hugged him again, slathering kisses on his cheeks. "Wait until the rest of the family hears. I'll have to run to the store to get enough food and things for dinner tonight. You know they'll all want to see you, every last aunt, uncle, and cousin."

"Mom." He held her by her shoulders, waited for her to look at him. "It's too soon for that."

"Of course it isn't. They're your family."

"So are the people inside. Besides, you're here. And you and the four people on the other side of that door matter most to me. I'm not ready for everyone else. I will be. Just not for a while."

"I have to tell them you're back."

"Let's wait a few days. Will you do that for me?"

"Right now, I'd do anything you asked. My baby." She fell into his arms. He held her until her sobs subsided.

It was time to step into whatever waited for him inside.

He draped an arm around his mother's shoulders. "I'll want some time alone with Kayla before I see the kids. You won't mind?"

She patted his arm. "I'll make myself scarce, but don't make me wait too long."

"Where are my kids?"

"Playing out back."

Starks opened the door and let his mother enter first.

Kayla called weakly from the den, "Who was at the door?"

Lynn glanced at Starks, who pressed a finger to his lips.

When no answer came, Kayla said, "Lynn? Is everything all right?"

Smiling through tears, Lynn said, "It's better than all right." She veered left into the living room to wait until called. Starks, as quietly as possible, closed the door, as she'd started to sob again.

The hallway to the den grew longer with each step Starks took. This was, in part, a result of his looking left and right, taking in the framed photos on the walls. When Kaitlin was five, she called it the hallway of love.

People included in the life he'd had, and wasted for the most part, smiled and laughed from each photo he inched past. Still, it was a relief to see he'd been allowed to remain in the gallery of captured family moments, few as they were, as though he'd never left.

He stopped to look at the last family portrait they'd taken. The lump in his throat threatened to cut off his air. Kayla's inclusion in their life would freeze in time. No future images would be added that included her. Nothing to show how her middle years affected her beauty. No photos of her with silver hair and lines in her face she'd resent. He knew she'd trade looking like a shriveled prune, if it meant she could stay with them, could smile as she expanded the gallery with pictures of grandchildren they'd, once upon a time, planned to enjoy together. Each beautiful photo of her would one day be, not long from now, shadowed by the memory of what had happened. Would happen too soon to all of them.

At the entrance to the expansive den, he paused. Someone—he couldn't recall who—had once said regret was the only thing to fear. No way to erase the regrets that stuck to him like burrs, but he could do whatever it took to avoid creating new ones with Kayla.

He stepped forward and stopped. Kayla sat in a winged-back chair positioned at an angle in front of the French doors, arranged that way so she could look out, not at the exquisitely landscaped yard or the pool but at her three greatest accomplishments in life.

Starks stayed there, transfixed by the afternoon sunlight that bathed her pale face, making her appear incandescent. From the crescent of her face that he could see, she looked far more serene than he'd expected.

He believed he understood why.

If it were him in this situation, he'd be drinking in every detail, every laugh, every word, every mannerism of the three people he never wanted to leave. He'd done his share of that in his own way, when he'd been sentenced, but always with the belief he'd see them again. With the exception of the times he'd believed he was about to die, the hope of that day—this day—had kept him going.

He took another two steps. Next to the chair was a small table, its surface covered with medicine bottles, a paper cup half-filled with water, and a carafe beaded with moisture.

Starks walked toward Kayla, who either didn't hear his approach, or if she did, assumed it was Lynn. He stopped a foot away and said her name.

Kayla, as still as she was, grew even more so. She turned her head. Her aqua eyes widened as far as they could though pain and drugs. "Starks? Is it you, or am I hallucinating?"

Starks moved closer, glanced past the glass at his children, who remained unaware of his presence. He bent down and kissed her forehead, leaving his lips to linger a moment. He went onto his knees next to her, lifted her hand and kissed the back of it. "I'm home, Kayla. For good. I'm going to take care of you now."

For my sins.

ABOUT THE AUTHOR

Nesly Clerge received his bachelor's degree in physiology and neurobiology at the University of Maryland, and later pursued a doctoral degree in the field of chiropractic medicine. Although his background is primarily science-based, he finally embraced his lifelong passion for writing. Clerge's debut novel in The Starks Trilogy, *When the Serpent Bites*, received the Gold Medal Award from Readers' Favorite 2017 International Book Awards. The second book, *When the Dragon Roars*, received Readers' Favorite 2017 International Book Awards Silver Medal. *When the Phoenix Rises* is the third trilogy book. The trilogy books explore choices, consequences, and the complexities of human emotions, especially when we are placed in a less-than-desirable setting. *End of the World: The Beginning*, is the first book in a new serial, and became an Amazon #1 Bestseller two weeks after publication. Clerge's other novel, *The Anatomy of Cheating*, has also been well received by fans of his novels. When Clerge is not writing, he manages several multidisciplinary clinics. He enjoys reading, chess, traveling, exploring the outdoors, and spending time with his significant other and his sons. For more information regarding his books, please visit Clergebooks.com.